"Look at me for the truth!" he demanded.

My eyes went into his, slammed into them. His pupils seemed like two black motes sucking the world inside them.

"Follow me," he said. All my senses came alive with strange sensation: a dog barking, the smell of burning meat, a roofline above some trees.

"Follow me," Shiva cried.

And into those trees a fire explodes. Burning meat, a dog barking, fire, two bodies coupling.

No, came a whisper from deep within me. Do not follow him into that fire. He is a madman. . . .

THE DANCE OF SHIVA

THE DANCE OF SHIVA

William Deverell

BANTAM BOOKS
TORONTO · NEW YORK · LONDON · SYDNEY · AUCKLAND

*This low-priced Bantam Book
has been completely reset in a type face
designed for easy reading, and was printed
from new plates. It contains the complete
text of the original hard-cover edition.*
NOT ONE WORD HAS BEEN OMITTED.

THE DANCE OF SHIVA

*A Bantam Book / published by arrangement with
the Author*

PRINTING HISTORY
McClelland & Stewart edition November 1984
Bantam edition / February 1986

"The Legend of the Tandava" is a condensation of "Shiva
Nataraja," a chapter from *Stories of the Hindus*, ed.
James A. Kirk (New York: Macmillan Publishing Company,
1972). Reprinted with permission.

*Bantam Books are published by Bantam Books, Inc. Its trade-
mark, consisting of the words "Bantam Books" and the por-
trayal of a rooster, is Registered in U.S. Patent and Trademark
Office and in other countries. Marca Registrada. Bantam
Books, Inc., 666 Fifth Avenue, New York, New York 10103.*

PRINTED IN THE UNITED STATES OF AMERICA

H   0 9 8 7 6 5 4 3 2 1

This is dedicated to
the desperados of the courtroom:
my fellow criminal lawyers

THE DANCE
OF SHIVA

Lukey and Company, Barristers and Solicitors

1055 West Hastings Street, Vancouver, British Columbia. Telex: LUKEYCO

January 22, 1985

Arthur E. Beauchamp,
Barrister and Solicitor,
15 East Cordova St.,
Vancouver, B.C.

Dear Sir:

Re: Om Bay Massacre

I have yours of January 17th advising you have been appointed by the Legal Aid Society as counsel for Shiva Ram Acharya (a.k.a. Matthew Bartholomew James). On behalf of the Crown, I am pleased to forward you the enclosed copies of reports from the RCMP detachment at Tash-Tash Cove. When the Vancouver C.I.D. has completed fingerprint and ballistics work, I shall forward their reports as well.

Dr. Wang at Riverview is of opinion that the accused is mentally competent to stand trial, and I do not propose to undertake a fitness hearing. The Attorney-General has instructed me to proceed by direct indictment. There will be no preliminary hearing. Lest there be any misunderstanding, let me advise that the Crown will not be satisfied with an insanity verdict and seeks convictions on all 22 murder counts.

Yours very truly,

Leroy C. Lukey

Leroy Chalmers Lukey, Q.C.

Artie: As the flight commander said to the kamikaze pilot, "Rotsa Ruck." L.C.L.

Royal Canadian Mounted Police

Disorderly Incident Record

RCMP/GRC C-237 (4/14) 688

COPY: Crown Counsel
FILE: 84/003-1254

(Shiva a.k.a. James)

1.   On FRIDAY 7 DECEMBER 84, 10:20 hrs., under signed was at
this office when I observed that the old motor launch used by the
commune at so-called Om Bay for supplies was down at the
Government Dock.

2.   A man in raingear from the commune stopped at the Co-op
store, then came into this office before returning to the launch.

3.   He identified himself as George, blond, dirty long hair,
approx. 5'10" Cacausian, and under apparent distress.

4.   He requested my attendance at Om Bay (actual name
O'Malley Bay) and feared for the safety of himself and
others because the man known as Shiva, their religious leader,
was demanding control of their minds. Complainant reported
Shiva as saying, "With me you will commit the final suicide."

5.   As sole member of the Tash-Tash detachment, under signed
had numerous duties to attend to but advised complainant I would
go to Om Bay the next day, weather permitting, as there had been
snowstorms.

                                    E.S

                                    Edward O. Scanks,
                                    Corporal.
                                    11-12-84

ADDENDUM: I later iddentified the victim after looking at the
corpses as George Wurz from photographs shown to me.

                                    E.O.S.
                                    11-12-84

Royal Canadian Mounted Police

Disorderly Incident Record

RCMP/GRC C-237 (4/14) 6881

COPY: Crown counsel
FILE: 84/003-1254

(Shiva a.k.a. James)

1.   On SATURDAY DECEMBER 8 at 12:30 hrs., under signed in
the company of Auxiliary Const. Wendell Joiner and his brother
Tom Joiner departed aboard the police launch for Om Bay on
the east side of Poindexter Island, about twenty-three miles
sea travel. The weather was foggy and cold with snow again
overnight, and fog but no wind or chop. None of us knew what
to expect having not been to Om Bay since the under signed
attended there last fall when the commune was being set up
and was asked to leave.

2.   At 13:40 hrs., we came into the bay where we saw the
commune's old motor luanch tied to a buoey thirty meters offshore
the beach. The only other thing we could see was a shed, new,
about 10 meters square, just above tide-line, and some of the old
totem poles which had been here for fifty years. No persons were
present.

3.   Tom Joiner controlled the police boat and A/Const.
Wendell Joiner and under signed stepped ashore on a rocky beach
and proceeded through heavy snow, there being no path beaten in
it, toward the above-mentioned shed and we entered this shed
finding it unlocked and contained items of a food nature such as
bags of flour and powdered milk and construction tools, a
generator, oil drum, rolls of plastic sheeting. A full
inventory of these supplies is being made by members from C.I.D.
Vancouver. Also tools, axes, chain-saw, handsaws, rope, fuel,
etc.

4.   A/Const Wendell Joiner and under signed then observed
what appeared to be sounds coming from behind some small trees
and bushes, a male voice, singing or chanting, we continued on in
that direction where we observed five newly-built cedar shacks
including a big one like a mess hall, also some temporary
structures made of plastic sheeting and poles, and behind these,

a clearing where we could make out the accused dancing or
whirling around in circles, singing in a foriegn tongue.

5.   He stopped dancing and under signed could hear his voice
clearly as he said "DEATH KISSES YOU WITH LIFE, YOU WILL BE
REBORN AS GODS," as recorded in my notebook.

6.   At this point I removed my service revolver from its
holster and proceded with it in hand around the buildings to the
clearing which was tramped down and a mix of mud and snow.

7.   We then observed the victims. 21 corpses all dressed in
outdoor clothing except for one under a sleeping bag, blood on
their faces, hair etc., 17 of them laying on their sides, approx.
three feet apart in a row, wrists and ankles tied by cord in the
manner of hog-tying. Apparent bullet wounds to the back of the
head, exiting through the faces or foreheads and numerous
.303 cartridge cases in the mud near the bodies. 4 others were
not tied but had bullet holes in chests and backs, and one of the
17 tied-up victims hed a bullet hole in the right thigh.

8.   The accused SHIVA RAM ACHARYA, known also as MATTHEW
BARTHOLOMEW JAMES, was standing by the bodies with his back to
us, and a .303 Lee Enfield British army rifle with a ten-shot
magazine with three live bullets in it not far from his feet. I
heard him say these additional words, "BECAUSE I LOVED YOU, I HAD
TO KILL YOU." As he said this he began to dance again, kicking
his legs, very wild, jumping in a frensied way. He is a
Caucausian male, about fifty, long curly hair and greying
beard, about five-ten, stocky build, white robe, very dirty with
red blood streaks in his face, a circle of blood around his mouth
blood on his hands, and he was crying as he stopped dancing and
looked at us.

9.   Under signed apprehended the accused and gave him the
usual police warning. I asked him what happened and he made no
response. There was no smell of alcohol or marijuana on his
breath, he was steady on his feet although crying and his eyes
were bloodshot. He offered no resistance to handcuffs.

10.   Victims were all examined for vital signs, none were
breathing, pupils staring vacantly or rolled into backs of their
heads although bodies were still warm and rigour mortis had not
set in. Of the 17 hogtied, many had faces partly blown away.

The 4 others not tied were shot in the heart, it appeared, and
one of these was the George Wurz from the visit of the previous
day.

11.   Nothing was taken or removed pending radio instructions
from senior officers and arrival of a C.I.D. unit by planes and
helicopters. Except that plastic sheeting from the shed was laid
over the bodies and over the scene of the incident.

                                    Edward O. Scanks,
                                    Corporal.
                                    11-12-84

ADDENDUM: On the boat while waiting for reinforcements, under
signed asked accused why he had done this and he said, "WHYS
CANNOT FIND ANSWERS. WHY ARE WE? WHY IS THE COSMOS? WHY IS
GOD?"

                                    E.O.S.
                                    11-12-84

Royal Canadian Mounted Police

Disorderly Incident Record

RCMP/GRC C-237 (4/14) 6881

COPY: Crown counsel
FILE: 84/003-1254

(Shiva a.k.a. James)

1.   On 13 DECEMBER at 08:15 hrs, under signed, alone manning
the detachment at Tash-Tash Cove, received a call on the
emergency band from Joe Whitegoose, fisherman, about 12 miles
southeast of here re female person in extreme conditio n,
malnutrition, exposure, etc.

2.   Under signed made radio contact with members of Vancouver
C.I.D. still attending Om Bay and made rendezvous with Insp.
Storenko, officer in charge, at 09:12 hrs. at Joe Whitegoose's
place, a tipical rundown Indian shack, Insp. Storenko and other
Members attending also by police aircraft. We observed body
still warm with many bruises and cuts, presumably from the heavy
bush, torn peasant-type dress, a light sweater.

3.   Whitegoose is single, 75 yrs., native Indian. He
reported he saw victim crawling on hands and knees to shoreline
from the bush, not far from his shack, trying to tear muscles
from the rocks and eat them. He carried her to his home where
she expired.

4.   We believe this victim is Emelia Cruz, as identified from
a family photograph, who must of escaped from the shooting at
Om Bay.

E.S.

Edward O. Scanks,
Corporal.
14-12-84

PART ONE

○

The Summer Solstice

Except for the point, the still point,
There would be no dance, and there is only the dance.
                                                    T.S. Eliot

1

o

The Longest Day

Mr. Justice Anthony Montague Hammersmith was seventy-four years old, clinging malignantly to his seat of power. The end was ten weeks hence, on September 2, 1985: his birthday and his mandatory retirement. I planned to solemnize this judicial milestone appropriately—for Hammersmith I would get unrepentantly hammered.

But this judge, my nemesis, was very much unretired on the twenty-first of June: he was on my case, literally and in the argot. I had drawn him for a writ of *certiorari* to quash a search warrant, and he was riding me all about the courtroom, digging his spurs in.

"Charter of Rights?" he hissed at me. Little pork-chop lips. Behind glasses, monkey eyes, nearly sightless, squinting into the murky distances of Court 54 of the Vancouver law complex. "Was it drafted by a panel of gods, Mr. Macarthur?"

"No, just ordinary people like us, my lord."

"You come here preaching it like some evangelical gospel. The new panacea. I have heard the Charter invoked in favour of every, ah, perversity that the law forbids, whether it be intercourse with animals or spitting on police officers. Now it is offered to advance the cause of mass market pornography."

You can see how my day was going—a long day. By chance it happened in fact to be the longest of the year, the Summer Solstice.

"Alleged pornography," I said.

"Counsel will forgive me." Mr. Justice Hammersmith's voice was scritchy, fingernails on slate. "Alleged, ah, obscenity. But the exhibits appended to the Crown affidavit material might suggest a certain, ah, *prima facie* case exists—in proof

3

that the publications exploit sex to an extreme and disgusting degree."

Leroy Chalmers Lukey, Q.C., was seated placidly at his table, not a notebook or text in front of him. This devious prosecutor had picked a few of the raunchier pages from some of my client's pulp paperbacks, filed copies for the judge to read. Doubtless this, ah, literature had inflamed Mr. Justice Hammersmith's tinder-dry passions.

I had been arguing that the morality squad was using its powers of search and seizure as a bludgeon to force my client, the president and sole shareholder of A-OK Books and Novelties (1979) Ltd., out of business. That business being mainly wholesale books and magazines *ad captandum vulgaris*. Plus certain novelty items (fart cushions, dribble glasses, rubber Brian Mulroney masks, pop-up spiders). The police, frustrated at being unable to get convictions against retail stores, had seized every scrap of published material in Tony D'Anglio's warehouse on a search warrant which, my argument went, was invalid.

I continued to thrust away with my blunted lance, the new Canadian Charter of Rights (whose clear language prohibits suppression of free speech) but, frustrated, I found I was beginning to repeat myself.

"Yes, yes, I have you. I'm not simple." It was true: his mental facilities had not receded as quickly as his senses. "I'm not with you, Mr. Macarthur. I'm not with you at all. The writ will not go. I do not need to hear from you, Mr. Lukey."

Leroy Lukey: rising like a genial old bear to a semi-upright stance, grasping at the edge of the table to do so. A deferential bow of his head, and he slid ponderously back into his seat. Has Criminal Code, will travel. An overweight hired gun, Wyatt Earping for the Attorney-General. This was really a piddling case for him. He was on line for the Fall Assize to prosecute the Big Case, the Shiva cult murders.

Hammersmith gave brief judgment dismissing my motion to quash the search warrant. I sat there bemoaning my lot. Why did I always draw that misanthropic dinosaur? Had Mr. Justice Hammersmith asked the Registry to send him *every* case upon which I appeared as counsel in the Supreme Court of British Columbia? Two dozen judges up here and I had drawn Hammersmith four times in the last six months. His retiring mission as a judge: destroy Maximillian Macarthur the Second. I knew whence came his special enmity toward me: two years ago I had successfully argued in the Court of Appeal that the defence had been deprived of fair answer in a jury trial because Hammersmith had shown extreme bias toward the Crown. Here is a man who takes such things personally.

"Application is dismissed," he repeated. "Is there anything else to clean up, Mr. Clerk? What happened to the other counsel who were here?" The beast was still hungry—were there no more Christians to be devoured?

"It's after four-thirty, my lord," said the clerk in a Bob Cratchit voice. "Everyone else has gone."

Including, thereupon, me. Outside the courtroom I was blinded by the sunlight that streamed through the massive diagonal face of aluminum tubing and glass that combined as a window and wall to the western sky. It is not a courthouse, it is a giant greenhouse. It is too odd a structure even to be referred to as a courthouse, and so it is called the Law Courts Complex. It is Arthur Erickson's act of vengeance against the pillared pomp of long architectural tradition. A symphony of triangles, open space, tiers, long, trailing vines. An outdoors *Vancouver* feeling.

In the barristers' changing room (a musty, indoors feeling), I was forced to engage in banter with Lukey.

"Good try, Mighty Mouse, but arguing Charter of Rights in front of him is like jumping out of a plane with a Polish parachute." Pink lips working around the bottom area of the great round flush of his face. "You heard of a Polish parachute? It's the kind that opens on contact."

"That's a good one, Leroy."

Lukey, in his undershirt, slapped a fat, damp, intimate hand on my shoulder. "Come on, I'll buy you a drink at the Lawyers' Club," he boomed. "Maybe the whole bottle."

I mumbled something about the only bottle I wanted was rubbing alcohol for the bruises. "Actually I have clients," I lied. Translation: I would as fain spend the declining hours of a cruel Friday afternoon with this closet bumboy as I would swamping cesspools. I had friends to be with. I did not want to be dragged into the Lawyers' Club like a hunting trophy.

Lukey released me, and I went down the tiers to our company locker. The prosecutor followed, doing up his shirt. "Stupid damn law," he said. "Throwback to the seventeenth century. A man should be allowed to read what he wants, whatever kind of muck. But there it is, there it is." He winked a fat wink that said: we poor minions of the law must do our crazy duty, uphold the laws even if they're ridiculous.

Lukey wandered back down to his own locker, saying jovially (to himself, I guess), "Yes, sir, there it is. Whys cannot find answers. Why is the cosmos? Why is God?"

What was that all about?

I removed my black gown and vest, wing collar, tabs, collarless shirt, the armour of the costumed lawyer in high court. The armpits of that shirt were damp with the sweat of futile struggle.

And with something else.

Let's face it—fear and loathing in the mansions of justice.

Was the courtroom doing me in? Was I, after only five years of this work, becoming an emotional cripple, a victim of the harsh practices of the law? I did not want to become one of those human shells that the courtroom casts out, men and women broken by the tension of the courts, unable to keep the pace, to fight off the Hammersmiths and the Lukeys. Many of my friends—young lawyers like me—were already on the road to destruction: alcohol, pills, knotted nerves. Others couldn't buck it and so were buying it: the system. I didn't know if I would survive. I would never buy the system but I was inescapably a part of it. Someone had to play the role of the civil rights advocate, the fellow who gets his butt kicked across the courtroom floor by the protectors of decency and responsibility.

That noble task had been assigned to Maximillian Macarthur the Second, myself, an absent-minded masochist just turned thirty, just moving into that terrible decade when men and women are made or broken. Or so my friend, Ruth, a psychologist, liked teasingly to tell me. She who had also just entered her thirties, but was fighting them, moving backwards; she who was hot-tempered and nervily independent; she whom I was wedded to in heart.

Anyway, I was just depressed. Losing does it to you. Always. I would have cried, but I possess brave Scots genes, and had been brought up to believe that tears, like masturbation, were not healthy.

I stuck my courtroom clothes in the locker, removed my light cord suit, and dressed. It was a rank place, this locker, containing the detritus of myself and two less disciplined men, Brian Pomeroy, who lives moment to moment in dread of the impending holocaust, and John Brovak, known in the legal profession as The Animal.

Within the confines of this, our firm's assigned locker in the changing room for gentlemen barristers, might have been found—buried in the murky compost of yellowed shirts and collars, aromatic gowns and vests—such clues to our collective personality as an occasional empty mickey of Smirnoff (It *does* take your breath, says Pomeroy); a nerd of afghani black (Brovak: "Where did I leave that stuff? I had it when I went to the courthouse"); a ham sandwich still in its sealed plastic wrapper, the meat probably as hard as pemmican (mine—sometimes I can't eat); a jar of Vitamin B Complex tablets; a copy of *Hustler* Magazine (Brovak again); a few scattered aspirins; a copy of Chandler on Impaired (can't remember whom we borrowed it from, can't agree on who borrowed it); another book, entitled *How to Survive the Eighties* (Pomeroy); the remnants of a twelve-pack of lubricated Sensitols (I admit having borrowed a few from Brovak's supply—Ruth had recently gone off the pill); five books of unsold raffle tickets: Civil Liberties Association, passage for two on an Alaska cruise (ultimately, I knew, I would feel guilty, and buy them all).

Two other partners used a locker in the lady barristers' changing room. They were Marx and Sage. Sophie Marx was murder in the courtroom, had excellent tools. She, Pomeroy, Brovak, and I had been law school pals but Augustina Sage was three years our junior, bright yet oddly naïve.

Pomeroy, Marx, Macarthur, Brovak and Sage. Preferred area of practice: civil rights and crime. (Funny how the two go hand in hand, says my father, a big corporate lawyer.)

I am the shortest person in the firm—I'll get this over with now—a victim of heightism on the part of bigots. I am five foot five and two-fifths inches tall. I am not proud of it and I am not ashamed of it. I am not particularly handsome—all ears and forehead—but I am personable.

Brovak is six foot four and looks like John Travolta.

Pomeroy is six-one. Sophie Marx is five-ten-and-a-half in her socks, a large-boned woman who could break your arm. Augustina Sage is only an inch taller than I, but her frizzy Afro, an explosion of brown curls, adds two inches.

It has been a long battle, my inner struggle over sizeness. But as I emerged from my uncertain twenties, I found myself winning it. The measure of a man in that most contemptible of planes—the physical—is the poorest kind of standard in a just world.

* * *

Pomeroy was at a table by himself against the back wall of the El Beau Room (truly, it is so called), his eyes sunken and red as a result of what I divined to be defeat.

"Ambush," he said. "They took no prisoners."

Pomeroy had a thin, cavernous look, his face hollowed out, a crescent moon. His voice was dark and resonant, gloom-laden, like a TV news announcer's.

"Who did you draw—Judge Dracula?" I said. "You look drained." I sat down beside him and ordered an Urquell Pilsen. Brian and I would be brothers in defeat, offering solace to one another.

"I drew Innes," he said, and pantomimed a face from a bad Hollywood horror movie. "Why do I always draw Innes?" He clutched at the lapel of my jacket and said urgently, "He comes to me every night now. Caroline wakes me when I start to scream."

I wanted to tell him about the evils that had taken place in Court 54, about the travesty of it all. But Pomeroy was three months senior to me at the bar and had first go. "Really bad in there, huh?"

"Hell might be worse." He took a big slug of his Marguerita. "My guy's an insurance agent, spiteful bitch of a wife, he goes out and has one too many one night, creams a parked truck, allegedly leaves the scene. Crown forgets to prove one of the essential ingredients of the offence, namely that the object that Mr. Borcovitch was in care and control of was in fact a *motor vehicle* as defined in the *Code*. Only thing ever mentioned in the Crown's case is the word Mustang. A judge can't take judicial notice a Mustang is an automobile." Brian was submitting hard, as if I were a judge on appeal.

"Guess who I drew?" I said.

"The Crown's evidence only proves—this is me, making my no-evidence motion—that the accused was driving a Mustang, which, as the whole world knows, is a wild horse and defined by every dictionary of the English language as such. Never defined as a motor vehicle. Can you believe it—Innes rejects my no evidence."

He called hoarsely to Samson Loo, the waiter: "More."

"My *certiorari* came on this morning, the one to quash the search warrant for A-OK Books and Novelties. Guess who I drew?" It was time now for Brian to share my burden, as I had his.

"Can you believe it? All the Crown had proved was that my client was driving a wild horse which damaged a parked Cadillac. Why do I always draw Innes? I said, when the trial was over, I said to myself, looking up at Innes's cold blue eyes, 'I will arise and go now, and go for Innes, free.' What does it matter, we're all going to be reduced to alpha, beta, and gamma rays any week now. And Innes will be standing there in the dust giving the accused a month to pay or thirty days. You know what he said? 'Mr. Pomeroy,' he said. . . ."

I gave up, allowed my moody partner to babble on as I peered around into the cool gloom of the El Beau Room, retreat of criminal lawyers and other riff-raff.

One of my partners, John Brovak, was carrying on expansively from one of two joined tables. He was surrounded by members of the Ramirez-Johnson cocaine conspiracy, a trial now into its seventh month, a war of attrition in which two of the twenty-four accused were John's clients, the balance shared out among another twelve lawyers, feuding bitterly with one another over tactics, a giant ego scrum, with Brovak being driven to ever-grosser courtroom excesses because of the sheer boredom of it all.

The cocaine conspirators (alleged) were brazen, showed lots of flash around their necks and fingers and earlobes, plus they had three or four pretty hookers fluttering around there like moths. The case, a Lima-Seattle-Vancouver hook-up, involved interminable paperwork and wiretap and surveillance, twenty pounds of Peruvian flake, a lot of guilt by association.

I worried about John. There he was, in the midst of them, roaring at his own scrofulous humour, disdainfully defying a directive from the Law Society instructing criminal lawyers, the untouchables of this profession, to shun the company of criminal clients in "social situations." Let the benchers of the Law Society charge him, he says. He would make a shambles of the disciplinary hearing. To Brovak, benchers are like cops. Brovak hates cops.

"He wouldn't believe my client, of course," Brian Pomeroy was saying. "'I was so drunk I didn't know I hit the truck.' An honest defence, forthrightly given. No intent to escape civil or criminal liability. Innes's mouth is saying, 'I find the accused's version could not possibly be true. I am satisfied beyond a reasonable doubt that the Crown has made its case.'" He mimicked Provincial Judge F.T.E. Innes's voice, a soft speech that sends shivers. "But his eyes, those distant, dying stars, are saying: 'You see, Mr. Pomeroy, if he were truly innocent, the police wouldn't have bothered to charge him, and how can I possibly believe the words of a man who has been charged with a criminal offence?'" Brian moaned. "Why do I always draw Innes?"

I just looked at him, not pity for this man any more. I had my own suffering to wallow in. A fourth straight loss. A bad streak.

There is no lower a low than losing a verdict. It is what makes the practice of law so bloody, so hard on the psyche. A few straight losses and suddenly you are suffering from what Ruth calls a siege mentality, judges and prosecutors coming at you with fifty-millimetre cannon fire.

But winning—ah, that is a different thing. There is no higher a high than winning. Only those who have practised criminal law—and I do not include the three-piece-suit pansies from the uptown firms, not real lawyers, basically solicitors who stick their toes in the water timidly once in a while—can ever know the almost narcotic rush you get when you walk out of that courtroom, your heart pounding blood to a flushed face, the words of the judge—"I must regretfully find that the Crown has not made out its case"—ringing like gongs in your ears, the client babbling happily behind you, the prosecutor left sulking at his table. John McEnroe has never known that feeling on the tennis court, nor Steve Podborski on the hill. Nor Sebastian Coe at the break of the tape.

If it's a big case, the kick can be almost orgasmic. And sometimes there are reporters waiting outside the courtroom door. . . .

Dream on. At the time I was still waiting for the big case, the headline-crunching murder that would make my name. I had never done a murder. Pomeroy did *his* first one three months ago. His guy only went down on a manslaughter, five years, pretty good. Brian had squeezed a little ink from *The Sun,* maybe half a column.

Skid road murders like that one are pretty common around here. But there was only one big case coming up in the Vancouver courts this year. The Om Bay cult murders, set to open the Fall Assize on September 2. This was a twenty-two count murder case that promised to sweep everything before it in a tidal wave of printer's ink. Matthew Bartholomew James, alias Shiva Ram Acharya, had been charged last December with killing every sole member of his small commune. He was being defended by the great Arthur Beauchamp: so eloquent, so in control of the courtroom, alternately charming and slashing. It was known that the more he drank, the better he got, and there was always Beefeater gin in the pitcher on the counsel table. I was planning to keep free days in September so I could watch him in action.

And thinking about Arthur Beauchamp, I conjured him just like that. He came striding in through the Hornby Street entrance of the bar, glowering, looking about as if for someone to vent spleen upon. He was still wearing, under a plaid jacket, his black court vest, wing collar unclasped, tabs hanging loose. His attention focussed on two plainclothes guys, Peake and Chekoff, lounging by the corner of the long bar: morality squad, drinking ginger ale, probably on duty. I could see that Arthur was chiding them a bit. These two policemen, famous for their love of overtime (they arrest everybody they can on the emptiest of cases to pick up that time-and-a-half for going to court, and they boast sixty-thousand-dollar-a-year incomes) are not like the wise-cracking, merry crowd in Barney Miller's precinct. They are a humourless duo who can never quite pick up on the barbs.

Finished with his sport, Arthur Beauchamp swirled majestically around the corner of the bar while I scrambled up to fetch a chair for him. "This used to be a decent establishment," he said. "Now they allow every kind of low-life in here including Constable Gavin Peake and Constable Henry Chekoff. Peek and Jerk-off, I believe they are called: those long, soul-destroying hours in the hotel-room closet, peering through the keyhole. May I join you gentlemen?"

As if he had to ask.

"Might one of you young fellows examine the top of my head for recently deposited fecal matter?" Arthur said, sliding with a groan into the chair. "I feel I have been dumped upon. I've just returned from the Court of Appeal, where their lordships and I engaged in controversy over an extorted confession. I fear the Chief knows as much criminal law as my three-year-old grandson, and is far less charitable."

Samson Loo scurried up with a Beefeater and tonic in a tall glass.

"In a word, to sum up, to culminate: I lost." Arthur's one good eye looked balefully at the drink being lowered to the table in front of him. His other, the glass one, stared somewhere else, perhaps at Samson Loo's feet. "Sam, whatever these gentlemen are having, please."

I wanted to say no—I had my run to do yet—but it would have been insulting to refuse. My gaze drifted over to Brovak and the conspirators: I saw one of them, Twelve-Fingers Watson, slip a small bindle packet to my partner, a transaction quickly completed between hands dangling down beside chairs. I glanced at Peake and Chekoff. They were not looking at Brovak; instead were glaring at Arthur, then over to me. Suddenly, uncontrollably, I felt guilty, as if in observing a crime I had been an accessory to it.

Unlike Pomeroy, Arthur gave avid ear to my tale of heroic struggle in Hammersmith's court. I related to him my arguments on *certiorari* and the judge's judicial depravities in response to it.

"You will appeal *that* of course," said Arthur with an indignation I knew was not feigned. "You have been screwed by the Hammer, unmetaphorically speaking. Thank God he is retiring. I won't have him for the Shiva trial this fall. I have Mr. Justice Baynard Carter." Arthur brought his hands together in a prayerful gesture, glanced skywards, and muttered a *bene dictum*.

Samson Loo came quickly with another gin for him. "I saw you praying," said Samson. "So I came." And, inscrutably, he left.

"Maximillian Macarthur the Second," said Arthur, savouring each syllable of my name, "upon those few privileged occasions when I have seen you in court, I have observed a doggedness. I have observed the exercise of a rational mind, rare enough in this decade of the eighties. We *experience* now, do we not? Thinking is a frivolous business, so we *experience*. I have admired, Maximillian, the way you prepare your—you will pardon the expression—briefs. I need a young mind. May I borrow yours?"

When Arthur Beauchamp prepared for a case, he eschewed the law library (a bleak place where no drink was sold), instead referred his problems of technical law to the young minds that sought refuge at the El Beau Room bar each day. I was his favourite, a crazed addict of the law's illogic, an inveterate reader of authorities. I assumed Arthur was not about to elicit from me an opinion. Among lawyers, they are always free.

"If you've got a problem, I'll find an answer," I said. Pretty cocky, but I believed one could find an argument in the books to support any position. It was simply a matter of hard work. No one ever accused me of being lazy.

"I should like to borrow your mind for a rather long time. Perhaps a few months, including preparation. Am I being presumptuous in asking if you might be able to clear your calendar in September?"

My mouth fell open.

"I have approached the Legal Aid Society. They are prepared to allow two hundred dollars a day for junior counsel. I know it is a pittance to a young man capable of earning that much per hour. . . ."

I was in a state of shock, unable to concentrate on his words. The Shiva mass murder case—Arthur Beauchamp was inviting me to assist him in the defence! My past few years of feeding Arthur snippets of law in the El Beau Room were paying off. I had given, now I was to receive.

"Serving as I will under the benevolent reign of Mr. Justice Carter, and knowing how much he loves the play of law and technicality, I should find you of immeasurable aid in feeding me lines, and delivering some of them yourself. I can't adjourn down to the El Beau Room every time I must seek the latest word on exceptions—they seem so varied and numerous—to the hearsay rule."

I was suffused with a rapture. Under Mr. Justice Baynard Carter, the defence would pillage the Crown's case. Carter was of that rare genus, the defence-minded judge. A scholarly man and a strict interpreter of penal statutes. My tribulations of the day were forgotten.

A smile opened up on Pomeroy's usually mirthless face. He was happy for me. The big case, and working at Arthur Beauchamp's side. We both knew what Arthur wanted of me. I was a library workhorse, and Arthur knew I would live and breathe the case all summer long, all September until the verdict.

I was embarrassed to find I was rubbing my hands together— an almost childlike gesture characteristic of Max Macarthur when he is excited. "Where are the particulars?" I said. "Let's go to work."

"Might we finish our drinks first?" Arthur smiled fondly down over me, like a favourite uncle.

There is not a criminal lawyer in Vancouver who would not trade his set of Daumier prints for a chance to peek at the particulars of the Shiva case. The particulars: that is our jargon for the minutes of evidence that convention demands the Crown provide to the defence. The profession was thick with rumour about the nature of the case against James, or Shiva, one of the strange new messiah-like folk who have been turning up recently. It was believed he was trained in the East, had taken on a "spiritual" name upon becoming a disciple of Bhagwan Shree Rajneesh, but had broken away, collected nearly two dozen followers and set up a wilderness ashram in the rainforest of Poindexter Island, about 150 miles northwest of Vancouver, at a place they called Om Bay.

About the murders, all we knew was this: on December 8, the RCMP had arrested Shiva at his ashram, standing in a pool—it was said—of blood of his twenty-one followers. They were young people, most in their early twenties. Seventeen had been tied up and executed with bullets to the brain, four others shot in the heart. The twenty-second victim had expired after crawling lost for five days in the bush. Otherwise the public had been told nothing. Inspector Frank Storenko, in charge of the investigation, had put a tight press clamp on everything. Om Bay: Canada's Jonestown.

Never once during his easy ramblings in the El Beau Room had Arthur Beauchamp let slip any of his insider's knowledge. What his client had told him was, of course, absolutely privileged and confidential. Arthur was a man of limber but not loose tongue.

As Brian Pomeroy slipped over to Brovak's table to tell him about my new client, Arthur leaned toward me and said in a soft voice, "Lined up against us will be the usual array of forensic psychiatrists. We have only Mundt, and you know how dangerous Mundt is with a jury unless he can be reined in. I can't find another local expert willing to back us up, and Legal Aid cutbacks prevent us from going outside the province. Anyway, Shiva doesn't like to talk to psychiatrists, finding most of them, I suspect, to be insufficiently spiritual. He will not even talk about the killings to me, Max. I think he prefers to be defended by God, although he is too polite to say it. He says he follows the 'wayless' way, and that way does not include a side trip to the witness stand."

"He refuses to give evidence in court?"

"He will not testify. The charges, the trial—these are worldly things and have nothing to do with what he calls the 'eternal present.' I want you to try to talk to him, Max. Perhaps you are more spiritual than I. Perhaps the two of you can *relate*." He fixed me sadly with his one good eye. "I fear we engage upon the defence of the impossible. I am pleased to have you at my side."

Not as pleased as Max Macarthur. I was about to defend a mass murderer (alleged). It was one of the happiest moments of my life.

2

○

Anniversary

Until the next afternoon, when I would meet with Arthur, the secrets of the Shiva case would remain temptingly in their file. I phoned Ruth Worobec from the bar to ask if she wanted to catch a movie this evening.

"We'll catch one here," she said. "*French Lieutenant's Woman* on SuperChannel." Her kind of movie. Ruth, beneath it all, was a romantic. "Also because Jacqueline is going out to a party tonight, and I want to be here when she gets home. Early. Listen, come for dinner."

Jacqueline is her fourteen-year-old daughter, the issue of Ruth and a married hit-and-run artist she encountered when she was only seventeen. Abortions had been illegal and dangerous in those days, and Ruth had refused to give up the baby, struggled through an M.A. program in psychology at the University of B.C. She was fanatically independent. I stayed over a couple of evenings a week, but never pushed it. A weeper like *The French Lieutenant's Woman* would probably keep me in her apartment for the night. I would tell her about the good news over one of her excellent dinners.

I left the El Beau Room as day was merging with evening, too much beer in me, and put off going to the office, where I knew Amanda, my secretary, tended to leave nagging reminders of things undone. Instead I did my run.

Six days a week, rain or shine: seven miles around Stanley Park seawall. Usually in the early morning, but on a day when I have a big case, late afternoon or evening. I keep my strip at the YMCA, drive (drive, don't walk, don't run) through the exhaust clouds of West Georgia Street, park in the lot below the zoo, then chug counterclockwise around the wall:

16

Brockton Point, north around Prospect Point, Third Beach, Second Beach, back along the isthmus by Lost Lagoon, charging hard toward the end.

I am not popular among the cyclists—I run them off onto their own side of the seawall path, going straight at them if they are on my side of the white line. They, too, like the view side, but it has rightfully been assigned to the walkers and runners. I do a thirty-eight minutes and forty-five seconds, down to just over thirty-seven for the six miles, pretty good for a criminal lawyer. I also do the marathons, Vancouver, Victoria, Seattle, and on occasion the Hawaii or Los Angeles. I rank high. I beat out a whole hell of a lot of guys who are a foot taller than me. I love it. I love what it does for me. Yes, I'm one of *them*.

The beer slowed me to thirty-nine and a half minutes. After doing a few quick cooling-off exercises, I jumped into my aging Daimler—which Jimmy the Gritch, with his unbounded skill, keeps running for me in exchange for retainers—and I returned to the Y. The Daimler is right-hand drive, imported from England. People are always craning their necks, looking for a midget in the left-hand seat. The law becomes confused, too, always coming up to the wrong window. (As a matter of principle, I fight all my tickets, even the parkers. I beat half of them simply because the police can't bother to show up in court for the minor cases.)

A quick visit to the office to pick up my messages and examine Amanda's angry memos. The messages: Mr. Williamson: "When is my trial date, please call." (Why do they always forget?) Mrs. Bowerchuk: an ominous call, "Get my boy off. Phone if in doubt." Plaintively, from Civil Liberties, first, "Call if possible before three," then, "Call anyway, at home. Greg."

I was on a retainer (the kind without a fee) to give quick advice whenever Greg Ranjeet, the executive director of the Civil Liberties Association, had to have it fast. I would call him later, from Ruth's. The other calls were from lawyers and could wait until Monday.

There was also a note from Amanda: Tony D'Anglio had been in. He would be wondering about the outcome of my motion to quash the search warrants against A-OK Books and Novelties (1979) Ltd. He would have to be persuaded to front some money for the appeal: a high principle was at stake here. But when was I going to have the chance to prepare the factums? I had to shed clients, not take on more business if I were going to give Shiva my best.

A final note: "Your Dad called. He was steamed."

What about, this time? Poor up-tight Dad: Maximillian H. Macarthur, CBE, OBE, colonel of the Air Force Reserve, ex-president of the B.C. Progressive Conservative Party, stern Presbyterian, old Shaughnessy. I come from a background of privilege. My father was a lord high poobah among corporate lawyers on the West Coast, the son and grandson of chief justices, headed for the bench one day himself. Macarthur and Oswald, that's his firm. Don't be fooled: the bigger the firm, the smaller the name. Macarthur and Oswald were seventy-three in number, at last count. It's a factory. Conversely, the bigger the name, the smaller the firm, e.g., Pomeroy, Marx, Macarthur, Brovak and Sage.

With such a background, why have I become such a rabid liberal? I, the epitome of male WASPness, a descendant of the powerful merchant Scots who opened up the Canadian West. Why, it might be wondered, does Maximillian Macarthur the Second tilt so hard at the windmills of injustice? Is it because I wish redemption from family guilt? Is it because I am five feet five and two-fifths inches tall? Or is it, as my psychologist girlfriend gently suggests, an oedipal aggression against my father and his values?

I called my father.

"This morning," he said, "I was called away from a bank directors' meeting to answer an apparently urgent telephone summons. The call was from a certain Mitzi Lovemore, if that is his or her or its real name. He, she, or it wanted to know when his, her, or its trial for gross indecency was scheduled and sought to meet with me in my office."

I could see him in his den, slippered, briar-piped, red-faced, fuming.

"Sorry, Dad, she's a client of mine. Transvestite."

"As I divined from the baritone tremolo of his, her, or its voice. And earlier in the week, the proprietor of what is apparently known in the trade as a head shop interrupted a meeting of the trustees in bankruptcy of Hastings Assurance and Indemnity to seek advice on the sale of a product he referred to as synthetic hash. Do you not offer the courtesy of your own phone number to your clients?"

"Sometimes they lose it. Sorry. How's Mom?"

"They say two more weeks in the cast. It's embarrassing

enough that I find your name in the paper almost every week—my name, too, I must regretfully add—championing the cause of a multitude of perversions in the name of so-called civil liberties—"

"I didn't raise my son to be a communist, huh, Dad?" I interrupted. "Maybe Mom should see a therapist." She had fallen over a hall table while sleepwalking. "She could have walked outside, right into the pool, you know. I think she sleepwalks because she's unhappy. Ruth says it's a signal of loneliness, a subconscious search for contact with others. Maybe she wouldn't feel so lonely if you talked to her more."

As I lectured, I could literally hear my father fuming. A lippy, blacksheep son: a cruel Macarthur legacy. My elder brother, Tom, had not turned out well either. A college drop-out, he was now running the family ranch near Kamloops, much too unambitious and happy. (As far as our father and us: many communication breakdowns.)

"Perhaps you might consider doing the same thing yourself, young man, instead of restricting your visits to Thanksgiving and Christmas. We are expecting you the weekend of July 6. Kamloops. A *very* important family get-together."

"Do you ever take her out, Dad?" I was unrelenting. Ruth says people pussyfoot most with those who are close to them.

"You know how she despises social functions."

"A movie. A weekend at Harrison Hot Springs."

"I didn't raise my son to be a marriage counsellor either. I suppose this is your friend's influence." There was always that inability to say her name.

"Ruth. Ruth Worobec. Yeah, well, if Mitzi Lovemore calls again, tell her I'll be adjourning her case until after September. I'm going to be working on the Shiva case, Dad."

"The *what*?"

"Junioring Arthur Beauchamp for the defence."

"The what? Shiva? The lunatic who killed all those people?" It sounded as if he were choking.

"'Cult Killer Arrested in Bloodbath.' That one. Maximillian Macarthur for the defence." I chuckled. "You're going to see your name in the papers, Dad."

"Max, you have to think of your—"

"Reputation," we said in unison.

I think my father loved me but there was no way I could really tell. We chatted unamiably about reputation for a few minutes, agreed to continue the battle two weekends from now at the Kamloops ranch. We hung up, both of us feeling unresolved. *Don't be so hard on him,* a little voice whispered within.

Sophie Marx was the only other person in the office. That she was there at all—at half-past six on a Friday evening— credit the fact she was to begin a big trial Monday. Her client was alleged to have picked up a teenage hitchhiker in his black van and committed what the Code now calls an aggravated sexual assault. Rape, in other words. 'A *consent* defence," she moaned when the Legal Aid contacted her. But you don't turn these things down on principle. It's like the Civil Liberties Association defending the rights of Nazis to march. People find it hard to understand; I get tired trying to explain.

I paused at the library door. Sophie, a large mole, had burrowed into a mound of law books. She squinted at me through bottle-bottom glasses. "He is a misogynist, an ego-deficient brute who hates all women, including his lawyer. I'm going for an all-male jury: twelve ego-deficient brutes."

Sophie Marx had a handsome, animated face, but had long ago given up (had she ever tried? As a teenager?) looking beautiful. Her attire could be described only as being baggy. So, alas, could her body. She was all lawyer, had no time for much else except a little disastrous dabbling in stocks, for she considered herself a competent capitalist. Sophie and I were the two hardest workers in the firm. We competed—not out loud, but quietly, with dignity.

"You going for the lesser verdict? A sub-section two assault?" I knew there was only ambiguous evidence of violence.

"I'm going all the way, Max. The thing is, he actually *is* innocent. The woman was so stoned she tore her own panties when she was taking them off, then fell and bruised her arm against the door of the van." Sophie sounded convinced of her client's version—but criminal lawyers are always prepared to believe their clients, even if they don't believe *in* them. "Trouble is," she sighed, "he didn't mention that to the police. I've got to put him on the stand, and his record will come out."

"What's the record?"

"Previous rape." She lit one cigarette off the butt of another, went back to her labours.

* * *

"I've got some good news and some bad news."

"What's the bad news?" Ruth asked.

"The bad news is we are going to have to postpone our canoe trip this August."

"Aw, Max, we've been planning a wilderness holiday for almost a *year*. I have my holidays set for all of August. What's the good news?"

"I am defending the infamous and so-called cult killer, that guy Shiva from Om Bay."

"Psyche*delic*," said Jacqueline, wolfing her vegetables.

"What's the good news?" Ruth glared at me.

"That's it. I'm junioring Arthur Beauchamp. But I'm going to need the month of August to prepare." She had always told me to be up front in all my dealings with her. Shiva was more important than a three-week canoe trip in Bowron Park. Into my mouth I forked the last broccoli *à la polonaise,* a vegetable so delicately cooked it melted on contact with the tongue. The main course had been *sauté de veau aux champignons*.

"How can you defend someone who murdered all those innocent kids?"

"How do you know he murdered anyone? You were on the scene?"

"Oh, don't lay any of that lawyer gobbledygook on me." I could see she was really peeved about the canoe trip. "I know the game. You've been playing it so long you've started to believe the real world is somehow accurately reflected in a courtroom. He's guilty. The police don't make a habit of charging people with murder unless they're guilty, even though it can't always be proved in court. One thing I've learned since you became a factor in my life—"

"A *factor* in your life?" Jacqueline said. "Jeez, Mom."

"—is that a good lawyer, which I suspect you are, gets crooks off. That's not just a popular misconception about lawyers. It's true."

"I do not get crooks off." This was an ancient, wearying battle.

"Oh, yes—they are innocent until proven guilty, and because someone forgot to dot an 'i' on count fifty-six of the indictment, they are not *proved* guilty, so therefore they were never crooks in the first place. So *that* ridiculous fiction goes. It is no wonder lawyers are distrusted by all normal-thinking people. I don't trust them, and I hang out with one."

"*Hang out*, Mother? You don't just *hang out* with this factor in your life. You sleep with him. Be up front."

Jacqueline had a lot of fourteen-year-old lip. She was my friend and constructive critic.

I got up and started piling dishes, feeling very comfy in the tummy. The appetizer had been onion tart. The side dish had been sweet potatoes with a lemon sauce. Ruth Worobec, counselling psychologist and gourmet chef. But usually she was too bagged out at the end of a working day to cook like this. What was the occasion?

Ruth was a tightly strung person, bright, cynical, phobic. Her appearance was what one would call striking, not pretty. She was tawny, her skin the colour of creamy ivory, and her dark eyes were oval and hooded. An Indian princess's high cheekbones. Some ancient Tartar blood mixed in there with her Polish genes? She is five foot five and a half inches tall. After five years, I was still in love with her.

"Okay, darling, I'll be up front," she said. "Maximillian and I *fuck*. Which is something you do *not* do. And particularly that you will not do tonight at Hester's place. Nor will you drink beer, nor will you smoke pot, nor will you dance in such a way as to allow boys to rub against you."

"I will do *none* of those things, Mother. I am aghast. Do you think I am some kind of bawd?" The buzzer sounded. "It's Jennie-Lou." She got her coat, then bussed me high upon the forehead where a worrying early bareness of scalp was showing. "They say bald men make terrific lovers," she said. Thus she would tease me. But Jacqueline could get away with anything.

"Have a good time, Jacqueline," I said. Ruth and I were forbidden to call her Jackie.

"Don't miss the last Seabus." Ruth pulled her daughter's face toward her, smeared a finger over her lips. "The modern freed woman does not use lip rouge."

"Mother, it's a jungle out there. I have to *compete*." Hardly. She was as quick and sweet as a swallow, explosive and dark like her mother, and tonight she was daring that mother with a mid-thigh mini. Ruth gave her a kiss, then looked intently and threateningly at her.

"Be good."

"God, her stern, *wroughth*ful visage will be haunting me every minute of the evening. Why can't you just say, 'Have a good time,' like Max?"

"Have a *nice* time, dear."

"See you at breakfast," Jacqueline said to me, tumbling out the door of the apartment. "You *are* staying the night, aren't you?"

She was already gone as I was saying, "I don't know. Sometimes it's a jungle here, too."

"Well, Max, I *am* disappointed about the holiday. We were going to be absolutely alone for three weeks. Like dessert?"

"There's dessert?" How had she done this? All those killing hours trying to repair busted-up relationships, and she comes home and creates *haute cuisine*.

"Chocolate mousse. You have room?"

"Let me think. Well, yes, just to be polite, I *will* have some chocolate mousse." This was, after all, why I ran every day. So I could enjoy the good life and not feel guilty. Great guilt-cruncher, running. "I'm sorry, honey, but it's *the* big case. I can't be paddling around the Bowron lakes just before it starts."

"I feel I've been jilted in favour of a psychopathic killer. He's a phoney, that Shiva. They all are. Enlightenment, surrender of the ego. I've studied all that mystical, mindless wump. U.B.C. offers *courses* in it now, for God's sake. Psych 500, alteration of behaviour and mood utilizing the tantra yoga approach, with emphasis on encounter and self-revelation. Psych 501, finding the inner self, emphasizing the techniques of Gurdjieff and Lao-tzu."

Ruth had a very Western-oriented approach. More Adler than Freud, more Maslow than Jung, existentialist, pragmatist, individualist. She had finished her Masters, was two years into her Ph.D., picking up classes when she could.

"You know, in mental hospitals you'll find all sorts of people who are a cult of one. They haven't found any followers—that's the only difference between them and guys like your Shiva. It's a mystical supermarket out there now, Max, hundreds of people with full-blown delusional psychoses playing therapist. No training or qualifications. It's always the same line: drop your ego now; surrender yourself to the good old godly guru. The whole thing negates what I try to do in my work: give people a sense of responsibility for their own lives."

"All great religions start out as tiny sects," I argued. "Who can tell who will be the next Mohammed or Christ?"

She shook her head wearily and laid out something in

dessert glasses that looked like chocolate orgies. I poured coffee for us, and some Benedictine from the bottle I had brought.

"It's easy to convince people to let their hands be tied and their brains shot out when you've got complete control over their minds," she said. "I know what you'll probably do, trot that forensic womanizer Werner Mundt onto the witness stand to testify that a disease of the mind rendered your client incapable of appreciating the nature and quality of his acts. Shiva is found not guilty by reason of insanity. A psycho is turned loose." She was taking it out on me: the lost holiday.

"That's *not* what happens. He would be committed to Riverview. Until they . . . cure him." A verdict of not guilty by reason of insanity could be a hollow victory. Shiva could spend the rest of his life behind hospital bars. Still, it was the only defence, however weak. It would be a battle of psychiatrists, the Crown doubtless led by Eric Priestman, always ready to do a hatchet job for the prosecution, the defence gritting its sets of teeth as its star, i.e., sole, witness, Werner Mundt, buries himself ever-deeper in the mysteries of psychodynamics, talking arrogantly down to the jury.

"They were executed, shot in the back of the head, that's what the newspapers said," Ruth went on. "That's too deliberate for someone you claim is insane. But Mundt, *he'll* say he's insane. He thinks *everybody* is insane under the M'Naghten Rule. He'll testify the Queen of England is insane if he's asked to. I despise the man."

Dr. Werner Mundt, professor, therapist, professional witness, had taught Ruth a course on aspects of deviance. She had described to me his practice of seducing the less strong-willed of his female students. "Good marks are guaranteed to the co-operative," she had said bitterly.

"The Queen of England—and Canada—has retained to do her dirty work a fat sadist named Leroy Chalmers Lukey, Q.C. My *bête noir*." I had already told her of my loss that morning to him.

"I hope he takes you to the cleaners. That'll *really* do it for your career. Why don't you ever prosecute, work for the good guys for a change? You're becoming known as a hireling of all sorts of criminals. I even get thugs phoning here and asking for you. I wish you wouldn't give my number out."

"I've given it only to trusted clients who could need me in a hurry and who are not thugs."

"Sure, like that Mafioso Tony D'Anglio. Phones me at my *office* today. Treats me like a *moll*. 'Ha ya doin', sweets, ya gonna be seein' da mout'piece tonight?'"

"Jesus, I forgot." Those phone calls. We had half an hour before the movie began. I reached over to the counter that divided kitchen and dining room and picked up the phone, began jabbing some numbers on the panel.

"It never stops," Ruth moaned. "He never leaves the office."

Tony D'Anglio's staccato voice. "I got a couple of friends, had bad beefs laid on them by morality, they work for the Baths, they ain't hustlers, I'll send them over in the morning, I a'ready heard the bad news." One phrase flowed into the other.

"Yeah, we lost, Tony. The judge we drew was a dinosaur. Born in 1000 A.D., beginning of the Dark Ages."

"I know you did your best, Maxie. Quote me some numbers for the appeal, and I'll shoot you up an advance on Monday."

"It'll go ten and disbursements, Tony."

"Okay, I'll give you five big ones on Monday, the rest Friday, although wit' no books to sell I am startin' to get embarrassed financially, but listen, I got some new stuff comin' in from the States, I want you should look at them, they're kinda like ticklers, little hard rubber warts on them, stretch them over the vibrator, pussy goes ape. Customs is givin' a hassle, claims they're banned under a tariff act or some law like that. I'll drop one off. I want a opinion."

"Well, uh, okay." We hung up.

Ruth had just stared at me through this with her dark, Oriental eyes, sipping her coffee. "Very funny guy, Tony the Angle. The friendly neighbourhood mobster. And here is his Lancelot, Maximillian the Second, fighting the good fight for freedom of the press—let us not consider for a moment the ten-thousand-dollar retainer—so porno magazines can be openly sold to perverts. Gambling and white slavery and—what's this new club he's got? A whorehouse massage parlour?"

"A private club for gentlemen. Tony's Roamin' Baths, down on Homer Street."

"Two-dollar memberships at the door. Makes his money off the hookers with herpes upstairs. God, ten thousand bucks. That's why you're so active in the Civil Liberties Association, you get all this business. It takes me two and a half months of tears and pain to earn that much, what you get for walking into a courtroom for one day."

That was unfair. She had no idea what went into a case.

"Yeah," she went on, "what about the civil rights of people who are *forced* to read the smut that guy puts out?" She had her face close to mine, her chin jutting out combatively.

"*Nobody* is—" I started a sentence but she cut me off by reaching over and kissing me on the mouth.

"Talking about it makes me horny," she said with nibbling lips.

I had been falling for her tease. "What about *The French Lieutenant's Woman?*" I said.

"They'll show it again."

"I've got one more phone call," I said guiltily. To Greg Ranjeet, to whom I was supposed to be only a telephone line apart all weekend.

"You make that call and I will never talk to you again as long as I live." She rimmed her liqueur glass with her pretty tongue. Somehow that did me in. Greg Ranjeet could wait. Human rights and civil liberties could take a long coffee break.

Ruth tickled my nose with her tongue, and said, "Happy anniversary, Max."

I looked at her warily. "Um, which one is this, exactly?"

"You louse. Five years ago I first invited you to stay the night. The shortest night of the year. The Summer Solstice. I believe I nearly raped you."

"God, you're right." Then I understood: the *sauté de veau aux champignons*, the chocolate mousse. "Okay, I forgot. I'll buy you dinner tomorrow night. Le Fleuve Loire."

"Unless you had plans to go to the Roamin' Baths." She gave me a sweet, shy smile and tripped off to the washroom.

I stared contentedly out of her big plate windows as she showered. Her apartment was on the twenty-third floor of a concrete tower on Upper Lonsdale, North Vancouver. It looked out on the cold north side, but rewarded with a spectacular view of the divide between Grouse Mountain and Cypress Bowl, with the twin peaks of the Lions thrusting between them, breast-like, eight thousand feet, snowtopped still in June.

Despite the beating I had taken in Hammersmith's court that morning, I felt good. Here was an important young man. Here was a bright criminal lawyer about to embark on the biggest defence of his career. Here was a bright criminal lawyer with a smashing and madly unpredictable girlfriend in the shower. I stood there rubbing my hands together, happy as a kid.

Ravishing Ruth. We had met when I was under articles, fighting the fundamentalists who were trying to take over the Vancouver General Hospital board to undermine its therapeutic abortion committee. She had been a women's rights activist, Catholic but pro-choice. The struggle had spent her—there had been a nervous breakdown. Max Macarthur had been her nurse. In the five years since, there had been several hints from me that we might take up joint living arrangements. Self-reliant Ruth always demurred sweetly.

Self-reliant Ruth, standing by the bed with a towel wrapped around her, giving me a sultry come-hither with a beckoning index finger.

I showered and joined her.

* * *

"You can."

"Oh, I don't think I can."

"You could if you really *wanted* to," she teased.

Only one of us had enjoyed release. Perhaps I had been over-energized by all that chocolate mousse.

"I'm not going to let you go until you say yes." She had her legs wrapped tightly around me. I was, well, on top of her, in limp condition. I thought of Tony D'Anglio's rubber wart-armoured vibrator.

"I'm not going anywhere," I said.

"You're not going or I'm not coming." She wiggled beneath me, sending shivers that gave me hope.

The bedside phone rang.

Without thinking (honestly, this was an automatic, unreasoning response), I reached for the receiver and spoke into it. "Hello?"

Ruth grabbed the receiver from me, hurled it over the side of the bed. "You dishrag," she said.

She pinned me to her with sinewy arms. A distant voice kept calling. "Max? Max? Ruth, you there? Jacqueline? Somebody? The family dog? Am I speaking to the family dog?"

Ruth still had her legs wrapped around mine, and she was

laughing. I broke free, pulled the receiver up by the cord. "Hi, Greg."

"Oh, I got it," he said. "Ruth threw the phone at the dog just as I rang. The dog's name is Dishrag."

I pictured Greg Ranjeet at his work table surrounded by Schopenhauer, Dewey, Russell, Sartre, and a pile of unsold Alaska cruise raffle tickets. Last year he had been denied tenure in the philosophy department of Simon Fraser University. Because he was a faculty maverick and a Trotskyite.

"I thought I heard some moaning when the phone fell," he said. "You weren't making love, I hope. I should feel veddy guilty." Greg mimicked an East Indian accent. He loved turning stereotypes in on themselves.

"What's up, Greg?" I asked. Ruth was not quite smothering giggles into a pillow.

"What is up I have a veddy good guess, indeed, yes."

"Can it, Greg."

"I've got another cult kidnapping. The Unification Centre in Burnaby. Vigilantes hit there about eight o'clock this morning, hustled away a girl called Astral, in a vw camper dressed down as a hippy van. There was a bit of a fight. Some of the Moonies want to lay kidnap and assault charges. But hold onto your pants, er, figuratively speaking. I have news for you."

"Was it the Reverend Wheaties?"

"Yes, Wheaties and his two sidekicks, Wimpy Morgan and the Body Beautiful."

This had been happening too often. The Rev. Bill Wheatley ran the biggest deprogramming operation west of Ontario and north of California. I'd heard he charged parents five thousand plus disbursements for each kidnap-and-deprogram. A contribution to the works of his True Gospel Pentecostal Church—that is how he puts it to reporters. Those reporters, and the public in general, eat this guy up, a former God-fearing linebacker with the B.C. Lions, now a fundamentalist pastor (although a two-fisted, beer-drinking guy).

Since the cause of freedom of belief and religion remains unpopular in this smug part of the world, I am the heavy when I go to bat in court for the sects on behalf of the Civil Liberties Association. I had been against Wheatley a number of times in court, seeking injunctions, fighting guardianship applications, trying to prefer criminal charges. The police, so eager to make arrests of such reprehensible outlaws as mari-

juana smokers and nude sunbathers, were nearly impossible
to budge when complaints were filed against Wheaties—the
name had stuck since college—and his bunch. These were
straight guys just like the police, trying to save the world
from the creeps.

But the smart people in town know that Wheaties is just
another religious fraud, belting the Bible on Sundays and
fleecing his flock the other six days, selling non-voting shares
in his various Christian corporations. He has half an hour
every Sunday morning on Channel 12.

"You're sure it was Wheatley? They can identify him?"

"Wheatley, Morgan, and Calico. From their pictures in the
papers. If you want more evidence, they've got a wallet. It
fell out of Wheatley's jacket during the scuffle. Some big bills
in it, I'm told."

"All right, are you in touch with the Moonies?"

"Sun Myung Moon believes the telephone belongs to
Satan, yet they phone me every hour. They talk to me about
the Divine Principle. It's deep. I'm hooked. *Mansei! Mansei!*"

"I'll open up shop at ten tomorrow morning. Tell the head
Unificator to bring witnesses and wallet, and in the meantime
have them take some fast Polaroid shots of their bruises. How
old is the girl?"

"Nineteen."

"Okay, she's of age to make her own decisions."

Here I was earnestly carrying on business on the phone,
making appointments, giving advice. Ruth just let go, an
uncontrolled, rolling laughter that welled up from under our
joined bellies.

"I hear someone laughing," Greg said. "Is that Ruth?
Veddy strange, veddy, indeed. Listen, Max, this will blow
you away. Do you know who Astral's father and mother are?"

"Who?"

"Clue one: her real name is Melissa-June. Clue two: she
comes from Bos—"

"Holy shit," I interrupted. "Melissa-June M'Garethy?"

"The lost Boston heiress herself."

"Holy shit." The story of how this young woman had cut
family ties, the kind that didn't bind, and had fled into North
America's psychic jungle of cults and religious families had
made spicy headlines for the tabloids a year and a half ago.
J.J. M'Garethy, a billionaire (plastics, textiles, banking, and
politics—he was ex-Governor of Massachusetts and chairman

of the Democratic Fund for the u.s.) had offered a fifty-thousand-dollar reward for information as to where his daughter had disappeared.

Late last year, Melissa-June had sent her parents a postcard from Vancouver, no return address, and notices of reward were posted throughout British Columbia.

Greg said, "I assume her father and mother are with Wheatley, assisting in the deprogramming sessions. Your assignment, Max Macarthur, will be to rescue the damsel from their clutches."

"Not exactly a popular cause."

"You want popular causes, join the Boy Scouts, not the Civil Liberties. Don't forget to throw Dishrag a bone, if you've still got one. Yuk, yuk."

3

○

Moon and Madness

The hectic practice of Pomeroy, Marx, Macarthur, Brovak and Sage occupies the floor above an ancient warehouse in decadent Gastown, an area inhabited by a mixed bag of junkies, drunks, punks, and criminal lawyers. This is the historic old belly button of Vancouver, and it's kind of *comme il faut* to have, here amidst the refurbished slum, a nice office with sandblasted brick and red cedar trim. Also we have got cheap rent: not many businesses want to be above a late-night hotspot. That great echoing space below our office has gone through turns as The Warehouse, The Stomp Place, Sweetlips Disco, the Kit Carson Cabaret, and now, God help us, the Shillelagh and Shamrock. Fifteen men and women dressed up like leprechauns comprise the band, nine P.M. to two A.M.

My own office, looking over Maple Tree Square, was a woodsy place with *ficus benjamina* branches shading my desk, grape and English ivy vines crawling up a wall with rust-red, chipped bricks. I was swivelled around in my chair behind that desk on the morning of Saturday, June 22, peering through the branches and out the windows over the square, and down onto the hat—pigeon-shit white—of the founder of Gastown, Gassy Jack Deighton, a fabled drunk of his day. His bronze statue gives the area its special tone.

Gastown is visited by many young wanderers and is a good place to sign up recruits, so there were usually one or two religious groups represented down on the square on any given day. I wondered if Astral née Melissa-June M'Garethy had ever been below my window passing out tracts.

I was waiting for the Burnaby Moonies to show up. There

31

had been nothing on the news so far: the story of the
kidnapping of Melissa-June M'Garethy had not broken. But a
media circus could be expected if I got charges laid against
Reverend Wheatley and his two bully-boys over the M'Garethy
case. Criminal lawyers thrive on ink. I would be happy to
share some with the famous M'Garethys, who had recently
earned many unhappy headlines in their hunt for Melissa-June.

These were the notorious facts: J.J. M'Garethy and Edith
Winters had merged great inherited fortunes upon their
marriage twenty years ago. He was Boston, she New York,
and a renowned hostess at their luxurious midtown Manhat-
tan co-op and at their seasonal home in Monte Carlo. They
were powerful voices in lay organizations of the Roman
Catholic Church and the Democratic Party. They had lived
busy and happy lives, raised a perfect daughter, their only
child, Melissa-June. Who did not come home one day eighteen months ago.

At first it had been believed the girl had been kidnapped.
Front page stuff, I recalled. The M'Garethys were waiting
for a ransom note. Weeks passed; none arrived.

A month after her disappearance, a note arrived from
Melissa-June: "Mommy, I am happy. I am with Jesus." That
was all. Her signature was verified. The fifty-thousand-dollar
reward was offered. Detectives were hired. Nothing.

I recalled that eight months ago, *People* magazine did an
exceptional job of chequebook journalism on this family, with
interviews from not-so-friendly friends and not-so-loyal ex-
employees. The M'Garethys had been sleeping separately
for the last fifteen years, had engaged in raging warfare all
that time. Daughter Melissa-June, a "slow learner" according
to a former private tutor, had fled a loveless home to find
shelter in the arms of a new Messiah: she had surrendered to
a man who called himself Brother Julius, a former New York
taxi driver who, during a trip down Seventh Avenue, realized
he was Jesus Christ returned.

The magazine traced her wanderings with Brother Julius
and his twenty young disciples, her departure from him into
the Children of God, then into the Unification Church, who
were believed to be hiding her from the bounty hunters. Her
trail had been followed to the U.S. Southwest, to California, to
B.C., and had dried up.

The M'Garethys, doubtless enraged by the article in *People*
had, I assumed, made contact with professional deprogrammers.

around the continent, people who knew the terrain. And Wheaties had scored. For how much? I wondered.

From their offices, I could hear Harry Pomeroy and Sophie Marx interviewing clients. Saturday is always a good day for that, a day when people don't have to take time off from work. John Brovak had clients in the waiting room, a couple of boys from the Ramirez conspiracy, but whether The Animal would show up on a given Saturday was chancy, and he did not honour all appointments.

But I heard a grunt behind me, and I realized he indeed was there. I swung my chair around and looked at a figure of grotesqueness in the doorway. John Brovak, bare of chest and foot, a toothbrush in his hand, his hair tousled, his nose running, his eyeballs pinned, his hands shaking. Six feet four inches of physical damage.

"Slept on the floor of my office," he muttered. "Too fucking wrecked to get home."

"Wrecked? A truck? You get the license number?"

"What happened is I was working late and decided to go down and check out the Shillelagh and Shamrock. You wouldn't believe the shit that goes on there. I've got to wash up. There are a bunch of zeros for you in the waiting room. I'll get them."

Before I could stop him, he disappeared, and a moment later I heard his raw, phlegm-choked voice from the waiting-room area. "You want Max, he's down the hall. Hey, Jake, Charlie, what's happening, man? Give me half an hour to shave and have a shit. There's coffee in the coffee room."

Five Moonies glanced uncertainly back in Brovak's direction as they filed into my office. Three young men, two women, dressed as neatly as job-seekers, scrubadub clean, little red and white badges pinned to their lapels with the spider-web design of the Unification Church.

The Moonie team leader, a man about my age, extended his hand and offered a vacuous smile. "I am Robert," he said. "Mr. Macarthur, our house was visited by Satan yesterday." His voice was Moonotonic.

"A Justice of the Peace will not issue a summons against Satan." These people had that glassy-eyed, drugged-on-religion look. "The wallet," I said.

Robert handed me a fat brown envelope, sealed at the flap. I asked each of them to initial it where it was sealed.

"Why?" said Robert.

"Just do it."

They did it.

"Have you gone through it?" I took a letter opener to the opposite end.

"No. A little."

I didn't like the hesitancy. "How much money is there?"

"I saw some thousand-dollar bills. Mr. Ranjeet told us not to open it up." Robert gave me a guileless stare. The wallet was brown leather, stitched with thongs, a little snap to hold it shut. I opened it and counted out forty one-thousand U.S. dollar bills, and twelve dollars Canadian. What a fool, I thought, to carry his fee on his person when he goes to do his hit on Melissa-June. Behind the bills was a folded piece of paper, with handwriting on it.

I put a tag on the bills, stapled them together, had the Moonies initial the tag. I have seen careless lawyers burned in similar situations.

"Astral—Miss M'Garethy—how did she come to join your centre in Burnaby?" I asked.

I made notes on lined sheets as I extracted from them the story of how eight months ago some Moonie leaders from Northern California drove Melissa-June up to relatively safe Canada and deposited her within the bosom of a church centre on Vancouver Island, later one in the interior, finally Robert's group in Burnaby. The Moonie organization was aware, from the M'Garethys' widely publicized search, that they had a very hot property on their hands, I presumed. Doubtless they wanted to hoard valuable Astral until she could somehow be cashed in.

I knew how they had kept Melissa-June: they had provided her with a substitute family, far more loving than the series of babysitters, nannies, and other custodians of her early growing years. Ruth had studied the process: reparenting—the recruit is love-bombed. "Take off your shoes; be silly. Turn off your head. Just feel it, feel it." Hymns with Pentecostal fervour and a rock beat. Let the family do your thinking and worrying. God loves you; we love you; everybody but your hateful parents loves you.

Anxious, stress-ridden, and love-starved kids, these were the fodder for the Moonies, who drew heavily, according to statistics Ruth had read, from college-educated youngsters from good homes. The Moonies, like other cults, imprinted people into an extended, substitute family, taught them to believe their parents were instruments of the nether world.

I wondered what she was like: unhappy, wealthy Melissa-June. With all her so-called advantages, just another member of the space cadets.

The kidnapping had been swift, my Moonies told me. An innocuous and beat-up vw van, not Wheatley's famous Winnebago, had been parked down the street from the centre, and as Melissa-June was taking an evening stroll with these five friends, three men barged out of the vw, and a struggle ensued. Wheatley and his two Brobdingnagian pals finally got her into the van and drove off.

I knew the average deprogramming required four days of non-stop, non-sleeping badgering. To avoid interruptions by police or harassing visits by fellow members of the religious group, Wheatley ran a floating deprogram shop, one of those road-hogging Winnebagos. He claimed eighty per cent effectiveness, his sessions usually concluding with an ecstatic moment of reunion between child and parents. The young person, having, to use Wheatley's phrase, "come out of it," would always decline to press charges.

So there had been few prosecutions for kidnapping. Only two of these ever ended in verdicts, one in Vancouver, one in Seattle, and both times Rev. William Wheatley and his two confederates were acquitted. No jury was ever going to jump on these guys for saving a child from the hypnotic clutches of Sun Myung Moon or whatever guru happened to be the villain of the piece. "They're all frauds," Wheatley tells reporters. "Moon, Moses Berg, Erhard, that Krishna Consciousness guy, they brainwash these kids until their minds are in cold storage, send them off to beg and sell plastic flowers, while they wallow in luxury theirselves."

Well, he was right, to a point. I carried no flag for get-rich-quick gurus. But the fundamental question involved not merely freedom of religion, but freedom to believe any kind of bullshit you want, and sink in it, too. That's one of the things a democracy is all about, isn't it?

"My wild eye-rish rose, the sweetest flow'r that grows. . . ." Off-key song came from the little shower stall next to a sauna down the hall.

The Moonies pretended not to listen as they showed me their bruises. Robert and another man had fierce, raw scrapes on their arms and one of the women a large, yellowing

contusion on her inner thigh. A mean place to aim a kick, I
thought. Wheatley, Morgan, and Calico had lived up to their
reputations as bruisers.

Brovak had moved on to *MacNamara's Band*, repeating the
chorus again and again. The Moonies smiled serenely at me,
unflinching in their goodness. I told them to meet me at the
Burnaby Justice Building in two hours.

"Father thanks you," said one of the women.

"Father, huh?" I just looked at her empty face. Ego-
deterioration, Ruth would say.

After they left, Brovak came in, a towel wrapped around
his middle. He was humming, seemed jauntier now.

"Hey, a retainer," he said, spotting the pile of bills.

"Belongs to Reverend Big Bill Wheatley. He dropped his
wallet doing a hit."

"'Oh, the drums they bang and the cymbals clang. . . .'
Sure and we have down below a band that plays all the gud
Irish music, me bucko. And a lead singer who is obscenely
well-framed. And who I got to chatting up during her break."

"And whom you brought up here last night, to the coffee
room, and snorted the snow that Twelve-Fingers Watson laid
on you in the El Beau Room yesterday afternoon."

"How do you know all these things?" Brovak said this with
a bored voice. He had a world-weary face, handsome and
bony, a face that easily woos the unwary female victim.

"The mirror was still on the coffee table, with finger smears
on it. A lipstick stain on one of two unwashed cups. Pecker
tracks on the couch. Your nose was running a little while ago,
before you did up in the sauna."

"I say, Holmes, this is really too much, dewn't you know,
what? Listen, John Brovak does not try to make out on a first
date. It is too trivial, too cheap. However, it is true that a
little gram of dust on first meeting does ease the pain of
shyness and pave the pathway to ultimate love." He began
singing again. 'There's no business like "snow" business.
There's no business I know.'"

I picked up Wheatley's money and wallet and followed
Brovak from my office to the clothes rack beside the sauna,
where most of us kept extra sets of street gear. "John, as
friend to friend, I think you should start thinking about your
septum. I'd hate to see what you look like when your whole
nose goes into meltdown. It will if that trial doesn't end
soon."

"Another year and a half, the way we've got it planned."
John gave me a look of mild contempt, one he reserves for
people he believes are straight. He began dressing up like
someone in an Old Spice commercial: ascot, tweed cap.
"Too-ra-loo-ra-loo-ra, too-ra-loo-ra-lay. She's never ridden in a
1953 MG before. A foine day, me b'y, for a droive up the
Garibaldi Highway."

"The Ramirez-Johnson conspiracy knows they're going down
whenever you get to finishing that trial. And so they're
dealing all night long—I've seen how bagged out they look in
court—and my guess is they've got fifty kilos of nearly pure
stashed somewhere, and what they're hoping to do is put a
fortune in hundred-dollar bills into the ground and wait until
parole sets in. I know it's all in hundreds because that's exactly
what a gram is going for in town these days. Way, way down.
They're flooding the market. But certain guys don't pay piss all.
And they get highest quality. It's always too easy for lawyers,
John. Especially when you get too close to your clients. Those
two dealers who are sitting in the coffee room, they're from the
trial. They're not even your clients, they're Lubor's. You seeing
them socially or something? Off some where to share some
toots?" I was heated. This had been simmering.

"Climb off my back. It's strictly business. Lubor is fading.
He's gotten depressive, and Jake and Charlie don't have
confidence he can hang in there any longer. I'm probably
going to be picking these two guys up. Jake and Charlie like
my style. They like the way I kick the prosecutor around and
get the judge laughing at the same time. It's another thousand bucks a day. That's a little more than Civil Liberties pays
for helping Moonies take Bill Wheatley to court. Now I'm not
being critical, I know you bring in clients, but I'm just letting
you know that the conspiracy is a barely tapped gold vein.
Especially the way Boynton, that suck, is plodding along for
the Crown. He dots every 'i' and he's got twenty-three more
wiretaps to prove."

"I'm just telling you you're too close to your clients. You're
going to end up getting wired, doing up five times a day in
the courthouse washroom."

"Hey, there must be forty or fifty G's U.S. here," he said
flipping through the stapled bills. "Where does Wheaties get
this kind of money? What are you going to do with that wallet
and stuff? You going to return it to Wheatley?"

"I'm going to make him sit up and beg for it."

* * *

At the Burnaby Justice Building, the J.P. wasn't rushing into judgment about accepting the kidnap and assault complaints from my Unification Church people. Across the public counter he watched my clients with suspicious eyes as they wrote out statements for him, then drew me aside.

"I want the prosecutors to look at this. Bill Wheatley could sue me for malicious prosecution."

"You're an officer of the court, not a policeman taking instructions from prosecutors."

"Wheatley is a kind of hero around here, Max."

You Crown toadie, I thought. And not smart. The name of Melissa-June had rung no bells for him. "Just take the complaints and issue summonses, please. Okay?"

He fingered through my clients' statements and the Polaroid photos of their injuries. "Well, I don't think I will. Need more solid evidence. Some witnesses."

"Damn it, you don't have a discretion." I was near rage. "If you want to get your name in the law reports, I'll slap a *mandamus* on you." I told my clients to call me, then stormed out of there, went to the "Y," then to the park for my run, trying to steam my anger away. Damn, I didn't need all this—affidavits, petitions, praecipes, service, a half a day going to be shot getting a *mandamus* order to force this bureaucrat to do his duty.

* * *

Arthur Beauchamp's office was east of Gastown, in the unvarnished part of skid road. He had relocated there two years ago, and the wise uptown lawyers said his move to the skids was symbolic. Beauchamp had hit them. His week-long drinking bouts were storied, boisterous benders, and it was said he had drunk his way from uptown to downtown, from an established firm to a decrepit single practice in the unit block East Cordova, a ramshackle streetfront that had been a daycare centre before all the recent funding cuts.

It was also said that Arthur's politically connected ex-partners—a real pile-driving firm, about twenty lawyers—could no longer handle the bad rep, and they had paid him off, bought out his share of the partnership. But that was just

the wise lawyers' talk. I knew different. In the El Beau Room
he had confided this to me: he and his partners had started
off in the late forties as a radical muckraking firm. As lawyers
they had been good, and success had come, and wealthier
clients. But the firm grew soft and conservative, and only
Arthur Beauchamp was left to handle its diminished criminal
practice—a trade that tended to tarnish the firm's mobile
uptown image.

Arthur had been playing the game: a Bencher, the right
clubs, the right people, the right wing. But there had been
an inelastic marriage that rattled from crisis to crisis, and an
even unhappier marriage to his partners. Arthur hadn't been
pushed out, he had simply gone through a personal revolution two years ago. He had quit—quit the firm, his unhappy
wife, the lifestyle he had gamely tried to hang onto for
decades. He decided it had all been a life of dross: huge
properties and huge mortgages, partners savagely chasing
dollars, a faithless wife who tore his heart apart. He gave
up his partnership, his West Vancouver manse to his
wife, cashed in everything and paid it all to her in a
lump-sum, court-approved settlement. All he kept was his law
degree.

He was happy. Doing shit cases for poor people. Outside
the court, mostly drunk. But happy.

At four o'clock that day, I arrived at his office, surprisingly
comfortable with soft armchairs and chesterfields bought from
nearby second-hand stores. His inner office, where he ushered
me, was like an overstuffed living room, circa 1948, pleasant
in a cushiony, slightly musty way. He lived in a suite on the
floor above.

He offered me a drink from a Beefeater's bottle displayed,
not shyly, on the counter behind his desk.

"No, thank you, not being a prig, but I limit myself."

"It is widely rumoured that I do not. A former partner
once said of me that he didn't know I drank until I came to
the office sober one day." He topped off his own tumbler of
straight gin, pulled a file from a drawer of his desk and
flipped it open.

"To look at these," he said, "it is *necessary* to drink.
Memento mori." A soul-shrivelling array of colour photographs, bodies on the ground, at the scene, the same bodies
on morgue slabs. Closeups of broken wounds, faces starkly
white, twisted with the death masks of rigor mortis. Youthful

middle-class seekers, seeking no more, their bodies desecrated. Thirteen males, nine females, the oldest thirty, the youngest nineteen.

Here was a picture of Emelia Cruz, the twenty-second victim, who had expired after having tried to crawl to freedom through the heartless Pacific forest, and who died, the newspapers had said, in a fisherman's cabin. There was something distantly familiar about this young woman's sad, pallid face. Had I met her?

"'Did he kill everyone?' Those were her dying words." Arthur looked at her picture with a baleful right eye.

"To whom?"

"To the old fisherman, Joe Whitegoose. "The full text: 'Did he kill everyone? Am I alive? Am I alone?' And then, according to the particulars, she dies on his bed while he was making some soup."

"It's inadmissible, not a true dying declaration, not in contemplation of death."

He shrugged. "It's excessive to their needs, anyway."

I pored through the photos. This is the stuff the prosecution thirsts to get in front of juries. "I guess we want to admit the identity of the bodies," I said, my stomach crawling. As far as stomachs go, a criminal lawyer needs one as strong as any wartime surgeon's.

"Even if we admit identity, Lukey will argue the pictures are relevant—to show the precise entry points and paths of the execution bullets." Arthur pulled out reports from a team of doctors who did the autopsies. "Our learned friend will, of course, seek to show that only a functioning, sane mind—twisted though it might be—could have so efficiently dispatched those twenty-one persons. Look at them. Children. Innocents. Poor, dreaming God-seekers."

He was upset, tried to mask that by activity, poked into a package of Players, found it empty, rescued a long butt from an ashtray, and lit it.

I riffled through the pathology reports. The cause-of-death conclusion in seventeen of them was massive brain damage as a result of gunshot wounds that penetrated just below the occipital brain. The coroner's team concluded that time of death was between eleven A.M. and one P.M. that day: best estimate, noon. Of those not tied up, one had died from a rifle bullet in the anterior chest, the other three from bullets in the back.

"The theory of the Crown," said Arthur, "is that Shiva ordered one of these fellows, George Wurz, to tie people up, then Wurz was shot in the back and everyone executed. There are rope burns on Wurz's hands, and Hair and Fiber found filaments of manila on his sleeves. All the rope used to tie them was manila, same as the rope found in the storage shed."

He passed some blown-up fingerprint photos to me.

"A complete left-hand palm print was found on the stock of the Remington rifle. Also our client's left middle, ring, and little fingers, and the left thumb, all impressed into the dried blood. The old English army rifle that was found near the feet of Shiva, according to a police check, had been stolen last summer in Vancouver. How it got to Om Bay, no one knows. Oh, yes, the soles of his boots were matched for impressions in the mud. His footprints were near each of the bodies, and ballistics says all the spent cartridge cases in the area came from the .303 at his feet. Not one of your skimpy circumstantial cases. Blood on his hands, robe, around his mouth, for God's sake—oh, what a grisly portrait for a jury. *Flagrante delicto*."

It was ironclad. "All they need to top this off is a confession," I said.

Arthur found the police reports from Corporal Scanks, the ones I opened this history with, and quoted the words that Scanks had overheard Shiva speak. "Because I loved you, I had to kill you." Arthur sighed. "I asked Shiva if he said those words, and what they meant. He just shook his head and stared at me."

I read through Scanks' reports. "He was dancing?"

"Shiva, the Dance Master. Are you up on your Hindu mythology, Max?"

"Gods being exiled into the forests and wrestling with tigers. There's an elephant-headed god. All sorts of wonderful characters who take each other's forms."

"All of them incarnations of the one God, it is said." He settled back with his drink and another burning butt. "The great triad consists of Brahma, Vishnu, and Shiva. The omniscient Brahma; Vishnu, the god of goodness, of social order, harmony. Shiva, the god of destruction."

The newspapers had picked that up. Matthew Bartholomew James in his incarnation as the god of destruction.

"Shiva is the god of the terrible, of death, of the disintegrative forces of the universe. The myths have him as a hunter, a flesh-eater, a god who calls for human sacrifices. It is said he burned Kama, the god of love, with a glance from his third eye. He is also the god of the joke."

"The joke?"

"A great humourist, it's said. The fables are rife with episodes of practical jokes he's pulled on his fellow gods, not to mention on lowly mankind. Would that the Greeks and Romans had favoured us with such gods. We of the West have inherited a lacklustre lot."

He emptied his glass.

"But he is also the great ascetic, the king of the yogis, the god of destinies, of the forces of the soul, of nature. And in his aspect of Nataraja, he is the lord of the dance. Shiva is supposed to have danced the universe away, and danced it back again—so he's also the god of regeneration. His seat is high in the Himalayas, and the Ganges is said to issue from the snows at his feet. Our client's first name, Acharya, that means teacher. Ram—that's the Hindu root word for fire. I asked him why he chose his name. He didn't know. Odd fellow. After you meet him you will ask the question: Could he have done this?"

I was still looking at the police reports. "'Death kisses you with life. You will be reborn as gods. Whys can't find answers.' Well, that stuff will help the insanity defence go."

"We have three medical letters from Werner Mundt. Weak stuff. The Crown has a battery of medical people to testify."

"Where are their reports?" I was rummaging for them. Everything was in disarray in this thick file. I would get it into proper order for Arthur.

"Leroy had been playing Scrooge with those, and makes unintelligible arguments about his right to deny disclosure. We have a pre-trial scheduled for this Friday in Mr. Justice Carter's chambers. Some law might come in handy."

"Cases on disclosure of medical evidence. Okay, I'll find some."

Arthur's glass eye looked somewhere down at my belt, but his good one looked squarely into mine. I felt I should say something encouraging about all this, but suddenly I felt fatigued, felt the weight of this terrible case pushing me down.

"All these children, lying there, a killer moving among them, and *God*, how terrified they must have been," Arthur said, and his hand shook. A splash of gin, embarrassingly, wet his waistcoat. "It does not seem that this killer was hallucinating, seeing demons and shooting wildly at them. Where is the jury that will feel sympathy for our client, Maximillian?"

"Anything can happen with a jury, Arthur. You've said that many times."

"It might help if the client would co-operate. I think he has given up on me completely. Too ruined is my soul. I will never reach the state of being he calls purposelessness."

"I'll work on him. Tomorrow is Sunday, I'll go up to Oakalla and chat with him. I'll also go up to Tash-Tash Cove as soon as I can and talk to some of those witnesses. Maybe those Joiner brothers, the amateur cops, can add something—Shiva had to have been acting crazy on the boat ride back to Tash-Tash." The file had contained no witness statements from these two men.

"Yes, I was hoping you might. We can't afford a private detective, so if possible, visit that old Indian fellow at whose shack Emelia Cruz died. I guess I have left a few of these things a little late. You probably want to say that, but you're too kind. Well, it's good to have you on board for this one." He stretched out a hand. "The S.S. Purposelessness."

* * *

I walked the two blocks back to my office, clutching my booty in my arms. I would have Amanda make a copy of everything on Monday, but in the meantime I made myself comfortable at my desk—it was early Saturday evening, and the band below had not started up—and got into Dr. Werner Mundt's reports.

"On examination, subject presented as slightly overweight, blue-eyed, red hair, and beard with grey, five feet nine inches, weighing 180 pounds. There was no clouding of consciousness at first, but apparent disorientation later. He was oriented, polite, and poised. His thought processes were organized, his speech coherent, and it became apparent that he was interested in my field, even able to talk with intelligence about various manifestations of behavioural disorders, although clearly he had only a lay understanding. On testing, his memory seemed intact, but he refused to discuss the events at Om Bay. He was able to retain a remarkable fifteen digits forward. His intelligence is extremely high, and he speaks or at least reads, he says, some ten languages, including Greek, Latin, and Sanskrit."

Mundt complained that in the course of each of several interviews he conducted, Shiva's attention seemed to go missing at the end, as if he had disappeared "into some inner state of consciousness."

Shiva had spoken openly to Mundt about his background.

He had been born fifty years ago in Central China, the son of Dr. and Mrs. Trevor-Towne James, American Methodist missionaries. He was christened Matthew Bartholomew. When he was a two-year-old child, his parents woke one night during the Sino-Japanese war to find looters in the house, who then murdered them. The infant was rescued, taken to Hong Kong, then flown to New Hampshire to live with his grandparents near Concord. He had been a much-disturbed boy, but seemed to settle outwardly, and in school had been bright, achieving prizes, scholarships. He selected St. Andrew's College at Harvard, and studied for the divinity. He lived comfortably, and would continue to do so for years, upon a trust fund set up by his then-deceased grandparents.

He had been reclusive, living chastely, absorbed in Christianity. But at the age of eighteen, two years into a Bachelor of Divinity program, he left his dormitory, rented a room, and began to audit philosophy courses at the university. Revelation of a basic kind had come to him. He could no longer accept the Christian God.

After recovering from an emotional breakdown—Mundt promised to locate a medical history of this and send it on—James studied philosophy and psychology at Princeton for a while, then at Chicago, then the University of Southern California. "A young man hungering for belief," Mundt instructed.

In 1961, at the age of twenty-four, Matthew Bartholomew James met his first master, Chongyam Trunga Ripoche, a Tibetan lama. James attended a lecture by Trunga in Los Angeles, then followed him to his seminary in Wyoming. Trunga, an odd manner of lama, brought, of all things, worldliness into James's life. The guru chainsmoked and often got drunk on saki, was unpredictable.

"Subject reported that Trunga showed him how to empty his mind, destroying all assumptions with, in James's words, 'the masterful illogic of Zen.' Subject said that from Trunga he learned this truth: 'The only hope is hopelessness. Once one knows that, all paths are open.'"

Matthew James, catching America's spiritual wave even before the swell, was an early adherent at the Meher Baba Spiritual Centre in Myrtle Beach, California, and he moved from there to the much larger Meher Baba community in India. He travelled even the cliché route of searchers for self—the southern Himalaya Mountains—without achieving a completeness. But finally he did. In Poona, in the fashionable suburbs of that city inland from Bombay, he found Bhagwan Shree Rajneesh.

"'I achieved. I was reborn in ecstasy. I burst like a child into tears. I entered the eternal present.'" As quoted by Mundt. "Subject," said the psychiatrist, "then accepted his spiritual name."

But later the eternal present seemed not to offer eternal joy. Shiva served Rajneesh for twelve years, in India and later in the Rajneesh spiritual centre at Antelope, Oregon, before the break came. "Subject made sorrowful references to the opulent lifestyle of this Bhagwan, his hunger for material goods (including twenty Rolls-Royce automobiles). I quote him: 'Greed is the hunger of the ego. Those who talk of humility yet relish having long lists of followers who lavish gifts upon them—their greed is deep.'"

And Shiva James left Antelope. He took with him a dozen followers, and ultimately they journeyed to Poindexter Island, on the inland waters of British Columbia, to a twelve-acre parcel of land that they collectively bought. Others joined him later. The Shiva commune began building at Om Bay in August of last year, four months before the murders. They lived on a few donations and the last of Shiva's inheritance.

As to Shiva's philosophy, Mundt was caustic. "The man offers a mixed and not totally comprehensible grab-bag of ideas: Hinduism, Zen Buddhism, a concept of timelessness, living without future or past; a dialectical approach to human behaviour that seems to owe as much to Hegel as to Lao-tzu; a merging of a mixed salad of Western and Eastern thought; enough Freud and Jung to give credence to the saying that a little knowledge is a dangerous thing. He preaches destruction of the ego, negation of will power, of knowledge, of logic. He teaches that only through total surrender, *samarpan*, can enlightenment be achieved. He denies Western therapy, claims it fails because it seeks to adjust the individual to society! He says: 'Through psychiatry, humans adjust to madness.'"

I could see that Mundt was ferociously belittling the goods being offered by the competition. Our head doctor, the centrepiece of the defence, might prove to be a nasty piece of business on the witness stand. Too hostile to the client.

But Mundt was at least not vague in his opinion as to insanity. Subject was psychotic to an extreme degree. No surer evidence of this could be found than in the mad dancing, the talking "in tongues," the nonsensical phrases in English, the ritualistic behaviour, the tears.

Mundt quoted from one of his interviews: "'Surrender means going mad. This madness is the ultimate leap. Jesus was a madman. Mohammed was a madman. Buddha was a madman. I am mad, too.'"

Said Mundt: "Subject with this classically schizophrenic delusion of his own grandeur demonstrates the wide dimensions of his illness." He concluded abruptly: "In the manner in which subject presents himself, in the formulation of his thinking, in his excessive delusional indulgences, Shiva manifests himself as a person suffering from a severe psychotic breakdown, fuelled by the early deaths of his parents and his loss of faith, triggered by some as yet undivined factor into a terrible bloodbath. I am of the opinion that for the last twenty years of the subject's life he has been unable to appreciate the nature and consequences of his acts or to know that they were wrong."

It was a typical Mundt report—pages of interview, an unkempt garden of weedy hypotheses, a snap opinion at the end. He promised follow-up.

Because Shiva was in isolation at Oakalla, I arranged by phone for my appointment tomorrow. What otherworldly phenomenon was I to encounter? Would he have messianic eyes, would he attempt to kidnap my soul with mystical powers? Or was he just some kind of unbalanced fraud, the poor man's Sun Myung Moon?

I skipped across to the late-night health food restaurant and ordered a sloppy avocado and salami sandwich and a bottle of beer, then returned to the office for a go at some of the police reports. I delved into death while the Shillelagh and Shamrock below pounded out Irish music.

At eleven-thirty the telephone rang.

"Hello."

"I'm going to bed."

Oh, oh.

"Or did you make the reservation at Le Fleuve Loire for after midnight?" Ruth's voice was choked.

"I can explain!"

"Yes?"

"I . . . I *can't* explain. I was working. I forgot, Shiva—"

"Happy fucking anniversary, Maximillian."

Click.

4

o

The Dance King

Oakalla Prison Farm is set squat on a hill in the middle of the suburb of Burnaby. Its view from the upper tier is pretty: rolling farm fields, a manicured park beyond the outer fence, Sunday sunbathers stretched along the beach at Deer Lake. The building itself, however, is as ugly a red brickpile as man with his genius for the morbid can create, and it sends vibrations of misery and anger down the hillside to haunt the people of Burnaby.

It is a good place to talk to your client, however. The huge centre hall has interview stalls in the middle of the room. We know they are not bugged—the Trial Lawyers' Association had the area searched.

Oakalla is a switching station for all kinds of people doing time. Its jailers have seen everyone and everything. It is hard to shock an Oakie screw.

"When he's finished screaming they'll bring him down from isolation," said handlebar-moustached Rolly Toews, the guard in charge of central hall this Sunday.

I was ready for anything.

"He screams from nine to nine-thirty. Then he leaves his body. Sometimes they bring him down here, he ain't with his body. I don't know about today, whether he'll be in or out, all you can do is wave a hand in front of his face to see if he's recording."

"Is he dangerous?" Would he go for my eyeballs?

"He don't seem dangerous," Rolly said, "unless you count the twenty-two hippies he wasted. He screams, 'Who? Who? Who?' For fifteen minutes every morning. Maybe he thinks he's an owl. Nuttier than an almond bar."

This was good news. "Who's he been seeing besides Arthur Beauchamp?"

"Shrinks. Your guy, Mundt, a few times. Priestman. Wang."

I hoped Arthur had instructed his client to avoid talking to Priestman and Wang. These were tough Crown-minded professionals, ready to blow down any flimsily constructed edifice prefabricated for an insanity defence. Mundt was smarter than those guys but lazier, and arrogant on the stand.

"Has Shiva been talking to Priestman and Wang?"

"He just gives them his wasted expression from outer space."

I liked this. Maybe he would flip out on the stand, let the jury see how psychotic he was.

Beside one of the interview booths was sour old Hank Hooper, known as Dumptruck. He hung around Oakie a lot, picking up legal aid clients, then dumping them in provincial court with fast guilty pleas for easy money. Judges loved him. He didn't make them work. He knew no law.

Hooper said some encouraging last words to a client, then ambled up to me. "Missing your yachting today, Macarthur?" He peered down and tried to read my letter of introduction to Shiva from Arthur. *This guy you had to watch like a hawk. He will steal your client from under your nose. Also, he thinks I'm an upper-class effete because my name is Macarthur and I come from an establishment family.* "Shiva? You're going to talk to him?"

"Yep."

"I'd like to see that guy in the flesh. What's happened, has Artie quit the case? Is Shiva back on the legal aid list?"

Sure Hank, glom the client, dump him in front of Mr. Justice Carter with twenty-two fast guilty pleas. "I'm junioring Arthur." Hooper had been around a lot longer than me; he could call him Artie.

"Case like this can screw a man's career and his good name, Macarthur. You'd be better off sticking to dirty books— gives you a better image. Jeez, there he is, the butcher of Om Bay."

"South wing!" The guard behind the barred door yelled to get Rolly Toews' attention. Toews went to the south-wing door and unlocked it, and ushered out a shuffling Shiva, who was shackled at the ankles. I felt a little lurch, as when a crowded bus accelerates. A strange sensation, and I blinked.

Shiva's eyes roved slowly about the central hall, never

seeming to light on anything. Was he smiling? The expression was very subtle and I wasn't sure. Photographs had not introduced the man well to me. A rounded, rather jolly face, ruddy cheeks, rust-coloured hair in full curls that cascaded below his shoulders like clusters of ripening grapes. A beard that was darker, a full, rich, salt-and-paprika bush. And his eyes were not messianic at all—they were calm, unpained, assured, hemmed on either side by the kind of crinkles laughter sculpts. He was dressed in a washed-out green shirt and coveralls, standard prison garb.

I motioned him to a seat at the table. I took the other side and placed Arthur's letter in front of him to read. But he didn't look at it, and his gaze drifted out past my left ear.

"My name is Maximillian Macarthur. I am a lawyer who will be helping Mr. Beauchamp with the defence.".

Shiva had a faraway look and that smile that was not quite a smile. Is it a good place that he has gone to? I wondered. I should have felt uncomfortable but instead I found myself relaxing, as if I was breathing some strange ether from him. I felt no urgency; I was prepared to drift along with this man, not push anything.

Ten minutes passed with him just looking past me, with me looking at him, determined to be nice to him, to "relate," as Arthur had put it. Then his lips spread in a true smile, direct, no irony in it, no tight little muscles working at the corner of his lips. Good-looking teeth as in a chewing gum commercial.

"Thank you, Mr. Macarthur. Thank you for the peace that you permitted me. Maybe you don't suffer from the mad urgency to consume time that our friend Dr. Mundt displays upon his visits. It's hard to maintain a calm when anxious egos are boiling and bubbling around one. So you're a lawyer, and you aren't here to psychoanalyze me. I'm bored with being kicked around the forensic football field by Mundt and those fellows."

His voice was penetrating and pellucid, yet soft. A worry nagged me: this man was sounding too rational to be the subject of a make-it-or-break-it insanity defence. "You were meditating."

"Indeed, I was at the penultimate state of dynamic meditation when they came for me. And you were kind enough to permit me the freedom to complete. Freedom: that word takes on magical dimensions in this building. But iron bars do not a prison make, unless they be the bars of the brain, stronger than metal. Please describe the day to me."

"It's, uh, beautiful. Sunny, a few clouds in the mountains. A good day."

"Ah—white clouds?"

"Yes."

"And what do the white clouds do?"

"They just kind of sit up there. Move around a little. Bump against the mountains." This was a weird conversation. Quite pleasant.

"What is the purpose of white clouds?"

"I'm not sure."

"You must watch the white clouds, Mr. Macarthur. They drift, with nowhere to reach, no goal, no destiny. They exist without past or future, in the eternal present. The path we call pathlessness; the way we call waylessness."

This was crazier, therefore better. Or was he saying something that made wonderful sense, something my unfreed mind was missing? How to handle this? Shiva had refused to talk about the killings to Arthur or Mundt. Could I bring him out by exhibiting an interest in this dynamic meditation? I was about to frame a question, but he anticipated.

"Morning is best for dynamic meditation. Before breakfast. It's difficult to meditate on a full stomach without being forced to meditate *upon* that full stomach." That smile. Pretty dazzling. "In the first stage, which lasts ten minutes, you breathe very deeply, quickly, without rhythm, and your body becomes a whirlpool around a still point, the centre. The unmoving centre of your moving maelstrom. Do I see disbelief in your face, Mr. Macarthur? Please feel free to show it."

He had me there. "I'm sorry. I'm a typical Western sceptic, Shiva. But a good sceptic keeps his mind open."

Shiva seemed to like this. A soft laugh. "That's a very good beginning. One must be honest with oneself before one can reach understanding. And your politeness is a graceful mannerism. But perhaps with your open mind you will try this, Mr. Macarthur: breathe chaotically and find the still point. Feel the tensions fall away. If you get nothing else from it, you will have had therapy."

I remember getting high like that as a kid. Never found the centre, though. I guess I hunted for it when I was seventeen

(Zen, brown rice, hair down to my fifth vertebra) but never got very far. "What comes next after fast breathing?"

"Then you dance."

Nataraja, the dance king. I tried to imagine this man dancing wildly among the human sacrifices. . . . It wasn't coming together.

"Or if you wish not to dance, you may laugh. Or cry. But you remain at the centre, re-experiencing what you've repressed and freeing yourself from its grip. That second stage also lasts ten minutes, as does the third, where you find the energy to soothe the turbulence of the mind by shouting the Sufi mantra, Hoo, to unlock the sex, the tantra. Then you enter the fourth stage, which is where I was when you introduced yourself to me: allowing the sexual energy to flow upwards, to work within me quietly."

"Sexual energy?" I inquired. A nervous voice.

"Tantra proclaims it to be the only energy. Sex is the bottom layer, but it can become a higher energy, the energy of love and compassion. The ultimate flowering we call divine energy, God. But it is the same energy that moves."

He smiled. I smiled too, unblocking a repression.

"The final stage is celebration. You may dance in joy, you may sing, you may just quietly be. The stage lasts for fifteen minutes."

"Am I interrupting it?"

"No. You have been a part of it." He spread his hands towards me like a fan. Long fingers. The hands did not shake in the least. In fact, he did not exhibit the slightest sign of fear. Maybe this is how it was when a man was quietly being.

The maximum sentence for murder was life imprisonment with no parole for thirty years. Shiva would be eighty if he survived such a sentence. If he were found not guilty by reason of insanity, he might never see the outside of a locked asylum. Yet he was celebrating.

It was time to move back to basics and down to earth. "Shiva, you are charged with twenty-two murders. If our defence does not succeed, you may never see the outside of a prison again. I would like to talk to you about that defence."

He offered a quizzical expression that might have been asking: who is *really* in prison, Mr. Macarthur? He shrugged. "I'm in prison because I can't be anywhere else. This is how life has happened. You're here, Mr. Macarthur, because you can't be anywhere else. This is how life has happened to *you*.

One goes like the white cloud, not where the will leads but where the wind leads. If you realize this, then you're not afraid, then life passes through you, and you become an empty room."

What passed through me was a warm shiver. I did not know where it came from. It wasn't fear.

"There's the story of the master who was celebrating his one hundredth birthday," Shiva said. "Someone asked him, 'Why is it that you are always happy?' He replied, 'Every morning when I wake up I have the choice to be happy or unhappy, and I choose to be happy.' I, too, make that choice each day. I made it again this morning." His voice had poetic rhythm. I was determined to meet his look, not to waver. I would show him my trust. Why did it feel as if his eyes were boring into my brain?

"You have talked to the psychiatrists."

"Mundt. Wang. Priestman. Oh, yes, I talked. But they don't wish to learn from me. I'm a teacher, Mr. Macarthur. I prefer to be with those who wish to learn."

"Dr. Mundt, uh, is of the opinion that you suffer from a disease of the mind that has rendered you incapable of appreciating the nature and consequences of your acts."

"Yes, the M'Naghten rule. And what acts are those?"

"The alleged murders."

"Ah, yes, the alleged murders."

"Shiva, believe me, it is important that I know about them."

"To whom?"

"To you."

"Or to you? Why is it important to me? I accept totally. Acceptance is prayer."

"Prayer won't win in court. Alone."

Shiva sighed. "Mr. Beauchamp seemed not interested in my teachings. Dr. Mundt sought to convert everything I said into evidence of insanity. But do *you* have interest, Mr. Macarthur?"

"I am interested in dynamic meditation. I'm interested in your philosophy."

"I haven't any philosophy." Shiva folded his hands, talked easily. He indeed seemed to like the role of teacher. "All philosophies are wrong. Because all philosophies begin from a wrong premise: seeing life as a problem. If life is a problem, there can't be any solution to it. But I don't see life as a problem but a mystery. You can't solve it, but you can become a part of it. Yes?"

I found myself nodding, coaxed into agreement.

"You're a lawyer, Mr. Macarthur, a man who worships at the shrine of logic. You wish to change mysteries into problems, because with problems you are potent, in control. With mystery we are impotent, we can't manipulate. But with mystery, we are open to the wonders of ecstasy."

I felt myself swimming a little. Was this guru sending me little teasers to get me hooked? Was I going to become one of those glassy-eyed wretches whom the Civil Liberties Association sends to my office? I had a vision of myself in Big Bill Wheatley's Winnebago, being brought out of it.

"I'm not allowed to be with other prisoners here so my thirst to teach is unquenched. 'I myself having reached the other shore, help others to cross the stream,' Buddha said. We aren't liberated until we liberate others. The one I once followed was known as Acharya, too, as teacher. But he changed his name to Bhagwan, which means emperor." He spoke with scorn. "He collects followers like baubles at a market. I teach. I *teach*."

I heard these as words of entreaty. After a while, I said, "Okay, Shiva, I will do a deal with you. I will learn from you and you will learn from me. I will tell you about how a jury trial works, and what a client must do to defend himself. I'll come here again in two weeks, and after that I'll try to come every weekend this summer, and you can teach, and I will try to understand. But in the process you must tell me what happened. Maybe it won't help. But if you were in a hallucinating state, not in your right, uh, mind—"

"A line of testimony presents itself." Shiva smiled wearily.

"Shiva, tell me what you can."

There was a long silence now. He seemed to be assessing me. I could hear a distant clang of cell doors and Rolly Toews somewhere off behind me talking on the phone. These sounds seemed detached, sounds distant from the little world of Shiva and Macarthur. I felt strongly that I had connected with him, that he was about to release to me that which he had withheld from Arthur.

He began talking in a soft and dreamlike way. "Nature in its wisdom doesn't allow you to remember past lives. Otherwise you'd go mad—unless you have achieved, unless you're so close to the divine that nothing disturbs you. Nature saves us from that madness with an amnesia. I can recall events of seventeen past lives, however, because I'm at *satori*. My first memory goes back to the time of Hammurabi."

His voice lowered. "Nature has determined that I must be saved from the pain of *this* lifetime. I can't remember any of the events at the asrama last December. Mr. Macarthur, I have meditated upon the mystery, dissolved myself before it, have become part of it. But no door has opened. I remember nothing of the deaths, nothing until a consciousness of pain overtook me as I was standing among them, in blood."

An amnesia—I didn't like that. Juries tend to think witnesses who claim amnesia are lying. Was Shiva lying? Maybe he killed them and couldn't remember.

He sighed. "I had shattered my ego into a million parts and sent it whirling from me like smoke. Yet it seems there's something left, a kernel of ego to be protected by amnesia. And so for many hours each day I meditate upon it. Here, at least, there is time to do that—between meals. It will come, Mr. Macarthur."

"It will?"

"It will come suddenly like lightning in a dark night. I will see the whole."

"What is the last thing you remember?"

"I had, shall we call it, a temple, a *chaitya*, at Om Bay. I went there alone in the morning. It is above the asrama, atop the escarpment. I climbed up to it in the snow, I meditated. And I was transported to a land of silver, dancing angels."

"I see."

"You don't see, Mr. Macarthur. All I pray is you be not blind."

"You were . . . transported to a land of silver angels." This could be a spectacular insanity defence, the kind lawyers dream of. Somehow we had to get this fellow on the stand to give his crazy evidence. But what about those distressing lapses into rationality, that soft, too-lucid sense of humour?

Shiva was waiting for me to ask another question.

"You were transported *out* of your body?"

"Do you think I packed my body into a suitcase and carried it with me?"

"This is like astral travelling?"

"So to speak."

"And is it like amnesia? Can't you see your body?"

"I wasn't able to. As I say, nature protected me."

"The temple?"

"Oh, yes, it is a great cathedral that is six hundred years old, and its steeple rises nearly half that distance in feet to the sky." Try to keep an open mind, Max, I told myself. But sometimes it was really hard. "Behind the asrama is a rocky hill. From our encampment, we cut a path to the crest. That's where the tree is, a hollow tree. You'll know it if you go there."

A tree. God, there were so many more questions to ask, and here was Rolly Toews coming and it was eleven-thirty. Oakalla had strict meal-time rules.

"They got to have him for lunch, Mr. Macarthur," Toews said.

"I hope they find me truly delicious," said Shiva smiling, rising with dignity, the chains around his ankles clinking.

I stood up, too. "A week from next Saturday. I will come early."

"That would be a pleasure, Mr. Macarthur."

"Maximillian."

We shook hands. I felt a sensation of flowing as our palms touched. From him, from me, I wasn't sure. But perhaps I was imagining it, caught like some teenager in this man's mystery.

He walked slowly to the south-wing door, his chains making plaintive music. From behind the west-wing door, other prisoners stared at him with cruel eyes, and I could see them murmuring to each other. And suddenly I felt empty. I knew that whatever the result of the trial: a penitentiary or an asylum—Shiva would never be allowed the company of other human beings. He was a target for death in jail.

I drove back to my office in a contemplative mood. *Nature in its wisdom doesn't allow you to remember past lives. Otherwise you would go mad.* How mad was *this* man? Astral travelling. Sex, the only energy. The Sufi mantra, Hoo. Well, who is to say about reincarnation, astral travelling? We once had a Prime Minister who believed in mediums and spirits. You meet a lot of people these days who are into such things. Lawyers even.

This Shiva had shown both madness and an intense and enigmatic intelligence. If a man commits murder while he thinks he is astral travelling, can it not be said that he was deprived of reason, and is therefore not guilty by insanity? Intriguing, perhaps, as a legal question.

Next visit I could start gently persuading Shiva that he must give evidence. We had been getting along pretty well in there. Not a bad guy for a man capable of cold execution—in his body or out of it—of nearly two-dozen people. (Had there been no resistance? Had seventeen of them simply allowed themselves to be bound and then shot?)

Perhaps he had been playing with me, a maniac with a fraudulent mind. Amnesia: murderers often claim that.

Then I realized: I have this man already convicted of twenty-two murders. I have done what no lawyer must do and still be able to live with himself: I have declared my own client guilty. Ah, damn, why couldn't he have said: I had nothing to do with it, in body or mind?

5

○

Love Affairs

From my office I phoned Le Fleuve Loire and made reservations for tonight. That done, I softly chanted the Sufi mantra, Hoo, seeking strength as I dialled Ruth's number.

It was Jacqueline who answered. "She's not speaking to you right now. No, Mr. Macarthur, not if you come crawling on bended knee, clutching roses in your teeth and plant them between her toes. Also, you set me up for a night of holy terror around here by breaking your date—"

"For *Christ's* sake—"

"Also because I thought you and she were going out, I had some friends over to rehearse a play for the club, and we had to deal with her *weeping* and *moping*. Using *language*."

"I have reservations. Tonight, seven-thirty, Le Fleuve Loire. I'll be by at seven. Tell her." I burped the message out like a fast telegram.

"Call late next week and she may be willing to talk to you." She shouted, her voice away from the mouthpiece: "I said *may* be, Mother."

"Who are you, her private secretary? Let me talk to her."

"Sometimes a woman needs a friend."

And that was it. She hung up on me.

What's the goddamn big deal? I asked myself. Ruth has to try to have a little understanding. I'm on a big, big murder.

I muttered such feeling-sorry-for-myself thoughts while dictating on tape my petition and affidavit material for the application to force the Burnaby Justice of the Peace to lay charges against Wheatley, Morgan, and Calico. I brought from a locked cabinet Wheatley's wallet in its torn-open envelope. I was going to put the contents through the copy machine, affix everything as exhibits to the affidavit.

I paused at the library door, and I saw Augustina Sage there, sitting sadly in the debris. (Our library was chaos, with everyone blaming everyone else for the mess. The library committee—Brovak and Macarthur—was riven by factional dispute.) Augustina looked as if she had been searching for a text, had become enervated in the hunt.

"What's the matter?"

"Oh, heck, I don't know." Her pretty pug-nosed face was cowled by a great halo of frizz. Around her eyes, which usually had a wide-awake, astonished look, were swollen areas.

"They took the Jimmy Bob baby away from her mother last week," she said. "Because the baby had been born an addict. Oh, God, poor Mrs. Bob."

Augustina had been doing most of our juvenile and family court work—not strictly criminal, but gruelling in its own way. John Brovak believed she didn't have the toughness that trial lawyers need to survive. "She hasn't got the balls to go for the kill," was his way of putting it.

"Are you going to appeal it?"

"I don't know; I've been trying to find some law." She had an open binder in front of her, and one note page was full of doodles. "Oh, Max, I'm *afraid*. They'll have the whole Department of so-called Rehabilitation up there with their fifteen-hundred-dollar-a-day lawyers. It's Big Brother against junkie mother, her hopeless legal aid counsel standing there just falling apart. I'll break down." She went rigid. "I've been getting the weeps."

And just then she did. I stood there feeling stupid, grasping Rev. William Wheatley's wallet.

"What *is* the matter, Augustina?"

She changed the subject. "I hear you're junioring on the Shiva case. Congratulations." She sobbed between words.

I walked over to her, boosted my bottom onto her desk, and made her look at me. "What's going on?"

"God's mercy, I'm in love."

"Well, great, it's a wonderful feeling. The heart flies like a bird."

She tried to smile.

"He's married," I said.

"No. Even worse."

"What's worse than married? He's a priest?"

She shook her head.

"Tell me, Augustina. It's going to feel better."

Another shudder. "Oh, God. Max, remember last March you asked me to do an interview out at Oakalla for you? You'd just got retained on those bank robberies?"

"André Fortin. Dropped two, copped two, three and five years consecutive. I did a real good deal for the Errol Flynn of bank rob..." I paused. Oh, no, I thought. "André Fortin?"

She burst into tears again.

"But you've never seen him outside a *jail*. He's in a maximum security institution, for God's sake."

"They let me interview him. In a private room."

"Augustina, you don't."

"Oh, *no*. We just touch a little. I'm not sure when it started, whether it was that first interview, but I remember he looked so vulnerable in there, and after that he sent me a message asking me to see him, and so I did, just before the guilty pleas. He didn't want to talk about the case at all. We talked about everything else. He opened himself up to me a little bit."

I listened in pain to this outpouring.

"He is a man with some real humanity, Max, not like the police reports had it. He writes me letters in French, and I don't read French that well, but they're like poetry. I think he is an artist."

This was very bad. Fortin had a string of fourteen convictions, false cheques to bank robbery.

"Max, I know it's wrong. I know it's stupid. I know it's disastrous. My brain tells me all these things."

"But your brain isn't doing the talking. I'm going to make a suggestion. I think you should adjourn all your cases and take a few weeks in Hawaii. I speak to you like a brother in this matter. You need to get away by yourself. You need to think things over." There were handsome blond brutes on the beaches there. Men with surfboards and heavy gold chains around their necks. She would find romance on the rebound. "My folks have a condo in Kauai. It's empty right now. I'll get you the key."

"How am I going to adjourn all my cases? They're urgent. I have women whose kids are literally starving because I can't get a date for a maintenance hearing. And if I leave, everyone around here will complain. Sophie in particular. We all have to be out there, earning our way—money, money, money."

"Anything that's urgent, I'll take."

"What about the *appeal*?" She waved an arm at her incompleted work.

"I'll argue it. Just go. Augustina, you've gone off the deep end with this one."

"I know. I *know*. That's the trouble. Okay, he's a criminal." She raised her voice. "But you never really got into his head, did you, Max? He's different."

Sure, like barracudas are different. "The firm will pay for the airline tickets. Everybody will understand."

"Oh, God, don't tell anyone. Not Sophie, especially. She'll hate me." Augustina lived in fear of the nineteenth-century capitalist baron Sophie Marx.

"Okay, I'll think of something else to tell them." Don't let her hesitate, I thought, get her on the plane. Don't let her get another hit of that addicting André Fortin narcotic. Narcotic. That would be the next step, Augustina smuggling dope into Kent Maximum.

I made reservations, CP Air, for the next morning, and to keep her distracted for the rest of the day I asked her to help list the documents that were in Bill Wheatley's wallet: driver's licence, pocket calendar, various credit cards, memberships in two political parties, pictures of wife and three kids. A laminated card, next to the driver's licence, identifying him as Reverend William S. Wheatley, pastor of the True Gospel Pentecostal Church. A lifetime pass to the B.C. Place Stadium. A *bubble gum* card showing him in a B.C. Lions uniform and listing his stats on the back (the card just *behind* the driver's licence, in case the traffic cop hasn't got the point by now). A paper showing he was Cloverdale Kiwanis Man of the Year for 1980. A group of restaurant, airline and taxi receipts, doubtless for income tax purposes.

And forty thousand U.S. dollars plus change. Both Augustina and I initialled the list and put the date on it, ran off extra copies of everything, even the credit cards and the currency.

The wallet seemed empty, but I dug with a broken pencil into the pockets and from one of them I came up with an additional receipt, a little crumpled Visa form which had been mashed into the back of the credit card pocket. I ironed it out with the side of my hand. Tyee Rent-a-Craft in Campbell River, Wheatley's carbon-copy signature, the sum of $185.73.

I was about to add it to my list as a postscript, but then I didn't. I brought the receipt to the light. The date on it was "8-12-84." That was the day the RCMP arrested Shiva on Poindexter Island.

And I thought: Campbell River. That's not far from Desolation Sound, and Desolation Sound is not far from Poindexter. How much time by fast boat to Om Bay? I stood there lost in speculative thought.

"Max, are you there? Want me to copy this?"

"Yes, make a few."

Reason returned: the man had probably been on a fishing trip. I had once seen his picture in the paper, holding a big spring salmon.

We initialled those copies, and I hand-rolled the Visa receipt from Tyee Rent-a-Craft into its original condition, stuffed it down into its pocket, stuck in the credit cards that had compacted it there, and put everything back in original order, including the stapled packet of money.

Had Wheatley been somewhere in Desolation Sound when these young men and women had died?

"Max, is there a problem?" Augustina said.

"No, no."

Life, says Shiva, is not a problem but a mystery.

* * *

Augustina and I spent the rest of the afternoon going over her files, seeing what could be adjourned, what could not.

To keep her from arranging one last evening appointment with André Fortin, I insisted she go to dinner with me tonight—I still had the reservations at Le Fleuve Loire—where I would occupy her mind with idle lawyer gossip.

I then phoned my father to arrange for the condo. ("I don't want to hear any last-minute, long-distance bailouts. Don't forget dinner, in two weeks, at the ranch with the whole family—you'll come Saturday and stay the night." "Yes, sir, I'll be there." "You can take the Piper Cherokee. It's in the hangar at Fort Langley." "Thanks, Dad." "Your mother's anxious to see you." "Me, too, Dad." Why wasn't *he* ever anxious to see me?)

I called Greg Ranjeet and took solace in the fact that there were no new civil rights wrongs to be righted tonight. I would be at Le Fleuve Loire, I told him. I should not be

disturbed unless the incident involved something of the level
of a fascist coup in Ottawa.

"*Mansei!*" said Greg. "What's happening with the Melissa-
June M'Garethy case, Max? Nothing in the press yet."

"Wheaties et al are probably still hard at their spiritual
gang rape. How could someone as big as J.J. M'Garethy stoop
to hiring someone as low as Bill Wheatley?"

"J.J. M'Garethy can afford number one. Listen, he could
afford to buy *me* out."

"There will be press. I'm going to *mandamus* that muscle-
bound Elmer Gantry into Supreme Court tomorrow."

Business done, I drove Augustina around Stanley Park,
along the perimeter road, wistfully glancing at my deserted
running track on the seawall. I tried to entertain her with my
account of the interview with Shiva.

"He asked you to describe the day for him?"

"Yes. He wanted to know about the clouds, what they
looked like."

Augustina began to cry again. "André told me about solitary," she said.

Thus it went. The weeps.

After we parked and got to the entrance of the restaurant,
she burst into tears once more, and raced into the ladies'
washroom, off the entrance foyer.

The *maître d'* came from the dining room and began
hustling me back there with him.

"Hang on, Alain, I'm waiting for someone."

"Ah, but Mr. Macarthur, your other party has already
arrived."

My head was still full of Shiva and Wheaties and M'Garethy
and this ghastly business of Augustina and her jailbird lover.
Dull-witted and dazed, I stared into the dining room. At the
smiling face of Ruth Worobec. Alone at a table for two.

She waved at me gaily. I didn't move.

She gave me a funny look, then got up and walked up to
me. "I did some thinking. Oh, do up that little button. Too
much chest hair. You'll never make it as Burt Reynolds." She
did it up for me. I was frozen. "I'm *supposed* to be a
specialist on relationships, after all. I just sat down with
myself this afternoon to get my head back on straight. I'm
always telling my clients that it takes two to strain a relationship."

"Uh, how did you know I'd be here?"

"Called Greg. Anyway, I said to myself, okay, I'm being

unfair. I forget I have a temper. It's a weakness, I've got to admit that. And I've got to remember that Max is the most absent-minded guy I know. He has important things on that absent mind."

Augustina came out of the washroom, a painted woman, her tear marks mascaraed away. She smiled nervously at Ruth. Ruth's face went white. She looked from Augustina to me.

The *maître d'* nervously wrung his hands.

I began to stammer. The only defence was truth. I was guilty of nothing. But the defence speech opened pitifully.

"Augustina is flying off to Kauai tomorrow, going to be staying at, uh, my folk's place—"

"So, are you going with her?"

"Table for three, Alain. Look, we had to have a talk, Augustina is—"

"God, I'm naïve sometimes. Is that the stuff you like, all that paint?"

"Look," I said with some heat, "let's stop jumping to all sorts—"

"Have the chef make him a shit pie, Alain," Ruth said as she slammed into the cloakroom and grabbed her coat. She whisked out the door into the night.

"Aw, heck," said Augustina, her makeup running.

6

○

In Gods We Trust

I never did get my run in on that difficult Sunday in June. But I got up the next morning at five-thirty and did a punisher all the way from False Creek, over the Granville Bridge, down to Beach Avenue, around the seawall, down the lower harbour road to my office in Gastown. I showered, changed, got going on the phone.

The thing that would save me this week was a four-day hole that had opened up because a hash conspiracy prelim had had to be set over. One of the other lawyers on the case was on sick leave. Three weeks ago he had been grabbed by Nanaimo police officers while running from the courthouse wearing a cowboy hat, a lawyer's gown, and nothing underneath, yelling, "Void *ab initio*, void *ab initio*." (Marriage breakdown, plus the tax man.)

I spent half the day on the phone, explaining to lawyers that Augustina was sick. Say no more, was the attitude of most of them, happy to free up a day on their own calendars. Amanda, who does my work and Augustina's, also does our lying, phoned the clients, told them Ms. Sage was going in for a delicate operation, vaguely implying some gynecological dysfunction. I told my partners she had had a work exhaustion breakdown.

"You joking?" said John Brovak, who had glided into my office to try to snitch my copy of *Martin's Code*, the library copies all having become extinct.

"Fuck, who pays for *my* holidays in Hawaii?" He tried to grab the Code from my desk but I whisked it from under his hand. "You were complaining to me about *me* being a little close to my clients."

"You've heard something?"

"Grapevine. We can't support her forever, Max. She wants to fuck Jack the Ripper or Fu Manchu, I don't care. She just isn't bringing in her share, and she hasn't got the jizz for court. Come on, man, I'm going to be late for the conspiracy. Somebody took the last copy from the library."

"Take it up with the library committee." I hugged my book to my chest.

"Hey, what's this?" He opened the box of gadgets that Tony D'Anglio had delivered this morning. "Hey, a little perverted, man." He pulled out a French tickler with hard rubber knobs on it. "Never thought this was your style, Max. Gosh, I didn't mean to look."

"Tony D'Anglio says the girls go ape. He wants an opinion."

"Well, listen," John said, thrusting the ticklers into his jacket pocket, "I'll give him one."

Somehow during the day I found time to get short notice to bring on my Wheatley-Morgan-Calico *mandamus* in Supreme Court chambers on Tuesday. Those three guys were probably still holed out in their Winnebago somewhere, deprogramming away at Melissa-June M'Garethy. I couldn't get them served in person, but I had our process man drop copies of the petition and affidavit off at Wheatley's home and had another taped on the front door of the True Gospel Pentecostal Church.

I also got the A-G's office, had them appoint Crown counsel. Wouldn't you know—Leroy Chalmers Lukey, Q.C., who seemed to get all the Crown referral work in Vancouver. It's that big Social Credit connection. Lukey, horrifyingly, was judge-bound.

"Your *mandamus* won't work," he said to me on the phone, "*Coughlan ex parte Evans*, 1970 Eight Criminal Reports." He could always spout these citations, had an enormous library of case law in his head. (I never said this man was a dummy.) "The language of Section 455.3 isn't imperative. But I'll concede you have a right to go before a regular provincial judge, make the application afresh. Want to saw it off that way? They don't call you a little saw-off for nothing, do they, Max?"

"No, they pay me."

He was offering what the bull leaves in the meadow, trying to buy me off with a pyrrhic victory. The *Coughlan* case was bad law.

"I'll see you in court," I said.

I spent the rest of the day at the U.B.C. library, reading microfilm newspaper files from December. An interesting side-note from *The Sun*, December 12: J.J. and Edith M'Garethy had come to Vancouver, apparently worried their daughter had been among the young persons slaughtered. They were even shown a corpse in the morgue—a girl said to resemble Melissa-June.

Emelia Cruz, I suddenly realized. Yes, looking at that photograph of her, I had been bothered by the thought I had seen her somewhere before. Sallow, thin-faced like the M'Garethy heiress, whose photos I remembered from the press. But Emelia's parents turned out to be a doctor and his wife from Sacramento. Did this resemblance in any way relate to the murders?

* * *

I arrived at Court 38 at ten the next morning, my five clients in tow. There was a pack of reporters here—Wheatley was stale news around town by now, but the M'Garethys added a spicy new angle to his misdoings.

My *mandamus* had been put in front of Mr. Justice Santorini, an unpredictable ex-trial prosecutor, a grouch on the bench this morning. He went after Lukey right away. "Are you opposing this?" A tone of irritability, pleasant to my ears.

"Yes, m'lord."

"*Mister* Lukey, if a citizen has reason to believe an indictable offence has been committed, why can't he force the authorities to act?"

Lukey began piling on the law. Santorini interrupted him, trying to get at the principle. It was looking good—Santorini had obviously read the affidavit. The wallet would be the clincher: all that money. Irrelevant to my application, but the kind of nothing that perks a judge's interest.

I had hoped the knowledge that the wallet was being turned over to the court would flush Wheatley out. He wasn't going to want to lose his bubble gum card with his picture and statistics on it, and he wasn't going to want to lose the forty grand. I wanted to find out if he had taken any fishing trips out of Campbell River last winter. But Wheatley was not here, had not risen to the bait.

My Moonies were on the front benches, neat as pins,

exuding holiness, along with a dozen media people, exuding
something quite different.

"*Mister* Lukey, you can stand there and you can tell me
straight-faced that citizens do not have the right under the
strict wording of the Criminal Code to prefer charges. Well, I
have heard you address juries more times than I want to
remember and consistently you have made hay with that
truism that not only criminals have civil rights, but ordinary
citizens have them, too. Do you say a person accused of
kidnapping cannot be brought to the courts? What about the
case of a woman with a rape complaint. . . ."

There was Lukey clutching the *Coughlan* case like a life
preserver, going under for the third time. I felt warm all over.
I was rubbing my hands with glee under the counsel table,
where no one could see.

Santorini was charging along at his obloquious best when
Bill Wheatley's lawyer paced energetically into the courtroom. Foster Cobb.

"My apologies, my lord," he said, "I have just received
instructions. I am here as counsel to the parties named as
respondents, Messrs. Wheatley, Morgan, and Calico. My
lord, I wonder if counsel may have a few minutes."

The judge knew a deal was about to be attempted. He
nodded and left the courtroom.

Cobb, Lukey, and I gathered in a corner, out of general
earshot. "Withdraw the complaints, Max, and the girl can go
back to her friends." Foster Cobb was a kind of Gary Cooper-
looking guy with a drawn face that had seen many wars. His
toughest had been with the needle.

"Melissa-June didn't deprogram, huh?" I said.

"That's it, then," said Lukey, "the girl is freed, drop the
mandamus, no damage done. Money saved for the taxpayer."
The harassed taxpayer—his champion being that leach upon
the public purse, Leroy Lukey.

"So the deal I am being offered is this," I said. "The
kidnappers will return the live body of the victim and we will
drop kidnapping *and* assault charges. This is starting to sound
like a terrorist hostage-taking." But I didn't blame Cobb. He
was trying to do a job for a client. Cobb used to be a
prosecutor, now heads up a good little criminal office. "Where
is the girl?"

"She's out in the hall with her parents, talking to them,"
Cobb said. Jesus, while I had been in here enjoying a public

paddling of good old Leroy, Foster Cobb had been out in the hall doing his work: getting the parents to persuade Melissa-June to drop the charges. Cobb continued: "You don't have to subject the girl to a trial. She and her parents have been through enough. Let's not make a bigger media circus of this than it already is."

I could see the hungry wolves of the fourth estate prowling around the back of the courtroom. I felt a little sorry for Melissa-June's billionaire parents. When all was said and done, I knew, the decision to proceed with the kidnapping charge would be up to Melissa-June.

Cobb brought in J.J. and Edith M'Garethy. In their middle years, they were both puffy of face and dragged out, ravaged by an ordeal from which they had not power nor money enough to escape. J.J. M'Garethy was a neat, compulsive-looking man, with a sense of strength about him, but cold and analyzing eyes that betokened a closed, sterile personality. His wife had a brittle, attractive face, was not ashamed to be dressed in a Vancouver courtroom as if she had just walked out of a Paris salon. She was the kind of person who should have looked a lot younger than she actually was, but today she didn't.

Two men in suits came into the courtroom with the M'Garethys, looking like guys you see hanging about the U.S. President. And behind them came a girl mousey-looking but defiant, taut, seeming as if she was about to shatter.

Such pain among the three M'Garethys.

"Hey, Astral, hey, we love you," came a whispered voice from one of my Moonies. She gave them a weak smile.

What had she gone through? Wheatley's process, I had heard, involved a relentless browbeating about Reverend Moon, painting the man as a fraud (easy for Wheatley; he knew the turf), with evidence from videotapes, recordings, voices of the formerly moonstruck, now awakened and returned to life.

The hammer of guilt is struck time and again: guilt at running away from those who love you most, guilt at despising one's parents, guilt at rejecting them. Guilt: Bill Wheatley does it the Judeo-Christian way.

Melissa-June M'Garethy came up to Cobb, Lukey, and me. "I want this to stop," she said in a whispery voice. "I know

God wants it to stop. It's a hassle." She looked as if she had been through the religious wars, but her eyes still had that distant look, that thousand-mile stare.

As we three lawyers withdrew into a corner, Melissa-June joined her friends and they cooed over her. Her parents slid wearily onto a bench at the back of the court and stared at us, Mr. M'Garethy seeming like a proud man broken, Mrs. M'Garethy a kind of painted sculpture, expressionless. Something in her stomach stronger than mere valium, I thought.

"Okay, Max?" said Cobb. "We'll have her say it to the judge, if that's what you want."

I wasn't going to push it. "There are still the assault charges. They're not Miss M'Garethy's to withdraw."

"Maybe the judge won't give you *mandamus* anyway," Cobb said.

I gave a hearty chuckle. "He's been ripping Leroy to ratshit, wants to strike a blow for justice while the press is here. Not even going to call on me."

"Santorini didn't take his ulcer medicine this morning," Lukey grumped. "Come on, Max, give us a break, go for the deal. I could get instructions to appeal this."

"Are bold Robin Hood and his merry men lurking somewhere outside the courtroom, too?" I asked Cobb, ignoring Lukey's ridiculous bluff.

"I have them in an interview room. Max, you've won, you've got the girl back."

"I'll bet Wheaties wants to get something back, too," I said. "His wallet. With that fat forty grand. Stick with this client, Fos. He will make you rich and happy, plus full of the holy spirit." I knew I had him. Wheatley's wallet was a hostage. "Yes, sir, if Leroy appeals, that wallet is going to be tied up here for months. Need it as evidence anyway for the assault trial. On the other hand, we can by agreement get it released today. Good way to get your fees paid fast. Wheatley will be really happy to get the serious charges dismissed."

We dispatched the clerk to find the judge while Cobb fetched his three clients. Wheatley strolled in quite amiably. He pantomimed a pained grimace when he caught my eye, then smiled as if to say, boy, am I naughty, keep getting into these darned scrapes. He wasn't the kind of preacher to show off the cloth, had on an open-necked brown shirt under a sports jacket.

At forty-three, much of Wheatley's beef would seem to

have been transformed into fatty amino acids. A beer-pouch protruded frontally, and his neck seemed wider than his head, a sturdy, knobby item that was jammed turtle-like into the rest of his body. Maybe he had delivered too many helmets to the stomach in his playing days, I thought. He always had a flashy smile, giant pearls under a trim moustache. However, if you were to look for happy little crinkles at the corners of his eyes, you would find none. Cloverdale Kiwanis man of the year for 1980.

Wheatley slid along the back bench so Morgan and Calico could join him. His boys needed a lot of room on that bench because they were giants, too. Cowardly giants, the kind who have to pick on kids, that had been my experience of them.

Wimpy Morgan weighed in, God help me, at about fifteen per cent of a ton. He had a holy, oval, smiling face, unhappy, heavy-lidded eyes. Beautiful goldilock curls modishly rolling over his collar. Morgan was also an ex-football player. He had come up from the Cougars of N.C. State, big all-star prospect at defensive tackle, but just didn't have the speed for the Canadian game. He beat around with a few teams, another of those pray-to-God-before-the-game guys. While serving time on the B.C. Lions, Morgan met Wheatley, and now helped run some of his Christian businesses: a chain of laundromats in the Fraser Valley, an investment service for parishioners with idle money, a forty-unit condo, the deprogramming business. This and that.

Though Wheatley and Morgan were both imports from the U.S., they fit well into the curious cosmology of West Coast Canada: a part of the world where fundamentalist Christian crooks had been indispensable to the social fabric for generations. Throughout the green reaches of the Fraser River Valley, it was known that Wheatley and his friends were more shearers of sheep than shepherds. This is an acceptable practice in this fair province.

The third of this professedly holy trinity was Jack Calico, who had a club foot. His scene, believe it or not, was body beautiful. Yes: Mr. British Columbia Lower Mainland four years running, getting points for courage with his club foot. He shaved his head bald so the judges could enjoy the perspiration on his scalp. The body of an almost-Adonis, but the head of Quasimodo, impacted features, puffy balls of lips, a fat frog smile. Calico had come to Jesus and to Bill Wheatley during the course of a fast one-and-a-half day deprogramming session. Calico had been, the story had it, an adherent to a small group that believed credit card companies ruled the world and would soon be lasering a number onto everybody's left hand.

Mr. Justice Santorini came in, sat down, took a view of the new people.

"The application is withdrawn as to the kidnappings," I said.

"Crown doesn't oppose the writ for the assaults," said Lukey.

"The writ goes then on that basis," said the judge.

"Respondents apply for release of the wallet, exhibit number one to my learned friend's affidavit," said Cobb.

"Agree," said Lukey.

"Agree," said I.

"Mr. Wheatley gets it back then," said Mr. Justice Santorini, cocking an eye at the pastor in the back row. He called to him: "Mr. Wheatley, that's a lot of money to be carrying around when you go calling on people who might not feel friendly to you. I find banks are useful. You keep your money in the bank, then you've got records to help you with your income tax at the end of the year."

That was a neat little ice pick that Santorini used. Wheatley probably wasn't giving receipts for most of his donations. The judge knew a charlatan.

I could sense Cobb was praying his man would keep his mouth shut. But no, it was never Wheatley's habit. "Well, if anyone wants to know, your honour, I had over sixty thousand dollars when they stole my wallet. It was a donation from friends to the True Gospel camp for orphans."

I could tell Cobb was wanting to walk back to where his client was standing and slap some tape over his mouth. Wheatley glared at the Moonies, on the front bench, then at me.

"I don't know if Sun Myung Moon has the rest of the money," he said, "or maybe one of his lawyers—"

I snapped at him, enraged: "You lying, slanderous bastard!"

I have this handicap of flying out of control when my name is sullied. A lawyer's good name means everything—especially in front of a throng of reporters. Lukey was making urgent motions to me to cool off, but I yelled again, "Take that back!"

Santorini, in a cowardly display, ordered the court recessed and gingerly stepped out, cooling tempers only for a moment.

When the judge disappeared, I started advancing on Wheatley, saying, "Court's not in session now, reverend, so anything you say can open you up to damages—punitive damages. If you're insinuating that I stole twenty thousand dollars from you, I want you to state those words clearly in front of everybody in this courtroom. I'll slap you with a writ so fast you'll be gasping."

Cobb by now had reached his client and, kicking the courtroom door, he pulled him through it.

Love had never been, as could be seen, lost between Wheaties and me. I followed them out, Lukey behind me, probably enjoying this, but grunting false words of caution to me.

Cobb was talking furiously to his clients, trying to work them toward the elevator doors. "Let's hear it, man," I shouted, as reporters poured into the hallway to take in this fun-filled show. "I want you to repeat it. You're a coward, Wheatley, repeat it!" I was steaming; it was no act.

I had picked the right word: coward. To some tormented bulls it is a crimson flag. Wheatley whirled around and bore down upon me, stopped, hovered, a six-foot-four dirigible.

"Mr. Macarthur, I don't know who stole my money; I guess it's not you, so it's got to be the zombies. Sell flowers and candies, steal money from wallets, don't matter to them, it all goes into Moon's pockets. I guess I got out of hand, Mr. Macarthur, but I also guess I don't like folks snooping through my wallet and hanging everything that's on the washline for everyone to see." His voice was loud enough so the reporters got it all. "And I guess I'm tired of someone putting charges on me like this all the time." He billowed above me like a dark thundercloud.

I wasn't flinching, not for this guy (I wasn't exactly alone with him in a dark alley). "Maybe if you'd stop acting like a vigilante, you wouldn't *get* charged all the time. What happened to poor Melissa-June? You had her four nights and three days and she didn't break."

"She floated. We almost had her back, and then she floated." He lowered his voice, although not in intimacy. Melissa-June M'Garethy was down the hallway, surrounded by a cocoon of Moonies, who were staring at us.

Cobb tried to take him by the elbow. Wheatley shrugged

him off. "We lost her. We lost her to Sun Myung Moon, the Christ reborn in this century, and Melissa-June M'Garethy is going back there to get her brain washed some more, and they're gonna train her how to get more people sucked into his maw." Wheatley was getting into his preacher voice now, playing to the media.

"You see those dead batteries standing down there, Mr. Macarthur? They've given their minds up. They got no free will, they got their minds in a strongbox. You want a world of spooks?" He raised his voice, started declaiming. "That's when the Russians are going to come. When the spooks have taken over."

"You're right, the Russians are behind everything."

"Moonies, Hare Krishna, Scientologists: zombies! All the power to think for theirselves is sapped from their minds!"

Wheatley seemed to be reaching ignition point. There was a sense of something a little nutty and dangerous in his voice and I was concerned. I could see Cobb was really pissed off. Morgan and Calico were helping pull the resisting Wheatley toward the elevators.

"What kind of world do you want, Macarthur? Empty, gutless zonk-outs? Brain-sapped fodder for the welfare lines?"

"Listen," I hollered, "if I have a choice between worshipping Reverend Moon or worshipping a parking meter, I'll choose the parking meter. But I want to live in a society where I have the right to make that choice. Who's next after you clean up the Moonies? Jehovah Witnesses? Doukhobors? Mormons?"

"I need the strength of the lord in me right now, Mr. Macarthur, just to still the anger I feel about you saying that." Walking backwards, Wheatley held his two big fists in the air in front of him as if he were pleading to God for that strength. "I'm talking about the *crooks*, my friend, the *frauds*."

They had him at the elevator now, and Wimpy Morgan was punching the down button, while he and Calico held Wheatley's arms. I was striding toward them, kind of enjoying the theatre in all of this. Cobb was coming back to ward me off.

"Who gives you the right to judge the frauds, Wheatley? What court do you sit in? Where do you get the goddamn right to think you can pronounce upon others' beliefs?"

"I work in a higher court than you do, Macarthur. The highest court there is."

"Praise God," came the voice of one of the reporters.

"Yes, praise God," Wheatley shouted as the door opened. "God sees his name being used in vain here. He sees you, Macarthur, and he knows you're doing the devil's handiwork for the cults." The door closed.

"Step outside and repeat that, Wheaties, I'll tear you apart." A bold Max Macarthur spoke defiantly to the elevator door. I turned to Cobb and smiled tensely. "Why don't you tell your client to take a flying fart up his own holy asshole? Self-appointed linebacker for the good lord Jesus." I mumbled epithets as Cobb and Lukey drew me aside. I was breathing hard, a teenager who had emerged from a schoolyard punch-up.

"Sorry about that," Cobb said. "I can't understand it—he's usually pretty lovable around me. But I'll charge him extra for having to endure his bad manners, and we can have a few drinks over it."

"Hey, speaking of cultish things," Lukey said, "I hear you're joining us for that tussle with Shiva alias James in September." An ebullient voice. He had recovered from his horsewhipping in court.

"Yes, I'm junior defence." I spoke proudly: "Arthur asked me."

"The butler did it, Max, my boy, the butler did it." Lukey chuckled, a man confident of his case. "I hear you have Werner Mundt waiting in the wings to say your man's not well in the head. Trouble with Mundt, his courtroom monologues are so bewildering they sometimes confuse a jury into acquitting. Well, we've got Priestman and Wang to straighten everything out, and half a dozen more if we need them, and our guys are going to say your client is sitting out there in Oakalla trying to fake insanity with his hoo-hoo-hooing and his singing in the cell. Crazy as a fox."

"We wouldn't mind seeing those opinions, Leroy. Maybe I should come down to your office with you and run them through the Xerox."

Lukey put his hand on my shoulder and squeezed it. "I'll show you mine, little guy, if you'll show me yours."

"We'll see what Mr. Justice Carter has to say about that this Friday."

"You boys will need all the pampering he can give you."

"Lunch, gentlemen?" said Cobb.

"I'll get my file, talk to my clients, then join you," I said, and went back into the courtroom. There were still a few

people here, the clerk, shuffling through papers; the M'Garethys
and their bodyguards. One of the tragedies of the rich—you
are never alone. And I thought of Astral out in the corridor—
nobody can guard you from the mind-snatchers but yourself.
And her parents had never given her the weapons of
self-protection.

Mrs. M'Garethy had her face in her hands. Her husband
had a stiff arm on her shoulder but seemed unable to give
comfort. They had clearly had little sleep during the ordeal
with their daughter. I picked up my file, went up to them.

"Damn, damn," Edith M'Garethy was muttering.

"I'm sorry," I said.

"I am sure you are," said J.J. M'Garethy hoarsely. "Let me
tell you something, my friend. We will get her back. We are
seeking a guardianship order in your courts. I understand it is
used when persons are no longer able to manage their affairs.
And if you are really sorry, as you say, you will not encourage
your clients to remove our daughter to another jurisdiction."

"What you have to do, do the right way, Mr. M'Garethy. By
law."

"We will get her back. Let us go, Edith."

"Damn. Damn. Damn." She repeated that word again and
again, did not seem able to get up. She looked up at me, her
eyes livid with running colour. "I gave her *everything*," she
said.

I stopped where my people were gathered, and the
M'Garethys walked past, he not looking at his daughter, his
wife whirling about suddenly, shouting at her, "For God's
sake, Melissa-June, we love you!"

"My name is Astral now, Mommy."

They disappeared down the stairs. I turned to Robert, the
bland, blond team leader. "Did you take twenty thousand
dollars from that wallet?"

He shook his head.

"Robert, tell the truth for God. God want you to tell the
truth to your lawyer."

He looked around at the others, got blank stares back.

"You won't lie to Astral, will you? Tell her if you took
twenty U.S. thousand-dollar bills from Wheatley's wallet."

Astral was looking at them strangely, frowning.

"It's for Father," Robert said finally. "We put the money in
the bank for Father, the perfect father. It was a gift from
Astral. It came from her, uh, former parents."

"Will you get it out of the bank and give it to me, Robert?" Astral asked in a thin voice that matched her face, very pinched. She looked like that photo of Emelia Cruz, all right. "I want to talk to Mr. Macarthur alone," she said.

And we walked to an alcove. She began talking in a rambling, monotonic voice. "I guess what you said to Mr. Wheatley was right. I don't know. I thought for a while he was a good man, and then he began playing these awful tapes about what God, Father, I mean, was doing, and he argued with me about the Divine Principle, and the unified family, and I guess I didn't study it hard enough, and then I began to hate him, and I began to cry and I was afraid I wasn't loving Father enough and I hadn't given to Father enough, and then he brought in some people who had belonged to our family and they said they had been deprogrammed, and they argued with me, and I got really confused. They said that Father taught it was okay to steal, and I didn't believe them, and now I'm not sure again."

"What are you going to do?"

She caught her breath. "I don't know. I've been wondering. I think I want to be myself for a while. Sometimes I want to be with people and then I want to be with myself. There's something out there."

My eyes followed hers, looked at a blank wall. "Where?"

"I mean, there's something out there. We all have to find it. Maybe I haven't found it. I thought I had, but it's hard. Do you know what I'm talking about?"

Robert and the others, like a slow-moving tide, rolled in toward us. "We should go home now, Astral," Robert said. "We can relax and be silly. We'll sing *Zip-a-dee-doo-dah* and play Messiah tag."

"I'm tired," Astral said.

"Father loves you," Robert said tenderly to her.

7

○

Wins

June 26. Wednesday. Winsday, as it is known in the Western Lottery, and Winsday for me in the lottery that is court. I took both ends of a double-header from Her Majesty's team: soliciting beefs against the two hookers from the Roamin' Baths whom Tony D'Anglio had referred. Also, in another court I got a ruling I wanted on a complicated wiretap I had argued a month ago.

I quit while my luck was running, adjourned a drunk driver until the fall because of a long docket in 615. I joined Arthur Beauchamp in the El Beau room, discussed defence strategies for Shiva, did my run, went home.

Early that evening, shaved, showered, and smelling gently of the musk of repentance, I attended at the front door of Ruth Worobec's North Shore highrise. She had refused calls to her office, and her bodyguard, Jacqueline, had deflected the ones I had made the night before.

"Who is it?" inquired Jacqueline, scratchily, through the speaker.

"Singing telegram."

"Sing it on the street. She still doesn't want to see you."

"Tell her I have tickets for the Bolshoi touring company on Friday."

"How many?"

"Three. I'm taking her daughter, too. Good seats. Forty dollars each."

"This is tempting. Let me confer."

"I'm coming up anyway, Jacqueline. I've got my own keys." Ruth and I had traded each other sets of apartment keys.

On the twenty-third floor, I could get the door open only two inches. It was chained from inside.

Ruth's baleful eye peeked at me. "Yes?" The voice was of one used to dealing with Jehovah Witnesses and vacuum cleaner salesmen.

"You are like Judge Hammersmith—you convict without hearing the evidence. I will tell you the truth, the whole truth, and nothing but the truth."

"I will be pleased to hear an airtight alibi. Make it good."

"Augustina Sage is now working on a sunburn at Hanalei Bay, trying to recover from a total nervous breakdown which you, for all your skills, failed to diagnose."

"It's not enough that he attacked me emotionally, now he attacks me professionally."

"She had been in that washroom to repair damage to her face. She'd been crying all afternoon and evening. Listen, it's easier if I talk to you inside."

"Ballet tickets alone don't get you inside. Only your story will. As I say, make it good."

I lowered my voice. "She's in a bad way over a guy. A bank robber from Montreal who's doing long time. That's what she's having the breakdown over. I took her to the restaurant to cool her out until we could get her on the plane in the morning."

"That's a pretty good story. It makes me look like a heel if it's true. What about the evidence of a long-standing, at least two-year-old flirtation that has been going on every time I see you together at a party? And the time you went skiing together last winter?"

"She just happened to be at Whistler on the same weekend."

"She's in love with a robber? That's real good, there's no way I can disprove that, is there?"

"As for forgetting the anniversary, all I can say is I'm sorry." I slipped the three ballet tickets through the doorway. "*Swan Lake*".

The door closed, came unlatched, opened again to let me in. Ruth had changed into her evening wear—blue jeans and a T-shirt. She was trying to look stern.

"You should have asked to see the tickets before you let him in, Mom." Jacqueline was squatting on the floor, doing homework. "What's the story? It seemed to work."

"He denies having an affair with Augustina Sage. He says she is making it with someone in a jail. It's an unbelievable story, but I am a fool, and I'm going to give him the benefit of a reasonable doubt. If I find he has lied, I will excise his manhood."

"I'm glad to see you're back in the picture, Max," Jacqueline said. "You're absent-minded, kind of dumb, but not intentionally wicked."

"You've got gall," I said. "I called every night and got blocked out of the play by you each time. You'd make offensive guard on anyone's all-star team."

"Max, when are you going to evolve from first-stage male to second-stage?" Jacqueline said. "You'll never make third-stage, you just have no insight into a woman's soul."

"I'm going to tell you guys all about Shiva. I finally met him."

Jacqueline perked up. "Oh, yeah?"

"Do you want to stay for dinner?" Ruth asked.

"Oh, haven't you eaten yet?"

"Yesterday's borscht is warming. There's enough for six, never mind three."

"Borscht, the Russian way, beets and sour cream?"

"Yes."

"Thank you, I'd be delighted."

Winsday.

* * *

Thursday was less joyous. I had hoped to have that day free to work on the Shiva file, but ended up filling for John Brovak in the Ramirez-Johnson cocaine conspiracy. It was July 4, a holiday to be celebrated in the States, and John had plans to too-ra-lay down the Oregon coast with his Irish lullaby.

"If you are carrying any coke across the border, you're crazy."

"Nobody at customs has got the jam to stick his finger up a used French tickler. If they find it I'll say, honest, sir, I didn't know it was there, I borrowed the tickler from my good friend Max Macarthur. Come on, Max, please, it's only four or five hours of listening to bullshit, and they're not sitting on Friday, and you've got nothing in the book for today. I'm in love, man."

I had no excuse. He has done the same for me over the years. So I did a Thursday shift, listened to wiretaps all day. Ramirez-Johnson was the kind of case you could walk into cold, as I had done many times. Even people who had been involved for the seven months of the trial could no longer understand what was going on. The twelve jurors were embattled hostages of a war without end over a thirty-seven-count indictment. Bannister Boynton, the federal prosecutor, saw conspiracies lurking everywhere, especially in the brief-cases of the defence. The lawyers on the other side were making good per-diem rates and made no admissions. It was the Iran-Iraq war.

Next door where another, more fiery battle was in progress, Sophie Marx was pinning the opposition down with her machine-gun mouth, tying her rape trial up in a two-day argument on the law of recent complaint while the jury cooled its heels at home.

I worked late that night, putting together some case law for the encounter on the morrow with Leroy Lukey, Q.C. The pre-trial hearing would give both Crown and defence a chance to air grievances and iron out bugs before the trial, and to fill in Mr. Justice Carter on the issues.

* * *

"They've got the whole thing," Lukey complained. "A hundred and forty five-by-seven glossies, all the fingerprint charts and ballistics tests, all the pathologists' reports, the whole darn set of notes from Corporal Scanks."

"But they don't have Dr. Priestman's report," said Mr. Justice Baynard Carter, a benign expression on his pink, cherubic face. "And they don't have Dr. Wang's report. They don't have any of your evidence that might relate to an insanity verdict."

"They don't have a right to that evidence, m'lord. With respect," Lukey said.

I whispered to Arthur's ear, "*Kabob versus Boland,*" and handed him a photostat. It was the leading precedent.

"The Crown is not, under our happy system, allowed to wait behind a poplar tree to dry-gulch a hapless accused," said Arthur, scanning the headnote, doing a quick read. He passed the case to Judge Carter and said confidently, "That's what the Supreme Court has to say on the matter, Leroy. The Canadian Supreme Court, not the Supreme Court of Utter Pradesh or wherever it was you quoted your law from."

"*Kabob* doesn't relate to the issue here." Lukey was sitting in a characteristic way of his: arms stubbornly folded across his chest, a defiant and righteous posture. "Why does the Crown have to walk into the courtroom stark naked all the time, m'lord? Insanity—that's *their* defence. I've got a right to hold back evidence in reply. That's always been the rule, damn it. Excuse me, m'lord, I swore."

"Not at all," said the judge. Everyone so courteous and smiling here in Judge Carter's chambers.

He read the *Kabob* case, raised his eyes. "It says here that where the insanity defence is obvious, the Crown has a duty to anticipate it with its own evidence, and I think that means the Crown has a duty to disclose that evidence. You should give them copies of your forensic-psychiatric material, Leroy."

Yes, Leroy, don't be a pig with your goodies.

"I may as well just give them my briefcase and they can forage in it," he whined.

"Come, come, Leroy," said Arthur. "*Veritas nihil venetur nisi abscondi.* Truth fears nothing but to be hidden."

We were pleased. With these reports, we would be armed for cross-examination of the Crown alienists.

"Any other issues, gentlemen?" Mr. Justice Carter smiled at everyone.

"You've got no worms hiding in the woodwork, Leroy?" Arthur asked. "You're not suppressing any evidence?"

Lukey took that as a joke and chuckled.

"The so-called dying declaration of Emelia Cruz," said Arthur. "It smells. From it wafts the odour of counterfeit. We haven't seen any signed statement by this old fellow Whitegoose."

Lukey said, "You have all the statements I've got."

That had the feel about it of a lawyer choosing words carefully. At Poindexter Island I would talk to Joe Whitegoose, who had been the last to see Emelia Cruz alive.

"A ghastly business," said the judge, ushering us to the door.

I hadn't yet told Arthur about the Tyee Rent-a-Craft receipt in Bill Wheatley's wallet. So Bill Wheatley was fishing near Campbell River on December 8 last year: I didn't want Arthur laughing at my naïve speculations.

As Arthur and I walked down the courthouse corridor we were overtaken by Sophie Marx, who was radiating good cheer. "Lunch, guys? Allow me to treat." She was dressed in her street clothes, a pair of baggy slacks and a wool sweater

with cigarette burns in it, ashes spilling from the one between her lips. She locked her arms in our respective elbows
and marched us out of the courthouse, down to one of the
Robson Square restaurants.

"Why so happy?" I asked her.

"A win," she said. "I got the judge so tied up with his own
bad rulings on evidence, he had to bail out. He called a
mistrial when one of the cops mentioned, right in front of the
jury, that my rapist had a record. They're going to have to
stay the charge. They won't put the complainant through *that*
again."

I was jealous. It was a good win. Her client had clearly
been guilty.

But so much more fulfilling, I thought, to fight the good
fight for the innocent, to enlist lawyerly ego in a righteous
battle for justice. Tomorrow, Saturday, I would be meeting
with Shiva. How hungry I was to believe in him, to be allowed
to fight not for a guilty man, not for one insane, but for that
rarest of all courtroom species, a person of uncompromised
innocence.

8

o

The Third Eye

July 6. My game plan today was to continue my seduction of
Shiva, to draw from him more detail, dissolve his mystery,
refresh his shattered memory. If indeed his memory of bloody
Om Bay had truly been lost. Criminal lawyers are sceptics:
after you have been burned a few times by the lies of your
clients you begin to listen to them with jaundiced ears, as it
were. Amnesia? If not, who was he protecting? Well, I would
maintain my vow to keep an open mind. Get the facts, size
the man up, work on him hard, convince him to co-operate.
And let's see how well the defence of insanity floats. I would
be in control today, sly and subtle.

That was the game plan. But, tense from the past week,
nervous about the family scene this weekend, I erupted as
soon as I saw Shiva shuffling toward me in the central hall at
Oakalla. I shouted to Rolly Toews: "I want those ankle
bracelets off. It's demeaning that a man awaiting trial has to
be shackled in front of his lawyer."

"What d'ya think, I make the regulations?" Standing there,
twirling his handlebars. I was infuriated by his attitude.

I wreaked legal havoc at Oakalla that Saturday morning,
dragging the deputy warden down there on his day off upon
threats of habeas corpus and Charter of Rights. I finally got
him to pronounce an edict permitting me to talk with Shiva,
shackles off, in a small, locked room off the centre hall. "If he
gouges out your eyeballs, it's your lookout," he said. "I want
that on record."

Flushed with success, I was breathing heavily when I sat
down across a small table from Shiva.

"Did you search for your still point?" he asked, composed and genial.

I remembered. In the middle of the maelstrom was the still point. "No, I guess I was busy."

I read into his expression a subdued disapproval. *Too busy to search for the still point? The still point of the whole turning world?*

"You should really try the dynamic meditation, Maximillian. You will not see God right away. You really have nothing to fear."

I smiled. "I'm not afraid."

"I sense that."

Shiva looked so directly into my eyes that I felt as if he were crawling into my head through the sockets. I felt again that strange essence pouring from him. But I was determined that he would play my game; I would not play his.

"I sense also there is a seeker within you," he said. "You don't thirst but you're more than merely curious. Yes?"

"A little."

"Inwardly, perhaps you seek completion. But you're going to have to turn East for completion. Home, Maximillian. The East is home, the East isn't burdened by the tragedy of the divided soul and the anguish that accompanies it—our farcical Greek heritage of repression, self-torture, and sin."

"I want to talk about the insanity issue, Shiva."

"But we are. I'm telling you why there's so much insanity in the West, so much psychotherapy, so many Mundts and Priestmans. We're born ecstatic, Maximillian, but we're nurtured on misery. The West simply won't acknowledge ecstasy. We are born gods; we die madmen."

I had an agenda; he could teach later. I pulled one of Mundt's reports from my file.

"Let us talk about *your* supposed madness. Mundt quotes you as saying surrender means going mad and that Buddha and Jesus were madmen, and that you are, too, and he says you suffer from a schizophrenic delusion of grandeur."

"How asinine of him. Only the inferior suffer from superiority complexes. The godly see themselves as quite ordinary. Surrender means going mad because all who are imprisoned in their logical minds will *think* that your ecstasy is madness."

Mundt had misread Shiva's irony. I tried to rake together the dying coals of our insanity defence. "The comparisons with Christ—"

"How presumptuous of me, is that the thought?" he interrupted, smiling. "Christ heard voices. Christ talked to the sky. Christ declared himself to be the son of God, and the king of the Jews. How presumptuous of *him*. And how schizophrenic, because in the next breath he says, 'Blessed are the meek, for they shall inherit the earth.' Maximillian, I said surrender is the ultimate leap, I said Jesus had taken that leap, Buddha had. And that I had, too. And thousands have done so and thousands are prepared to do so, to try their wings. There are also those who, like you, stand at the edge, nervously fluttering them, wondering what it would be like to soar."

I sat there with my fixed and purposeful smile, humouring him, yet enjoying this cosmological blarney. He was good: how easy it must have been for his followers to escape into his world of surrender.

"The leap can be made only by one who is receptive to change, Maximillian, a risk-taker."

Shiva seemed to enjoy challenging my ego, that terrible part of a criminal lawyer that rises to the contest. This jailhouse guru knew me well enough to guess that he could dare me to take the bait. "I'd guess I'm a risk-taker."

He softly jabbed my shoulder with his finger and chuckled. "Yes, you're a peaker, a transcender. It's something I knew, Maximillian, on the first day you came here." His eyes locked with mine; I refused to withdraw my gaze.

"Among certain beings of this earth, Maximillian, exists an intense affinity, a longing for communion with others who harbour—this is perhaps unrecognized by themselves—the need to join in a mass evolutionary consciousness. I see that in you, my young friend, and I pray you, too, will find *jivanmutta* one day and join the small colony of the mad."

"*Jivanmutta?*"

"Liberation while alive." His voice took on an almost precatory tone: "Perhaps one day in a welling forth of that mass consciousness, the millions will join us in our madness. An enlightened earth, an earth that has made that first cosmic step, like an infant, a baby, discovering how wonderful it is to walk, how joyful not to have to endure the fear of falling." His voice was mellifluous, rich.

I looked out the window at Rolly Toews bustling about the centre hall, locking and unlocking doors, the tinny clash of metal so forlorn, so terrible. These were not the doors to enlightenment. They were the doors behind which Shiva might spend the rest of his life.

When I looked back at Shiva he was staring at me, his eyebrows arched.

"Perhaps," I said, "I could try to become enlightened." By pretending to play his game, I would have him playing mine.

He began to chuckle softly. "Please do not let me persuade you of anything, Maximillian. And please do not *try* to be enlightened. That's *prasad*, a gift, God gives it to you—you can't snatch it from His hand. Enlightenment descends when you're ready. No one can persuade another to change because each of us guards a gate of change that can be unlocked only from the inside."

I blinked. I realized I had been drifting a little. Back to firm ground.

"Shiva, you and I have a contract, and it allows you to be a teacher half the time and me to be a lawyer half the time. There are some things I want to know—I'm going to Poindexter Island next weekend—and then it can be your turn."

"Yes, our contract. How honourable it is to deal with a lawyer."

"I know this may be painful, taking you back to Om Bay."

"It is only the aversion of pain that hurts. I've given myself to my suffering, surrendered to it, and no longer endure its bite."

"I want to go over Corporal Scanks' reports with you, to see if anything jogs a memory." I became lawyer-like, trying to dispel a mood. "Two days before the killings, a young man named George Wurz came into Tash-Tash Cove on a launch for supplies."

"A gentle young man."

"He went to Scanks and complained that you, Shiva, were attempting to control their minds."

"I find it hard to conceive he would say such a thing."

"He is no longer able to tell us about his motives."

"Perhaps."

"'With me you will commit the final suicide.' That is what he quoted to the corporal."

Shiva began to rub his pudgy nose. "'The final suicide'—it sounds like something I might say. In fact I'm sure I've said it at one time or another to my *chelas*. I teach the delight of disappearance of self, of *anatta*, no-selfness. I teach that in order for one to blossom forth, something in him must die.

Transformation is a kind of suicide, and it is frightening because the ego dreads its own demise. But George Wurz was not afraid of me—he was afraid only of himself."

I worried. If Lukey could somehow get this final suicide hearsay in front of the jury, it would, unexplained, make Shiva appear to have been plotting a mass killing. But if Shiva *did* take the stand to explain, would not even the most undiscerning of jurors realize that this man was too rational to be found insane?

"'Death kisses you with life. You will be reborn as gods.'"

"I may have said those words. I was standing among them, weeping."

"'Because I loved you, I had to kill you.' Did you say that?"

"I had been travelling, dancing with the angels, Maximillian. I had just returned to my body. I might have been saying anything, but I cannot think I would have said those words on such an occasion, even metaphorically." Had Corporal Scanks been editing Shiva's babblings, picking out the juicy phrases? It is what police often do.

"Had you ever meet the corporal before December eighth?" I asked.

"In August when we first began clearing and building, he visited. He was vaguely unpleasant. We showed papers of purchase. We offered him a sandwich, but he declined it."

"Arsenic in the bologna."

"A bland cheese, I'm afraid. We are not meat eaters."

"The hunting rifle?"

"We hadn't a rifle. We took no animal's life. We believe in *ahimsa*, the doctrine of non-violence and non-injury to all living, breathing, sentient creatures. The *Isa Upanishad* says the wise man beholds all beings in the self. If we are one with all life, we cannot kill."

"You had not seen the rifle before?"

"At the least, I was not aware of it. It would not have been permitted."

So how did that stolen rifle get there? "It had your fingerprints on it, pressed into the dried blood."

"I am a religious man with little zest for logic, but if my fingerprints were impressed into dried blood—"

"Then it would seem the blood was already drying on the rifle when you touched it. Yes. Your bootprints all over the mud—do you remember dancing, Shiva? *In* your body as well as out of it?"

"As I returned to an awareness of the physical plane, I was standing, looking over the snow and the blood and the mud and the desecration. I spoke some words. I was crying. I was aware of blood on my hands and on my robe and in my hair and on my face. I can't speak for it, it wasn't mine." His voice lost its melody, became toneless, distant. "I turned around. The police were there."

"Let us go to the morning of December eighth, when you arose."

"We have an agreement, Maximillian."

"I know we're running late, but I'll make it up. After you woke up that Saturday, what did you do?"

"I rose before the sun, began a fire, put some water on for tea. I donned my robe, threw my sleeping bag over my shoulder, pulled on my boots, and climbed through the falling snow to the *chaitya* on the clifftop. I felt the need to be alone, to pray. The temple, the hollowed fir tree, was dry, bare of snow. I assumed the lotus position. I meditated."

"And you were transported. Tell me about that journey."

Shiva closed his eyes, and it suddenly seemed as if he weren't here. A trance? "I travelled between spheres and transcended mortality. I descended within a brilliant light into a land of amber moons, a cool land, with air that smelled sweetly pungent, and my tears were dried by the touch of their long and gentle fingers upon my face."

The haunting echo of vast distances was in his voice. I felt some turbulence, as if on a small craft in bad weather.

"They showed themselves to me in the *maya* image of men and women, naked, their skin with the sheen of silver. These angels tried to still a terror that kept thrusting at me, a terror that tried to draw me back to our angry, other world. And then the dance began."

His eyes still shut, he extended, slowly, his right hand, taking my left one in it, holding tightly. I had a sense of vibrant communion, a current that quickened my pulse. It was frightening, but I didn't withdraw.

"We began the dance slowly, and the silver angels carried me into it, and I became enraptured with the dance, and felt the moons and stars begin to move, and I became one with the pulsing rhythms of the cosmos. I danced the *tandava*, the

Dance of Eternity, the dance of universal death and joy, and I felt an electrical awareness of myself with all life."

I, too, felt an electrical awareness just then. A jolt. It scared me. I wanted desperately to withdraw my hand from his, fearing I had been connected into him like a socket. But something Scottish and stubborn and unyielding in me refused to let me draw away from him.

"There was awareness with the superlife," his voice was saying, "and with the godhead. All was one. Brahman and Atman were one. And I, for a timelessness, was one with God."

As he talked, I felt and saw and smelled and heard—for the most fleeting fragment of a second—what? A vision, an hallucination, a mirage: a bubbling creek, the sun tinkling golden from it; a gnarled willow; birdsong; a wild garden of foxglove, daisies, purple thistle; the rich odour of country.

"And I danced the silver gods away, and when the dance died, too, I was standing alone, amidst the ruins of my *chelas*, my disciples." His eyes opened, bright beams. "And there was a man in uniform placing handcuffs on my wrists."

But I was not among birdsong and flowers, I was in the greyness of prison. I could hear my own shallow breathing, felt little balls of body waste coagulating in my bowels, straining for freedom. He withdrew his hand.

"I said to them: 'You will be reborn as gods.' But of course they already had."

A long pause. My heart was thundering. "What powers *do* you have?" I asked softly.

"None that you have not, although you're blinded to them." He smiled. "Maximillian, we're on a channel, you and I. Very good reception. It is strong. I receive even when you jam the frequency."

I took a deep breath. "I think I had a vision just now. Countryside, a tree, a small stream, sun, flowers."

"You are going to Om Bay? Perhaps you should watch the white clouds when you're there."

"What happened? What did you just do?"

"Maybe you've seen representatives of my namesake, the god Shiva: five faces, four arms, a third eye at the centre of the forehead. The eye was said to have burst forth to save the world from darkness when Shiva's wife Parvati stole behind him and playfully covered his eyes with her hands. But it wasn't unknown to the Christian apostles. In Matthew it's written, 'If therefore thine eye be single, the whole body shall be full of light.' You must learn to exercise the third eye, Maximillian."

"I see," I said, not seeing. I was still shaking. "Okay, Shiva, you have got my attention. Tell me about . . . the way."

He smiled. "You cannot ask about the way. You have to travel it."

And I smiled, too, nervously. "But what is the route?"

"Meditate upon it."

"The route is through meditation?"

"And love."

"And love?" That dangerous word. I saw Rolly Toews coming. Lunch time.

"Gyana yoga and bhakti yoga—the path of wisdom and the path of devotion. The ways are only two. Meditation can be done alone. Love needs another, not oneself, because love for the self is merely ego. The ego is insatiable, a parasite. The more love you feed it the more it demands. You are better rid of it."

"I think I would feel naked."

"Maximillian," he said softly, "once your boundaries are destroyed, you are infinite."

* * *

Still spinning from that strange encounter with Shiva, trying to repress it in the appropriate Western way, I was determined to brave the weekend with the family. A high-class soap like *Dynasty*.

Early Saturday afternoon I flew Dad's Piper Cherokee float plane into Kamloops Lake, where Tom, my older brother, picked me up. Looking even shaggier than his car—an old gas-eating Chevie station wagon—was Tom, garbed in denims and cowboy hat: he managed Macarthur Ranch Ltd., his main chore being to maximize the write-off.

"Hey, there, Maxie, aw-*right!*" Tom grabbed my hand in a palms-up grip. His hand was horny and scarred, his face red with wind and sun. Marijuana was on his breath. Tom and I were fond of each other, but he was six years senior to me, and we'd never made the connection that brothers closer in age do. He had not enjoyed school, had faded out in the second year of university, drifted around the world on an allowance. A bit of laziness, I'd say, and Dad had been hurt that Tom had not shown more Macarthur pride. But he was happy running the ranch.

"Chief Justice Tooley is visiting, no missus," he said. Dad was a good friend of the Chief's. I knew I would have to be careful, not drink too much.

We sped west on the Tranquille Highway, then north onto a gravel road, into the hills, scrubby and barren and hot. These were drylands, but so was most of British Columbia this rainless summer.

"How's Mom?" I asked.

"Same. Still got the cast on. How *you* doing?"

"Good. Real good. Maggie?"

"Fine. She's been cooking up a storm. She's real nervous about the company, you know how shy she is. She and Mom are a pair."

"Not pregnant yet, huh?"

"Naw, we've about given up."

More such idle family chat as we moved higher, toward four-wheel country, greener, pine-clad. The station wagon bumped over cattle guards every few kilometres.

"Want a smoke, Maxie? It'll make it easier." He had a half-smoked joint in his hatband.

"No, thanks." Not after that encounter with Shiva, that was drug enough.

A final cattle guard, and the forest broke into clumps, finally gave way to lonely pine spires, and we were on the ranch, thirty sections of grassland, polled Herefords roaming it. Tom finished the roach to a nubbin, rolled it into a ball between his fingers, and flicked it out the window as we circled around the stable with its fifteen riding ponies, past the shed where Dad had parked his Beechcraft (he had flown in with Mom and Chief Justice Tooley), and pulled up in front of the sprawling new ranchhouse. There was my father at the door, looking awkward in an over-embroidered Western shirt and starchy new blue jeans.

"So good of you to grace us with your presence."

"Nice to see you, Dad."

"Hope you can stop for half an hour between murder trials."

I gritted my teeth in a smile. An afternoon and evening with Mom and Dad and the Chief Justice. *You cannot ask about the way. You have to travel it.*

* * *

I have memories of the afternoon, little images that I have not suppressed. My father showing his paternal devotion in his peculiarly roundabout way: "You're leaving tomorrow *morning*? Your mother had expected you would at least stay the whole day." Him making a silly sleepwalking joke about Mom's accident, suggesting she had something going with the neighbour at night. Her giving me that dryest of Scots busses on the cheek, no emotional effusions in this family. Tom talking Judge Tooley into wearing a sombrero and getting on a horse for a picture. Lots of laughs over that. Maximillian Senior going for a gallop, proving to Tooley, that grandson of an Irish immigrant, that the Macarthurs were above him, upper class and horsey.

My mother stood out of the way most of the time, looking lost, wearing a melancholy smile. She didn't seem to have any friends these days, refused to socialize with lawyers' wives, hated that scene. Something was much troubling her this weekend. Mom, I love you, please be happy, I wanted to tell her. But the Macarthurs and Frasers don't use such strong language, don't mouth such words as "love." Scottish rock monoliths, Ruth says.

Hors-d'oeuvres and champagne on the terrace. Getting it on with Chief Justice Tooley, roly-poly and bald, not much taller than me, an ex-pork barrel Liberal who turned down a seat in the Senate and chose a senior judgeship instead. A tendency to mumble, which made conversation awkward. Not exactly an in-court heavyweight, but pretty good, not as reactionary as most. I drank champagne and laughed at his jokes about people such as the redhead, the rabbi, the priest and the atheist, well aware that from time to time I am called upon to argue cases in front of this man.

I remember getting impaired enough to try to relate with my mother, but felt I was being put off, deflected from target. Standard expressions of interest in me of a superficial kind. This ritualistic question: "And Ruth, she is well?" Meaning: are you still seeing her? Not once in the five years I had been going with Ruth had my mother expressed any feelings about her. Of approval, disapproval, anything. They were opposites— Ruth: emotional, blunt, opinionated; Myrtle Macarthur, née Fraser: in a word, dour. My father had stolen her away from a microscope forty years ago—she had been a botanist, had

written a couple of papers. Perhaps she wished she had stuck
to the cell structure of pollen; perhaps she had been content
in the loneliness of a laboratory.

Mother and Father weren't talking. All afternoon, the
subliminal screams between them. . . .

By dinner time I was drunk.

The six of us were sitting around the perimeter of a
laminated maple round which was the dinner table. Maggie
was to my right beside Tom, with his stoned, effortless smile.
To my left was Chief Justice Tooley; then Mother, stiff and
mannered, and Father, slashing at the NDP and the unions
with his steak knife.

I smiled seraphically, pretending to listen with interest to
my father's sound and fury, hoping that in my drink-demented
state I would not be called upon for brilliancies.

I heard from my left what I thought were the words,
"Polish it." I turned to Chief Justice Tooley.

"Politics," he repeated.

"Yes, Chief Justice?"

"Politics. Next step, young man."

"Nex' step?"

The table linen was wet and purple under my wine glass. I
had not a steady hand.

"Your Dad made the right move going Conservative. Break
with family tradition, of course, but the Tories look like
they're the future. If I had to start off today, I'd choose that
route myself. Too late for me, a man can't change colours
when he's almost finished the race. Yes, I think the Conservatives, Max. That's where the judgeships will be coming from
for the next twenty years. Too many of us Liberal hacks up
there now anyway." He expected me to chuckle at this
truthful bit of self-disparagement. I managed to do so.

"Praecipe, of course." Perhaps the judge's tongue was thick
with drink, too.

I leaned my ear closer to him. "I'm sorry?"

"It's the price you pay, of course."

"What's that, Chief Justice?"

"Politics. Being a Macarthur. Four generations in the House
of Commons. Part of the job of being a Macarthur, eh? I'd say
go against an NDP member next outing, give it your best,
don't hope to win first time out, but get your name up there.
You're about thirty. Parliament by thirty-five, that's the ticket."

"Have to think about that, Chief Justice." I would as fain

run for the Conservatives as for the Baader-Meinhof gang: that's what I wanted to tell him.

My father had moved onto the subject of the anti-nuclear crazies demonstrating in Europe. I drunkenly assumed he was trying to bait me, to get me into a fight. I sipped more Bordeaux.

"Got to worship a smidge."

I leaned toward the judge. "Sorry?"

"Got to worry about your image. Right thing of course to do a few criminal cases. Civil rights, got to stand up for them, no question. Fooled a little with radical things myself when I was your age. Part of being young. Can't get bogged down, though. Those obscenity cases."

"Yes?"

"That sort of thing starts to say something unsavoury about the people connected to it."

"You mean—because I'm the lawyer?"

"See your name in the paper. Acting for the smut peddlers, that's what it looks like to the public, eh? Working for prisoners' rights, acting for these strange sects—wrong kind of constituents, see what I mean?"

It was Dad's speech. I wondered if he had put him up to this. A wooziness had overtaken me. I felt the need to excuse myself, but my father was drawing back his chair, sticking his fingers in his belt, seeming about to say something portentous. I drank more wine.

My memory of this was poor, and was reconstructed on the way to the plane the next morning by Tom. It seems my father did have an announcement to make, and he went about it in a rambling way, talking about the pressures that are put upon a man in making life's choices. I remember having a paranoid thought—my father was talking about me, had lined up a Conservative nomination in some constituency like Okanagan-Similkameen. Then I realized he was talking about himself. He said he had come upon a crossroads.

And I remember realizing this was the judgeship. The time had arrived in the Macarthur life cycle; tradition had to be observed; judgeships were in the genes. This is why my father wanted me here so badly tonight. I think he wanted me to be proud of him.

"Of course, all of you have the right to know first. Ernie here, Chief Justice Tooley, will be taking a place on the Supreme Court of Canada. I will be replacing him. I want to say to his face right here that I feel honoured to follow him—honoured, Ernie, deeply honoured. . . ."

I was later informed that we had all been cautioned to secrecy because the announcement from Ottawa would not be made until the end of August.

Tom described to me how Mother, almost dutifully, gave Father a peck on the cheek. (This was why she had been so down: she couldn't bear the thought of being the Chief Justice's wife—the committees, the teas, the honorary patroness, the horrors of entertaining.)

I, apparently—for the memory is a blank—brought myself unsteadily to my feet, my newly filled wine glass in my hand.

"The path of wisdom," I am said to have said, "and the path of devotion. The ways are only two." And something to the effect: "Enligh'enment is a grace. It descends on you."

And saying that, I turned, knocking my chair over, losing control over my wine glass. Three ounces of dry red wine descended upon Chief Justice Tooley's tie and shirt.

"You cannot ask about the way," I said. "You mus' follow it."

9

○

The Doodle Dandy

July had begun and stayed limpid and hot: wonderful summer days under a benevolent warm front. But they were stressful days for me as I continued to keep both Augustina's and my practices afloat, continued to labour in the trenches of the criminal courts, continued to run the Stanley Park seawall almost every day, continued to put together the Shiva defence.

I remained troubled by that psychic episode—whatever it was—that I had endured with Shiva, and I declined to accept the mystery of it, sought reasons: my strong imagination had got to me, someone had slipped peyote into my morning omelet, I was having a stress breakdown. Or I had been hypnotized. (That's crazy, I told myself—professionals have tried and failed.)

On Saturday, July 13, having phoned ahead to Tyee Rent-a-Craft to reserve a boat, I organized myself for Vancouver Island, four hours by ferry and car. Into my faithful Daimler I packed my briefcase with the Shiva file, a trolling rod and some gear, marine charts, and topographical maps. I took the ferry from Horseshoe Bay, drove up the Island Highway, working in and out among road-cluttering campers and trailers, showing my fast car's ass to them when I found clear stretches ahead.

I found Tyee Rent-a-Craft a mile or so south of Campbell River: an office, a marina, not many rentals still in dock. This was one of the world's hottest fishing areas, and salmon and their human predators gather here in multitudes.

The proprietor, a Mr. Barney Hinkle, was about fifty, had a Rotarian manner about him, showed good spirits, business

being excellent. "Mostly Yankees. I keep that Stars and
Stripes out there like a red, white, and blue hootchie.
Americans are real patriots, not like us. You want the full rig,
Mr. Macarthur?"

"I've got my own gear. It's about two hours, would you say,
to Tash-Tash Cove?"

"That's why you want the big engine and the extra tank?
There's coho running nearer, up by Reid Island. What are
you going fishing for at Tash-Tash Cove?" He looked at me
suspiciously.

"Some facts." I had given Hinkle my card. "I'm acting for
the defence in the case involving the murders out at Om
Bay." I could see this fellow suddenly going on the defensive,
hairs bristling. I hoped he was not one of those people who
almost instinctively distrust lawyers. "You do much business
in the winter, Mr. Hinkle?"

"You get a rent here and there."

"How about two and a half weeks before Christmas last
year, couldn't be much business. December eighth, to be
exact."

"You acting for the guy that killed those people?"

"Yes, I'm his lawyer." He looked impressed. I hoped, after
his initial wariness, he would become intrigued about this,
want to open up a bit, want to play a role. *Yes, Martha, he
started asking me these questions about Om Bay. He's the
defence attorney for the murderer.*

"No, I guess I don't mind."

"December eighth. Your records show any boats go out?" I
smiled pleasantly at him.

He went to a cabinet and flicked through what looked to be
monthly records of accounts. He pulled out two pieces of
paper stapled together. "December eighth. A boat went out.
One of the big ones. I got three twenty-two-foot cabin
cruisers, the *Yankee Doodle,* the *Doodle Dandy,* and the
Macaroni."

"Can I look at that? I don't want to take anything, I just
want to look at it." Make no unreasonable demands.

He placed the documents in front of me. One was a
rental-receipt form under the letterhead of Tyee Rent-a-Craft,
similar to the one the car rental outfits give you. It bore Bill
Wheatley's signature. The other was a merchant's carbon of
the Visa form, bearing the same notations as the copy I had
found in Wheatley's wallet. A hundred and fifty bucks a day

plus gas. Out: five-thirty A.M. In: eleven forty-five A.M. The day of the murders. But the chief pathologist's best estimate of the times of death was noon, only fifteen minutes after Wheatley had returned this boat.

"Do you remember him?" I asked.

There was a pause. Hinkle studied the forms like a witness stalling. "Well, I guess I know who he was."

"Yes, Mr. Hinkle?" I stared out the window, past his shoulder, watched a column of fish boats chugging their way north, past Savary Island.

"I guess that would be Bill Wheatley."

"That's what the documents say."

"The football player guy. He's a preacher. I seen him on his TV show."

"Anyone with him?"

"Well, he had two friends, two big guys."

"Know their names?" I wasn't taking any notes; this had to be very informal.

"They're fighting the cults. What's this all about, Mr. Macarthur? Maybe I should talk to my own lawyer. I don't want any bad publicity."

"Not as if you have anything to hide, Mr. Hinkle. Barney, isn't it?" I pressed. "Did they say where they were going fishing?"

"No, they didn't say. They didn't have much in the way of small talk. It was awful early in the morning, maybe they were grumpy. I know I was, at five-thirty."

"What gear did they bring?"

"Can't say. I wasn't around when they were loading the boat. It was dark."

"Doesn't say here you rented any gear to them." I indicated the receipt.

"No. Can't recollect I did." Funny how people start off so talkative, then retreat into shells when they get questions.

"What about when they got back? Talk to you then?"

"Can't say they did."

"Did they bring anything back with them? Any fish?"

"Can't say I remember any fish."

"What about when they returned it, did you see their gear?"

"Can't say I paid any attention."

"See any deer carcasses?"

"What?"

"Deer carcasses. It was still hunting season. No wolves on some of these islands out by Desolation Sound, lots of deer. I'll bet you get guys coming up here in hunting season, want a boat to get over to one of the islands."

"I wasn't watching when they unloaded the boat, Mr. Macarthur. I don't remember seeing no rifles, if that's your next question."

"What was their mood?"

"Only talked to Mr. Wheatley, and he didn't invite no conversation. I just filled in the amount, put the Visa through. They left in their Winnebago. A Minnie Winnie, it was."

"There's a place to stay in Tash-Tash?"

"The Lodge. Firetrap Arms, they call it. What time you going to bring the boat back tomorrow?"

"I'll see how the fishing goes, Mr. Hinkle."

"There won't be no bad publicity?"

"Won't be if you keep your mouth shut."

He took me out to my boat. "It's the same one they had, the *Doodle Dandy*."

* * *

The inside passage. Cultifornia North, its nearly deserted shores sprinkled with groups of society's opted out, communes of alternative life-stylers scattered among the bays, escapees from our ravaged civilization.

At the wheel of my cabin cruiser I sped through the green sea into the awesome spectacle of Desolation Sound, so thrilling, so eerie. The air was still. The snowy spires of the Coast Mountains were mirrored in the satin sheet of the sea. Islands clad in a hot summer dress of brave, unwilting green dotted the sound, islands disappearing behind islands, islands fading into the haze where the mustard-yellow sky met and coloured the ocean. My wake spread behind me in an endless fan.

I had come here often in my boyhood. The private school to which my parents had consigned me for four terror-stricken years was on upper Vancouver Island. In studying for one's manhood, one must learn how to handle yachts, and I and my fellow trainees for society's upper establishment had sailed the school sloop in Desolation Sound. The area seemed preternatural to me then, and seemed so now. Lovely and loveless.

But I had never sailed as far north as Poindexter Island, which began to emerge from the smoky distances. I got my charts out so I could get in as close as possible to look it over, avoiding the rocks and reefs of Chaco Point.

Close in, I cut speed and putted north along the steep western slope of the island, where Douglas Fir and western red cedar hung over rockfaces twenty feet high. The island seemed not to have been logged for many decades. It was a North Pacific jungle, a tangle of cedar spurs and salal and rotting trunks. Somewhere, in one of these little bays, lived Joe Whitegoose, the old fisherman to whose cabin Emelia Cruz had come, and where she died. I would visit Whitegoose tomorrow after a trip to the other side of the island, to Om Bay.

There were few beaches along this western shore, few places where one could easily or safely walk. The summer sun blazed now, but what had it been like in the pitiless, penetrating, wet cold of the rainy season? I thought of that eighteen-year-old girl scratching and crawling her way for five days and nights last December to Joe Whitegoose's cabin. The distance had been seven or eight miles if she had followed the twisting contour of the shoreline, God knows how many miles in the bush. That she had lasted so long was amazing. That she had died without unburdening herself of her anguished story lent her tragedy an additional sadness.

After a while I came around a little point and slackened speed as I pulled around into Tash-Tash Cove. The village comprised about a hundred small houses scattered on the hillside, shacks of greyed, untreated cedar, sombre yet ramshackle, most of them, and some larger buildings built around the cove on either side of a government wharf. Smaller wharves spread like fingers from the government dock, and fishing boats were bumpered against them: seiners, trollers, packers, runabouts, skiffs. At the top of the wharf was a squat, white-painted wooden building, advertisements on it, that I guessed was the co-op store, and beside it, up the hill, was a one-storey brick building so spare and unattractive it could only have been the government building.

To the south stood the fish plant with its own dock, partly hidden by a wooded promontory. I saw the RCMP launch there: Corporal Scanks was in town. To the north, away from the village, at the end of a boardwalk raised on piles, stood an ancient, two-storey structure I took to be the Tash-Tash

Lodge. Its shingled walls seemed to have taken root in the soil, were part of the ragged forest. Incongruously, a huge dish antenna was perched on the roof: technology intrudes upon funk.

I found a spot between two fishing boats and I slithered in. A couple of Indian boys jigging for cod or sole stared as I tied up, grabbed my briefcase, and made my way up the planks. Some men stopped mending nets to gaze at me. This is a town where not much happens, I could see. The presence of a stranger with a briefcase gives an edge to the day.

I wasn't expecting much from Corporal Scanks. He would be familiar with the RCMP routines: don't talk to defence lawyers, they'll only use it to screw you around on the stand. My attitude was: no harm trying. You don't get unless you go for.

The red brick building housed, from one of a pair of front doors, Post Canada, and, from the other, one of the little tentacles of the long arm of Canadian law, the Tash-Tash RCMP detachment. I went in.

A counter, a couple of desks behind it, a back door with a barred window which I presumed led to a cell. The Queen stared reproachfully down at me from the wall. A man I took to be her temporary representative here glared at me from beside the police radio, to which he was listening with headphones. He had a face that looked not so much weather-beaten as beaten upon: nose askew, left cheekbone purpled with old scar tissue. He wore a khaki toque—indoors on this hot day—and a stained T-shirt and blue-mirror sunglasses that gave his face an other-worldly glow.

"There's nobody here," he said in a loud voice.

"Nobody here but you." I smiled. "And me."

"The corporal's out to lunch."

I looked at my watch. Three-thirty. Long lunch. I thought: this guy is tending the store for Scanks. He must be Wendell Joiner, the auxiliary policeman mentioned in the reports. He and his brother had accompanied Scanks to the scene of the massacre. I tried to read this man: Coors belt buckle, that little army commando toque, those big blue pilot glasses, his brain plugged into the police radio. This would be your basic frustrated cop, not enough wherewithal to get into the force but infatuated with the role, made virile by it.

"Can I talk to you?"

The man grunted and removed the headphones. I decided

to play this one a little differently, and to worry about my ethical position later.

"Name is Macarthur." From my briefcase I pulled the copies of the police photographs, and the photostats of Scanks' reports, given to us by the Crown. "I'm being paid by the government. I'm here to take some statements on the Om Bay case." There was untruth in intent only. I *was* being paid by the government—through the legal aid system.

He got up, came to the counter, looked at the police reports, and accepted my outstretched hand. His manner changed from cool to obsequiously fraternal. I was okay. I was law and order. I flipped open my wallet to my Law Society card and said, "I'm one of the attorneys for the trial coming up. I guess you're Wendell Joiner."

"Wendell, yep." He didn't seem like a Wendell. "Yeah, I help Eddie out. Jeez, I thought we wasn't supposed to be interviewed by you guys until next month. August fifth, the letter said. You in Mr. Lukey's firm?"

"Different firms, but we're both going to be doing the same trial." If this man smelled out my lie he would dry up. I wanted to milk him a little before Corporal Scanks got back. "While you've got a moment, Wendell, mind if we go over a few details?"

"Am I really going to have to go to court?"

"'Fraid so. I'll explain how it works after we go over your evidence."

"Eddie saw everything. Nothin' I can add. Waste of time for me to go to court, far as I can see." He glanced idly at the pictures of the dead bodies on morgue slabs. "It's enough to make you want to puke." He showed no signs of doing so as he flipped slowly through the book of photos, studying each naked body in turn, then the pictures taken at the scene. "All these dead fuckin' wind-up dolls. Hey, a guy could sell some of these pics to a magazine for big bucks."

I began making notes on a lined pad, talking at the same time. "Okay, you arrived at Om Bay, Eddie's report says, on, let's see, 8-12-84, at, uh, thirteen-forty hours. Tell me what you did and what you saw."

"Well, it's like in Eddie's report there. I seen it. I got a copy. It's how it happened. There it was, that Shiva guy, the bodies all around, the rifle and like that." Lukey would have to coach this witness carefully. Only a dim bulb burned here.

"Did you hear Shiva say anything?"

"No, I wasn't close enough to him, only Eddie. Well, later I heard Ed ask him why he done this, and he said, 'Why can't be answered.' I remember that."

Perhaps, I thought, I could get something out of this goon to bolster our insanity defence.

"Shiva was acting awfully strange when Eddie arrested him, I guess."

"Have to say his brain was fried. He just sort of babbled on, but I didn't really get none of it. Didn't give no resistance."

"He didn't seem to know where he was, that the idea?"

"Sort of, I guess, yeah. You could say that."

I pressed with the kind of question I would not have dared in a courtroom unless I knew the answer. "Did he say anything about having killed anyone, Wendell?"

"I guess not, no."

I scribbled down that helpful answer.

"Like I can't help much, Mr. McCarthy. It's just a waste of time far as I'm concerned to go down to Vancouver for a trial. Who's the stupid lawyer who's defending? Why doesn't he just cop a plea and get it over with?"

"Well, there's the insanity defence."

"Insanity. Sane or insane, he did it. Cocksucking attorneys, dragging everything out for their fees."

I was about to ask about Bill Wheatley when I heard the scrape of footsteps outside the door, then heard the squeaking door-hinge behind me. I turned about to face a man in RCMP brown, no tunic, shirt open at the neck, sweat patches at the armpits.

"Hey, Eddie," said Wendell Joiner, "this here's one of the prosecuting attorneys for the Om Bay trial."

A time of decision. The game of deceit becomes more intricate when played against an officer of the peace. Was there some obscure criminal charge that could be laid? The offence of impersonating a prosecutor? Would Scanks recognize my name from somewhere and blow my delicate cover?

"Eddie Scanks, this is Mr. McCarthy," Wendell said.

"I hope there's no confusion," I said, preparing to give myself an out.

"What do you mean?" said Scanks. He shook my hand in a gruff way, studied my photostat copies of his reports.

I decided to go for broke. "We were supposed to get together on August fifth, but I decided to come up early. The case is too big; we can't wait."

"You should've phoned ahead, Mr. McCarthy. I might not have been here. I got a fair bit of range to patrol." This man was not your laid-back country cop. He was skinny, hypertensive, had rashes and scabs on his elbows. He was short for a Mountie, with close-cropped orange hair, neat moustache, impacted features. Close up, what smelled like lozenge-sweetened beer breath. A parade sergeant's voice.

"Mr. McCarthy, I'm forty-five years old and I've been in the force since I was nineteen. I hate the fucking work and I hate the fucking jerkwater shacktowns they send me to, and I hate the fucking courts. And if you'll forgive me, I hate the fucking lawyers, but I know I got to put up with them. I saw you come in by boat. Attorney-General too cheap to fly you in?"

"Thought I'd do a little fishing this weekend."

Scanks gave a little snort. "I hate all the fucking fish, too. You live above a pile of fish guts, you learn to hate the fucking fish." He ushered me around the counter, sat me beside a desk, went to a nearby filing cabinet, and opened the bottom drawer, pulled out some thick files.

"Can you do it from the top, corporal, without your notes?" I was pretty nervous playing counter-spy for the defence.

"My name is Edward O. Scanks, Corporal, Royal Canadian Mounted Police, and was such on December eighth last year, stationed at the Village of Tash-Tash Cove, in the County of Vancouver, in the Province of British Columbia." He smirked. "I've been to court a hundred thousand times. Only thing I'm worried about is Arthur Beauchamp. I hear he goes for the gonads. What's he going to ask me? If he asks if the guy acted crazy, I'll have to say I'm not an expert. What do you want me to say?"

"Just be truthful."

"You're not much help. I don't want this guy getting off." He sat down across the desk from me, scratching his left elbow with four fingernails. "What's that weirdo going to say on the witness stand, that's another thing I want to know."

"Shiva? I'd like to know, too." Truthfully.

"I don't want to lose this one, Mr. McCarthy. I got my very own fucking mass murder here, and I want to get some respect. This is a big collar."

"You left Tash-Tash at half-past twelve. What had you been doing earlier that day?"

"There'd been an all-night party at a cabin up in the

woods, they'd just come from a logging camp, had cocaine and everything, and the damn party was going to continue all day Saturday if I didn't shut it down. I know it's going to look bad I didn't take the trip to Om Bay earlier in the day, with what George Wurz had told me about being scared of Shiva, but they didn't post Superman to this detachment, they posted Edward O. Scanks. I got to deal with seabillies and weirdos all up and down hundreds of miles of coast. I even got other communes. I'm getting off the force, Mr. McCarthy, just going to finish my year. Screw it."

He switched elbows halfway through this splenetic speech. "From the top then, corporal."

He recounted his day at Om Bay like a good cop, everything memorized, in chronological order: the bodies, the dancing, chanting Shiva, his strange statements. Wendell listened, his eyes flicking back and forth. I made notes.

At the end, I said, "Okay, we have seventeen people executed by bullets through the backs of their heads. We've got four shot in the heart, two in the back, one in the chest, one of the young men executed also had a bullet through his leg. What do you make of that?"

"I don't make anything of it. That's your job."

"You think he shot some of them up and after that they simply allowed themselves to be tied and executed?" I wondered if the Crown had a theory for that.

"They were all space cadets. They'd walk into the ovens for him. I saw them here in town, I saw them once out there." Scratch, scratch at his elbow. "Okay, my bet is that George Wurz, the guy who came to town to warn me, he tried to lead a revolt, and some of his buddies got shot up by Shiva and he was forced to tie all the others up. We got rope burns on his hands. Shiva shot him in the back afterwards, then greased everybody else, and Emelia Cruz got away, the only one. What I'm interested in is, what's Shiva gonna say on the stand?"

"You checked everyone for signs of life?"

"They weren't in rigor yet. They were fresh dead. You seen the pictures of their faces, blown out by bullets."

"I want to explore the possibility of there being other witnesses that we haven't heretofore considered."

"Wendell and me, that's all, and Tom Joiner out on the boat."

"Any other boats around that day you didn't recognize?"

"There was fog all over. We had boats almost colliding."

I took the plunge. "Know of a guy named Bill Wheatley?"

Something changed in Scanks' expression. A soft shielding of the eyes as they glanced away from mine, down to his files. Something in those files about Bill Wheatley?

"Why are you asking that question?"

"Has he ever been seen around Poindexter Island?"

"Why are you asking? I want to know."

"Let me ask the questions, corporal."

"No. I'm asking the question. What about Wheatley?"

Why so defensive? Suddenly Scanks picked up his files, put them back in the drawer, and brusquely pushed Wendell Joiner away from the radio desk. "G.I.S., Vancouver," he said into the microphone.

I was getting adrenalin rushes. I glanced nervously at that back door with the barred window. Would I be allowed my one phone call? Scanks made his connection and told someone at the other end to patch him through to Inspector Storenko. This was bad. Storenko knew me. I could vault over the counter, might make the door on time. I wanted to be where witnesses were.

"Corporal Scanks, inspector, sorry to bother you. There's a man here by the name of McCarthy, came unannounced, says he's assistant prosecutor on the Shiva case, and he's got copies of all my reports and stuff. . . ."

"McCarth. . . . Is his first name Max, by any chance?" Storenko had gone to law school with me, sent there by the force after a dozen years in criminal investigation. With his LL.B., he made inspector fast, at forty-two. "Little guy, sandish hair, kind of aggressive?"

"That describes him," said Scanks.

Wendell was looking at me stupidly. What was happening, he wasn't sure, but he could be depended upon to be very disappointed in me when he figured it out. I got up and went towards Scanks, who made sudden motion with his hand, tried to ward me off.

I called into the mike, "Hey, Frank, how's it going? How're the wife and kids?"

"What are you trying to pull off, Max? If I find you've been looking at privileged records—"

"Cool it, cool it. There's obviously been a mistake here, a little verbal confusion. We've just been chatting about the case, nobody's got any secrets, right, Frank? So you still

coaching the midget baseball?" Scanks glowered as he held
the microphone for fast talking me.

"Get that little son of a bitch out of the office, Scanks.
You've got nothing more to say to him. Call me later.
Understand?"

"Yes, sir."

Storenko clicked off. I took a slow step back. Scanks put
the microphone down and looked sharply at me. Wendell
seemed to inch up from his chair.

I chuckled and took another casual step toward the passage
past the counter. "Good old Frank. He and I are going to
have a drink and a laugh over this. We went to law school
together, you guys know that? A real gentleman, honest as
the day."

Scanks hadn't moved. Wendell swivelled around, his rear
just a little raised from his chair. I could see by his expression
the dawn had broken. I slowly strolled to freedom, around
the counter, toward the door.

"You better get on your boat, McCarthy, and paddle your
butt out of town," Scanks said. "Get out of here."

"You're not the sheriff of Laramie, corporal; you don't run
people out of town." I was standing by the door then, feeling
cocky now that Scanks seemed committed to nonaction. And
I hate being challenged.

"Get out of Tash-Tash before I lay a charge of obstructing
on you." Scanks' voice had lost its bigness, was squeezed and
tense.

"You'd be the laughing stock of the RCMP if you tried that,
corporal. I'd sue your brass buttons off you." I opened the
door and slipped outside into the late afternoon sun.

I could sense Scanks and Wendell Joiner staring out the
window at me as I trudged down the planks to the dock,
toward my boat. I could imagine their little grunted curses,
giving way to self-congratulatory remarks. *Looks like we
scared the piss out of the little fucker. He's going back to his
boat.* I imagined their eyes squint and their smiles disappear
as they saw that I was only collecting my overnight bag,
coming back up the dock, whistling a merry tune.

I would not change my plans in a display of insipidity and
cowardice. Those plans had me staying overnight at the
lodge. A not-tall person like myself knows it is never wise to
show fear. If the dogs scent it, they come after you.

The Tash-Tash Lodge. I checked into a little room on the

upper floor whose walls bore stains from winter rain-leaks. It looked down over the bay, a pretty view from here, little boats scuttling about, gulls crying their anguished cries. Although it was high season, I seemed to be the only guest. Had some 1920s romantic dreamed of tourists here, believing that tourists might go where no highways go?

After having eaten a portion of dead and cooked animal in the dining room, possibly something of a bovine nature, I discovered the true purpose of the Tash-Tash Lodge; in the worldwide scheme of things: a dispensary of drink, a place where the citizens exercise their inalienable right to get creamed and fall on their faces.

The bartender, bland-faced and bald, was not a fount of information.

"What goes on in this town?" I asked.

"Nothin'. I don't get involved."

"You working here the day all those people got shot up on the other side of the island?"

"Don't know nothin' about it, Mac."

The locals must just have had their mid-July payday because about fifteen guys from the fish plant or off the boats were at three joined tables in the lounge, powering their way through huge pitchers of beer. Eight or nine full ones were on the tables. At another nearby table, with friends, was Wendell Joiner. The television set had the sports channel on. Two flyweights were battling noiselessly above the barroom din.

I chose the opposite side of the lounge—which I picked up quickly was the Indian side—and sat down at a little terrycloth-covered table, held two fingers up to the waiter. I looked at my neighbours: four men and a woman seated to my right, a young couple to my other side. I said, "Hi," to the folks on my right, "Hi," to the young couple. Everyone gave shy nods and hellos back. The waiter dropped two glasses of draft in front of me (no Pilsen Urquell in here, I'm afraid), and five glasses for the party to my right, plus a little pot of something that looked, well, putrid. With crackers.

Wendell was pretending not to notice me, swilling beer with the rest of them over there. He would be hostile to us in court as a result of my charade, but he was frightened of the courtroom and would come clean if handled right.

The young couple to my left were talking to each other in a soft and languid way, sneaking little looks at me: Stranger in

Town. The woman, plump and pretty, giggled a lot. Did she find me funny? I turned to one of the older men to my right.

"Tash-Tash," I said. "Is that Salish? What does it mean?"

"It means the two places of drawing water," he answered in a voice so low I could hardly hear it over the bar noise. "It is from the Kwakiutl story of the two springs of life."

An ancient Indian legend. I was about to get into it when Wendell Joiner, tired of ignoring me, got up and strolled toward the men's can, not far from where I was sitting. As he reached the door he made elaborate show of noticing me. "You still here?" he growled. His voice full of beery bravery.

"I fell in love with this town."

"If you ask what I thought, I thought he was sane."

"Scanks tell you to say that? It's not what you told me, Wendell. You said Shiva's brain was fried."

"You think you can come around here and play your smart-ass lawyer games, hey?"

"Perish the thought."

"Why you hanging around this end of the pub, Mr. McCarthy? Looking to get laid tonight? Susy there, she'll give you a go." I could sense Susy and her boyfriend stiffen. "If you can stand the smell."

"Wendell," I said, "aside from being a racist and a sexist bigot, you are an unmitigated and contemptible boor. And do you know something else? If you don't tell the truth on the witness stand, we're going to slice you into thin bologna."

Wendell opened his mouth as if to phrase a rejoinder, closed it, opened it again, noiselessly like a fish, then walked into the toilet. A few minutes later he came out, passed by without a word.

No expression had shown on the faces of the people at the tables near me during that little encounter. All remained silent after Wendell returned to his chair, angrily sloshing beer from the pitcher into his empty glass. Finally one of the men to my right turned to me and said with a gentle smile, "You like to try this?" He was pointing to the little pot of fish-smelly goop on a dish ringed with crackers.

"What is it?"

"Ooolichan grease."

I felt my stomach curdle. I recalled from somewhere: the oolichan fish, so oily the Indians used to make candles from them.

"Makes you strong, healthy, tall," said the man, passing the dish. The contents looked like moldy guts, smelled rank and awful to my untutored nostrils.

I poked the edge of a cracker into the oolichan grease, holding my breath. From the adjoining tables, seven pairs of eyes watched, fascinated. I knew this was a test. Was I man enough to sit with the Kwakiutl? I remembered Richard Harris in *A Man Called Horse*.

A hush fell on our side of the beverage room. I brought the cracker carefully to my mouth, grimaced as the stuff slipped like goo down my throat. The Indians seemed to enjoy the awestruck expression on my face.

"That's . . . good stuff," I said, passing the pot and dish back.

There was another time of silence. Then the young man at the table to my left, in the soft, whispery accent of the Coast Indians, said, "What was that you called him? Contem . . . contemptible boor, I got that part."

"Unmitigated and contemptible boor."

He grinned, looked me in the eyes, then shyly away. "You the lawyer for that guy at Om Bay?"

"That's right."

"I heard the cop say he don't like you."

"Corporal Scanks? What did he say?"

He glanced at his girlfriend. "It wasn't nice," he said. She giggled. "I hear him talking, you know, outside." A pause. "We should have a lawyer in Tash-Tash."

"Do you think there's a lot of work for a lawyer here?"

"Nobody knows what to do. When the judge comes every month, we just go to court and do what the police says."

"My name's Max."

"Mine is Benjamin Johnson. This here is Susy." Handshakes. I joined their table, and we sipped from our glasses.

"What's with this Scanks?" I said. "He seems a little edgy for a man who broke a big mass murder case—a police hero."

"You see the guy in the white shirt and tie?" Benjamin twisted his head in the direction of a rambunctious fool who was drinking straight from a beer pitcher. "He's Mr. Cosgrove, the manager at the plant. Don't listen, Susy." He whispered into my ear: "He puts it to Mrs. Scanks."

Susy giggled. "I know what you're talking about."

Now I understood the eczema on Scanks' elbows. He was a neurotic with a cheating wife, the subject of local gossip.

"That Scanks, he got in a mess over a property deal,

partners with Wendell. Wendell, he thinks he's John Wayne
or something."

I figured that about summed it up. John Wayne in oilskins.
"Is his brother Tom over there?"

"You see the big guy by himself, with the long hair and the
bad hand, like?"

I saw him. Tom Joiner was staring into what looked like a
beer-and-tomato juice, either very drunk or very meditative.
His hair was tied back into a ponytail. One hand was a stump
with a thumb and part of the small finger.

Benjamin said, "He was working trawler up north, an' he
got his hand stuck in the hooks when they was winching. He
got his own boat and used to have a crew, but he's alone now.
Best fisherman here, not counting me and Susy."

"Not me," she said.

"Tom Joiner don't talk to nobody much since last December. Guess what he saw at Om Bay changed him. He used to
be sort of like Wendell, but I hear he goes to the Catholic
church out by Refuge Cove on Sundays now."

Tom Joiner raised his eyes, looked at us, looked quickly
away. I realized he was not drunk. Maybe he was drinking
straight tomato juice. I had a sense that this man hid more
than terrible memories in his deepest mind, and wondered if
it had something to do with Bill Wheatley.

I pulled out the photograph of Wheatley from my wallet.
"See this guy around here last winter?"

"Yeah, he was in to see Mr. Scanks."

I almost sloshed my beer. "You mean you saw him?"

"But I think November," Benjamin said. "Maybe the end
of November. The Chief will know, he remembers everything." He got up, walked around my table, and showed
Wheatley's photo to the gentleman who had introduced me
to oolichan grease—the Chief, I gathered, of the nearby
reservation.

"Bill Wheatley," the short, portly man said. "I seen him on
the TV on Sundays. Useta play for the Lions. Well, he come
here twelve days before the big snow, I remember."

"Can you recall what day that was, Chief?" I asked.

"Day before the Grey Cup, that was it, wasn't it, Jimmy?"
he asked one of his friends.

"Think it was," said Jimmy.

"November twenty-fourth, around there," said the Chief.
"A Saturday. I remember thinking, Grey Cup day tomorrow,

and here is Big Bill Wheatley, useta play for the Lions, coming into the cove on a plane. Flew in by hisself. Yes, sir, we was sittin' right here, and from that there window, you could see he went up to the RCMP, stayed in the office there for, oh, about two hours, then took off in the plane again."

I was excited. "Did anyone see him around again? On December eighth, the day of the murders?"

They all shook their heads. "Never saw him again," said the Chief. "The day those murders—nobody flying no planes then. All foggy. Except the RCMP—they made it in."

"Were you here when Scanks left for Om Bay on the eighth? About half-past twelve?"

"Susy and me, our boat is just down from where his is tied. They came running up the dock, coming out of the fog, like, with their uniforms. Three hours later, helicopters, everything."

"Any strange boats in the area on the eighth?" I asked.

"Nobody was out around then except Tom Joiner," said Benjamin. "Tom and his crew were fishing. Don't know what they saw."

"His crew—where are they?"

"Vancouver, I guess, haven't seen them around for months."

"Well, you could talk to ol' Joe Whitegoose, down by Storm Bay," the Chief said. "Think he was out puttin' out some traps, think he may have seen some boat, but he don't say very much, so I'm just guessing, you know." Yes, I would be talking to old Whitegoose.

I chatted a while longer but found out nothing else. I got to bed by eleven o'clock, but my spinning brain and the noisy fights that erupted in the bar below conspired to withhold sleep from me.

Wheatley had been here two weeks before the murders. On what mission had he met with Scanks?

The final fight broke out a half hour after closing time, spilled outside my window. Then the last of the fishermen wandered to their boats, their profanities drifting through my window. Then only the hoots of prowling owls. Then sleep.

10

○

Locus Delicti

The sun broke and entered my room at a quarter to six, slapped me awake. I struggled to the window to close the curtain and, glancing out upon the rustic charm of Tash-Tash Cove, I saw that my rented boat was half-submerged.

I dressed and raced outside. Benjamin, my young Indian friend, must have heard my footsteps thundering along the planks of the wharf, because he poked his head from a transom of his small purse-seiner as I raced by.

The *Doodle Dandy* had three feet of water in it. The engine was probably salt-water soaked, and that meant I would not be going to Om Bay today. Had someone taken an axe or a pike to the fibreglass hull?

Benjamin, buckling his pants, came up behind me. "Looks like someone left the water on," he said. And I saw: the snipped end of the green garden hose that served as a fresh-water feed to the boats along the wharves was hanging over the gunwales of my boat. Benjamin pulled it out. Water was still pumping from the hose. "Yes, sir, looks like someone cut through this here water hose." He looked sadly down into my boat. "Gonna take a long time to bail."

I stood there dumbly while he went back to his seiner. I heard the engine start, *blurp, blurp, blurp*, warming up. A few minutes later he came alongside my craft, got some chains under my port rail, and winched the boat up by that side, and the water gushed out over the starboard rail.

"I'll go get Charley Bill, and he'll dry out the engine for you. Lucky it wasn't salt water."

"It will take all day." Things were floating in the bottom.

"Where do you want to go?"

"Om Bay, and to Joe Whitegoose's house."

Benjamin nodded. "Susy, she'll make breakfast on the way." She was standing by the cabin with that soft smile, her eyes lowered. "You go to get your things from the Lodge, I'll get Charley Bill."

The hell with this town, I thought, as I checked out of the Firetrap Arms. I wasn't going to waste my time by making a complaint to the local corporal.

"What would you like for breakfast, Max?" Benjamin said. His fish-boat was dark green with a lemon trim, comfortable, looked-after. The name on it was *The Lazy Susy*.

"I like everything."

"Good. Oolichan grease today."

He saw me go white, and he chuckled. "Maybe bacon and eggs instead," he said, patting me on the shoulder.

We decided to circumnavigate the island, go to Om Bay first, then drop in on Joe Whitegoose on the way back. The day was nearly cloudless—a few puffy wanderers only—and the peace was barely disturbed by the soft *chug-chug* of *The Lazy Susy*'s engine, and the cries of questing gulls that followed us down the coast for a mile before giving up on us.

I had time to relax and think. My mind last night and this morning had been constructing what it secretly feared were improbable scenarios. A client somehow framed. Deprogrammers on a rampage. A police cover-up. *Know of a guy named Bill Wheatley? Why are you asking that question?* Why had Scanks so suddenly become defensive? Why was he protecting Wheatley?

I stood in the wheelhouse with Benjamin, who recounted the local lore about Om Bay. At the turn of the century there had been a homestead there, a family of seven raised by an Irish-Indian couple known as the O'Malleys. He was a totem carver: thus the old poles near the death site that I had seen in the photos. After they passed on, their children sold the property for the taxes that had accumulated on it, to a speculator from Vancouver, and it was from him that the Shiva commune purchased it. The bay was not named on maps, but had been known around Poindexter Island as O'Malley Bay. After the arrival of the strange new settlers, it became locally known as Om Bay.

"Coming up here, the whirlpools," said Benjamin. "Not bad now, but watch out when the tide is flooding." We were ploughing through a channel at slack tide, yet currents grabbed at the little seiner twisting it left and right. "Then after the narrows, Om Bay around the corner."

I went onto the deck to take pictures as we came around a point into the bay. A long wedge of sea, a bottleneck, widened into a deepwater cove, two tiny islets at the centre, a pebble beach at the head. A small stream splashed down from some rocks and bubbled across the stones into the sea. Most of the area was in second-growth timber, but three acres near the beach were cleared, covered in high, brown, seed-bearing grass and by patches of thorny bushes: great green tangles of salmonberry and blackberry. A few grey, paint-peeled totem poles leaned over a clearing in haphazard fashion.

"I don't think there's nothing to see," said Benjamin. "Everything burned by some people from town."

"The commune had a boat. What happened to it?"

"Same people who came by after the cops left, they burned the buildings, scuttled the boat."

Vandals. I remembered: the police had claimed to be distressed—but quite understanding of the anger that the local people must have felt at a deed so black as the Om Bay massacre. My guess was thrill-seekers from Tash-Tash on a beer-filled Saturday.

Susy was almost rigid with apprehension as we anchored about thirty feet from shore. Benjamin, I could tell, didn't like the idea of going ashore but bravely rowed me to the beach in the dinghy. "I'll wait here, okay?" he said, pulling it onto the beach.

I climbed up the creekbed to a grassy bluff. There had been an orchard here: I saw a dozen old, gnarled fruit trees, their branches struggling to free themselves from the chokehold of the twelve-foot-high thickets of blackberry.

Doubtless paths had been trampled by the curious after the massacre and by the hordes of reporters that had descended. But grass disguised those paths now. Seven or eight beer cans were scattered about. Just at the edge of the bluff was a large patch of burned area—the former storage shed, I assumed. It had held provisions—flour, powdered milk, tools.

Between the totems, a cut seemed to have been made through the heavy bushes, a path which opened into a large clearing. I heard a soft, crashing sound, and saw the white end of a mule deer springing through the air into the trees beyond the clearing. Then an eerie silence. I remembered this place from the police photographs. This was the place of the dead.

White heads of wild daisies struggled for sun in the foot-high grass, bravely lying to the world about what had happened here. A white-crowned sparrow added to the chicanery by singing a sweet song. Nature's cover-up. The grass grew thickest where the blood had been.

I walked about, idly peeking under fern fronds and vanilla leaves as if I'd find an undiscovered clue. I took a few photos of the burned areas here, foxgloves growing along the marges of the burns, a hummingbird diligently farming the white and lavender blossoms, fragile bells.

I listened for the moans of wandering spirits and heard only the whisper of the wind. I looked for the dance, and there was only the waltz of the green-glitter hummingbird. Was a part of Shiva's transported mind still floating about here? Somewhere above, among those frilly white clouds?

Watch the white clouds, Maximillian.

White clouds, drifting from the west, over the trees, and seeming to dissolve under the baking July sun. I picked one out, a fragile white puff that resembled a big toe with a wart on it, and I stared at it and into it and through it. And became, I guess, transfixed. The cloud drifted, and I drifted, too. The cloud transformed into a fat chicken with a little head. I don't know what I transformed into, but I lost track of time, just stood there a part of space, and the universe was the clouds, the sun, Max Macarthur, the white-crowned sparrow making inquiries, and I felt at one with all of this, peaceful and happy.

How beautiful it was here. How distant seemed the horror.

An awesome calm enveloped me.

Crack!

A noise like a rifle shot.

Soul and mind rejoined, I stood gaping.

My cloud was a fat man laughing, and beneath it, atop the escarpment which rose steeply from the clearing, a giant tree, an enormous Douglas fir, was rocking in the sky, stones falling away from loosening roots.

Another crack. The trunk split jaggedly.

And slowly, with a rending cry of splintering wood, the top half of the tree, an eighty-foot length of trunk and branch, ripped away, toppled, parting finally from the rest of the tree. It plunged down the bluff face into the forest below.

A squawking of frightened birds from that forest. Then stillness.

I looked up at the jagged spire, a hundred feet of brown, scarred, branchless trunk. And at the point of the break, I saw a hand. A jagged fist of splintered wood, and a long index finger pointing toward the western sky, accusatory, the tree's dying declaration.

Benjamin came trotting up beside me. He, too, stared at the great, maimed fir.

"Tree went over," I said.

"Yeah."

"It's funny—not much wind."

"Yeah, it's funny," he said. He looked a little spooked. Which is how I felt. But I was letting things get to me. All that had happened was that a tree, perhaps diseased, at the edge of an escarpment, tilting by inches across the decades as the ground loosens beneath it, no longer able to support that lopsided weight, suddenly shattering high up on the trunk. . . .

Logic destroys the beauty of mystery.

And I thought: the *chaitya*, the sacred place. That living temple where Shiva used to go to explore the inner sun. . . .

I saw an opening in the thicket near the hillside, and I slung my camera bag over my shoulder, and willed my body to uproot itself, and, Benjamin following, went that way. I could see that a path had been chopped through here, small alders cut away. Then the trail sliced through a patch of salal, ascended into cedar and fir. It became steeper, and we groped upward, grabbing at trunks and branches, finally coming to the bluff-top, which was covered with a cushion of brown moss.

And there: the tree, some of its great roots breaking free from the ground but still clutching at the earth and rocks, still anchoring this thick, heavy-barked arm and its eloquent finger. It had been what the foresters would call an unhealthy tree, and that is why it had been spared the chainsaw when these acres had been cut many decades ago. The trunk was about twelve feet wide at the base, but the centre had decayed away and the heavy russet bark, blackened by an ancient fire, furled around a four-foot-high opening, leading inside to a hollow. I moved with trepidation closer to that doorway. The rest of this behemoth could go any time, I knew. A three-hundred-year-old Douglas fir as my coffin: was that stern finger a message for me? A warning against foolhardiness?

I crawled onto the bend of a root, peered into the hollow tree, saw that it opened out as well to the opposite side, a window through which could be seen the clearing below, the black, scarred squares where the commune's buildings had been. The sad, tilting totem poles.

This had indeed been the *chaitya* of Shiva. Evidence was the melted nubs of three candles on the bare, dry ground. I took pictures, then took a deep breath, then ducked into the little amphitheatre, six feet in diameter, the ceiling high and dark, an area to the side covered with dried cedar boughs, like cusions. Through the window I could look down over the clearing, the beach, the totems, the *Lazy Susy*, the islands in the bay, the narrows, islands beyond islands.

And again, although I did not will it, I felt myself drifting, felt myself being pulled away. I panicked a bit, brought myself back. What was this? I had not been trying to meditate, yet stuff was happening again. And I was scared to surrender myself into that strange state of calm that had enthralled me down below. What was going on? Learn how to do it, then you can't stop it. Bliss threatening to come at you like hiccups.

Om Bay, so tragically beautiful at my feet, its rich green surface speckled by blinding bits of sun, the cloud's shadow now moving across the waters, swallowing the two islets.

I don't know where it came from, but suddenly an understanding hit me with all the power of a thunderbolt. A belief. A faith. An acceptance. Shiva Ram Acharya alias James was innocent of all charges laid against him. It was not a conclusion from the evidence. It was a truth. The fact was suddenly *known* to me.

I felt an enormous welling of relief. And as I powered myself back into contact with those faithful but neglected friends, mind and ego, I saw the cloud's shadow pass across the grassy banktop above the beach. It left another shadow: the maimed, thrusting arm of the tree within whose bowels I was lurking, the jagged hand, the accusing finger. The tip of that shadow finger was touching the creekbank just above the beach.

Benjamin following, I scrambled down the escarpment, jogged across the clearing toward the creek at the edge of the beach. I found the shadow of the broken tree, followed it to

the fingertip, looked up and saw the sun bathing the torn
stump in a brilliant halo. And I discovered my bare arms
were smarting: I had wandered blindly into a patch of sting-
ing nettles. Benjamin, looking concerned, was standing a few
feet away.

Now I was staring in the direction of the little creek. *Déjà
vu.* I had been here before. The old willow tree, the foxgloves and daisies, the sun sending diamonds from the water.

"You all right?" Benjamin said.

Is this what I had seen through Shiva's third eye? I was
feeling weak.

"What are you looking at?" Benjamin asked.

"There's something in the water there." I pointed.

Benjamin went around the nettles, waded into the creek,
bent down. I went closer. He had picked something up. He
stirred around the rocks with his hand and found something
else, extended his palm to me.

Two brass cartridge cases. A rifle had been fired here. The
police had found plenty of .303 cases but all in the vicinity of
the bodies, about two hundred feet inland. But these were
not .303s—they were from a .30-.30. "Dominion .30-.30"
stamped on the cartridge heads. I took a picture of Benjamin
pointing to the spot where he had picked them up.

We searched around for a while. Benjamin found two
more cartridge cases, both at the foot of the willow tree,
within twenty feet of the creek. Both .30-.30s. Obviously
the police had not searched this area—assuming that the
cartridges were here then. But there had been that snow-
fall.

What to do? Leave everything as it was and alert my friend
from the local RCMP? I had little faith in and lots of distrust
for Scanks. I had little conviction, moreover, that the police
in general, with their smugly air-tight case, would follow up
any new leads. So after taking pictures of the scene from
different angles, marking the spots with pennies, I wrapped
the cases into my handkerchief.

At least four shots fired from the creek above the beach.
Why?

I looked up at the *chaitya* tree of Shiva. I was dazzled,
awed, frightened. *You are a transcender, Maximillian. Perhaps one day the millions will join us in our madness.*

* * *

The little cedar house of Joe Whitegoose—the "typical run-down Indian shack" described in Scanks' report—had a cozy, hand-built look, was decorated outside with old bumpers and floats that the man must have fished from the sea. Joe Whitegoose himself was outside mending nets when we chugged into his little bay. He looked about seventy-five, had skin like worked leather. He radiated Indian mystery and legend.

"This here is Joe," said Benjamin. "This guy is Max, a friend."

Joe's hand was as smooth as rubbed silver.

He sat down on a bench and pulled from his coveralls pocket a package of Export A's. I declined his offer of a cigarette, and sat down beside him. I was still buzzing from my otherworldly journey to Om Bay, but denying it, refusing to think about it.

"How's the fishing?" I asked.

"Not so good now," Joe said. "Some daysh good, some daysh bad."

"Hard life here by yourself?"

"Gettin' t'roo it."

I told him I was a lawyer from Vancouver.

"Been there once't. That's enough."

"You may have to go back. To go to court."

"They ask me."

I told him I was here to talk about the day that the young girl found her way to the beach in front of his house. Last December 13.

Joe looked up at Benjamin, back at me. "They say not to speak to nobody." He seemed apologetic.

"It's all right," said Benjamin. "Max is a good friend."

Joe Whitegoose nodded. He rested his crinkled eyes on my face for a long while. Then in his soft, worn voice he began his story of having seen young Emelia Cruz, wounded and near death from exposure, emerge from the thick salal by the shoreline, and stagger down onto the rocks, from which she appeared to be trying to rip mussels. By the time Joe had got to her, she had fallen unconscious. He had carried her into the house, put her on his bed, hurried to his boat to radio the Tash-Tash RCMP, returned to his cabin to make some soup.

His words poured slowly, like syrup. He was without expression, but I could sense the old man had suffered in those minutes that Emelia Cruz lay there. "The police says not to talk to no one, but you are a lawyer," he said respectfully. He seemed to like me.

"She regained consciousness?" I asked. "I believe she said some words to you?" The particulars had her saying to him: *Did he kill everyone? Am I alive? Am I alone?*

"She opens her eyes. I says to her, 'I am making some fish soup.' She moves her lips, and I can't hear so good, and I come close, and she says, 'Did they kill everyone? Am I alive?' And her voice fades, you know, and her eyes roll back. And she says, soft, 'Am I alone?' I feel the presence of her forefathers. She don't eat no soup."

"You absolutely sure of those words?" My heart was racing.

"Didn't hear too good, you know."

"It was, 'Did they kill everyone?' not 'Did he kill everyone?'"

"Maybe something else I don' hear. I don' know."

"'Did *they* kill everyone?'" I urged. That *was* it, wasn't it, Joe? Tell me what I need to hear.

"Yes, I t'ink . . . yes."

I was excited. "You repeated those words to the police when they came? Inspector Storenko, you remember him?"

"Yes, Storenko. He comes in airplane to speak to me and take the body. I tell him what the girl says. He writes down, like you are doing. I sign the paper."

"Did you read it?"

He was silent. I had offended him; perhaps he could not read and was embarrassed about it. I said, "Never mind. I am writing out another statement for you. Benjamin will read it to you, and if it is right, you can sign it."

"Yes."

And I drew up the statement, feeling elated—feeling, perhaps, the ecstasy of the logical mind, not the empty mind, the thrill a lawyer gets when a case begins to break for him. I pressed my luck. I asked Joe if on the seventh or eighth of last December he had seen any boats in these waters that he did not recognize.

"Rented boat, I think, mister, from out of Campbell River. *The Doodle Dandy.*"

"What time?" I was almost stuttering.

"About three hours after sunrise. About eleven, maybe. I was setting out traps down by Chaco Point, she passes me the other way, going toward the West, t'ree, four men in it. In the middle of the channel, no fog there. I look t'roo the binoculars. T'ree, four men, big men, I'm not sure."

"Where is Om Bay from there?"

"Up behind, maybe t'ree miles."

"How do you remember this?"

"Police asks. Mr. Scanks from Tash-Tash. When he come to interview. He say, 'Remember all the boats you saw on those days.' And he writes it down, but says not to speak to nobody."

"And you haven't spoken to ... nobody, except for me, here, and Benjamin?"

Old Joe studied me for a while. "You are the lawyer for the man they say he killed all those people?"

"Yes, I'm one of them."

"Mr. Scanks says not to speak to a lawyer at all. I have never talked to no lawyers ever. You seem like a good young man. I just want to tell the truth what I know."

"And you seem like a good young man, too, Joe. Thank you."

We smiled at each other, and Benjamin smiled, too. I felt blessed to have such excellent friends. I was bubbling with joy. Benjamin read over to Joe what I had written—two statements, one about the dying words of Emelia Cruz and one about the sighting of Wheatley's boat—and Joe Whitegoose took my proffered ball-point pen and painfully scrawled a couple of marks on each paper. Benjamin witnessed.

* * *

Did they kill everyone? As I looked across the greenness of the inland sea, I saw Joe Whitegoose's lips, soft and creased like leather pouches, form the words that must have formed on the dying lips of Emelia Cruz. I heard the old man's voice, whispery, velvety, sounding in my inner ear as *The Lazy Susy* chugged back around Poindexter Island to Tash-Tash. I had wished him good health as we left him mending his nets. Good health, old Joe. You will make a remarkable witness at the trial.

I had those signed statements snugly folded into a back pocket of my wallet.

Arthur had confidently declared Emelia's words to be inadmissible. Now we must scramble up the shrouds of the good ship Justice, set sails to tack the other way. I thought back to my law school days: the dying declaration—that rare and quite conditional exception to the rule against hearsay evidence. That rule prohibits a jury from hearing statements from third parties: persons not before the court as witnesses. But what a person says, knowing he or she is soon to die, can be offered as credible evidence—if the judge can be convinced to allow it.

I must hit the law books hard, prepare a brief in favour of admissibility.

And the business about Wheatley. We had him and his buddies heading in the direction of Om Bay and not three miles from it shortly before noon on December 7. How to follow it up? I could hardly wait to get back to Vancouver to hash this out with Arthur Beauchamp.

When we got back to the docks at Tash-Tash, I saw that Charlie Bill, his tools out, was reassembling my engine after cleaning and drying it. Tom Joiner was working with him, dexterous despite his maimed right hand.

Joiner looked up at me, his face grease-stained. "I didn't have nothin' to do with this."

I squatted on my haunches on the planks. "Who did?"

"I ain't sayin'. I ain't sayin' I even know."

"You're Tom Joiner."

"Yeah." He wrenched a bolt into place.

"Well, thanks. Thanks for helping."

"I figured you was done a wrong." He had a cross on a chain around his neck. He seemed quite different from brother Wendell.

"She's another hot one, eh?"

"She's hot," he said.

A pause.

"Mr. Joiner, I'm doing a job here. Why do some of the locals seem so upset about that?"

"I don't know. I don't know nothin' about nothin'. Can I talk to you for a sec?"

"What about?" I said. "You don't know nothin' about nothin'."

His ponytail bobbed behind him as he jerked his head in the direction of a spot down the wharf out of earshot. He climbed from my boat and walked with me there.

"It's about the nothin' I can say in court, Mr. Macarthur. I was on the boat all the time, I didn't see nothin', didn't hear nothin', didn't do nothin' until I saw Wendell and the corporal comin' back with the prisoner, and then all I did was turn the boat around and come back here. I don't see why I have to go to court."

"It's not up to me. If the Crown calls you, you've got to give evidence."

"You can say you don't need me."

There is a certain kind of person who dreads court worse than hell. Tom Joiner seemed that type.

"What is it you're afraid to tell the court, Tom?"

"Nothin'." That supremely loaded word.

"Let me ask you nothing, then. Were you out fishing around here last December eighth? The morning before you took Scanks and Wendell to the murders at Om Bay?"

"There was a closure."

"Nobody's going to charge you under the Fisheries Act, for Christ's sake. Were you out by the east side of Poindexter Island?"

"No way. Anyway, real foggy that day."

"If it comes out now, Tom, the jury won't think you had something to hide. Scanks told you not to say anything, right? He's got no business telling you that. We don't want to have to embarrass you in court." He just looked at me. "Tom, did you see a little sport-fishing launch—just like mine there— somewhere out in these waters on December eighth?"

With the little finger of his claw-like right hand, he wiped a drop of sweat from his greasy, sunburned face. "I didn't see nothin'."

"Tom, have you ever been on a witness stand? I've seen people forget their names after two hours. I think I should tell you we have a dossier on you—every stupid, shitty thing you've done in your life. There are going to be a hundred newspaper reporters in there. Your life story doesn't have to come out in court if you'll be frank with me now." This was bluster of the most insupportable kind. "Are you hiding something, Tom? You and Wendell and Corporal Scanks—are you protecting someone?"

"Your boat should be fine, Mr. McCarthy. I'll just help Charlie clean it up."

11

o

Trial Run

Monday morning. Aside from the sound of secretaries scuttling about, gathering files for the day, there was calm in the jungle community of Pomeroy, Marx, Macarthur, Brovak and Sage. We lawyers huddled inside the coffee room, afraid to break out, afraid to face the beginning of the work week.

Sophie Marx: devouring cigarettes and cinnamon buns and sugary coffee, making great slashing notations on a transcript, mumbling, "These are lying buggers, lying buggers."

Brian Pomeroy: groaning through the daily tabloid's menu of dismal headlines. "M-X's going into the ground in Wyoming. SS-20s in place in the Ukraine. I give it eight, nine months. Global suicide." Brian had finished a long case some weeks ago with a group of nuclear disarmers charged with causing a disturbance. The case had made him a fanatic. "God saw how it was going in ancient times. Thus, the flood. God sees how it is going in these times. I'm going to get myself a spaceship, call it Noah's ark."

Augustina Sage (newly returned to the bosom of the firm, her skin splotched and peeling): "I can't tan worth a darn." Pointing to her legs. "These are chigger bites. Over here, sand fleas." Had she rid herself of her infatuation with André Fortin? The affair was known to all the partners now; Brovak had talked.

John Brovak: wired, jumpy, offering little scattered snatches of talk: "Get laid a lot in Kauai, Augie? Sun, sand, and sex, that's the trip, man, you bet. How was *your* holiday, Max? Find any more bodies on Poindexter Island? Hey, Augie, stop scratching them; they'll fester. Max, I fucking near came getting cited for contempt Friday. Called Boynton a shit-faced

126

liar, had to retract it. Barry Lubin hit the dust—the trial's blown his marriage; he's gone off to Vegas to try to track her down. Jake and Charlie—remember them?—another six hundred a day into the office pootpail. I bring in thirty grand a month, I take home five or six. Something wrong with this system."

And Max Macarthur: spaced out on spaceship earth, Om-Bay-mind-boggled Max Macarthur, trying to clear his head for a Section Nine, Narcotic Control Act. On in twenty minutes. Fearful of lapsing into a meditative state in the middle of the trial.

The receptionist comes in with messages. "A Mr. Jordan has been calling—"

"I'm not here," Brian says, looking terrorized. "Out of the office all week." Jordan is an income tax man.

"And a Mrs. Lippman is in the waiting room—"

"I'm late for court," Brian says, and sneaks out the fire escape window, the secretary standing there gritting her teeth. Brian has lost Mrs. Lippman's insurance settlement forms.

"They've got no case," says Sophie, slamming her transcript shut. "Flimsy tissue here."

Brovak, Augustina, and I evacuate the coffee room. We are brave soldiers off to the front.

*　*　*

I'd arranged to meet Arthur Beauchamp at four-thirty that afternoon after court. At first I didn't see him in the dark expanses of the El Beau Room, but Samson Loo led me to a back table, where sat Arthur, a sick, ashen-faced man.

"You don't look great," I said.

"I am on the wagon. Hanging onto the railing by my fingernails." His eyes were bloodshot and the lids drooped. He was a man finding the going heavy. "I am determined to ride that wagon for a few weeks. It is a trial run." He had a full glass and an empty bottle of Perrier in front of him.

"I'll have grapefruit juice," I told Samson. "Bring another Perrier. A trial run?"

"If I can last three weeks, I know I'll be able to last out the trial in September." The ashtray was full of stubbed butts. He was chainsmoking.

I didn't like this cold turkey business. I'd seen Arthur stop drinking before for several weeks at a time. Each period of abstinence ended in a week-long bout of grandness and majesty. I didn't feel I should say it to him but I'd have preferred he sip a little during the trial than be enduring it in pain.

"I stopped two days ago, Saturday," he said. "On Sunday Annabelle phoned. She wants to see me. About what, she wouldn't say. That has made the last two days even harder."

Arthur was quite obviously still in love with his ex-wife—a gold-digger, in my judgment. Very attractive, classy, twenty-odd years Arthur's junior.

"Maybe things are not working well with her new enamorato," he said. "A stockbroker who wears a medallion instead of a tie and cultivates chest hair. That man is a contemptible fool. What possessed Annabelle?"

I was wishing that Annabelle Beauchamp would run away and hide until the trial was over. Anyway I had news to get Arthur's mind off his troubles.

But I had decided not to mention the seemingly preternatural aspects of my short stay at Om Bay. He would not understand. I did not understand. Coincidences, daydreams, psilocybin in the oolichan grease: there were limitless explanations.

"Arthur, I've been to Tash-Tash Cove and Om Bay. I've found out some very interesting facts. I am going to run something by you."

"Run something *by* me? As if I am a reviewing stand? Don't talk like an advertising salesman, Max, it makes my headache worse."

"I have a scenario, Arthur. A perhaps not-so-hypothetical case. You know of the Reverend William Wheatley, alias Wheaties?"

"Yes, a rogue. You have told me something about your adventures with him."

Samson brought the drinks. "On the house," he said.

"Arthur, the scenario goes like this. Bill Wheatley and his sidekicks in the deprogramming business negotiate a deal to kidnap one of the members of Shiva's little group at Om Bay."

"Do you know this?"

"No, but look at these." Photographs of Emelia Cruz and Melissa-June M'Garethy. "A resemblance?"

"Yes, yes, there is."

"The M'Garethy girl was believed to have been in British

Columbia. Her parents got a postcard from her last October, mailed from Vancouver. M'Garethy had announced a hefty reward. I think it's possible that Corporal Scanks spotted Emelia Cruz buying groceries at Tash-Tash, described her to Wheatley on November twenty-fourth—"

"Slow down, you're jumping about like a rubber ball."

"That's one possibility. Or maybe Wheatley had a contract with relatives of one of the other victims. We can phone all the parents, twenty-two sets, find out if any of them had entered into contracts with Wheatley. Okay, let's assume Wheatley's services are being sought by someone. He has never been to Poindexter Island and decides to do a reconnaissance. November twenty-fourth, a Saturday, the day before the Grey Cup, in fact, Wheatley flies in his private plane to Tash-Tash Cove. He spends a couple of hours there *relating* to the RCMP officer, Scanks. It doesn't take him long to size Scanks up as your basic hippie-basher, a fellow front-line fighter against the cults and freaks. Let's say Scanks promises to turn the blind eye of justice if Wheatley raids Om Bay to rescue one of Shiva's brainwashed victims."

Arthur looked at me incredulously. "Back up. Reverend Bill Wheatley was at Tash-Tash Cove two weeks before the killings?"

"I have proof, eye-witnesses. And I also have proof that on December eighth he and his two pals rented a launch in Campbell River. And I believe their boat was seen near there about eleven A.M., on the east side of Poindexter Island, by Whitegoose, the old fisherman. He can identify the rented boat but was too far away to see the occupants. Three or four men."

"Go on."

"My scenario suggests the murders were committed in the morning, well before noon."

"The bodies were not in rigor when Scanks got there."

"He *says* the bodies were not in rigor mortis. What does he know? Arthur, Shiva wasn't at the campsite when his people were murdered."

"Where was he?"

"I'm getting through to the guy, he's talking. Early that day, he went to his *chaitya*—that's a Hindu word meaning sacred place—a hollow tree on top of a nearby bluff. I don't know if he left his body or what, but that's what he says. He had a sleeping bag. When he came to he found himself standing among the bodies. We have to assume that at some point he picked up the rifle, put it down again, thus the prints. The sleeping bag found over one of the bodies was his. He had blood on his lips—maybe he'd tried mouth-to-mouth rescusitation. He was in a trance, he says, and can't remember anything."

"A trance? I don't like that. This Wheatley and his friends— would they be capable of doing such a thing?" Arthur was shaking his head in disbelief.

"I've heard it said that the ability to kill is in all of us."

"But why—what possible motive?"

I pulled out a sealed plastic bag containing the four spent cartridges. "A young Indian and I found them at the creek there. My theory is that is where the first shots were fired. Suppose this: Wheatley on going ashore meets resistance in his attempt to take his target. He threatens with guns. Maybe Wheatley or Morgan or Calico get clumsy. A rifle goes off, someone is killed: the guy shot in the chest. More shots, more deaths. Only .303 cartridge cases were found by the investigating team, Arthur. One for each murder and a few more. They never searched the area where I found these."

"The executions?"

"They are hog-tied at gunpoint, put to death to silence their witness to the deeds that came before."

"My God," Arthur whispered. "But Wheatley is a man of the cloth."

"He is a fraud."

"And a murderer? What is it we know about that rifle, Max? It was reported stolen."

"Registered to a man by the name of Durkee, retired major, British Army. An old army rifle stolen from his house here while he was back in England on a holiday. Maybe Wheatley knew it could not be traced to him, so left it lying around. It'd be interesting to find out if Wheatley or those other two guys own a .30.30 hunting rifle—and if we can match these cartridges with it."

"A marvellous, if grisly, edifice you have constructed, Max. But flawed, I think."

"I have more."

"I've seen no reference in the police reports to a proposed raid by Messrs. Wheatley, Calico, and Morgan on Om Bay. Surely, if Wheatley had spoken of his project to Scanks two weeks earlier, the police would have invest. . . ." His voice trailed off.

I was shaking my head.

"Scanks got scared when I mentioned Wheatley's name, Arthur. He went white. There's a coverup. I'll tell you what it is. Scanks knew as of November twenty-fourth that Wheatley was going to raid the Om Bay commune. He knew a crime of kidnapping was to be committed. Instead of acting to prevent it, he probably aided and abetted it by giving information to Wheatley. Anyhow, now Scanks is scared shitless and he's looking after his own skin. If word escapes that he permitted three dangerous men to commit the indictable offence of violent abduction, a crime which ballooned into a ghastly massacre, Scanks is going to go to jail for criminal negligence."

"Yes, yes," Arthur said softly. His expression told me he'd forgotten his withdrawal pains. His good eye was as wide as his bad one. He breathed out slowly through a little whistle-hole between his lips.

"Whitegoose was told by Scanks to say nothing to anyone." My words tumbled out enthusiastically. "And I think Scanks has told Tom Joiner, maybe under some kind of threat, not to mention he had seen Wheatley's boat on December eighth. You better know that this guy shits into his oilskins when he thinks of having to give evidence. Eddie is going on drunken binges in Tash-Tash and he's got a nervous condition of the elbows. But wait till you hear this. Well, read it instead."

I pulled a duplicate of the statements by Whitegoose, put them in front of Arthur. After a while he looked up, gave me a good one-eyed eyeballing. "Is this a joke, Max? Would you be taking the mickey out of old Arthur Beauchamp?"

"No joke."

" 'Did *they* kill everyone?' "

"Yep. Old Joe wasn't *exactly* sure, but it fits."

"It seems, Max, that to defend, we must prosecute."

"Prosecute. What a grisly concept. But if that's the way to an acquittal, well, here's to prosecution. And to justice." I raised my grapefruit juice.

Arthur, too, raised his glass. "*Fiat justitia, ruat coeium.* Let right be done, though the heavens fall." He grimaced, took a swallow of Perrier, grimaced again.

* * *

I did my run, six miles around the park. Then, that evening, took the cartridge cases up to the police lab on the third floor of the Public Safety Building (friendly local jargon for the police station), and asked Jack Hislop, the forensic scientist, to look at them through the comparison microscope.

"All four definitely fired from the same weapon," he said, peering through the scopes at the heads of the last pair of spent cartridges. "Same on all four: the firing pin impression— see that little lip, and where it bifurcates here? The extractor marks on all four rims are definitive, too. You got a rifle you want test-fired?"

"Not yet," I said.

He scratched his initials in to my four prospective exhibits.

* * *

Later that evening, Ruth came, unannounced, to the door of my penthouse condo in Kitsilano.

"What," she said, "have you been doing?"

I was struggling to catch my breath, panting like a dog. I staggered a little as I closed the door behind her. And led her into the apartment.

"Rapid breathing," I gasped. "It takes you to the centre."

"Max, my *God*." Ruth groaned. "Dynamic meditation. Shiva has you in his clutches, man. Soon he'll be getting you to sign over your Daimler, your savings bonds, and your inheritance. Meditation—that's how they get you. Empty your mind, and let someone else fill it for you. It's a tool, meditation, a tool of mind-control groups. Same thing as deep prayer."

"I'm open to experience—what's wrong with that?"

"I've been through it, darling." She gave me a peck on my sweaty cheek. "Human potential, the whole Fritz Perls dance. It's beautiful, but you've got to *work* at it, and you can't goddamn do it without pain in the old gestalt. McDonald's fast food transformation—that's what Shiva is selling. It's the loneliness business, Max. Only the lonely buy this narcissistic, me-generation pap. But you're not lonely. And you're more fucking integrated than I am, so stop fooling around. You're getting me worried."

"Look, I'm not saying I'm buying all this, but it's important to try to *understand*. I want this guy to relate to me. Then he'll have confidence in me, and help us out. I'm doing a very subtle psych job on him." I cleared my throat. I decided not to tell her about the weird things that had happened at Om Bay. Not yet. "He says he can remember seventeen past lives."

"Aw, come on, Max, reincarnation is the biggest piece of crap the East ever sent us."

"I think maybe he transmits thoughts through his third eye, Ruth." Her expression said she wasn't buying it. "Damn it, there's lots of stuff now that can't be explained in scientific terms. Yuri Geller makes the dials of clocks turn. There's an energy aura around people, it's been photographed. Mental telepathy—lots of cases."

"And flying saucers, too."

Yes, and tree temples that split with the sound of a gun, and wood-splinter fingers that point to rifle cartridges, and visions transmitted by the third eye. Now was not the time to discuss these things with this sceptical Adlerian. One must open her mind with reasoned argument.

"We were created with six senses, Ruth, but we've lost one, the ability to telecommunicate. Now you look at ants, how they walk along a file, with a touch of the antennae transmitting complex messages: like where the picnic is laid out. Maybe it's primitive, the most primeval of the senses."

"It's a good thing we lost it, then. We'd be one giant ant-mind."

"And astral travelling, well, who the hell is to *say*? We can't prove Shiva *didn't* visit some silver angels."

"No, but it does sound like something one might dream, doesn't it?" She stood up, began pacing, took off her jean jacket, searched through the closet for a free hanger. "What an unholy mess. Your whole apartment, Max, it's like your life—dishevelled."

It was true. Haphazardly scattered newspapers and books and records, socks and shorts, unwashed dishes. In furnishings I had tried for funk. Tasteful Ruth called it junk. But I had a nice view over English Bay and the mountains, and a sundeck outside, on the roof.

"You want a drink?" I asked.

"Yeah. A Caesar."

"You'll have to do without pepper, tabasco sauce, lime, Clamato juice, and vodka. How about some wine?"

"Wine will do."

I opened a Liebfraumilch while Ruth wandered through the apartment, picking things up, straightening.

I watched her for a while until she quit this little nervous dance, and I extended her a glass of wine. She looked wonderful. "I have an idea," I said.

"What?"

"Let's, uh, get married."

"Oh, Max." She began to laugh. "That sounded so enthusiastic." But she put her wine down and hugged me.

"I meant that pathetic-sounding proposal, Ruth. I love you."

"You almost sound as if you need some convincing of that."

"The tedious truth is I'm the kind of guy who settles sooner or later. I figure, why not sooner?" A man, I felt, needs some better place to end the day than the El Beau Room. He needs *sauté de veau aux champignons* and Polish cabbage rolls that melt in the mouth. He is a second-stage male who is prepared to wash the dishes afterwards.

She held me for a long while. "Have you eaten yet?"

"No. We could go out."

"Let's not. Got anything in the fridge?"

"I picked up some fresh shrimp at the market."

"There's lettuce?"

"Sure."

"I'll make a salad." She drew back and looked me over like an object on the shelf of a curiosity shop. "You're something, Max, you know that?"

"Yes or no?"

"Let's talk about it later."

"When?"

"After you get your mother's permission."

"Oh, come off it."

"Max, you know the problems."

"No, I don't know the problems. If this is the old song about how my family stifles you—"

"Max, the song is about the whole snobby Shaughnessy bullshit trip that has been laid ever-so-decorously upon me ever since I began *daring* to date you. The Macarthurs versus the daughter of Kaspar Worobec, foreman of the die-and-cut section at Coquitlam Machine Works."

"Your father could be chief shit scooper at the zoo, it doesn't make any difference."

She stepped back; I reached for her arm, but she was out

of touching distance. Her eyes had begun to spark. "Your mother spits on the ground I walk."

"She *likes* you. She's just a very withdrawn person."

"She hates me. She gave up a career and she sees in me the person she should have become." Ruth took a quick swallow from her wine. "Anyway, it won't work. We're not compatible. You're an up-and-coming lawyer with a birthright to the establishment, you need somebody nice and Anglo or Celt, with the right genes, play all the right social games."

"It really bugs me when you talk like that."

"I'm seven months older than you are."

"And three-eighths of an inch taller."

Afterwards, while in the throes of constructing a salad dressing from my kitchen condiments, she said, "We'll talk about it."

"When?"

"Come to dinner tomorrow."

We ate shrimp salad and drank wine and we talked into the night and we watched the lights blink on, little white and yellow ribbons across the North Shore, and we watched the moon rise over Seymour Mountain.

12

○

The Fourth Dimension

On the following day, Tuesday, I was able to visit Shiva when a client no-showed (bench warrant issued against Louie the Loot, six priors on his sheet for B. and E., and he had been facing pen time in the middle of a hot and busy summer).

"I have news," I said as the guard ushered him into our little interview room.

"News." He rolled that word around his tongue. "Why is the word 'news' used to describe matters of the past? Only the moment is news." His eyes shone strangely. "The moment is eternity, but it's also such a tiny, atomic interval that only a Buddha-mind can exist within it."

The guard raised his eyebrows, shook his head, locked the door, disappeared.

"And the moment is a river. You must surrender to it, Maximillian, let it take you, become the river. Wherever it reaches will be eternity. On the banks of the Ganges, you can see the villagers carry their dead into the water. What I seek to do is drop you alive in the Ganges."

Shiva sat down, held me with his look. His eyes were large, seemed hot with inner radiation. Had he been in some deep meditative experience?

"How are you?" I said.

"The body complains to be here, but the body is only a house where Buddha dwells. I live with Buddha. I am Buddha. You are Buddha, but Buddha asleep. The Koran says, 'Men are asleep. Must they die before they awake?'"

Shiva suddenly turned the brights of his eyes down and I felt myself relaxing, the pressure off. "I'm sorry, I've made you ill at ease," he said. "But I wasn't expecting you today,

136

and I have been in deep communion with the Brahman."
Then, seemingly able to tap into my transparent thoughts, he
said, "But you have things on your mind, as you say, Maximillian,
and we will delay our business with Buddha until we have
dealt with them. What, then, is the news?"

I told him of my journey to Poindexter Island. He smiled
as I related my encounters with the Tash-Tash locals. His face
glowed with pleasure as I told him of my strange encounters
with the beyond at Om Bay, and the discovery of the .30-.30
cartridge cases.

"And swiftly the lawyer's logical mind is shocked into the
realization of mystery. How beautiful. How wonderful. God
must be in search of you."

I sat silently for a while. "Is that all? Don't you have some
explanation?"

"What does it mean to you, Maximillian?"

"I'm not quite sure. I have been criticized for having a
strong imagination."

"Thus the lawyer wrenches the experience into formed,
understood shapes so his mind can deny the unknown. A
strong imagination indeed. That is something children are
told, Maximillian, not spiritual teachers."

"I'd like some help with this."

"Meditate upon it. Meditation is the key to all mystery."

"Actually, I've tried."

"Perhaps then an illogical theory. Perhaps I am still at Om
Bay, and I remain there as a witness to what happened there
last December. There is a me at Om Bay which has not yet
rejoined this me, a me who is the memory of cruel December
eighth, a me who cannot come home yet. A me who dwells
with angels who shine like silver. And who topple trees." He
laughed, and I pictured in my mind the God Shiva of Indian
myth, laughing, jesting, the god of the practical joke.

I sighed and told Shiva about the evidence I had collected
as to Wheatley, and about Emelia Cruz's dying words, and at
the end of that, I said, "Now we have hope."

"Hope is just food for the ego, Maximillian. The more hope
you feed the ego, the more it demands. I'm happily without
hope. And thus I'm freed from hopelessness as well."

I glared at him. "Who are you?" I said after a while. "I
mean, who *are* you?"

"Meditate."

"Are you some kind of witch? You have psychic power, I'll

accept that. I know there are phenomena science can't yet explain."

"That is because science looks outward, not within."

"I have to understand. Where do you come from? You told Arthur you didn't choose your spiritual name, it chose you. What is that all about?"

"Shiva has a thousand names and an infinity of form. He comes to some. He came to me as Nataraja, the Dance King. He named me. Acharya, teacher. Ram Acharya, teacher of fire. Shiva, in honour of him."

"He came in a vision, is that it?"

"In a vision."

"Well, a vision is maybe what I got from you on my last visit, Shiva. From your *chaitya* I think you witnessed those first murders and somehow, God knows, in some psychic way, you transferred into my brain the scene where those first shots were fired. And you helped me find some evidence, some rifle cartridges. I believe you could do this only if you saw the murders happen, Shiva. Look, I can't take the stand to say that although my client has amnesia, he has miraculously shown me the place where some people were gunned down. Even Mr. Justice Carter might conclude that sort of thing offends the rule against hearsay."

"What matters it to you that I can't remember? I shan't be participating in your trial, Maximillian. Arthur Beauchamp has assured me there is no power within the man-made law that can put me against my wishes onto the witness stand. He knows Latin. *Accusare nemo se debet, nisi coram Deo.* No one is bound to accuse himself except before God."

*　*　*

My nose was puzzled; it didn't recognize the smells that assailed it as the kind that customarily came from Ruth Worobec's kitchen. But they were wafting down her hallway from the open door of her suite.

"Hi, it's me."

Jacqueline, wearing an apron that advised: "I'd rather have a bottle in front of me than a frontal lobotomy," was looking dubiously into a pot in which heads and skeletons of fishes were swimming.

She graciously accepted my proffered buss on the cheek. "I know this stuff looks bad, but the book says you're supposed to put three or four pounds of fishheads and bones in the soup base. *Bouillabaisse à la Marseillaise*."

I put two bottles of Vouvray in the fridge.

Jacqueline pondered her cookbook. "God, I don't have all these ingredients. Mom, is there saffron? It says saffron, two big pinches." I pulled out of the way as she pinched me once in the arm, tried for my tummy.

"Spice rack," Ruth called. "Third row, under 'S.' Lord, learn your kitchen."

"Madam Benoit, I am not. My artistry lies in less mondo kinds of pursuits." To me: "How does this smell? Want to taste it?"

Tentatively, I sipped from the tip of a tendered spoon. "Mmm, that's pretty good." Memories of oolichan grease.

"This will be an hour yet. Why don't you make Mom a nice bloody Caesar?" Her voice went low and woeful. "She's in a *mood*. I told her I'd cook for a change, to cheer her up. Your role is to snap her out of it."

I brought the Caesar, a scotch and water for myself, preparing myself mentally for I didn't know what. Ruth was lying on the couch, a wet cloth over her forehead. She reached up, took her drink, sipped, groaned, lay back. "You never put enough tabasco in it."

"I'll add more," I said.

"Stay."

Dog-like, I squatted beside the couch.

"I've a dreadful headache," she said.

"Anything I can do?"

"I had an awful day. All morning with a weepy alcoholic mother, all afternoon with some stingy bureaucratic bastards from Victoria who are trying to chop the *fat* from the system. They see me as fat. More government jobs are on the line, including mine, it looks like."

She worked the bureaucrats over hard, detailing for me their egregious ways, their deficiencies. Ruth loved her profession, hated her government job, and in my view would be well rid of it. Max Macarthur would be only too happy to set his new wife up as a counselling psychologist in private practice.

I knocked back my scotch, went to the kitchen for another. Jacqueline was staring narrowly into the bouillibaise pot. "'Double, double, toil and trouble, fire burn and cauldron bubble,'" she said, raising her eyes to me. "That's from

Macbeth. I told you: it's been like the Rocky Horror Show around here since she got home. I think she's going through her middle-age crisis."

"She's thirty-one."

"You're not helping. Get romantic, for God's sake. You're so *yucky*, all you talk about is law, law, law. Sweep her off her feet, that's what she wants."

"Thank you, Ann Landers. Yucky, hey?"

"So what I'm going to do is I'm going to slip away to my room early after dinner so you can do a big seduction scene."

I returned to Ruth, who was sitting up now. "Max, I'm sorry about being such a bitch. I guess it's the job, it's the insecurity, it's the lost canoeing holiday. And it's just me. I think you're wonderful to want to marry me. I'm afraid to decide, I guess. I don't know why I'm afraid."

She pressed a hand to my mouth, smothered my words.

"This is my speech. Let me get it out in one go. I need time to think. Jacqueline is going to Montreal for August. I'm going to take my four weeks then. I think I'll go to the A.P.A. convention in Mexico City, then maybe trip down to Acapulco or somewhere. I didn't want to canoe the Bowron lakes anyway."

"Aw, Ruth."

"I'm just kidding. Honest, Max, I want to spend some time by myself and think, okay?"

I sighed. "Okay." I was hurt.

We managed to chug haphazardly through the meal, Jacqueline's bouillabaisse receiving mixed reviews (Ruth nitpickingly critical, I wimpily ecstatic). At the end of dinner, Jacqueline courteously disappeared into her room, and at the end of the second bottle of Vouvray, Ruth's humour had radically improved. She became light of heart and teasing.

Wine brought me the courage to tell her about my strange trip to Tash-Tash Cove and Om Bay, and I dared her credulity by speaking of the strange spaces I felt I had travelled in, the wave of calm, the vision, the apparent messages. I had no understanding of the processes that had occurred to me, and I told her that.

Ruth listened to all of this with a quizzical look. "Max," she said finally, "what do you and this Shiva talk about when you visit him?"

"Oh, everything, the cosmos, the mind, waylessness, and

surrender." I smiled. "You know. Those things. I've agreed to let him teach me."

"Surrender. I see. This kind of stuff can lead to a little loss of orientation, Max. Certain people—what William James calls 'self-surrender individuals'—they can't survive emotionally without structure. Some kinds of religious conversion can be pretty regressive, especially if they encourage dependence. It stunts the growth. And some of these people lose contact with reality, under the influence of a skilled mind."

"Look," I said petulantly, "I'm not under the influence of anyone's mind. I'm totally in charge of my own. But this guy is different. He talks about mindlessness, not mind control. It's a matter of *emptying* yourself so you can receive . . . awareness."

"I see." She was a doctor studying an unusual case. "Mindlessness. Emptying yourself so you can receive, eh?"

"I'm *not* a self-surrender individual."

She leaned toward me, stared into my eyes, touched my cheek with her hand. "Honey, don't get caught up. There are some tricky people out there. They can get you thinking all sorts of things that aren't real *are* real. You *have* heard of post-hypnotic suggestion, haven't you? Ever been hypnotized? That's when you start to see strange things."

"It's impossible to hypnotize me. Listen, the tree split just as I was standing there. His *chaitya*, his temple. He couldn't have hypnotized me into seeing that."

Ruth gave me zombie eyes. "Who-o-o kno-o-ows," she said in her ghost voice. "Look dee-e-p, dee-e-p into my eyes. Max Macarthur, you are my slave. I give you total fulfillment in return for total subjection. Render unto me your ego, and I promise you nirvana." And she put her lips to mine. And I surrendered. Nirvana.

* * *

On August 3, Leroy Lukey phoned me in a great temper. "You're like the midget in the nudist colony, Macarthur, getting in everyone's hair. I just got back from Poindexter Island. I find you were up there talking to Joe Whitegoose. Now he's changed his evidence. I think it's fucking unethical for a lawyer to be badgering a Crown witness into changing his testimony."

"Leroy, he volunteered it. 'Did they kill everyone?' "

"What did you do, buy him a year's supply of whiskey?"

"Isn't that funny, we thought you had doctored the particulars. We were going to tell the judge you were suppressing and/or fabricating evidence. Your calling me like this renews my respect for you, Leroy. Not that it had begun to flag. You're telling me you were caught by surprise."

"Listen, stretch, you're no good at playing the innocent. You goddamn well know we had a signed statement from him dated December thirteenth, when his memory was fresh. Taken by Storenko, and he's an honest cop."

"Well, we both have statements, Leroy. We're even."

"You want war, I'll give you war. Tactic for tactic. You'll be wishing you wore your jockstrap to court. Oh, by the way, Corporal Scanks thinks highly of you for posing as my junior. The short arm of the law, eh, Max? And now what are you trying to do—implicate Bill Wheatley in this? You'll get hoisted on your own erect petard. You're not going to get that dying declaration in, be assured of that."

"Mr. Justice Carter is a judge of liberal views. We shall see."

"We're going to pull out the stops. I'd been planning to bend over backwards for you guys."

"No thanks, Leroy."

13

o

Minnie Winnie

The dog days of summer. A dry season unlike any I had
known. In the north, terrible forest fires, like mythical mon-
sters, trod the wilderness, devoured everything green in
their paths. Even as far south as Vancouver, there was a dead,
yellow pall to the sky—from the burns that seared the spine
of Vancouver Island.

There is a psychosis about this West Coast: manic in the
summer, depressive in the winter. A flighty climate, coquett-
ish, as torrid and randy in this July as she had been despon-
dent and tearful in the winter. *Où sont les neiges d'antan?*
Where were the rains that had washed over us last January,
the rains that had chilled our bones and seeped into our very
guts as we carried on in aqueous stoicism under the toiling
grey sky?

Dog days on the West Coast. You will have to spend a
summer out here to understand how they can get. Small riots
on Granville Mall and on the beaches at English Bay. Complaints of police beatings: hot evenings, hot tempers, too
many unemployed young people, bitter, feeling betrayed.
The Civil Liberties Association kept me busy with referrals.

At work, free from Shiva's gentle pull, I lived not for the
moment at all, but lived with mind, memory, hopes, and
ego—and time crawled by, filled with tension. The pile of law
books grew higher on our library table: cases on dying
declarations, insanity, confession, and scattered about were
briefs for cross-examination, texts on pathology, ballistics,
fingerprints, notes full of the kind of reasoned arguments that
Mr. Justice Carter loves. As the trial moved menacingly
closer, I found myself sleeping less, eating more, drinking too

many Urquell in the El Beau Room. And running only every other day. What was this protrusion at the waist? A warning of potbellies to come?

The heat wave didn't break in August. In normal years, one feels a jolt then, as summer suddenly slips a cog, and there are morning mists, hints of damp. One sniffs the fall. But this year, as the weeks shuffled by and the days grew shorter, the sun mocked our expectations, remained brazen, continued to harass forest and countryside. The crowded city core became a sweating armpit.

By mid-August I was consumed by the case, driven by a passion which surprised and exasperated Shiva. I was schizoid, split into two, and our meetings were schizoid, too. For an hour I would be like a football coach beseeching my quarterback to get into the game, to give evidence, to *win*. And for the next hour I would be quietly nodding my head, agreeing that, indeed, a man who has no desires has come home, all that the mind carries is excess baggage to the soul, all that it tries to do is a futility. "Truth liberates, but the truth has to be your own, not a judge's, not a jury's, and not your ego's. The only law is *dharma*, the ultimate law. If you want to live according to the ultimate law, you must drop the legal mind."

I really did feel altered in the course of these sessions, I think. As Shiva began to speak, my anxious spirit became subdued, enclosed in the warm cocoon woven by his words, and his smile danced through me. I always left Oakalla pensive, less distressed than when I arrived.

But when I returned, neurotic after a week of staring goggle-eyed at law books, feeling coffee-shattered, menaced by the spectre of the looming Fall Assize, I would fall upon Shiva like a wolf, demanding that he see the nonsense of spending his life in a prison, demanding that he give evidence, demanding that he help save his innocent hide and put the true killers to justice.

He seemed pained that I had seemed to retain none of his teachings. The trial promised to offer an excellent argument, he said, in favour of purposelessness.

Ruth was still in Mexico, unheard from. Her daughter was in Montreal on a summer language exchange that her high school was running, and I had no contact from her either. I fretted. Had my girlfriend picked up a convention-goer in Mexico City so she could enjoy illicit escape from her stuffy, part-time partner? A perfidious fling with a rolfer from Esalen before returning to her Canadian wimp and his slavish proposals of marriage. Perhaps some brawny, smarmy gigolo who runs rats through mazes at Fordham.

My defence-building went poorly. I had exhausted the list of relatives of the twenty-two dead, had come up dry. No parent or guardian had contracted with Bill Wheatley for a kidnapping. Unless that parent were one of the M'Garethys. I was unable to get through to them, despite many long-distance efforts. J.J. M'Garethy's secretary refused to return my calls.

I had talked to the retired British major who had owned the Lee-Enfield rifle found at Shiva's feet. Mr. Durkee's Vancouver home had been broken into while he was on holiday. Nothing but the rifle had ever been recovered. Durkee had never been near Poindexter Island.

I spent many hours talking tactics with Arthur, who still looked and doubtless felt terrible, but seemed to be winning the battle of the bottle. His wife still had him strung by the gills on a line. He was seeing her for tea occasionally. He seemed hopeful about a reunion.

Arthur had let me take charge of the somebody-else-did-it defence, spent all his time preparing for the insanity issue. He came away from his sessions with Mundt miserable. "Delusions of grandeur—who suffers most, the client or the psychiatrist? How can a jury acquit on delusions of grandeur?"

My nights were spent alone, hot nights in sweat-stained sheets. My dreams were phantasmagorical. Laughing Buddhas, and all-pervasive god's-eyes, and rivers pouring into the oceanic mind. Nightmares, too, the kind where you are running slowly from distorted shapes. Such as Bill Wheatley or Wimpy Morgan? Almost every night, a dark, deep, threatening voice, a voice that in my sleep I believed I recognized but never did. The crack of a gun—or is it a tree splitting? Red-dappled snow, nature's measled surface.

* * *

The trial of Wheatley, Morgan, and Calico upon the charges of assaulting my Moonie clients was set for Thursday, August 29, in Burnaby Provincial Court. Melissa-June M'Garethy, alias Astral, telephoned me on the weekend before, to tell me she wouldn't be attending as a witness.

"I can no longer accept Reverend Moon as my personal saviour," she said. "He is a crook. He thinks it is okay to steal from God."

The combination of Bill Wheatley's heavy deprogramming session, and the theft of twenty thousand dollars from his wallet by her former comrades-in-religion, had caused a serious god-failure here, I could see. "Where are you calling from?" I asked. Her voice had come on the line only after much clinking of coins.

"I . . . don't think I should say."

"How come?"

"I think they are after me again. Mommy and Daddy. If I come to court on Monday, they'll find me. I am happy now. I am with my true sisters and brothers. I don't want to leave them. They're a *real* family. Mr. Macarthur, you were really nice to me in court. I think I should tell you something. The climax of the world is coming in four weeks. September seventh has been the day chosen."

"The climax of the world?"

"We auto . . ." I could hear her conferring with someone. "We auto . . . auto-eroto-destruct. Through the mass love conferred by Raba-urt-Jogan." That's phonetic, I think that's what she said. She was in a bad way. "Unless we acknowledge Raba-urt-Jogan, and love him in return."

"Who is he?"

"He comes from the star Antares. He is the true father. We are his first family on earth. He is love. He will come on September seventh. That's a Saturday. If you love him, Mr. Macarthur, you will not auto-eroto-destruct."

"Well, I'll keep that in mind for the seventh. Listen, Astral, are you sure you're all right? Are there any messages you want sent to anyone?" From your world to ours? To unhappy, wealthy J.J. and Edith M'Garethy, perhaps? I was now feeling badly about my role in saving this multi-billionaire heiress from her parents. Ego-deterioration had set in worse. Maybe this had become a medical case.

"I send all my messages to the stars, Mr. Macarthur. Now I know why I am Astral. It was intended by Raba-urt-Jogan."

"Listen, how can I love him if I don't find out more about him? Where's his head office?"

I could hear her conferring with her friend or friends. "When the sun dawns on the day of his coming, you must go to the top of a high hill, and call his name, and scream out your love for him. Go with Raba."

"Don't hang up! What is the name of your group?"

"Love Apocalypse. Go with Raba." She hung up.

Wow. I made a mental note to try to track her down, check on her.

* * *

Although I wouldn't be allowed to participate in the assault case in Burnaby (prosecution had to be done by a Crown lawyer), the trial would give me a chance to see Wheaties, Wimpy Morgan, and Jack Calico in court, see how they stood up. I had arranged to meet Robert the Moonie and his friends just outside court at ten A.M. At nine, before I could get out of the office, Wheatley's lawyer, Foster Cobb, phoned. He was going to ask for an adjournment.

"What grounds?"

"Wheatley is sick. He has a bad case of hives."

"What's he been rolling in instead of money?"

"Speaking of money, I just want to warn you that when your clients do take the witness stand, I'll be accusing them of stealing twenty thousand dollars from my guy. It will go to their credibility. Maybe they want to rethink these charges."

"Come on, Fos. What's this hives bullshit?"

"The reverend gets allergies. There is a lot of stuff floating around in the air during this hot spell. A lot of stuff that causes Bill to sneeze and break out in rashes. Some of that stuff seems to be coming from you."

"What is that supposed to mean?"

"He thinks you're trying to embarrass him over something to do with the Om Bay massacre."

"Where might he get that idea?"

"He might get that idea from Leroy Lukey, to whom parents of the Om Bay victims complain. They say you have been pestering them, asking questions about Wheatley. Thus he has hives."

"*Did* Big Bill Wheatley have a contract to deprogram someone at Om Bay?"

"Sorry, Max, I'm not saying what I know. I have to protect my clients' interests, but I'm going to try to protect yours, too. Max, you're barking up a wrong and dangerous tree. And Wheatley, Morgan, and Calico do not like the bad P.R. you

are spreading about them. He's my client, Max, and I have a
duty to him, but I don't carry his torch. He's a vindictive son
of a bitch with power, and he doesn't like you, and he can
cause damage. He's worried about his career. You and Arthur
should be worried about your careers, pal, if you're thinking
of developing this nonsense as a defence at the Shiva trial.
This is a very, very, very friendly warning. Don't say I didn't
tell you. I've got to get out to Burnaby. Meet me there. Seek
instructions from your clients. Perhaps they want to forget
about this whole thing."

We hung up and I sped out to the Burnaby Justice Building. What was with this very, very, very friendly warning?
Foster Cobb was known to be a lawyer of a certain slyness, a
master cardsharp when it came to the game of courtroom
poker. You *bet* he has to protect his clients' interests, I was
thinking. And the best way to protect them would be to bluff
me out of the action with some veiled yet grandiose threat to
career. Maybe he thought he was dealing with a courtroom
rookie. Clearly his clients had expressed more than a casual
annoyance at my investigations. Perhaps they had told all.
Foster Cobb wouldn't be the first lawyer to be forced by his
barrister's oath to keep terrible secrets.

That telephone call was more convincing evidence for the
convinced: Wheatley and his buddies were the butchers of
Om Bay. Now they knew the pursuit was on—that couldn't be
avoided. But perhaps they would get scared and run.

I could find no parking spot in the lot beside the Justice
Building, and I was already late for the opening of court. But
I knew Cobb and the prosecutor would wait for me, let me
have a chance to ask my clients if they wanted to withdraw
the charges.

My Daimler prowled up and down tree-shaded back streets
looking for a parking space.

There: just behind that big yellow-striped Minnie Winnie
Winnebago. Just enough room.

I slid in behind the metal monster, cut the engine, sat.

"I Found Him," announced the bumper sticker in front of
me. The windows at the back were shut and curtained. The
mobile home sat comfortably in the shade of a big-leaf maple.

I got out to look it over. The infamous Minnie Winnie
consisted of a not-so-minnie trailer built onto a Dodge cab,
and lacked the boxy look of the standard model. All windows
were locked and screened except the driver's door window,

open about the thickness of an arm. About the thickness of my arm, actually. Which was of a length that it could reach down and pull up the lock button.

Was I so desperate in my search for evidence that I might commit a crime? B. and E.'ing a Winnebago: was it listed in the Criminal Code? This street was deserted. Calico and Morgan would be with Foster Cobb in court; Wheatley would be hiding out somewhere with his alleged hives.

Lawyers get disbarred for less than this, I thought as I slipped my hand through the opening, reached down, found the button. I tugged. As it popped, something wet and rough slurped at my hand, and I jerked it up, wrenching my elbow, which was caught at the top of the window. I cursed softly. The springer spaniel which was scratching at the window—and for which, I gathered, the window had been left open—seemed friendly enough. He had refrained from chomping on a couple of fingers.

I was committed. Dogs don't tell tales. I slipped inside and locked the door. The dog, a tail-wagging non-barker, jumped playfully at me a few times, then followed behind as I crouched and went into the back. My elbow was slightly sprained.

I felt foolish all of a sudden, not knowing what I expected to find. What I did find were thousands of Bible tracts, boxes of them piled upon boxes. Here was a seventeen-inch television set, a videotape player. Copies of *The Divine Principle*, discourses on Scientology, Eckankar, the Hare Krishna, other groups. A book entitled *Brainwashing in Korea*. A table with some files piled on top. I would have a quick look at those after casing the place. I patted the dog, who was seemingly happy to have a stranger checking out his masters' goods.

A pair of sliding doors opened into a closet-cum-storage area. Inside: coats, other clothing on hangers, and a lot of sporting equipment. Some weights and springs for Mr. Body Beautiful, fishing rods and tackle boxes, a catcher's mitt, a soft football. And a rifle bag. And in it, a Winchester .30-.30 hunting rifle.

The label on the bag had Bill Wheatley's name and address on it.

Take it, I told myself. Have the rifle tested, then find some way to return it quietly.

The dog rushed away, up to the front. And I heard a loud voice outside. "I could do with a triple Mac and double fries."

The voice came to me louder as the driver's door clicked open. "And a coupla shakes."

I ducked into the storage closet, drew the doors shut.

Shakes, I had.

A lurch, as if an earthquake had hit: obviously Wimpy Morgan, on the plus side of three hundred pounds, mostly former muscle. I could hear straining creaks as he reached across and unlocked the other door; then another tilt, the other way, not as severe, as Jack Calico, only two hundred plus, climbed aboard. The doors slammed shut.

"October eighteenth, that's okay," came Morgan's voice, muffled but discernible through the thin wooden doors. "Mr. Cobb says they're getting scared, and they'll drop the charges before then." A southern drawl.

An indistinct response from Calico.

"What time do we have to pick Bill up at the airport?" said Morgan. "We got time for McDonald's, ain't we? There's one on Canada Way."

"We don't need to go to no McDonald's." Calico's voice was high-pitched, almost falsetto. "You got the sandwich you ain't yet ate I packed for you this morning."

"Well, if he's flying up to pay off Scanks, he ain't gonna be coming down until this afternoon anyway."

To pay off Scanks?

The rustling of paper bags.

"Peanut butter and strawberry jam." I think that's what Morgan said through a sandwich-muffled mouth. "I like that real heavy English kind of jam. Food industry, that's where we're makin' a mistake not putting our money into. Laundries, that's just pee. If the rich Mick pays off big, we'll get into food. Bill don't talk Dogan talk, that's how she floated last time. He should of had pictures of the Pope."

Words coming from between gulps. Had Wheatley a new contract to kidnap Melissa-June? Had they located her new commune—Love Apocalypse, the earth station of Raba-urt-Jogan?

Something from Calico I couldn't make out. But Morgan had a heavy, penetrating voice. "Now why'd you tell Mr. Cobb that Bill was out of town on a business appointment? Sometimes I think you got all your brains in your legs. The lawyer don't want to hear that. He wants to hear Bill is sick, so he can honest tell that to the judge. Lawyer ain't gonna do your lying for you, *you* gotta do it. I don't want to know about it, Mr. Cobb says. You wanna finish half this other?"

"No."

"He don't want to know more than Bill has got hives. I got some milk back there in the fridge, Jack, you wanna fetch it for me?"

"You could say please," Calico whined. He made his way back to the kitchenette. I heard the fridge door open and close. Outside my thin wooden doors, the panting of the little spaniel. I made myself smaller.

"You keep your mouth shut real good, Jack, but when you open it, the strangest stuff come out. What do we do every Saturday, Jack?"

"We work the laundromats. All day."

"And when do we do that, Jack?"

"Every Saturday."

"And the folks on the route, they know that, don't they? They see us every Saturday."

"Yeah, Wimpy."

"And if you don't memorize what we do on Saturday, your mouth is liable to get our asses in a whole lot of mess. You heard what Mr. Cobb said about those lawyers. They ain't playin' games unless it's kick the can, and it's our can."

Calico said something in an impatient voice.

"It's nearly lunch. Let's go to the McDonald's."

"It's only half-past ten."

"No, I feel the good Lord is pointing us to McDonald's on Canada Way. We got lotsa time."

The motorhome's engine started and the noise drowned their words. My mind was milling. A payoff to Scanks for his silence about Om Bay. Scanks, with financial problems, deep in trouble for abetting Wheatley's plan to raid Om Bay—he had obviously agreed not to interfere—was making the best of his awkward situation by blackmailing Wheatley. Or, to put it more generously, the noble Mountie was accepting a fair gratuity for his silence.

The Winnebago bumped along the road to Canada Way. Yes, McDonald's—I could slip out while they were pouring Ketchup on their chips inside the restaurant.

A flap-flap-flap sound against the closet doors, as if a dog's tail were wagging against it. Go away, boy. Good doggie, go away.

The Winnebago lurched down Canada Way, its stowaway crouched in the stern gunwales like a rat.

I felt the bump of a low curb as the mobile home entered the McDonald's parking lot. It rolled to a stop, then backed into a stall. The engine was cut.

". . . magazine article about this nigger who does deprogramming out of California," came Morgan's voice. "They're taking over. Try to get on a pro ball team these days, you gotta fight off the niggers. Smell that good smell? Hallelulah, I feel saved again." He chuckled. Smells wafted of Big Macs.

Should I take the rifle? How would I get it back to my car?

"Be real good to have a couple of these franchises," Morgan went on. "Bill says stocks, but folks is losing their shirts, look at that East Kootenay Silver we went for, down eighty cents in five months. Hamburgers'll never go out of style. Folks when they wanna eat, they don't wanna fuss. They just wanna eat." Doors opened. More lurches. "They don't make the shakes here as thick as the A & W. Okay, Ishmael, time for you to go out and find a tree. He'll be all right out here."

I assumed that Ishmael, the friendly spaniel, jumped out. The doors slammed shut. All right, James bond, let's get out of here. It will take McDonald's thirty seconds to fry up a triple Mac and three seconds for Morgan to eat it. Through a crack between the screens of the back windows, I could see the restaurant, waitresses and customers bustling about. The vehicle just to starboard was a rusty pickup, no one in it. In front, a high, wire-mesh fence, a thick fringe of weeds and ferns beside it.

I grabbed the rifle bag and gingerly opened the locked driver's door, poked my head out to see if it was safe, then got out, quickly shut the door, took a few crouching steps to the weedy area, and hid the rifle and bag there. I would come back for them in my Daimler.

Annoyingly, Ishmael came dancing up to me, body and tail wiggling with intemperate glee. "Stay," I ordered. The dog disobeyed, following me as I slipped along the fence, outside the line of parked vehicles, and headed for the street. I would have to find a taxi, but such promised to be sparse in this area. There was a payphone in the restaurant. I approached it as if coming from the street, left Ishmael wagging outside the door.

When I was inside, I thought to myself: so far, perfect. And here was an excellent chance to seek information from that dauntless duo who were just now taking their trays to a table. Yes, why not? Grab a burger at the counter, join them.

Armed with a Big Mac and a coffee, I walked over to them. "Hot out, huh? Some weather. Haven't seen a summer like this around here I can ever recall." A long pause. "You fellows got out of court real quick. Just back from there myself. Adjourned to October eighteenth, eh? Too bad, I suppose you boys wanted to get it over."

"I don't recall you asking if it's okay to sit," Morgan said.

"I sense hostility."

"You sense right," said Morgan.

"I offer no hostility, just being a lawyer who is doing his job."

Morgan's eyes were dark beads lost in folds of fat. But his hair was pretty: styled, golden curls cropped short at front but long in the back. His hands, slabs of beef with chubby tentacles, surrounded a triple burger with everything, which he slowly raised to his mouth.

Calico, a quiet type, was a healthy cole slaw and milk fellow. A bald gargoyle with a gimpy leg and a perfect body. He wouldn't look at me.

"We can be friends," I said. "'And to him that striketh thee on the one cheek, offer also the other.' St. Luke." I doubted that these tent-show carnies had ever done more than pretend to read the New Testament.

Morgan's face went into the triple burger and when it drew back again, he conversed between swallows and chews. Now I knew why they called him Wimpy. It had nothing to do with being a wimp. "You a Christian, Mr. Macarthur? The pastor calls you the handmaiden of Satan."

"Sure, I'm a Christian. I teach Sunday school. 'Jesus loves me, this I know, For the Bible tells me so.' What's in the Bible, that's literal, I've always thought. What about you guys?"

"We're Christians," said Morgan. Calico nodded.

I bowed my head. "Dear God, please bless the food that Ronald McDonald, through You, is providing to us this day." They ceased eating, bowed heads. They had been out-Christianed. These were humourless frauds who didn't know they were being taken for a ride. "The little things, like saying grace, they're too easily forgotten, especially in restaurants. You know how it is—people watching. But Jesus watches too, doesn't he? He wants to know the Spirit resides within you. I hope you guys understand that as a lawyer, I don't have any choice who my clients are. I'm trying to get them to drop these charges."

The last of the triple burger disappeared into Morgan's maw. "You believe in the Holy Spirit, Mr. Macarthur?"

"Of course. Actually I know someone who speaks in tongues. You fellows ever speak in tongues?"

Calico glanced at my face, and his eyes flicked quickly away. He munched his cole slaw like a rabbit with fast, nibbling teeth. Morgan attacked his first milkshake, double-strawing it, not coming up for air for quite a while. Then he said, "What church do you belong to exactly?"

"The Holier-than-Thou Assembly of the Gospel of the Only True Faith. The one out near Chilliwack."

Morgan just nodded. I couldn't believe this. Talk about zombies. Did Wheatley have control over their minds? Would they do his every bidding—even if it were murder?

"Bill Wheatley doesn't really know me, that's the trouble," I said. "We've never had a chance to get together outside the courtroom, where I can be myself. Where is he today? Sick at home, I hear."

Calico and Morgan looked at each other.

"Yeah, he ain't feeling well," said Morgan. "Hives." He wiped his lips with a paper napkin, went after the second milkshake while eyeing my untouched burger. A long, slurping pause. "Mr. Cobb says you been asking some questions to try to tie us in with that massacre on Poindexter Island," he said. "I don't understand that. Why would you do that? That ain't a Christian thing."

Wimpy Morgan seemed not at all soul-riven by the guilt of twenty-one cold, calculated executions.

"Listen, I forgot I had a big breakfast. You like to have this burger?"

Morgan eyed it. "You sure?"

"I'll just have the coffee."

His hand powered across the table and picked off the Big Mac.

"They make them real good here," I said.

"What about that, Mr. Macarthur? We know you're acting as that guy's lawyer, Shiva. Mr. Cobb says you're trying to drag a herring across the path. Because we help save people from cults, we're your marks."

I worried: could these dumb pseudo-Christians commit such an abomination? Guys with such a nice dog?

I leaned toward Morgan confidingly. "Listen, I told you: as a lawyer, I've got my job to do. The thing is, I know Pastor Wheatley made a trip to Poindexter Island. Last November twenty-fourth." This much Wheatley would already know I could prove. "I have to follow everything up or I'm not earning my fee."

"Mr. Cobb says people can get away with anything in court and not be sued for libel," said Morgan. "No, it don't seem Christian."

"Okay, I'll make a deal. If you tell me where the three of you were last December eighth, I'll promise your names won't be mentioned at the trial." I lied, but only to seek out *their* lies. An alibi had doubtless been concocted.

"You could've asked, you know," said Morgan. "Instead of talking to all sorts of folks who don't know us."

The quiet Calico added, "We wouldn't do nothing like that." He sounded hurt, a better actor than I gave credit for.

"We heard about the murders over at the pastor's place, on the TV news," said Morgan. "Jack and me was working the laundromats out in the Fraser Valley, doing the circuit all day, and we went over to Bill's home and had some pizza and some Chinese sent in, and we watched the hockey game, and we saw the murders on the news."

They hadn't guessed I had traced them to Campbell River and Tyee Rent-a-Craft. I was rubbing my hands briskly beneath the table. I pressed. "Any witnesses? Just for the record?"

Just then, Calico, who was staring out the window, said, "Hey, there's Ishmael. What's he got?"

My eyes followed his and my heart sank. There was Ishmael struggling across the car park, his jaws clamped upon the fabric of the rifle bag. He pulled it a few feet, stopped and panted in the heat, tackled it again. Ishmael was a good dog—he had found property that had the scent of his masters on it, and was bringing it to them.

Calico and Morgan climbed to their feet and headed for the door.

I decided to get the heck out before they started making some connections between me and that rifle. This was bad: upon being told about this episode, Wheatley, of more limber mind, would likely conclude I had been occupying his two underlings while my confederate jimmied his van, grabbed and hid the rifle.

Now he would destroy it, I thought, as I despairfully slipped from the restaurant and jogged down a back street. I had just lost the most valuable piece of evidence I could have had—the rifle which, ballistics tests should show, had fired the cartridges I found at Om Bay. Unless I could get somebody quickly inside that Winnebago.

I took off my jacket and jogged all the way back to the Burnaby Justice Building. My Moonies were still there, waiting for me.

"Would you care to buy some maple candy?" said one of them.

"No."

"It's for the perfect Father."

"No."

"Father thanks you anyway."

14

o

Ruthlessness

Man, reckless in the management of this planet, this single cell, this systemic whole, has caused a rent in the stratosphere, and the ozone layer has begun to leak away. A resulting greenhouse effect has caused ocean currents to alter ancient weather patterns. Thus the drought, said Brian Pomeroy. Friday, August 30, was day sixty-five without rain. The wet West Coast of North America would soon become the new Sahara.

It was the latest of Brian's dire predictions. The planet (it was never referred to as Earth, or the world) had skin cancer, and with its epidermis eaten away it would soon be as dead as all other children of our star. There was no hope.

Brian was doomsaying hard this morning because the cruel lottery of the judges' rota had caused him to draw Mr. Justice Hammersmith on this, his last day on the bench, the eve of the old troll's seventy-fifth birthday and his mandatory retirement.

Brian's clients were four underground warriors for the green movement who had been charged with contempt of court for disobeying an injunction Hammersmith had issued. His clients were said to have attempted to free some Orcas from the nets of licensed aquarium whalers.

"The quality of mercy droppeth as the acid rain in The Hammer's court," he moaned as he left the coffee room for the Law Courts Complex.

I had worries of my own that day. I felt helpless and unready for the Shiva trial, to begin following the long weekend. The defence was incomplete patchwork. We had Wheatley in the vicinity of Om Bay. But we had no motive.

We had confidence the jury would hear Emelia Cruz's words: "Have they killed everyone?" But we had no direct evidence of who "they" were. We had the beginnings of a reasonable doubt. But that doubt would vanish like thin smoke when the jury realized Shiva was not going to take the stand to gainsay guilt.

Arthur and I would go with what we had, hoping for small gifts of innocent proof from witnesses' mouths in cross-examination. Arthur was as ready as could be expected with the insanity defence, but it would stay on the back burner while we went all out in an effort to nail Wheatley, Morgan, and Calico. "Do we poke around, or go for broke?" I had asked Arthur.

"We nail Wheatley to his own cross," he said. He was excited about the chances for a complete acquittal, far more optimistic than me. I had imbued him with my own conviction as to Wheatley's guilt, and as to the payoff to Scanks, the Crown's chief witness. I could tell Arthur was looking forward to ravaging the policeman on the witness stand.

We knew we could ask for an adjournment to gain time to find stronger evidence to implicate the deprogrammers, but if we adjourned, we would probably lose Mr. Justice Baynard Carter and end up with a lesser judge and a less hospitable courtroom. Carter was a key to this case. He would let us run the trial the way it must be run.

And who knows what shape Arthur would be in if we adjourned. He was still on the wagon, a pillar of the legal community. He had truly got into this case, had spent long hours with Mundt and longer hours in that abhorred institution, the courthouse library. The Shiva case had given Arthur something to stay sober for.

Ruth was due back at three on this Friday afternoon. That is what she promised on the back of the one and only postcard I had received from her, which showed the waters of Zihautenejo bay, a bikinied woman para-sailing above the wake of a boat. "This is me!" was written in pen, and an arrow. I got the picture.

Ruth had been enjoying herself. Well, I guess that was good. But who had taught her to para-sail? Many possibilities of infidelity were to be read between the lines of her merry paragraph. Her P.S. asked me to pick her up today at three. "Long letter follows." That was an ill-kept promise. The postcard had come two weeks ago. No letter.

Amanda came to the door, interrupting my coffee-room self-flagellations. "Everybody wants you at once. A Mr. Lyons on three. Desolation Sound Air Charters on one. And your mother on six."

Mom told me she was coming downtown. She wondered how my time was. We arranged to meet on Robson.

Unhappy news from Claude Lyons, one of the best lock-and-pick men in town. "It was a picnic getting in. I could've brought you a catcher's mitt or a pair of barbells, but not the item for which requisition was requested. Sorry. Always helpful to be of service in any future endeavour."

Wheatley had got rid of the rifle, all right.

But on line one, I struck pay dirt. I had tried to think like a good detective, reasoned that if Wheatley was with Scanks on Thursday, they would have met where few witnesses might see them. So I had made calls to all air charter companies in that area. Desolation Sound Charters had told me they did a return trip from Tash-Tash that day, and now were calling back with details.

"The passenger was a Mr. Scanks," said the woman on the line. "Tash-Tash to Heriot Bay on Quadra Island. Left at ten A.M., returned at noon."

I rubbed my hands together.

* * *

Mom and I met at The Mozart on Robson.

"I don't suppose," she said, "we shall see anything of you for the next few weeks, however long your trial lasts. I just want you to know my wishes go with you."

"Thank you, Mom."

She sat there quite primly—pretty, proper, frail. So dignified, my mother.

"Your father, of course, wishes that you will do well. He talks about you, you know. He doesn't talk very well to you, can't seem to tell you how proud he is of you."

"One of these days we'll have to get together, Dad and me. I'm proud of him, too. Chief Justice of British Columbia—that's a great trust placed in him."

"The appointment will be announced in two weeks. I really can't bear the thought of it. I'm afraid I've been rather cruel with him."

"Mom, I share with you the horror you feel about the

judicial social twirl. But you married for better or for worse.
He'll be a wonderful judge. He's now a Charter of Rights
man. Let him have his shot at pronouncing wisely on the law.
I think he'll want to be remembered as a great judge."

"Oh, all that pomp and power, it's all so much poppycock,
Max. Why doesn't the man just retire? He's sixty-five, for
God's sake, when most men relax and reap the rewards of a
hard-working life. He'll work harder as a judge. I want some
time with him while we still have health. I am greedy about
that."

"I have your point, Mom."

We sipped our tea quietly. "How is Ruth?"

"I'm going to find out. She's coming back from holidays
today."

"It's been a long separation. A month?"

"Yes. Mother, what do you think about Ruth?" I was being
nervously bold.

"I think she's quite nice."

"She feels you don't like her."

"I hope I don't give her that impression. I *quite* like her. If
it's approval you want, you have it."

How old-fashioned I was. Approval, I realized, was exactly
what I sought. "I think you have reservations."

Mother sipped, dabbed her lips. "Let me put it this way.
It doesn't look as if Tom and Maggie are going to have their
own family. God knows they've tried hard enough. Ruth—she
already has a family, hasn't she? Jacqueline. I know she's a
lovely child. I suppose it would have been nice to continue
the line, and all that. I guess that's what I'm saying."

I left her with a breath of a kiss on her cheek and went up
to the courthouse to get Tuesday's jury list from the sheriff's
office. With time on my hands before going to the airport, I
wandered down to Courtroom 43 to observe the torment of
Brian Pomeroy upon the last day of the last of the hanging
judges (Hammersmith had sent two dozen people to the
gallows before the noose was abolished during a rare lucid
moment in Parliament).

Brian, standing at the courtroom door, looked as if he was
being stalked by a hit man. "We've recessed for sentence," he
said in his lugubrious voice. "Hammersmith has before him a
tribe of captured ecologists. Sacrifices will be taken to mark
the festive occasion of the judge's retirement. Entrails will be

examined. They will tell us why God chose Brian Pomeroy to drop his pants for Hammersmith's final butt-fucking."

Brian's clients were bronzed, outdoorsy Greenpeacers, with the cockiness of front-line revolutionaries. They joked about, leaning by the rail over the great foyer of the courthouse.

"The petitioners said they'd be happy with a nominal punishment," Brian said. "The aquarium people don't like the bad P.R. this case is giving them."

A reporter from *The Sun* came up to us. "What's the news?" I said, hoping to ward off his own questions, which would be about the Shiva trial. Sometimes these guys play on your hunger for ink to worm secrets out of you.

"Scandal in Victoria over contracts for the new Squamish Highway," the reporter said. "Your client is going to have to share the front page for a while. What's he going to say, Max? 'I didn't know the gun was loaded'?"

The court clerk called us in before I could decline to answer. I grabbed an empty space on the counsel bench as Mr. Justice Anthony Montague Hammersmith wobbled in, scanned the courtroom with squinting eyes, sat down. "Sentence," he said.

Would it be one of his famous rambling tirades that bespoke common cause with seventeenth-century values?

"We will have either a society of laws," he said, answering my question, "or we will have anarchy. Perhaps there are those in this courtroom who would, ah, elect for anarchy, but their views are condemned by right-thinking people everywhere. These four men proclaimed their intention to defy a court order, and acted pursuant to that proclamation. I divine no signs of remorse. Once people are conditioned into believing they may defy authority without recourse, we are opening the gates to, ah, terrorism. The respondents will have two days to get their affairs in order before reporting to the Vancouver regional jail where they will each serve a term of six months. Judicial orders may not be disregarded and disposed of like old newspapers."

"Who is the terrorist?" It was one of Brian's clients, Jerome Yates, standing, shaking with anger, a defiant university student with a long blond pigtail. "Who terrorizes the oceans? Who terrorizes the sentient species of the oceans—"

"Please control your client," Hammersmith ordered Brian. "This is not a town meeting. Court is adjourned." He got up and began to walk out.

"Order," called the clerk.

"Do you know what I think of your justice, your honour?" Yates must have had a martyr complex. "As a judge, I think you've shown about as much class as a fried-egg sandwich."

It was a still-frame. All motion stopped. Everyone in the courtroom had been getting to their feet, and Mr. Justice Hammersmith was about to take that last step down from the bench—his last step as a judge—toward a door being held open by a deputy sheriff.

I breathed out slowly. This would be The Hammer's chance to wreak one final act of judicial retribution. The unsubtle Yates still stood there, reckless in his youth and anger.

Hammersmith's expression didn't alter, and his eyes seemed to rove sadly about the courtroom. He looked to counsel table, at Brian, then at me behind him, at Jerome Yates and his comrades, at the crowded gallery. He said nothing. He went out the door.

"Let's get the fuck out of here," Brian said to me in a choked voice.

* * *

"Six months for trying to free a few killer whales," Brian said bitterly. "The whales get life."

We were delivering piss into urinals along the wall of the washroom at the Vancouver Hotel's Timber Room, where we had repaired to drink and eat.

"That miserable old fuck," he said. "He'd sentence Jesus Christ to life for treason for preaching the Sermon on the Mount. 'Perhaps there are those in this courtroom who would, ah, elect for anarchy.'" Brian rendered a squeaky imitation.

We washed our hands. "They didn't even have a retirement ceremony arranged for the old vulture," I said. "That shows how much everyone despises him, even his brother judges."

Brian suddenly uttered a savage guffaw. "'As much class as a fried-egg sandwich.' Aw, *Jesus*." Now he broke into hard laughter, which was infectious. We roared.

"The last words ever uttered in his courtroom—" I said, sputtering—"'You showed as much, as much class as a . . . as a fried-egg sandwich!'"

A toilet flushed from behind one of the closed cubicle doors.

When Mr. Justice Hammersmith emerged from it, Brian

and I stopped laughing. He didn't look at us. He calmly went
to the mirror and began adjusting his tie, carrying on as if we
did not exist.

* * *

At the airport, still flustered from that terrible scene, I
waited at the immigration out-doors and watched the line of
tanned and tired faces stream out, but the Western Airlines
flight upon which she had promised to arrive came in Ruthless.

Why wouldn't she have telephoned me with her change of
plans? (Whom had she changed those plans for? What was in
that letter that she had promised to mail? Dear John. . . .)

I found my way back downtown, to the El Beau Room. I
refused to sit with a merry tribe of my learned friends at
three big, joined tables, instead secreted myself among the
opposite-end-of-the-bar sports fans to watch the Friday night
football, Bombers against the Tiger-Cats.

Wasn't Ruth due back at her office on Tuesday? Was she
well and safe? That postcard had been oddly flip and breezy.
Had she suffered some kind of manic-state nervous breakdown?

Bombers moving the ball slowly toward the Ti-Cats' end of
the field. Bombers fumble the ball away. First half almost
over.

I should have been in the courthouse library, polishing my
evidence briefs, but I was down, moping, filling up with
Czechoslovakian Pilsen. And I was full of dislike for myself
over the incident in the Vancouver Hotel washroom. I had
not been thinking—the Timber Room was a judges' hangout.

Brian and I had slipped out of there like schoolboys caught
talking dirty about their teacher, knowing in our cruel hearts
that we would never have to face Hammersmith again and
that our mean words would be carried by him into retirement. It is one thing to malign a judge behind his back—as
all good lawyers do—but another for him to hear you. But he
had not acknowledged our presence, and we had not acknowledged his, and we had crawled out of there like snakes.

Ti-Cats stall on the Bombers' five and blow the field goal
with a slice off to the right. Hamilton penalized twenty yards
for rough play. Half-time interrupts this gridiron classic, and
we catch the news. More riots in Chile. Hurricane Thelma
hits Louisiana. One-man royal commission appointed into the
bribe-taking scandal over the new Highway 99.

I sat bolt upright. Mr. Justice Baynard Carter's picture was framed on the TV screen.

"... announced he will be taking immediate leave from his duties on the Supreme Court bench. Mr. Justice Carter says he intends to start a preliminary round of hearings within ten days. ..."

Oh my God, I thought. We've lost Carter.

"... was to have presided over the trial of Shiva James, charged with the massacre of. ..."

Then: an execrable apparition on the screen. I jumped to my feet. "No!" I screamed. "They can't do this to me!"

PART TWO

o

The Fall Assize

Awake! awake o sleeper of the land of shadows, wake!
Expand!
I am in you and you in me, mutual in love ...
Fibres of love from man to man ...
Lo! we are One.

William Blake

15

o

Time of Trial

The Brownie (our sheriff's officers are named for the colour of their uniforms), walrus-moustached and full of pomp, bawled in a theatrical timbre: "Oyer! Oyer! Oyer! All persons having business in this Court of Oyer and Terminer and General Gaol Delivery, holden here for the County of Vancouver, in the Province of British Columbia, this Third Day of September, in the year of our Lord Nineteen Eighty-five, draw near and give your attention and answer to your names when called. God save the Queen!"

Thus opened the Fall Assize. The medieval call to court and its conjurations of the assizes of Clarendon and Northampton, of special sessions of the hundred court, and of peasants hanged for stealing sheep, of innocence denied in pots of boiling oil.

God save the Queen. God save Shiva. God save me.

Mr. Justice Anthony Montague Hammersmith sat scrunched on his high bench looking balefully down at us, a desert hawk hunting for prey. His eyes settled beside me on the scowling person of Arthur Beauchamp, with whom I had shared a difficult working weekend. He had almost gone to drink again when he heard the news about the change in judges.

And O, that scene in the hotel washroom. Had I set us up for a sure defeat? I hadn't the courage to tell Arthur of that awful business.

I had fumbled many balls in the last few weeks. The rifle—that had been the worst. Its owner and his two accomplices were probably somewhere polishing their lies for court. Our strategy was to make enough of a case against them that Lukey would have to produce them in rebuttal, and then we

167

could draw and quarter them into ample proportions. And if
the prosecution refused to call them—the jury would wonder
why, and perhaps not wonder long. Not after having heard
Joe Whitegoose give evidence for the Crown.

Other witnesses would help make a circumstantial case
against Wheatley, Morgan, and Calico. Mr. Barney Hinkle
from Tyee Rent-a-Craft; Benjamin Johnson, who found the
.30-.30 shells and saw the tree temple; the Indian who had
seen Wheatley visit Scanks on November twenty-fourth—they
were all under subpoena, would show up on a day's notice.

"You gentlemen—and lady—will be aware," said His Lordship, "that I have been appointed supernumerary in this
court to help out, ah, temporarily in my brother Carter's
absence." His eyes travelled away from our table, to the right
of us, to prosecutors, Leroy Lukey and his junior, one Patricia
Blueman of the Crown counsel's office, a quiet rabbit of a
lawyer, not considered part of the Attorney-General's brain
trust.

Lukey brought his barrel-like body to a standing position.

"My Lord," he bellowed, "I cannot tell you how delighted
we are that rumours of your retirement, to paraphrase Mark
Twain, were greatly exaggerated."

Poor taste, I thought, the original word being death, not
retirement, but when the old farts around here crack jokes,
there's always lots of chuckling. Deputy sheriffs, lawyers,
reporters joined in.

Shiva, in green prison garb—he had refused any other
clothing—sat behind and above Arthur and me, in the prisoner's dock, surrounded on three sides by panes of bullet-proof
glass. He was looking about, absorbing the sights and sounds.
Being aware.

Court 54 is Vancouver's main assize court, huge, with
galleries to seat a hundred and fifty people. Every seat was
occupied this morning (there were a dozen parents of Om
Bay victims—so sad they looked) with latecomers still outside, behind a barrier of pocket-patting deputy sheriffs and
their walk-through metal detector. The sixty-five-member
jury panel was out in the hallway, too.

The interior of Court 54 is bland: beige walls and furnishings dominated at front by a Canadian coat of arms, beneath
that, the judge's chair, red as blood, to match his brilliant
robes. Red chairs for the jury, too, to the right. We were
separated from the judge by a long, raised table occupied, to

our right, by the court clerk, to our left, by the official court reporter, a Sphinx with a stenotype machine.

"I'm sure all of us in this courtroom will benefit from your lordship's vast experience in criminal matters on the bench."

The judge, no time to waste, cut Lukey short. "Let's get on with it."

Although Hammersmith disliked Arthur, he had a respect for his ability. But he held Lukey in utter disdain, a bully who tried to dominate the court—*Hammersmith's* court—with his blaring trumpet. We had determined, over the weekend, to work slivers into this one-sided relationship—Lukey, the loudly mewling sycophant; Hammersmith, scornful of lick-spittles.

The clerk rose. "Will the prisoner please stand?" Shiva just sat there, not quite smiling, but not very serious, either.

I got up and went back to him. "Stand, Shiva," I said in a low voice. "It's just part of the ceremony."

"Very well," he answered. "I enjoy ceremony." He had vowed silence during the trial (*Only silence is holy; only in silence does truth flower*) but at least he was talking to *me*. He stood.

The clerk read the indictment: twenty-two counts of murder. It was a roll call of the dead, their names being intoned to a courtroom hushed except for a few stray coughs. I sensed from behind me the unhappy resonances of the victims' parents.

Lukey stood again and entered his and his junior counsel's names into the record. Arthur stood, and announced the appearances for the defence. The judge gave two almost imperceptible nods of his head, to Arthur, to me. Yes, young Macarthur, I see you down there. *They didn't even have a retirement ceremony arranged for the old vulture, which shows how much everybody despises him*.

"Read the indictment to the, ah, prisoner," said Hammersmith. "Take his plea."

Arthur rose. "I have an application."

"Yes, Mr. Beauchamp?" The judge perched forward.

"I am applying to adjourn this trial to the next assize," Arthur said. "Certain matters have just come to our attention that require urgent investigation. They involve a new line of defence hitherto closed to us."

If Hammersmith gave us the adjournment, we could hope for a new judge. If he refused it, there would be at least a first, if weak, ground of appeal.

"What is that new line of defence, Mr. Beauchamp?"

"My Lord, the defence is disadvantaged if it discloses it now to the Crown."

"The trial will begin today, Mr. Beauchamp. An application for adjournment should not await the opening day of a trial when it inconveniences the state and its citizens, not to mention the, ah, court. I note with some interest that no adjournment applications were made by the defence when Mr. Justice Carter was under appointment to this assize." The Hammer had developed a self-pitying tone over the years: counsel were always trying to adjourn out of his court.

"I know it is not your lordship's habit," Arthur said coolly, "but you made a decision without hearing argument. I had hoped to make a submission on the law respecting adjournments."

Hammersmith checked himself lest he be taunted into a display of petulance that would give us ammunition for the appeal court, and simply agreed to hear the argument.

Arthur made his submission against a foregone conclusion. At the end, Hammersmith made a speech about how counsel, of late, have become so adept at, ah, dilatory tactics that no judge might feel secure in ever finishing a case. "Incessant requests for delay have been strangling the court system. Every reason is offered. I had a lady counsel in here who wanted one because she was pregnant." Dutiful laughter from the galleries. "When counsel have been retained nine months for a case, they are expected to be ready when it begins. When I prosecuted, we could get a murder on in a month, the appeal done in another."

"And hang the poor son of a bitch at sunrise the next day." Arthur had turned to me to say this, but his voice was a resonant instrument.

"What was that, Mr. Beauchamp?" The judge's hearing was not as bad as his eyesight.

"I'm sorry, I was voicing my thoughts aloud. I said, *Festinatio justitiae est noverca infortunii*. Hasty justice is the stepmother of misfortune."

"I have another one for you," said the judge. " 'Justice delayed is justice denied.' Take the plea, Mr. Registrar."

So it went, and so, I supposed, it would go until the end of this ordeal.

Shiva, when asked how he pleaded, maintained his vow of silence. Hammersmith merely sighed, and said, "I will record a not-guilty plea." That is the procedure upon a refusal of plea. "Jury selection. Let us proceed with the jury."

"This is going about as well as we expected," Arthur groaned softly. "I got on his bad side this morning."

"I forget, which is his bad side?"

For those familiar with the fastidious U.S. system of jury-picking, the Anglo-Canadian practice might seem like a crap-shoot. In the empanelling process only in unusual cases may questions be asked of prospective jurors. You have the name, the address, the occupation, and the rest is a guess when someone is presented to you for a quick view before you decide to say "content" or "challenge." The system is heavily weighted in favour of the Crown: Arthur and I had a limit of twelve challenges without cause—to be saved for particularly vindictive-looking types—but after those were exhausted, Leroy Lukey would have unlimited choice of the other sixty. This is the way our system works: all this Crown-oriented bric-a-brac decorating it.

Arthur and I had brief conferences as we studied each face in turn. I had determined to seek eye contact—that would often mean the person was more open than closed (although many good persons are shy). Over the years, Arthur had developed several additional rules.

Arthur: "Bogenhart, says he's a sales executive. Used auto-mobiles would be my guess. Look at that white blazer."

Me: "He looked right at me and smiled. Maybe he's done EST training, looks the type."

"The white shoes, Max. Never put a man with white shoes on a jury. That principle has guided me."

"But there's a half a dozen hard noses coming up behind him. We'll run out of challenges."

"We will have no white shoes on this jury." Loudly, to the judge: "Challenge."

Lukey, unscrupulous in his use of power, stood aside anybody who looked to us passable (e.g., a long-haired young man in his mid-twenties with an army surplus shirt and an open smile). Lukey was picking the educated, the mature, the respecters of the system. People who are not going to be hoodwinked by defence shysters.

Still, I guess we did okay—until we ran out of the chal-lenges. We ended with four women: an older but unretired nurse, a botanist, two homemakers of middle age. The great working class was represented by a plumber and a lathe worker. And we had a teacher, two professional engineers, and a young economist. But after our twelve peremptory challenges were exhausted, Lukey looked the rest of the panel over and chose two retired fellows, one with a brush cut.

After the jury was empanelled we were excused for lunch. Arthur lit into Lukey in the barristers' changing room.

"The brush cut—what did he retire as, a colonel?"

Lukey just chuckled. "Maybe you'll wish you hoarded your challenges more carefully."

"You've put an *ex-cop* on the jury."

Lukey pretended it was a joke on us, laughingly telling us that number sixty-three, McIlheny, the brush cut, was a retired RCMP training instructor, ex-Regina. "Don't worry, they tell me he's got a mind of his own. Tough as nails but fair, that's the word."

"I'll goddamn bet." Arthur stalked off to his own locker, saying to me in a low voice, "That man has a less-than-zero sense of fair play. Somewhere along the line I am going to pin him to the wall by his underpants."

At lunch Arthur and I discussed the list of witnesses the Crown had given us. Lukey intended to call the photographer first, to get the grisly stuff in early, so the jury would thirst for vengeance upon the animal who had done this. Then he would call Scanks and the Joiner brothers, the lab people, the pathologists, ending with Joe Whitegoose, the long list of attending officers, holding his psychiatrists ready to answer ours. I had seen Whitegoose briefly this morning, outside the witness room. He gave me a nervous smile.

Bad news to start the afternoon with: our jury had elected McIlheny, the ex-RCMP instructor, as foreman. If he were a skilled man, as he seemed, he would weave consensus his own way on the many issues the jury would consider. He sat straight-backed in the number-one seat in the jury box. About sixty, and tough and fit-looking, he took the measure of Shiva with bright, calculating eyes.

The afternoon was consumed by Leroy Lukey's windy opening. He used this chance to advantage: an opportunity to outline in fine detail the evidence he proposed to call against Shiva. Aware of the dangers of a mistrial being called, he avoided matters to be tested by the judge before being heard by the jury, such as the hearsay complaint to Corporal Scanks two days before the killings, the dying declaration of Emelia Cruz.

Hands over his belly, fingers interlocked, stomach resting against the rail of the jury box, Lukey put on his sad face. "What you will see and hear paints a most gruesome picture. I apologize for this. But I have a duty of proof, and sometimes it can be an arduous and distasteful duty. It will be best to get the photographs over quickly, so our first witness—"

Arthur got to his feet, interrupted. "The defence will admit the identity of each deceased and spare my learned friend what he refers to as the arduous and distasteful duty of proof." Arthur's voice was never loud, but always penetrating, easy and natural, like a good actor's.

"My friend is interrupting my opening," Lukey said.

"What is your position?" said Hammersmith. "It would, ah, shorten the trial."

"The Crown has no obligation to accept admissions by the defence," said Lukey. "*Castellani and the Queen*, 1970 Four Canadian Criminal cases, page 287."

"I asked for your position, not a page reference. Counsel have developed this habit of not being responsive."

"No, I won't accept the admission."

Arthur, still standing, said, "That gives the lie to my friend's protestations about distasteful duty. I expect he is only too pleased to lead us wading through the gore."

"That will be enough," said the judge.

Arthur sat down. An opening skirmish; defence gets the edge. There would be a few squeamish jurors who might blame the prosecution for having to be put through the ordeal of studying bodies on slabs, close-ups of their torn death masks.

Lukey, knocked off stride, seemed unsure where to begin again, then touched on the insanity issue, saying it would be for the defence to raise it, but that certain distinguished gentlemen—he raised his arm in the direction of Mundt, Priestman, Wang in the front row—would remain present throughout the trial to hear evidence, and perhaps later we would be privileged to hear opinions from them.

He tried to conclude with a joke. "Their being here reminds me of the two psychiatrists who met on the street. 'You look fine,' said one, 'how am I?'"

As Lukey sat down to an embarrassing silence (even his junior, Patricia Blueman, offered only a smile), Arthur stood up. "I hope no one asks their opinion about Mr. Lukey's sense of humour." The courtroom broke up.

* * *

That evening, from home, I called Ruth's apartment. Jacqueline answered. "Allo? C'est la maison Worobec. Puis-je vous aider?"

"Je suis Max Macarthur."

"Oui, je te souviens, L'avocat. Roger Bon-temps. That means Roger Good-times. It's a Quebec expression for Good-time Charley."

"I gather you had a good time."

"I broadened my mind. We are so provincial out here in the West, you know. We think the universe ends at the Rocky Mountains."

"Sounds as if you've bought some of that Eastern propaganda. But you should ace your French this semester."

"Vraiment. I saw your picture on TV. Walking into court with Mr. Beauchamp. Hey, you looked utterly dev."

"Dev?"

"Devastating. The gown! I dug it. But what about the wigs, you got to have wigs."

"No wigs in Canada."

"You could use one the way it's thinning."

"Where's Ruth?"

"Do I hear a possessive, almost threatening tone of voice? She called to say she'd be back by next week, Sunday. I've got to be responsible for a few days and make my own meals."

"Where did she call from?"

"From the middle of the Pacific Ocean, I think. It was a radio-telephone call. She's out on a schooner somewhere, heading south. Listen, I find this as strange as you do. Maybe she's going through her second childhood."

A red-bearded Norwegian, a sailboat built comfortably for two. In the silence Jacqueline sensed my vast decomposure.

"She says she's getting off in Puerto Rico or somewhere and flying back," she said. "She says she's thinking of us."

"Puerto Rico! That's in the Caribbean."

"Or was it Costa Rica? One of those piddly countries somewhere down there. She said, did you get her letter?"

"No."

"She mailed it three weeks ago. Seemed anxious you read

it before she comes back. Listen, can I come down and take some of that trial in? It sounds utterly outstanding."

"Yeah, sure," I said distractedly. "Find me and I'll take you into court."

16

○

The True Path

After Hammersmith asked the official reporter to prepare a
daily transcript of evidence, Lukey called his first witness,
Sergeant Mallory of Identification, the photographer, a familiar face in these courts, possessor of a cruelly honest camera.
He escorted the jury on an illustrated tour through hell.
Eighty photographs in five bound volumes, a copy for each of
the jurors. No one would escape. The sergeant's matter-of-
fact voice went incongruously with his descriptions of each
picture's awful contents: all those exploded faces. A few of the
parents shuffled out after a while.

Mr. Justice Hammersmith was studying Shiva in the manner of one who might be observing a wax Jack the Ripper in a
rogues' gallery.

I turned to Shiva. He smiled at me. He was good, wasn't
causing any scenes. No dynamic meditation. A renunciant
whose pudgy face and long, woolly hair, rolling over his
shoulders, merging with his beard, gave him an appearance
of a chubby Jesus.

Lukey insisted on telling the jury that he hated ever so
much putting them through this. Into the third book of
photographs, we had a problem. One of the jurors, a teacher,
an unimposing gentleman with a blond, see-through moustache, was fast losing colour, his lips going chalky.

I whispered to Arthur. "Number four, top row, Prebbles,
may have had the biscuit."

"And will soon be tossing them." He stood up. "May I
suggest we take a break, my lord?"

"I am almost at the end of this book of photographs," said
Lukey.

"Why?" said the judge, looking puzzled at Arthur.

"I'm not interested in embarrassing anyone, but I think one of the jurors may be in some difficulty."

Poor Mr. Prebbles nodded, his eyes pleading.

Hammersmith got the point, granted the adjournment.

Prebbles' troubles were of the stomach, we were told by a sheriff's officer conveying a message from the judge. "He says we'll come back after lunch, get the guy a chance to get hisself together."

"Lunch," Arthur said to me, "is entirely inadmissible, and I object."

"In that, I queasily concur."

Instead, we sat in the barristers' lounge and debated tactics. "We have got to get their attention away from all this blood," Arthur said. His hand was shaking as he lit his third cigarette in fifteen minutes. It was odd: Arthur seemed tense outside the courtroom, yet inside it—no matter what the stress level—was as comfortable as a man wearing slippers in his den. "We have to get them thinking not about what was done but about who did it. It is time, soon, to start dropping hints."

Sergeant Mallory did not complete his evidence-in-chief until mid-afternoon. Arthur issued a contented sigh as he rose to his feet and began his fumbling act—shuffling through papers, notes, photographs. He disarmed jurors and witnesses this way: a kindly old bumbler trying to do his best.

"We're going to chat about the weather," he said, wandering over to the witness stand, leaning against it, very friendly with the sergeant.

"Yes, sir," said Mallory.

"You arrived at Om Bay by RCMP Otter at about three-thirty P.M. on Saturday, December eighth."

"Yes, sir."

"And it had snowed there just before you arrived?"

"I don't know."

"How could he?" Hammersmith interrupted.

"You are an identification expert, Sergeant Mallory?" said Arthur, quite ignoring the judge.

"I am trained in that area."

"And you are trained to *observe*?" Arthur smiled up at the witness.

"Yes."

"And did you not observe that it had snowed at Om Bay that afternoon?"

"There was plenty of snow. Three or four feet of it. But I don't know about that afternoon."

"Would you look at photograph three, please? One that you took from the aircraft as you were circling, before landing. You will see the plastic sheeting over the bodies. And it appears to be well-dusted with a whitish substance. What would you call that substance?"

"That would be snow."

"Thank you. Now let us know something about your powers of deduction. What do you deduce from the presence of snow on the plastic sheeting that Corporal Scanks had laid an hour and a half earlier?"

"That it had been snowing."

"That's surely a conclusion for the jury to draw," said Lukey, feisty about the little things.

"I apologize," said Arthur. "I wouldn't wish to mislead the jury. The possibility exists that someone came by with a snow-making machine just before Sergeant Mallory arrived." Arthur got a round of laughter.

Mr. Justice Hammersmith squinted at photograph three. "What has this got to do with anything?" he said.

"It has got to do, my lord, with my client's innocence," said Arthur, abrupt and cheeky. "May I proceed?"

"Please get on with it."

"I am honoured to be allowed to do so." The jury was picking up very fast that these two men were not enamoured of each other. "Near the totem poles, those dark spots that form a line toward the top part of the photograph—they appear to be indentations in the snow, do they not? A track on the snow, as it were, leading from the clearing up the hill and into the trees?"

"Yes, I see that."

"Well, I don't," said Hammersmith, holding the photograph close to his face. "What is it you're talking about?"

I had earlier spotted the shadowy line in this picture. I explained to Arthur that in July I had walked the path that was marked by these tracks in the snow, the route to Shiva's aboreal temple. Shiva, we believed, had walked from his *chaitya* to the campsite shortly before his arrest. His footprints were still remembered in that light, indented line.

"I'm not sure what that is," the witness said. "It could be just the way the shadows work on the snow."

"I still don't know what you're talking about," Hammersmith said. "Can you see it, members of the jury?"

Heads nodded. The clerk stood up to help the judge, pointing to an area near the top of the photo.

"When you examined that area from the ground, I take it you could make out separate footprints, obscured somewhat by new-fallen snow?" Arthur asked.

"I never did examine it."

"You dod *not* examine it?" Arthur was clearly, the jury saw, taken aback.

"It was getting on to mid-December. The days were short. It was still foggy. I had lots of work to do before the sun went. Also, after these aerial shots were taken, quite a few members arrived, and with everyone searching about, a lot of the hillside snow got tramped down. During the on-scene investigation."

Arthur let this explanation stand for a long time, as if silently observing to the jury that this was shoddy police work indeed. Obliterating evidence.

"You cannot deny that the marks that compose this line might have been made by the foot impressions of a man walking in the deep snow?"

"Well, no, I don't know what it is."

"Maybe somebody's tracks going and then coming back," Lukey said, loudly, from his chair.

"My learned friend," said Arthur, "doubtless will take the stand himself and give his evidence under oath." To the witness: "I gather, then, sergeant, you did not follow this path up into the trees?"

Lukey interrupted again. "Nobody said it's a path."

"My Lord, while I am cross-examining, I wonder if learned and able counsel for the prosecution could remember this is not a tag-team match, and he cannot keep coming to the aid of his witness."

"Let us get on with it," said Hammersmith. His bad eyes were still working at the photograph.

"Assuming it's a path, sergeant, you didn't seek to follow it to its end, I take it?"

"No, I didn't."

"No other attending member did, to your knowledge?"

"No, sir."

Mr. Prebbles, the teacher, was healthier now, attentive. So were they all. McIlheny was leaning forward, still frowning. Perhaps he, too, thought there had been lazy work done here.

Arthur took a wild and highly improper shot. "What would you say, witness, were I to inform you that at the top of the escarpment, where the trail ends, there was a shelter beneath a tree—"

"I object," yelled Lukey.

"You know perfectly well, Mr. Beauchamp," said the judge, "that you cannot suggest such things. Counsel of late have adopted a tendency to be over-liberal in their questions. That sort of thing may be allowed in other courtrooms, but it isn't in mine." Arthur sat down. "Rules of evidence that have developed over the centuries aren't going to be disregarded in this courtroom just because we're nearing the end of a hot and tiring day." He looked down at the seated Beauchamp. "Are you finished?" he said.

"No, my lord, I was waiting for you to do so."

"We will adjourn," Hammersmith was fairly irked at Arthur.

"Order in court," hollered the sheriff's officer.

* * *

We trooped to the locker room, where Lukey was being his ebullient worst: "Why couldn't the Polish cheerleader get up after she did the splits? Because she stuck to the floor."

Arthur suffered the misfortune of being Lukey's locker-room neighbour, but mercifully I was able to retreat a few rows away from him, to the Pomeroy-Macarthur-Brovak locker. John was there, weary-eyed after another long day with The Conspiracy. He gave a quick glance right and left, tamped some powder from a packet onto the back of his hand and snuffed it up.

He held the palm of his hand up to me, as if to ward off my condemnatory words. "Don't nag, okay? I don't need it. I'm going around the bend in there. I had to have a straightener." He put the packet away.

"You're going to break, John, just like Lubor," I said in a soft, urgent voice. "I'll bet you couldn't cold turkey it for twenty-four hours without getting the screaming Marys."

We talked in hushed tones, Leroy Lukey bellowing over our words from the other side of a bank of lockers. "Artie, fine job on the cameraman, you got your red herring in front of the jury. What's the story—Shiva is up in a tree-house? Comes down and finds all these bodies, somehow gets his fingerprints all over the rifle? Are you guys jacking me around, or what? Little Macarthur, he's been up to Tash-Tash Cove, putting the hustle on my witnesses. Wheatley is a smokescreen. I *know* he's a smokescreen."

I sighed and began changing. John was already in his street clothes, a smile on his face now. "That's better," he whispered. "Takes the edge off the mouth-to-mouth combat with that Crown hack, Boynton."

"What was he doing at Tash-Tash, Leroy?" I yelled. "Why was he seeing Corporal Scanks?"

"I know why Wheaties was chosen for your jiggery-pokery," Lukey shot back. "You hate his guts, Max. I remember that slanging match between you guys last July."

"Keep a clenched anus," Brovak said softly, patted me on the shoulder, walked away whistling.

Lukey went on to Arthur: "All you really got for a defence is Werner Mundt. Why don't we offer a little show of forgiveness to the poor taxpayer? I'll drop twenty-one counts, Artie. You plead to one. Take your pick of the bodies. Yeah, I know one term of life imprisonment isn't much different from twenty-one, but look at it this way, you'll rack up twenty-one straight murder wins against one loss. It'll look good when *Lawyer Magazine* profiles you, Artie."

I joined them. "Leroy, here's the deal," Arthur said, straightening his tie, a cigarette dangling from his mouth. "You drop all twenty-two counts, and my man will plead guilty to practising religion without a licence."

"You haven't got Baynard Carter to baby you any more. Like the farmer said to the travelling salesman, cut your losses. You heard the story? The farmer finds the salesman in bed with his daughter, drags him down to the barn, puts the salesman's cock in a vice and breaks off the handle, then starts sharpening a knife. 'You're not gonna cut it off?' the salesman says. 'No,' the farmer says, 'you can do that, I'm going to burn the barn down.' Well, that's what I'm going to do to you boys, burn the barn down. Cut your losses, fellas. Take a plea. Wheatley—he's a red herring."

"It's an old defence trick," Arthur said. "Let the enemy think we're planning a landing for Calais and get their minds off Normandy."

"Make sure you don't try your landing at Dieppe, old buddy. The Wheatley business doesn't have me scared. I'm just laughing."

After a strategy meeting with Arthur, I went home to bed with a sore throat. I had forgotten to run again today. I was beginning to feel pretty beat.

* * *

Thursday morning: Arthur was lounging against the jury-box railing, very relaxed and in control of things. His back was just slightly to Mr. Justice Hammersmith, who seemed to be in one of his rare temperate moods. I wondered how long that would last.

"Sergeant Mallory, do you know what happened to the shacks and the sheds that are in your photographs?"

"I gather everything was burned down a few days later. By some people from the town."

Lukey stirred in his seat, grumbling softly about hearsay, but not making much effort to stop it. He looked like a bear coming out of hibernation. His junior, Patricia Blueman, seemed lost. I don't think she'd ever handled anything bigger than a dangerous driving.

"One of those former buildings was a storage shed?" said Arthur.

"The one closest to the water."

"What was in it?"

"Tools and foodstuffs mostly. Constable Dennis prepared a list of everything."

"You found no weapons in there?"

"No. A chainsaw, that's the nearest thing to weapons."

"No rifles?"

"No."

"No bullets?"

"No."

"In fact the only live bullets found in this entire encampment were the three left in the magazine of the Lee-Enfield .303, isn't that right?"

"Yes."

"Have you not thought it curious that there was not a single box of live ammunition found anywhere—"

Before Lukey could object, Hammersmith uttered a weary, "Sustained."

"That was very quick, my lord," Arthur said.

"What the witness thinks is curious is not of this court's concern," said the judge.

Arthur bulled on. "But conceivably, sergeant, the authors of these murders could have taken the rest of their ammunition with them when they fled—"

Hammersmith and Lukey talked over themselves, both ordering the witness not to answer the question. Arthur was getting everyone awakened in here. That's what he wanted.

"You know better, Mr. Beauchamp," the judge rasped. "You know better."

Arthur spoke with an injured, somewhat righteous voice: "My lord, the Crown seeks to prove an entirely circumstantial case, and the defence is entitled to suggest rational conclusions that go to innocence. The possibility that the real murderers left the scene before the police arrived is one such rational conclusion."

"You know better. You cannot ask such questions. This isn't argument. I remind you of rules, Mr. Beauchamp, I remind you of rules."

"I'll move to another area then." The jury was all attention, drinking it in—Arthur had determined to give them something to think about. "You described to us yesterday a terrible, soul-shattering scene of carnage, twenty-one bodies arrayed, most tied wrists to ankles behind their backs, all executed by .303 rifle bullets. How could just one person have done this, unaided—"

That caused a sputtering fusillade from both bench and Crown counsel table. Arthur stood his ground. The jury would see how the defence was being shut down.

"I know exactly what you're trying to do, Mr. Beauchamp," the judge was saying.

"What I am trying to do, my lord, is my job." Arthur sat down. "No more questions."

Retired British Major Swindon C. Durkee was brief, identifying his .303 Lee-Enfield by the serial number from the stock. In clipped phrases he described how he had returned from an August visit to relatives in Essex to find his Vancouver home had been pillaged: gone were rifle, coin collection, some silver, some old coins. The crime was as yet unsolved.

Constable Dennis, the chief exhibit man on this case, took hours, putting into evidence cartridges and slugs, the torn and bloodied clothes of the victims, the rifle, Shiva's clothing and boots, hundreds of items of little consequence taken from the buildings. The performance was dulling to the senses— only Shiva seemed alert, watchful.

But he was gradually becoming invisible in here, receding from view. Only when one turned directly to look at the prisoner's dock did one make him out: an ornament at this trial, like the coat of arms on the wall.

I felt a rawness from my little cold, felt it slowly creeping up my Eustachian tubes, a soft pounding in my temples.

Jurors and onlookers seemed to emit a sigh of shared relief as Lukey sat down and turned the witness over to Arthur late in the day, who began to put our defence in through him.

"Seventeen people shot in the brain by a .303 rifle, and four shot in the heart," Arthur summarized, "and we have also heard evidence, constable, that one of those twenty-one victims suffered another bullet wound, to the leg. But only seventeen spent cartridges were recovered, only seventeen slugs were dug from the ground—all near the heads of the hog-tied victims."

"Here we go again," Lukey mumbled.

"So it would seem," said Arthur, "the cartridge cases from the bullets that caused those four wounds to chests and one wound to the leg have not been recovered, nor have the expended bullets. Will you agree with my summary of this evidence?"

"All I can say is that we found seventeen cartridge cases and seventeen fired bullets, what was left of them, in the ground."

"And no sign of the other five cartridges?"

"There was snow everywhere, Mr. Beauchamp. We cleared it for ten metres around the area where the bodies were found, and we went over that area an inch at a time."

"To sum up, the bullets that were fired at close range—I expect we will hear evidence they caused powder burns to the victims—you found each of these?"

"Yes."

"But the other five bullets, which were presumably fired at longer range—there was no sign of them?"

Presumably fired at longer range—I liked that. Both Lukey and Hammersmith were too fatigued, it seemed, to complain. Was Hammersmith napping? His head was supported by one arm and his eyes were closed.

"No sign of them. They may still be there."

"Constable, I am producing to you a plastic envelope containing four items—what do those appear to be?"

Lukey lumbered to his feet, went over to the witness stand where Arthur was handing the envelope to the witness. "Let me see that," he said. "What's this about?"

"What are they, constable?" said Arthur.

"Well, they're obviously cartridge cases. Dominion .30-.30 stamped right on them."

"What's this about?" Lukey repeated, loudly, to awaken the judge.

"To quote from *Othello*, 'How poor are they that have not patience,'" Arthur said. "My lord, I propose to tender these cartridges for later identification."

"Exhibit twelve for identification," said the clerk.

"It's four-thirty," said Hammersmith. "That's enough."

A good day. Arthur had diverted the jury and slowed the thrust of the Crown's onrushing locomotive. Tomorrow, with Scanks, we would pry a few rails from the tracks.

17

○

Redcoat

Eddie Scanks was all polished up, but with his 1950s-cut orange hair and ill-fitting RCMP dress uniform, he looked like an aging punk rocker in stolen livery. Yes, the scarlet tunic: the Crown sends its important RCMP witnesses to court this way. The heroic redcoat fresh from tracking the thievin' injuns by dogsled. The jury remembers their history books: men like Scanks brought law and order to the West.

Well, if he's flying up to pay off Scanks. . . . That Winnebago conversation (hearsay, unfortunately) continued to intrigue Arthur and me. We had concurred in the implications to be drawn. Scanks—a bitter man with a cheating wife and a dead-end career, criminally negligent in failing to prevent the Om Bay massacre—had accepted a large cash payoff to protect the real murderers. And quite possibly was prepared to bend his evidence toward that goal. What kind of policeman was this skinny, jumpy man in scarlet?

His voice was falsely confident and loud as he took the oath, gave his name and rank, and declined bravely the judge's offer to sit while giving evidence. I observed that foreman McIlheny was squinting at him, his finger pensively at his lips.

Scanks didn't look at the jury, didn't look at the judge, but seemed to have his eyes trained on an invisible spot about four feet from his face. His answers to Lukey's questions had a confident, rehearsed quality about them, and his voice was a clarion. It was as if Lukey and Scanks were trading cannon shot.

The prosecutor began by taking him to Om Bay in August

of last year, his one previous visit to the commune before December 8. "What was the purpose of that trip?"

"A large group of people had arrived within my jurisdiction. I felt I should introduce myself to them, to let them know I was around."

"Why did you want to do that?"

"In case any of them should get into trouble and need my help." As Scanks expressed this clumsily contrived excuse for some old-fashioned hassling, I was staring at the jury, and I happened to catch the eye of the economist, Mr. Margolis, an intelligent-looking fellow in his late thirties. He smiled at me. I would work at trying to maintain eye contact with Margolis.

"What observations did you make?" asked Lukey.

"They were working when I came ashore, hammering, and somebody had a chainsaw going. Some trees being cut. A few of the buildings had been started, a roof already up on one."

"How many persons were there?"

"About twelve, I think."

"Did you notice anything unusual about them?"

"Their voices were expressionless. They seemed hypnotized, I think."

"For that matter, so does Corporal Scanks," said Arthur, rising. "Who's this witness to say anyone looks hypnotized? Is he an expert?"

"Objection is sustained," Hammersmith said grumpily. "You can do better than that, Mr. Lukey." I liked the way the judge hinted that the witness's obviously fashioned answer was Lukey's doing.

"Don't draw conclusions, corporal," Lukey said. "Just tell us what you observed about these people."

I saw Scanks' eyes flit down to our table and back. His head didn't move, just his eyes. *I hate the fucking courts, Mr. McCarthy, and if you'll forgive me I hate the fucking lawyers.* (Read *fear* for *hate*, I think.)

"Their faces were vacant. When I was talking to them, they didn't seem to be looking at me, but looking past me or something." Maybe Scanks realized himself was expressionless, because he glanced at Lukey, attempted a stiff smile, looked away again.

Their strategy was plain: build up a picture of mindless oafs who would agree to be tied up and shot through the head so that they might achieve ultimate purposelessness.

"Did you notice anything else unusual about them?"

"A couple of girls weren't wearing anything to cover their tops. They didn't seem embarrassed about it."

"Do you recognize anyone in this courtroom who was there on that day a year ago August?"

Scanks' head swivelled to the left. "Sitting there, dressed in the green," he barked.

"For the record he is identifying the accused, Shiva alias James," said Lukey. "In the course of your dealings with him, did he produce a document?"

"A real estate paper showing he and some others had bought this property, thirty acres."

"Mr. Lukey," said Hammersmith, "you know you can't call evidence of what is on a document without producing it in evidence."

"It's not that relevant, m'lord."

"If it's not relevant, let's not hear about it at all," the judge rasped. "Get on with it."

"Then what did you do?"

"Well, after a while I left. At their request."

"Did you later see any of the people from this commune?"

"Yes, two or three of them would come to town by boat once a week for supplies. I got to know one of them fairly good, a Mr. Wurz. He would stop by at the detachment office and talk. He didn't seem as out of it as the others."

"*Out* of it?" said Hammersmith. "Out of *what*? Mr. Lukey, does your witness speak English, or is this some kind of pidgin tongue he has learned in the course of his, ah, duties?"

Chuckles in the body of the court. I could see that Scanks hated being made fun of.

"Let's get ready," I whispered to Arthur. *With me you will commit the final suicide, the death of self:* Shiva's "threat" to Wurz, who had complained to Scanks that the guru was seeking control of their minds.

"And did you have occasion to see this Mr. Wurz in the month of December last?"

"On Friday, December seventh last year, Mr. Wurz and someone else from the commune came in by boat for supplies. He came up to my office. We had a conversation."

"May the jury be excused, my lord?" said Lukey.

After they went out, Lukey read Wurz's words from Scanks' report and told the judge he proposed to call evidence of the take-control-over-minds conversation. He claimed it was relevant to show the accused's mental state; tendered on that basis the rule against hearsay would not be breached. Of course there was only one thing in Lukey's mind—get those damaging, death-saying words before the jury.

"'With me you will commit the, ah, final suicide,'" the judge quoted, then peered in Shiva's direction, then down at Lukey. "Goes to the insanity issue, you say? These are words which show he was sane?"

"Perhaps the evidence will help the defence on that issue," said the generous prosecutor.

"I have learned, over the years," said Arthur, "not to look a gift horse in the mouth, especially when the horse is my estimable and learned friend, Mr. Lukey. The insanity question has not even been raised. And in any event it doesn't convert simple hearsay into any higher form of testimony. I have some case law on the matter."

Hammersmith looked balefully down at the fifteen fat casebooks that were in front of us—English and Canadian law on hearsay evidence. "Come back to me later with this problem, mister prosecutor," he said. "Come back to me when insanity is well in issue. I do not want to hear long argument while the jury is waiting."

"Damn," said Arthur softly as he sat down. "If the old bugger won't decide for you, he won't decide at all."

Scanks had been permitted to remain standing in the witness box while we argued, looking like an odd bird of bright plumage in this massive, dun and red courtroom. I finally caught his eye—his was a bitter look. *I don't want to lose this one, Mr. McCarthy. I got my very own fucking mass murder here, and I want to get some respect.*

We took the morning break. Outside the courtroom, looking winsome and lost, was Jacqueline Worobec. Yet—*was* it Jacqueline? Her hair was more orange than Scanks', and almost as short. Magenta under her eyes, a purple, floppy hat and a slinky black dress and high heels.

"My God, what have they done to you?" I drew her aside. Werner Mundt was ogling her.

"*Regardez la cosmopolitaine,*" she said. "*C'est l'aspect Montréal.* Don't I look dev?"

I grabbed her by the elbow and steered her away from the gaping throngs. "Look, it's none of my business, but if your mother sees you decked out in orange hair and dark eye shadow—and braless, my God—she's going to come after you with a couple of bricks of lye soap."

"*J'épate les bourgeois. Je suis gens du monde.* I am not under her thumb like a vassal. I'm entering a period of self-identification. Mother will simply have to understand that." She gave me a Martian smile. "Okay, fill me in, who's the good guys and who's the bad guys, and can you get me a pass to the twenty-dollar seats or what?"

"Aren't you supposed to be in school?"

"So I miss French and art. Here I'm studying life in the raw. Anyway I already know more French than Mrs. Mackelson, whose accent is simply incredulous."

"I don't want Ruth thinking I've encouraged hookey. What new news of her?"

"Oh, yeah, I should tell you. She phoned about midnight—from a bar in Costa Rica. I think she was drunk. I'm to call her office—she'll definitely be flying in Sunday, back to work on Monday. She asked about you." She pulled some tissue paper from her bag and gave my nose a deft wipe. "She'll call you when her plane gets in."

I ushered her toward the courtroom, stopped beside Arthur, who was chain-smoking. I introduced them.

"I'm his lover's daughter," she said, smiling prettily.

Arthur blinked. "How, er, delightful," he said. Otherwise speechless.

I seated her on a front bench, glared at lascivious Mundt, who gave me a snide wink.

After court resumed, Lukey took his witness through the events of December 8 at Om Bay, where he and the Joiner brothers had gone "as a result of" his conversation with George Wurz. Scanks, still staring stiffly ahead, described the events without notes, megaphoning them at the wincing jurors. He had memorized his reports, had probably been told to do so by Lukey; it's hard to trip a policeman who has memorized everything.

The jury was sent away for the rest of the morning while we conducted a *voir dire*—a trial within a trial—to determine the admissibility of Shiva's disconnected ramblings at the scene.

Asking Hammersmith to rule those statements inadmissible was like making argument to the wind. What Shiva had said in the presence of the police, he ruled, must be heard by the jury.

On that predictable note, we adjourned for lunch.

I bought Jacqueline a sandwich at a deli, fished out eighty dollars, pressed the bills into her palm. "I want your apartment bedecked with flowers on Sunday. The card with them will simply read, 'I love you.' Sign my name."

"Oh, how romantic. Why don't you give me a thousand more, and I'll buy a ring? Actually, it would be just superlative, you and Mother marrying. You're both so archaic it would suit you."

I had to rush. To the library to drop off some books. To the barristers' room to make some calls. To the locker room, to gown up.

When the jury returned at two o'clock, Scanks boomed out the first of the terrible phrases: "'Death kisses you with life.'"

"I'm sorry, can you repeat that?" said Lukey, suddenly hard of hearing.

"'Death kisses you with life.' Then he said, 'You will be reborn as gods.'"

"And then?"

"'Because I loved you, I had to kill you.'"

"I didn't quite catch that."

Scanks repeated.

"And then you say he began to dance again before you arrested him?"

"Yes, sir."

"And he said additional words while on the police boat?"

"I asked him why he had done this. He answered, 'Whys cannot find answers. Why are we? Why is the cosmos? Why is God?'"

"I see," said Lukey, shaking his head at the enormity of it all. He sat down. "Your witness, Mr. Beauchamp."

"Okay," Arthur said to me as he rose, "let us find out what has been going on."

He shuffled over to the witness stand and gave Scanks one of his eye-wandering stares. Then he leafed through some papers he was holding loosely in his hands—I don't know if anything was in them, probably nothing, but the idea was to persuade the witness we had secret information about him.

"Now, let's see—you've been on the Force for twenty-six years, corporal."

"Yes, sir." Addressing the air in front of him very taut.

"And it appears you've held the rank of corporal for eighteen of those twenty-six years."

"Yes, sir."

"That's a goodly time." Not much going for this man, career advancement-wise—that was the suggestion. Not super-cop.

"You've been posted to quite a few detachments—two-year stints over the province?" Arthur appeared to be reading this off his papers, but he knew that the standard RCMP tour was two years in any one place.

"Yes, here and in Alberta, Saskatchewan. Lots of places."

"Seen a fair bit of crime in your time." Arthur smiled. "If you'll pardon the rhyme."

"Yes, sir." Not a sliver of a smile creased that closed face.

"But nothing as gruesome as that scene at Om Bay."

"That's right." Short answers in cross-examination—that's how prosecutors coach their police witnesses.

"A very big murder case—and you captured a suspect."

"I captured *the* suspect." Scanks was prepared to scrap if he had to. How would he be if backed into a corner? It is when the rats are most vicious.

"And here you are, the main witness for the Crown."

"I may be—I don't know."

Arthur now wandered from the witness box to the counsel table, dropped his notes there, shuffled through a thicket of papers, pictures, notebooks, found nothing, shrugged, then ambled, smiling, up to the jurors.

"I had everything in order when we started today." He called to me as if we were pals in a bar. "Mr. Macarthur, would you be so kind as to form a one-man search party for that photograph of William Wheatley? Now, corporal, let's go back to November twenty-fourth last year. A Saturday. You were on duty that day at Tash-Tash Cove?"

"I imagine so. I'd have to check my records."

"Come, come. You have a memory for this. Two weeks before the Om Bay murders. You were on duty, yes?"

"A police officer is always on duty, sir. Especially if he runs a one-man detachment." Leroy Lukey thought that a clever answer and chuckled loudly, Patricia Blueman chuckling dutifully along with him.

"I want to suggest to you that a small plane flew into Tash-Tash on November twenty-fourth, and aboard it was a man known to you as William Wheatley."

Now Lukey delivered himself of a huge sigh and shook his head, letting the jury know that there was going to be some nonsense discussed here.

"Yes, sir," said Scanks. His eyes flitted to the prosecutor. Had they discussed this?

I found the photo, passed it to Arthur, who put it in front of Scanks' nose. "Is that him, Wheatley?"

"Reverend Wheatley, yes, sir."

Reporters were scribbling away. Wheatley was a right-wing folk hero, darling of the open-line-show set.

"He's a deprogrammer, isn't he?" said Arthur. "Involved in the business of helping parents get their children out of cults."

"He has that reputation. I read about him in the newspapers, seen a TV show on him. I never met him before that day, that Saturday."

Arthur asked to tender the photo as an exhibit. Lukey seemed as if he were going to make an objection, his bulk rising, then hovering and subsiding. "Mark it as an exhibit," said Hammersmith.

"And Mr. Wheatley visited you in your office that Saturday afternoon, two weeks before the murders?"

"Yes, Reverend Wheatley called on me."

"And the subject under discussion involved the Om Bay commune?" We were on the very border of hearsay.

"In part, yes." Again Scanks glanced at Lukey, who was poised to burst from his chair. How far could Arthur get before the boom dropped?

"And Mr. Wheatley showed you a photograph, did he not?" This was an educated guess.

"Yes, he did."

"Did you recognize the person in that photograph?"

A pause. "No."

"Are you sure?"

Scanks cleared his throat. "I didn't recognize her."

"But this picture that Wheatley showed you—you had also seen it in magazines and newspapers. That's quite true, isn't it?"

"I didn't recognize her as any person I had actually seen."

"Witness, I'm not in a playful mood. You know very well whose picture you were shown, isn't that right?"

We were getting to Scanks early. His left hand was working at his right sleeve, by the elbow. "Okay, yes," he said.

"It was a photograph of Melissa-June M'Garethy, the missing daughter of the Boston banker and industrialist, was it not?"

"I believe so, yes."

"And you were aware—it was common knowledge—that this nineteen-year-old girl was believed to be hiding somewhere in a commune in British Columbia?"

"I guess I was."

"And did you not tell Wheatley that you had seen someone from the Om Bay commune who resembled Melissa-June M'Garethy?"

"I did not."

"But you had seen most of these people, yes, with their visits to Tash-Tash for supplies?"

"I'd say so."

Arthur strolled back to the counsel table. I handed him another picture. He wheeled around and returned to the witness box. "There. That's a picture of Miss M'Garethy. Is it not similar to the one Wheatley showed you?"

"It's the picture I saw in the papers."

"And if you will look at the RCMP photo album here, picture number thirty-four, who do you recognize there?"

Scanks studied the exhibit. "That is Emelia Cruz, and I recognize this to be taken on the bed of Joe Whitegoose while I was there."

Arthur leaned against the edge of the court reporters' table. "Look at those two pictures. Study them."

I turned slowly about to take a peek at Jacqueline. She gave me a magenta wink.

"Quite a resemblance, isn't there?"

"Now that you point it out. But she turned out to be Emelia Cruz, didn't she?"

A long pause.

"Didn't you tell Wheatley you might have seen someone who looked like this young lady on Poindexter Island?"

"I did not."

"Something to that effect?"

"Definitely not." Now the other elbow. Surely scabs were coming off.

"I suggest that you agreed to co-operate in her kidnapping by turning a blind eye to it."

"I did not!" Almost too emphatic. "I told him I would not stand for any breaches of the peace in my jurisdiction."

Arthur had to be careful. Scanks was prepared to lie to protect Wheatley. We didn't want those lies on record—the key would be to provoke an objection from Lukey, make it appear to the jury the Crown was covering up distasteful facts.

"I suggest you described the layout to him of the commune at Om Bay."

"I can't remember doing that."

"Can't remember? Can't *remember*?" Arthur's voice was a rejoicing one. We had followed a liar to his lair: the last refuge, the emptiness of memory. "You remember very well indeed. Witness, I suggest that Wheatley announced to you the kidnapping was planned for Saturday, December eighth—"

"Objection!" called Lukey.

Arthur, who had already got the good stuff out, gave Leroy an astounded look. "There is an objection to this?"

Came the chiding voice of Hammersmith: "Don't stand there affecting an injured air of innocence, Mr. Beauchamp. You know you are asking for hearsay."

"Far from attempting to affect innocence, I am attempting to disprove guilt, my lord. I am shocked that my learned friend would take this position in a matter so critical to the heart of the case, and astounded that the court should countenance it."

"Mr. Beauchamp," said the judge, "you would be well to choose words more diplomatically. I'm just warning you."

"Let me try it another way," Arthur said. Heat seemed to rise from him as he turned to the witness. I looked around at Shiva. He seemed rapt in this theatre.

"You knew that the accused had a reputation for engaging in acts of violence known as kidnappings?"

"Wheatley is not the accused! I object!"

Arthur bulled ahead. "Yet you described the layout of the commune to him knowing he planned a raid upon it—"

"Objection!"

"—to kidnap a young woman from it."

"My lord, he won't stop," Lukey railed.

"That is enough," said Hammersmith. "You've gone too far."

Arthur looked innocently up at him. "My lord, I don't understand—why do my questions provoke such a storm of protest? I am simply attempting to advance a defence. If I am not allowed to ask questions, perhaps your lordship might indicate some role for me that would be less distressing to the court."

"I have warned you, Mr. Beauchamp," said Hammersmith.

"Am I being told that there is no way of finding out what these two men talked about on November twenty-fourth? I can understand my friend being embarrassed about evidence showing dereliction of duty by an RCMP corporal, because he is obviously engaged in a conspiracy of silence, but the court—"

"M'lord," said Lukey, "this is quite unseemly. The jury should be asked to leave."

But Hammersmith was odd with juries, rarely sending them out, letting them watch the lawyers scrap. Arthur had been working hard for their support, casting himself in the role of the underdog, the judge a tyrant prepared to throttle the defence.

"If the defence is not allowed to develop its case we may as well slap the shackles on the accused and all go home," Arthur said. I was amazed at the man's insolent bravery. He had more than a few times been cited for contempt in his four decades at the bar.

"Mr. Beauchamp," Hammersmith said, "I am close to the edge."

"While I find that regrettable, my lord, my client is here on a murder charge. Surely the rules of hearsay evidence must be relaxed in a murder case. *In poenalibus causis benignius interpretandum est*. In penal cases, law should be interpreted with leniency."

"Hearsay is hearsay," Hammersmith snapped. "I have heard you say that yourself."

"And by a strict interpretation of the rules of evidence, we are not allowed to find out why Mr. Wheatley was visiting Om Bay that day?" Arthur's voice was vigorous with rage. "My lord, I propose to put it to the witness that he was told the exact date was Saturday, December eighth—" Arthur continued to try to talk through the uproar—"Scanks agreed not to interfere—" Lukey was yelling, the judge ordering the jury to be removed, Arthur carrying on as if his control had left him. "If this evidence be not allowed, this courtroom will witness one of the most damnable deceptions in the history of the common law and a flagrant railroading of an innocent man. . . ."

It was a chaotic scene. The Hammer was pounding his

bench with the flat of his hand, Lukey was bellowing about getting the jury out of here, and slashing through it all came Arthur's voice, powerful, reverberant, his right arm punching the air, his index finger out. The jury seemed frozen in their seats as a deputy sheriff tried to get them to file out. Although Arthur was a consummate courtroom actor, this rage didn't seem feigned. Perhaps it was an explosion of pent-up frustration over this case.

"I want it on the record that the defence is being deprived of fair answer through denial of cross-examination," Arthur shouted. "I want it to be known that we are engaged in a courtroom farce."

By now the last of the jurors was out. The courtroom took on a hush as Arthur leaned against the counsel table, breathing hard.

"Defence counsel will show cause," Hammersmith said, "why he should not be cited for contempt of court. After the noon break. Court will adjourn for ten minutes."

He stormed out. Arthur stormed out. The courtroom buzzed. Jacqueline was standing in the aisle blinking. "Does this go on all the time?" she whispered to me. "It's a *rage*."

"Just a typical day in court, Jacqueline."

"Listen, I don't know what's happening here, but that RCMP, he's a liar for sure, and the judge is obviously in the pay of the police. Your client, man, I love him. It looks like a put-up job."

"You've got it exactly. Hang tight."

I tried to brush past Mundt, who was blocking my route to Arthur Beauchamp. The psychiatrist grabbed my sleeve. "Your most recent fling, Max?" he said, bending his head toward Jacqueline. "I didn't imagine you to have such eclectic taste."

I pantomimed a smile and moved past him.

Arthur was leaning over the balustrade, looking down at the business below, a swirl of humanity drifting around the Law Courts Complex.

"How can I show cause why I should not be cited for contempt? I have nothing *but* contempt for the man." He winked. "But that felt very good."

"What are you going to do?"

"Enjoy my slice of humble pie." He shrugged, took a deep drag from his cigarette. "Max, give me Quadra Island again."

"Population a few thousand, bunch of stores, hotel, bit of a

shopping centre. It's just off Campbell River, gets its
weekenders. I called some of the people down by Heriot Bay,
at the docks, but no one remembers Wheatley and Scanks
coming there Thursday. A couple of planes came in, that's all
anybody could tell me."

"Why would they meet there?"

"It's only ten air miles from Tash-Tash. Quiet enough place,
no crowds."

"We're talking about a big sum here, Max?"

"I'd say upwards of a hundred grand. Maybe twice that
much. Could be Wheatley had another big retainer from J.J.
M'Garethy. In U.S. thousands."

"Yes, cash for sure. Wheatley wouldn't have given him a
bank draft. Tell me, Max, do you think Scanks is the kind of
person to risk carrying all that money around, hiding it?"

"He's neurotic, I don't know."

"Is there a bank on that island?"

"I'll phone and check."

18

○

Rigor Mortis

When I re-entered the courtroom, Arthur was standing penitently in front of the bench, the jury still out.

"My lord, I must confess that emotions often conquer reason in the heat of battle. I wish to apologize. I cannot express my contrition in clearer words than by reference to the ancient Latin maxim, *Ignorantia judicis est calamitas innocentis*." And Arthur abruptly sat down, looking pious.

The judge peered narrowly in his direction, ran his tongue over his lips, said softly, "Very well, I will accept that. Call the jury in. Let's get on with it."

As the jurors filed in, Arthur gave me a nudge and whispered: "In the words of Ben Johnson, he hath small Latin and less Greek. But he is rather too vain to admit it."

"What did it mean?" I whispered back.

"'The ignorance of a judge is the misfortune of the innocent.'" He stood up and walked over to Shiva, said a few words to him, patted him on the shoulder, and took up position beside the jury foreman, McIlheny. That man, I noticed, was taking careful measure of Scanks, waiting in the witness stand for cross-examination to resume. McIlheny had been a cop for thirty-five years, a terror to the young recruits of the RCMP, according to some contacts we had inside the Force. I had begun to have a better feeling about him. If he were a proud veteran, he would not be pleased to see bad apple Scanks sully a great tradition.

Scanks was, if anything, tighter than ever, looking as if he needed a fast transfusion. I guessed his worst fears about the courtroom had been confirmed this day. He knew now that it was neither his memory nor his powers of observation that

were under attack—the standard targets when police take the
stand. It was his credibility that was in issue.

Arthur looked around the gallery for several seconds, as if
searching for someone, then turned to Scanks and began
asking stern questions about the corporal's visit to Om Bay a
year ago August. "How many of these people did you talk
to?"

"Two or three, I guess." Scanks' voice was not so loud now.
He was still staring straight ahead.

"But you described them all as having expressionless voices.
You said they seemed hypnotized."

"Those I talked to, anyway."

"Corporal, everybody was working, clearing, building, busily
creating a group homesite—that's what you observed, yes?"

"Yes, sir."

"Not a bunch of mindless automatons staring into space as
you would have us believe, yes? Now let's be straight with
this court. They didn't seem hypnotized at all, quite normal-
looking young people. Am I right?"

"I'll say that if that's what you want me to say. I have my
own opinions." Scanks' surliness was not entirely conquered
by fear.

"And no laws were being broken by these people—no
drugs, no one being held by force?"

"There were a couple of people practising nudity, partial
nudity," Scanks said.

"However morally repugnant you find the display of wom-
en's breasts, you knew this was private property and no law
was being broken by the two girls whom you took such care
to observe. . . ." Arthur's voice stopped in mid-flow as he
glanced at the back of the courtroom: a little flutter of
commotion there as the door opened and a woman from
1940s Hollywood stepped inside. Annabelle Beauchamp,
Arthur's ex-wife. He lost the beat of his cross-examination.
"I'm sorry, corporal, we were talking about Om Bay, last
August, that's a year ago August."

I could tell that Arthur hadn't the slightest recall of the
long question he had been asking. A Brownie offered seating
space to Mrs. Beauchamp (you'd have to say Celeste Holm,
in *Gentleman's Agreement*, circa 1947). Arthur made his way
back with difficulty to Om Bay, circa 1984.

"Yes, you visited there on that occasion, on no particular
business, found nothing there of interest save the female

breasts we have heard about, and you were politely asked to leave—because you were a trespasser." Arthur was getting it together again.

"I was requested to leave, yes, but it's a matter of opinion whether I was politely asked and whether I was trespassing. Your lordship, may I say something?"

"About what?" said the judge.

"Can I explain why I went there that first time?"

"He's already done so, in answer to my friend's questions," said Arthur. "The witness can make his self-serving statements on Mr. Lukey's time, not mine."

"We will hear the witness," said Hammersmith.

"I'm the lone law enforcer for a very large territory, your lordship, myself and an untrained, part-time auxiliary, and frankly there are quite a few groups like this, cults, scattered around the islands where I patrol, and you do get drugs in them and sometimes guns, illegal aliens. I have to do my job. I wasn't hassling anybody, sir."

"I had not wished to be so bold as to accuse you of *hassling*, as you put it," said Arthur. He gave a little fling of his gown as, fully recovered, he paced briskly across the courtroom. Lots of vim, with his ex-wife looking on. "George Wurz, whom you say you befriended, he seemed like a normal-enough fellow, pleasant to talk to, yes?"

"I'd say he was normal, except for the group he was with."

"And the people from Om Bay who came to town from time to time to buy supplies, groceries, mail their letters, they carried on quite normally in every respect?"

"I don't know. I guess so."

"No one wandering around as if hearing voices, you'll agree with that?"

"I guess not, although I have got my opinions as to that, too."

"Officer, be plain with me or we will be all week here. I put it to you that you were in error when you suggested there was anything about these people that could characterize them as appearing hypnotized, or under somebody's control." Arthur's voice was hard, demanding. "And you know that the merchants of Tash-Tash Cove can be called to this stand to testify to that, don't you?"

"They kept to theirselves, Mr. Beauchamp. I only knew George Wurz a little, and I'd agree he seemed okay. That's all I can say."

I caught the eye of the economist, Margolis. He smiled. I smiled back. A silent conversation. This juror was agreeing with me that Scanks was not an unbiased fellow, nor too reliable.

"When you arrived at the scene on the Saturday, December eighth, I take it you observed what seemed to be footsteps in the snow leading to the site from the hillside, from the escarpment?"

"No, sir."

Arthur tried to work him over with the aerial photographs, but could get nothing better than, "I don't know what that is, sir."

After some probing about Scanks' observations of the murder scene, the corporal never relaxing, standing stiffly on guard as if for the anthem, Arthur moved on to the tricky issue of time of death. The chief pathologist would testify, we knew, that all twenty-one deaths were sudden and the time of those deaths was between eleven A.M. and one P.M., most likely noon.

The pathologist had assumed that rigor mortis had not set in as of two P.M. when Corporal Scanks first examined the bodies. But limbs start to stiffen, generally, from within two to four hours after death. Our problem: if none of the bodies was in rigor mortis at two P.M., the deaths could not have occurred before twelve noon, when Wheatley, Morgan, and Calico were leaving Campbell River in their Winnebago.

"'Rigor mortis had not set in.' That is what you say in your written report." Arthur frowned at the witness.

"Yes, sir."

"Corporal, do you pretend to be an expert in any medical area?"

"No, of course not."

"You aren't able to stand up here and discuss how muscles pass into rigor as a result of contraction of the myosin and actin filaments of the muscle fibre?"

"I've seen corpses in various stages of death, also we had a course in training on sudden death, that's all. I think I know what it looks like."

"Yet the medical team which arrived an hour and a half later will tell us, I understand, that all these bodies were well into rigor mortis at three-thirty."

"Well, I guess rigor mortis started to come on after."

"Those who were tied—you didn't cut them loose?"

"I didn't want to disturb evidence, sir. If there was any sign of life I would have, any sign at all."

"You say the muscles were still flaccid, loose, when you came upon these bodies?"

"Yes, sir."

"But they were all tied tightly, wrists to ankles?"

"Yes."

"Their hands behind their backs, their stomachs arched forward?"

"Yes."

"In firm, rigid positions?"

"Yes."

"And you say this was not rigor mortis?"

"I looked at the faces. You see it first in the face."

"But almost all those faces were shot away by slugs which exploded through them. Come now, witness, be straight with us, you cannot say one way or another if there was rigor mortis."

"I have my opinion."

"For what that's worth."

"For what that's worth." I thought Scanks might leave it at that. He added: "The bodies were still warm." A pause. "I've felt cold corpses."

Arthur just let the ghoulish afterthought sit there. I felt my neck hairs prickle. So did, I imagined, the jurors.

"Perhaps we might take the break now," Arthur said.

As everyone withdrew from the courtroom, Arthur moved nimbly up one of the aisles to greet his wife and began an animated conversation with her. I had good feelings. Maybe a big win in this case would repair their marriage. She might inspire him to magnificence if she stayed on and watched. Scanks was already a much-diminished witness. Arthur merely had to keep him on the line until we broke for the weekend at four-thirty.

After the jury left, the deputy sheriffs placed handcuffs on Shiva and motioned him toward the prisoners' door. He turned and looked wistfully around, caught my eye, fixed it for a moment, then stepped from the dock.

* * *

The day's final round. Scanks came out of his corner glazed-eyed. Arthur glanced at Annabelle, svelte and cool in the

front-row seat he had arranged for her, on the shrink bench.
Do it for Annabelle, I thought. Show her the old form,
Arthur, the fancy steps.

"We have heard evidence that you met with William
Wheatley on November twenty-fourth. Did you meet him
again on December eighth?"

"No, sir."

"But he was in the vicinity of Poindexter Island—you knew
that."

"No, sir, I didn't. I don't to this day."

"You asked residents of the island about unfamiliar boats in
the area on December eighth?"

"I was assigned to do that, yes."

"And is it not true that you received at least one report
about a small boat that was strange to those waters?"

"Objection," said Lukey. "Hearsay."

Hammersmith: "Yes, it's what someone else said."

Arthur groaned. "Surely, my lord, I'm entitled to find out
the result of this man's investigations."

"No, you're not," said the judge.

"You talked to a man named Joe Whitegoose," Arthur
snapped.

"Yes, sir."

"A fisherman, a witness in this case. He told you of a
boat—"

Lukey was on his feet. "Cannot my friend be admonished?
He is running rampant."

"Objection is sustained," the judge said. Nothing more.

"Apparently, witness, I am not allowed to ask you what
report Mr. Whitegoose gave to you of an unusual boat in the
area, so I will simply ask you if you sought such information
from him."

"Yes, I did."

"And did you make a written note of his answer?"

"Yes."

"May I see that note?"

"Objection. Not a note to refresh memory."

"Yes, sustained."

"Where is the note?" Arthur asked in an exasperated voice.

"At Tash-Tash. I didn't bring it."

The foreman was staring at the witness with hard, beady
eyes. Most of the other jurors appeared confused. Why, they
were doubtless wondering, are all these facts being kept from

us? What kind of system of justice prevents defence lawyers from asking reasonable questions?

Arthur fired a hard one, a quick pick-off play at first. "You met with Bill Wheatley last Thursday, August twenty-ninth, isn't that right?"

Scanks didn't say anything, just looked ahead, stalling.

"Be careful, there are witnesses," Arthur bluffed.

"I can't remember." The last refuge of a cornered man.

"It was on Quadra Island, wasn't it?"

No answer. Scanks frowned as if trying to remember.

"You were in Quadra Island that day, weren't you?"

"I think . . . yes, that was my day off. Yeah, I think I did bump into him. In the lobby of the Heriot Bay Inn. I do business on Quadra. I don't know what he was doing there. We just said hello, that was all." Scanks had figured out this was all our "witnesses" could have known. Had they rendezvoused in a hotel room for the payoff?

"No, that wasn't all, was it?" Arthur's words were soft and sinister. He slowly walked towards Scanks, came around to the front of him, where the witness could not avoid a face-to-face confrontation. "That wasn't all. Was it? WAS it?" He roared at him now.

Scanks' face looked like an open wound.

"He paid you off. Be straight with us. He paid you off."

"What kind of question is that?" Scanks' big voice had turned faint.

Arthur began putting the theory of the defence to the witness. "I suggest, corporal, you were fully aware as of the twenty-fourth day of November, A.D. 1984, that the accused planned to raid the Om Bay commune—"

"Wheatley is *not* the accused," Lukey called.

"He should be," Arthur roared. He continued to suggest: to suggest that Scanks knew very well that Wheatley had planned his raid for December eighth; to suggest that he was guilty of negligence of the most wanton and criminal kind in rendering himself wilfully blind, in giving licence to an act of kidnapping that exploded into a mass murder.

Lukey was tap-tap-tapping the rubber end of a pencil. A great, black-robed monk, twitching to interrupt, but daring not, afraid by so doing to give credence to this dangerous red herring. Patricia Blueman was blinking her eyes as if bemused.

Nor did Hammersmith interrupt. He was awake though his eyes were closed. I could see facial movement. A pursing mouth. A twitch of nose to ride his glasses up a little. A frown.

Arthur suggested, and his finger stabbed forward like an épée. He was dominating the courtroom, owned it now.

"I am suggesting that Mr. Wheatley felt gratitude for the favours bestowed upon him by your inestimable self. I am suggesting that you accepted his gratitude, and that you let it be known that he might feel even more charitable in exchange for your continued silence."

"That is not true. Of course it is not true."

"Corporal, you bumped into Wheatley, as you put it, in a hotel on Quadra Island. In the course of that bumping, something changed hands. I put it to you."

"Not true at all." Scanks had his hands on the railing, and I could see the knuckles playing like piano keys.

"You do business on Quadra Island, you say?"

"Yes."

"And you keep an account in the credit union there?"

Scanks hesitated. "Yes."

"And you have a loan there?" A reasonable guess. Benjamin Johnson, my young Indian friend, had told me Scanks was seriously in debt over a business venture.

"Yes."

"You're heavily in debt?"

"Everybody's in debt."

"Despite seventeen years of service to Her Majesty, accommodation provided, you're in deep debt?"

"It's a mortgage on some land. Everybody's got a mortgage."

"And you were in that credit union on August twenty-ninth after you met with Wheatley, were you not?" The last three words were pronounced like shots.

"I . . . probably."

"And you signed in—to enter the safety deposit boxes?"

A guess, a dangerous question, but Arthur was operating on instinct now. If Scanks had gone to his safety deposit box, he had no way out but to admit it. But he was saying nothing.

"Cash, wasn't it? All cash, in very large bills?"

No answer.

"Tell me, corporal, how much is the silence of a uniformed man worth? How much are the lives of twenty-two young men and women worth?"

Foreman McIlheny looked at the witness through hooded eyes.

Continued silence from Scanks. Then a thin line, the colour of his dress uniform, began to trail down over his unmoving lips, over his chin: a nosebleed. Otherwise, he seemed to be in a state of rigor mortis.

I looked up at Hammersmith. God knows what was going on in his mind. "Corporal Scanks," he said, "you understand that you will not speak about your evidence over the weekend with anyone. You are under cross-examination."

Scanks nodded dumbly.

"I think we should, ah, adjourn," said the judge.

It seemed a perfect time to do so.

* * *

"Hey, this is great," said Jacqueline as I shepherded her to the elevator. "How do you get to be a lawyer, anyway?"

Yes, it was one of those good moments. There was no better job than to be a lawyer.

"You're going to get blisters," she said.

I looked down. I was rubbing my hands together viciously.

"Watch that cold." She waved, got into the elevator.

Lukey was not so chummy in the locker room today. "That jerk, I'd like to ream him with a hot poker."

Arthur said in a jolly voice, "If I hear one single whispered suggestion that you coached him this weekend, there'll be so much shit raining on you, Leroy, you won't know whether to duck or wipe."

Arthur and I were struggling to suppress joy. Scanks had crashed into the goalposts. This trial was starting to turn around on the prosecutor. My runny nose and scratchy throat seemed bearable now.

"I don't know what kind of a deal that clown of a corporal made with Wheatley," said Lukey, "and frankly I don't care. It's not going to make any difference to this trial." He stomped out.

Arthur gave me a wink. "Yes, not a bad day at all. If we have made the weekend miserable for Leroy, we have made it the more pleasant for honest people like ourselves. I have a dinner meeting tomorrow with Werner Mundt—you should come: we have to decide to abandon the insanity defence. The more it looks as if Shiva is innocent, the more insanity becomes a trap. The jury could seek an easy way out, compromise. If insanity becomes their compromise, we may lose an innocent man to a lifetime in the house for the criminally insane. What do you think?"

"I think we go for the gusto. Take no prisoners. Abandon the insanity defence." Scanks had been utterly shattered. Wait until Joe Whitegoose takes the stand. *Did they kill everyone?* Even if Lukey were to call evidence of the earlier, third-person-singular version, we could repair the damage in cross-examination.

"In most murder trials it is dangerous to limit a jury's choices," Arthur said.

"Murder one or nothing," I said. "I know it in my gut— Shiva isn't guilty. Insanity—that means he did it. But he didn't do it. Wheatley and his gang did it. I know that the way I know Leroy Lukey has an anal fixation. It's a given. A fact of nature and the cosmos. Shiva could never have done those acts."

Arthur shrugged into his suit jacket. "When we talk about abandoning the insanity defence, I want your views to be untrammelled by your alleged gut feelings." He was stern. "It is difficult enough to maintain a lawyer-like sense of clarity in our *non-professional* lives. Speaking of which, I have a date tonight." He looked at himself in a mirror, tried to brush away the wrinkles in his suit. "I need some new clothing. All my suits are old."

"You look just fine to me." I was proud of him. He looked like a king, as far as my idolizing eyes could tell. "She ever seen you in action before?"

"No," he said quietly. "She's never come to court before. Isn't that strange? She has never known but the one part of me."

"I hope she keeps coming."

I scurried down to the El Beau Room. A tall glass of suds—just to replace the day's water loss—then six miles around Stanley Park. Yes, I would run today, enjoy the unrelenting September sunshine. I would run hard, laughing off my annoying little cold, steaming those germ cells out of me. Making up for five straight days of runlessness.

"Heard?" said Brian Pomeroy, making room for me at the table.

"What?" I looked from Pomeroy to Brovak to Sophie Marx.

"André Fortin," Sophie said.

I looked again from face to face. "What? He was about to

be transferred to Kingston... He was shot in an escape attempt?"

"No," said Pomeroy, "he *escaped* in an escape attempt."

"Oh, God. How'd it happen?"

"It seems," said Sophie, "that someone slipped him a derringer. He had it in his boot in the wagon taking him to the airport. He forced the guards to take off his cuffs, to free him from the back of the van. Somewhere in Richmond. He ran off into the bush. They've tracked the whole area with dogs. He got away."

A silence.

"Augustina—where is she?" I said.

"Right now I'd say Weeps is approximately somewhere underneath André Fortin," Brovak said. He seemed a little high.

"Don't be a grunt, John," Sophie said. "We don't know, Max. She hasn't been in the office all day; we can't raise her at home."

"I went to her apartment," Brovak said. "I knocked, I shouted. Just echoes."

"When was her last visit to the penitentiary? To see him." I felt weak.

"We don't know," she said. "We're too scared to phone and ask."

Another silence. "She wouldn't have slipped the gun to him," I said.

Brovak humphed. "You don't know a woman in love, Max. Sometimes they go ape." He gave a sad-eyed glance to Sophie, who returned a cold look. "Just talking from my own experience, of course."

"Your experience of women, Brovak, is limited to the area explored by your four inches of male pudendum," said Sophie.

"If you don't do it, don't knock it," John shot back.

Things were getting out of hand. "Order please," I said. "What are we going to do?"

"That's what we had better talk about," Sophie said. "I have a feeling the police will want to see her. She hasn't exactly been discreet about the relationship. The screws at the pen know what's been going on."

I dragged myself home from the lounge many hours later, a little drunk and somewhat flatulent with a stomach full of bar nachos. All sinuses had packed it in; the nose was glowing. This, I remembered suddenly, was the eve of the destruction of the world. According to Melissa-June M'Garethy, otherwise known as Astral, we auto-eroto-destruct at dawn tomorrow unless we shout our love for Raba-urt-Jogan. I should not be dragging myself home to bed. I should be searching for a high hill where I could scream out my love for Raba.

Love Apocalypse. Poor girl.

The thought of auto-eroto-destructing must have made me jumpy because I almost climbed out of my skin when a figure approached me in the darkened upstairs hallway of my condo.

"It's me," came Augustina Sage's frail voice. "I turned the hall light out."

"I hope you're alone." No way was André Fortin coming into my apartment.

"Yes. Oh, heck, I'm alone, all right."

"Come in." I alcohol-fumbled the key into the lock, pulled her inside, locked the door again. I sat her on a hard kitchen chair, got out the drip grind, put some water on. "Better tell me everything. Did you help him?"

"I don't know." She was the colour of ash. "I may have."

"How?"

"I kited notes out for him. Usually mailed them to an address on Graveley Street. I didn't read them. Didn't want to know what was in them, I guess. I don't know how they got the gun to him." Her eyes were dry. There was no sign that she had been crying, no streaks. She did not have much expression. Her voice was a monotone.

"Did you know he was going to try to escape?"

"He told me he had to get out of there before they transferred him back East. We'd never see each other again if they sent him to St. Vincent de Paul. Aw, God, yeah, I knew about the escape."

I poured steaming water into the filter. Coffee, we needed coffee. I was pretty woozy.

"We arranged a . . . meet. I was to bring a suitcase full of clothing, an Air Canada ticket to Montreal—and a bit of money. He was going to get a place back East, and call me."

"How much money is a bit of money?"

"I got about ten thousand dollars together. I took a loan."

"Ten grand plus clothes and an airline ticket. You gave these to him? Tonight?"

She took a deep breath and blew it out. "Yep."

"Milk and?"

"Both, please." She smiled a gritty smile. "Kind of wild, huh?"

"Kind of. Can you be traced to any of this? You'll be suspected, Augustina."

"It doesn't matter. I'm out of this business. I'm giving up my ticket. I don't have it. Never will. Haven't got the 'right stuff,' as John puts it." She stared soulfully at her coffee. "Yeah, well, I'm sure the police will be coming by my place. That's why I want to stay here tonight. To get my head together. Can I?"

I was tipsy enough not to weigh too carefully the implications of this. I said, "Sure, you can stay." I have no excuse for the next thing I did, which was to take our coffees, a bottle of Benedictine and a pair of liqueur glasses, and move with her into the living room.

"You were not seen tonight?"

"No. It was dark—the airport parking lot. He had a suit and tie, he'd shaved off his moustache. I hardly recognized him."

"The airline ticket—you didn't put it on an AmEx, or something stupid."

"I paid for it in cash. Over the Air Canada counter. I was there twenty seconds. Bought it in the name of Mr. Charles Grolier."

"And are you going to visit Mr. Grolier in Montreal?"

"It turns out not. No, it doesn't seem that that is going to happen."

I sipped Benedictine, waiting for the rest.

"He said it wouldn't work out. He would try to pay me back, send me some money. He said he loved me too much to have to force me to live in exile with him. Exile in the underworld, is how he put it. Our love would cause us to be chained, and a poet cannot be a poet with chains."

"He said that?" I knew André Fortin would be hitting banks when Augustina's ten thousand ran out.

"And he walked away with the suitcase. And I just stood there, stunned. Just Ms. Augustina Stupid standing in an airport parking lot." She bit her lip. "This is crazy. I'm crazy. I couldn't help it, I followed him to the terminal, got up to the departure level just as he got to the ticket counter. I wasn't sure she was with him at first, but they were standing together at the counter, talking, and then I saw them check their bags together. Her bag and my bag. Then she took his arm. I guess she's the one who's been living at that Graveley Street address. Quite young, I thought, but made up to look older. Very French, I suppose. Kind of... well, you know she'd be flamboyant at a party, but she was being very cool, very Mrs. Charles Grolier."

Augustina sipped her coffee, stared into space. She looked like a pretty doll from a puppet show, abandoned by the crowds, by the puppeteer, her eyes vacant, without animation. She didn't cry. Grief beyond tears.

I put an arm around her. She came rushing against me, her arms circling my neck, her face buried into my shoulder, and I remember thinking how this woman's scent was different from Ruth's, how her skin seemed grainier, how there were all these tiny black curls that tickled.

"Make love to me, Max, please. Don't ask why. I want that."

Well. This is how life happens, as Shiva would say. Who knows how one prevents such things from happening? A man is high from a good day in court, he is high on alcohol, there hasn't been a woman.... But she was so vulnerable. And I knew that afterwards there would be guilt.

19

○

End of the World

A knock-knock-knock at the door. Very light, but causing me to sit bolt upright. An empty bottle of Benedictine was at the table to my right, two spilled glasses on the floor. Upon the sheet were sticky places that smelled of liqueur, perhaps other things. Augustina groaned and turned over, burying her face in a pillow. Rap-rap-rap. Who comes to visit at such an unholy hour? I looked at my watch: unholy indeed—seven A.M., dawn of the end of the world. We had been asleep for only a few hours, a night now embarrassingly remembered.

I staggered from the bed, into my pants, shut the bedroom door behind me. I had not slept off the alcohol, and my head was at the railway junction of drunkenness and hangover, my cold still rumbling down the track, drippy nose and fever.

Knock, knock.

"Who's there?"

"Police."

"Police who?"

"Police open the door." It was an old routine. "I forgot my key." I was beginning to auto-eroto-destruct. I had failed to call out my love for Raba-urt-Jogan.

"Ruth, you're back early."

"Came in last night," she hollered. "Didn't want to bother you, thought I'd make up time with Jacqueline. Say, it's great talking to a door like this."

Her clothes, her bag. A quick glance. Must all be in the bedroom. Did I smell of another woman's closeness? I unlocked the door.

"I have a hell of a cold," I said as I sneaked the door open. She was standing there, fit and smiling, brown as a hazel-nut,

213

her oval eyes running the length of me, up and down. She wrinkled her nose.

"A twenty-six-ounce cold from the smell of you. My God, wipe your nose. What have you been doing besides falling apart? You've got a *pot*." She stepped up to me, patted it. "Well, I'm suicidal." And she kissed me on the mouth, very sweetly. "I missed you."

"Uh, come in." Hide under the bed, Augustina. Slip out when the coast is clear. "I'll put coffee on. We can go out to the terrace. Lovely morning."

"It's a bit chilly for outside just yet. I'm used to warmth. I have to reclimatize. How can you live like this?" She was moving about the living and dining rooms, picking up. "Just leave your shirt lying on the floor like this?" My God! Beside the chesterfield. Augustina's shoes: little loafers.

I gave a great sneeze.

"Poor waif. I should put you to bed."

"No, no, I'm fine." Panic.

She swept past me into the kitchen. "Big nurse will get warm cocoa. You go to bed."

I looked about wildly, rushed to the bedroom door, stepped inside. Augustina was still sacked out, her head buried under a pillow. I grabbed some more clothes, shut the door, rushed out into the living room, kicked Augustina's shoes under the chesterfield, raced to the kitchen. "Thank God you woke me. I've got an appointment at the office. Only take fifteen minutes. Come down with me, then I'll buy you breakfast somewhere."

"Are you crazy? What's with you? Phone the office and cancel it. Hey, did you get my letter?"

"Letter? No, never did. Listen, really, it'll only take a few minutes, then we can concentrate on each other. I've got a lot to tell you."

"I've got a lot to tell *you*. You didn't get the letter?" She stopped her stirring of the milk atop the stove. "Gee, that was going to make things a lot easier."

"We'll talk about it on the way to the office. Let's take your car. Is it just out front?" I paused. "What do you mean, it was going to make things a lot easier?"

"You know how things are, Max. Sometimes we can't talk to each other, we have these silent spaces. I just sat down in the hotel bar in Mexico one evening, and I started writing down all the things I wanted to say about our relationship. It began as just some notes to myself, and then I found myself talking to you, saying things to you that I've always wanted to say. How it is important for me to be my own person, how there has to be a mutual recognition of two liberties when two people are . . . in love. I don't use that expression loosely, Max. I know you think I don't use it enough to express myself to you. It's hard for me. I'm so afraid of being dependent."

I guessed this gentle outpouring was something she had been holding back, was determined to say to me now. Guilt and fear gripped me.

"This sounds like a speech, doesn't it? Well, I kind of *did* prepare it. I hoped you'd have read the letter first, though. This is hard. Well, it's all leading to a question, and I'm not picking the time and place, I know, but. . . ." She glanced at me with a shy expression. "Hell, call off the appointment, and let's *both* hit the sack. I was a good girl for the last month. Too good. I *had* the opportunities, to be honest, but my heart wasn't in it. . . ."

Creak of door. A soft, female groan. "Oh, where is the bathroom?"

Ruth's expression of shock seemed to expand her face, while I felt my atoms shrivelling, my body collapsing inward like a black star against the rush of her astonishment and her hurt.

Warm milk washed down my face, over my shoulders.

The saucepan went careering into my crystal wine glasses. Ruth's mouth was open, but only one repeated word came from it: "You . . . you . . . you . . . ." Her tongue could find no epithet sufficiently foul to round the phrase off. A cup and saucer whizzed by me as I stumbled into the living room, where a frozen Augustina stood, my robe draped over her bare shoulders. Ruth came flying out after me, hurling dishes. Augustina ducked into the bathroom and I behind my two-sided bookcase. I do not know where Ruth found the strength to bring it down upon me. I lay smothered under the complete *Decline and Fall of the Roman Empire*, volumes one to six, as I listened to the front door open, slam shut.

Soon all was a stillness except for the moaning of Augustina in the bathroom.

* * *

Ruth, Augustina, the trial, Shiva, Wheaties, alcohol, germs: I felt twisted, the taste in my mouth as foul as corruption. After

a stinging-cold shower and brisk encounters with Messrs.
Macleans, Mitchum, Murine, Gillette, and Listerine, I bade
Augustina to stay in the apartment, to lock it against all
comers, to await word. And I walked ten blocks to Sophie
Marx's house, one of those 1920s wooden gargantuans that
hunch into the hill over English Bay.

Sophie. Sophie in a crisis. Sophie despite her dislike of
Augustina. Sophie because of her toughness, and more than
that, because of the softness deep inside.

She shared ownership of the house with her friend Harriet
Nikeratos, escapee from an impossible marriage, owner of an
exclusive women's wear shop. Harriet, on her way out to
work, met me at the door. She was the yang to Sophie's yin,
small-boned, delicate, dressy, and immaculate.

"Max, you look like you spent the night standing up in a
broom closet. Yeek, what a smell." She drifted by, blew me a
kiss, went to her car.

In the living room, Sophie was seated on a couch with a
bowl on her lap, spooning corn flakes into her mouth, leafing
idly, with an expression best described as sceptical, through
one of the *Vogue* magazines on top of an end table. I slid into
a low leather chair.

"I found her."

"Yuh."

"She stayed the night at my place. She's there now."

"Yuh." She looked at me oddly.

"This morning Ruth showed up."

Her spoon stopped moving, halfway to her mouth. "You
need an aspirin or something?"

"I need to have my head examined."

"I'm sure Ruth is perfectly capable of doing that."

"She would like to examine it. Embalmed in a jar."

"You lout. She caught you in *bed* together?"

"Strong circumstantial case," I sniffed.

"Is there a defence?"

"No."

"Macarthur, have you been feeling suicidal lately? Or
what?"

"Help me, Sophie."

"God, I suppose the police are looking for Augustina."

"She'll be okay if she doesn't panic. They don't have
anything on her." I honked into a Kleenex.

Sophie sighed. "Bring her here, I'll look after her." She

looked at me with scorn. "Don't worry—she'll be safe. I don't try to screw my own partners. I'll set something up with the horsemen, make sure they don't charge her. As for Ruth, well, I'll call her after I get Augustina straightened away. I'll make a case for you. I don't promise much, maybe you've really blown it this time. You're a snivelling, two-timing rat, Max, but you're my partner."

* * *

Hank (Dumptruck) Hooper was in the centre hall at Oakalla with a provincial court remand list, trying to whip up some fast business.

"Haven't seen *your* name in the papers, Macarthur. You doing any work in that courtroom aside from carrying Artie's bags and filling his gin jar? What's the point of having a big case if you don't get your name in the papers? So I hear your father is taking over the court of appeal. Passed on from generation to generation like an heirloom. Must be nice to be a Macarthur, have all the right friends in the right places."

I didn't deign to respond. Or didn't have the strength.

I dabbed at the rawness of my nostrils, glared at him with febrile eyes. Rolly Toews rescued me, taking me into the little room where Shiva awaited, who seemed in a soft, perhaps melancholy, mood.

"In a week, maybe by Friday, the prosecution will close its case. You are a teacher, an *acharya*. Teach this jury your truth, Shiva. You can't let Wheatley and those mad dogs get away with this."

"I haven't any lust for vengeance. It comes whether or not we desire it. If they've killed my *chelas*, they've cast the seeds for their own souls' lowly rebirth."

I was exasperated. "Bill Wheatley coming back as a garter snake doesn't save you from a lifetime in a penitentiary, Shiva. Take the stand. Tell the jury the truth: you saw Wheatley and Morgan and Calico. You saw them. I know you saw them. If you were in the tree, you saw them."

"I would not take the stand to say that even if I could."

"For God's sake, Shiva, we've got the jury begging for our defence. They're on the hook. Scanks as much as admitted he was bribed by Wheatley. Anything he said remotely damaging about you will be disregarded by the jury. And we've got

Joe Whitegoose to come. But we need *you*, damn it. *Reconstruct* the scene, that's all you have to do." I was a rabid, snapping dog.

"Reconstruct the scene? Does that mean to lie? Is that how far I am asked to play this game? You cheapen me by suggesting it, Maximillian."

"Tell the truth!" I raised my voice. "Tell the truth, for Christ's sake. Or for Buddha's sake, for Brahma's sake. Just for the sake of the *truth*, Shiva. Tell them you were in your *chaitya*, transported. But tell them you didn't kill these people." My fists were bunched in frustration.

He put both his hands over those tight fists. "Maximillian, you are in an extremely confused and unhappy state. Be calm."

I took a deep breath.

"If you lose this trial," he said softly, "it will be such a shattering experience for you. All of mind and ego are focussed upon it, and the focussing distorts, and you do not see that this little engagement in a Vancouver courtroom is a paltry *affair d'honneur* of infinitely small interest within God's infinite cosmos."

I took another deep breath. I slowed. I felt a headache release its talons from my head and take wing. Shiva's hands were cool upon mine.

"Maybe that shattering experience is something you must undergo, Maxmillian. A rebirth for you. A total ego-destruction. The actor dies. Tragedy and hopelessness descend upon your neck like a sword, and you are free of your head. And you'll then understand, as I do, that all this is nothing, the trial, your voracious hunger for victory, your hopes, your anger, all of less moment than a passing autumn breeze. For you to win, for you to so sacrifice yourself to your rapacious ego— why, God would be hard pressed to find you then."

I withdrew my hands. "You would rather I lose? You would be just as pleased as not to see Wheatley get away with this? Are you *crazy*?"

"I have no hatred for him. Love opens the mind. Prejudice and hatred close it. Maximillian, I tried to build a bridge to you, but never did complete it. You are the saboteur. Drop the mind! Give it up!" His eyes blazed at me. "Understand this, and understand this finally. I don't hope for acquittal. I don't hope for physical freedom. I have no desire to be fulfilled. I can die at this moment because I *am* fulfilled.

Death's merely the manifest moving into the unmanifest, and after death I'll remain, as my twenty-two disciples remain, a part of the uncreate, a universalized, liberated soul. I'm ready to be freed from karma, from the cycle of birth and death. I am ready." Passion in his voice.

"What is this talk about death, Shiva?"

He stared at me fiercely for a while, then slowly closed his eyes. "It's nothing," he said softly. "Death is nothing. It is merely the loss of information, an episode. It changes only the skin. Life after life we remain the same."

I was overtaken by a sadness that seemed to have little to do with my own troubles. We sat together quietly, I looking at Shiva, he looking into the inner sun, intensely, the muscles of his eyes tight. He did not share with me what was in there.

* * *

While junior counsel's personal world was unravelling at the seams like a worn sandlot baseball, senior counsel's world seemed to be coming together, freshly sewn. "Annabelle is fairly fascinated by this case," Arthur told me Saturday evening. We were at La Cantina, waiting for Mundt. Annabelle, invited along, was freshening up in the ladies'.

"Did I tell you she'd never seen me in action before? She told me she understood now why I used to drag myself to bed with no energy for her." He confided in me: "I went home with her last night."

Mundt arrived just as Annabelle returned from the washroom, and he looked her over in much the same manner as he later examined his fat, sauteed trout before giving fork to it.

Throughout dinner, Arthur, pleased with himself, with his trial, with thoughts of re-budding romance, did not pick up on the body language between Mundt and Annabelle. A pair of erotomaniacs: a lot of knee touching under the table while kindly, innocent Arthur called for more Bordeaux for us, Perrier for himself. I was stoned on antihistamines. I was refusing to think about Ruth, blocking everything.

Later, over coffee, Mundt made his pitch to us. "Frankly, if you want my opinion, and perhaps you don't, but I have some experience in these matters, I fear you're making a grave mistake."

"Commander Lukey has seen his gunboat take a torpedo

amidships," said Arthur. "He will be standing on the poop-
deck saluting as he goes under. I am not about to throw him a
life preserver."

"But you have two cracks at it, Arthur, for God's sake. If
the jury, for some reason, rejects innocence, then they can go
on to the insanity issue. Two shots at it."

"If we raise insanity with the jury, we leave compromise to
them. Oh, of course they're supposed to be unanimous on
either issue. But when twelve human beings get together in
debate, there exists always the tendency to indulge in the sin
of splitting the difference. No, Werner, unless something
happens in the next three days, we will be closing the
defence without raising the insanity issue. Sorry."

Mundt could see his chance for headlines slipping away.
"Arthur, I *know* I can swing the jury. I know it. Priestman,
he's just an automaton, looks like a stuffed shirt on the stand.
Juries can't stand him. Wang is worse. They're bookmen, not
an original thought has ever come out of their combined
cerebra."

"I want my client declared innocent." The rasp in Arthur's
voice warned his good humour was being tested. "I want to
take no chance on losing an innocent man to either a prison
for the sane or a prison for the insane."

"He's not insane," I put in. "He's psychic."

"Psychic." Mundt gave an irritated shake of his head.
"What a crock of shit. He *is* insane. He *should* be treated.
My God, it's the classic delusion of grandeur, the God
complex. These people used to dress up like Napoleon, but
Christ is back in fashion in the wards these days. Long hair
and flowing robes. He had one heavy breakdown we do know
about, when he was eighteen. They threw him into a clinic in
Philadelphia. I phoned yesterday, the report's coming. He
was under heavy drug therapy."

"A nervous breakdown at age eighteen doesn't make for an
insanity defence thirty-odd years later," I said.

"He was manic-depressive," Mundt said. "Very sick."

I could see Arthur did not like the way Mundt—Arthur
having missed his chance—snapped his lighter open, held it
to Annabelle's cigarette. She daintily placed her left hand
over his extended one, and gave him a look as the flame
flickered.

Mundt glanced grimly at me, at Arthur. "If you gentlemen
trip over your own guns and shoot yourselves in the feet,

please don't call me out of bed at night. I work with heads, not feet."

We made merry at his little joke, in a strained way. Arthur picked up the bill. Mundt argued, then insisted on returning the favour. If Mrs. Mundt would be pleased to accompany her husband Monday night.

20

○

Rectum Esse

Court was half an hour late getting under way on Monday morning. While the judge was doubtless fuming in his chambers, Leroy Lukey and Inspector Storenko met with Arthur and me in one of the crown counsel rooms. The news: Eddie Scanks had gone AWOL. A warrant had been issued for his arrest on corruption charges.

"Frank will fill you in," Leroy said. His face showed a splotchiness this morning, layered shades of pink. His case had fallen apart.

"Personally, I'd like to fill Corporal Scanks in," said Storenko. But he seemed relaxed, giving off, as he always did, an air of easy authority. A dispectic, pipe-smoking policeman, giving us the facts.

"Frankly," he said, "Scanks wasn't the only one around here caught off guard by your cross on Friday, Arthur. Leroy, I gather, lost ten pounds of hot sweat. I was at my office, didn't get the story until half-past five. By that time, Eddie had flown charter to Quadra Island, where he got into the credit union safety deposit and out, and back on the plane. Very fast police work. On his part. Not so fast on ours."

"He got away with the loot?" said Arthur. "The not-so-stool pigeon has flown the coop."

"It might have been different," said Storenko, "had some quiet information been imparted to us."

"You'll catch him," Arthur beamed. "I have great faith in our federal police force."

A deputy sheriff came to the door. "He's building up a head of steam."

"Tell him counsel are discussing ways to shorten the trial,"

Arthur said. "The roof has fallen in. The Crown's case is *caput mortuum*. There may be a stay."

"Just tell him counsel are in urgent session," Lukey said, and the deputy left. "There aren't going to be any stays, gentlemen. Don't get the wrong idea."

"When the members from Quadra detachment got there, the credit union wouldn't let them search records without a warrant," Storenko said. "By the time we got the warrant, Scanks was somewhere in Victoria—that's where his plane took him. He paid the pilot with a U.S. thousand-dollar bill, no change asked for. He was carrying a satchel and a suitcase."

"How much was in the safety deposit box?" I asked.

"We haven't a clue," said Storenko. "He left mortgage, home, job, wife—although apparently he was losing her anyway."

"Bill Wheatley—had he been seen on Quadra Island?" I asked. "The Heriot Bay Inn?"

"August twenty-ninth," said Storenko, looking at me with his cool, blue eyes. "But you have that information. We've been open with you. Now how about you being open with us?"

"We'll be honoured to co-operate with the police," said Arthur, "as soon as we know what dispensation is planned for these charges. Come now, Leroy, pride goeth before a fall. You've proceeded on a wrong premise, accept your fate like the sort of gentleman I truly believe you to be, and drop the charges. Think of the poor taxpayer."

"I am not quite sure what's been going on between Scanks and Wheatley, Artie, but whatever it is, it's not enough to take us out of the game." Lukey exchanged with Storenko a heavy glance. "The case may be shaky, but it's still got legs."

"Aw, come on," I said, "this is crazy. You're going to proceed? Why haven't Wheatley and his two cronies been questioned? *Arrested* for Christ's sake." I paused, thought. "Or are you using this trial as a way of collecting a case against them?"

"We've talked with them," said Storenko. Another glance from Lukey, this one with warning in it.

"And they gave you the bullshit about doing a coin laundry route," I said. "And watching the news of the massacre on TV while they were eating pizza and Chinese food, waiting for the hockey game to come on."

"You should join the Force, Max," Storenko said. "Skilled investigators are rare."

"Frank, I've known you since law school, you're a straight guy." Storenko had been one of those bright officers the Force picks for advancement. With his legal training, he knew how to put a case together and to do it fairly. He was straight. Brighter than bright. Cleaner than clean. Oxydol. "Why are you playing a part in this charade?"

He leaned toward me. "Your man is guilty. Guilty as hell."

"Look, Frank, I know this case is your baby." I talked urgently but nasally through a stuffy nose. "I know you worked twenty-four hours a day on it for the first week. I know it started off as a cinch. But you're a horseman on a dead horse."

"Your man is guilty. We—"

Lukey put a restraining hand on his shoulder. "They don't play, we don't play. Gentlemen, if you want to give us what you know about Wheatley, we'll be happy to consider our position. As things stand, we proceed."

"And Wheatley?" said Arthur.

"We're looking for him, to ask a few more questions," Storenko said. "There seems to be some evidence of bribing a police officer."

"*Some evidence?*" I almost rose from my chair. "What's going on here? Wheatley has skipped, too?"

"Nor Wheatley, nor Morgan, nor Calico are about," Storenko said. "Big Bill missed his Sunday sermon. Maybe he's aware of the penalties for bribery."

"Boy, this is getting to sound more and more like a malicious prosecution—"

Arthur interrupted me. "We will let them do it their way, and we will do it our way. Proceed at your own risk, Leroy."

Again the deputy sheriff. "He's becoming—"

"Apoplectic," Arthur said, "Let's get on with it."

As Lukey and Arthur chugged off to court, I remained behind with Storenko. "Let me ask you one thing. You took a statement from Joe Whitegoose when Emelia Cruz died."

"I did, Max, but I'm sorry, I'm under instructions not to discuss the evidence with you outside Leroy's presence. By the way, Max, watch your ass on this one."

I didn't like the seating arrangement on the front row of the gallery: the shrink bench. Annabelle Beauchamp was perched rather dangerously close to Werner Mundt and she seemed to be enjoying his witty whisperings.

The jury looked, by and large, a little bedraggled on this Monday morning. They were already feeling the stress of this trial. Most of them were staring hard at Shiva, with wondering expressions. (If they only got to *know* this man, what a difference it would make.) When Shiva turned to them, most looked quickly away. He seemed sad this morning.

"Calling Mr. Wendell Joiner," said Lukey.

"I think it should be explained to the jury," said Arthur, "that Corporal Scanks has deserted us."

"We'll deal with that in open court at the proper time," said Lukey.

"He's flown the coop," Arthur broadcast.

"Let's proceed," said Hammersmith. "Corporal Scanks can be recalled."

A Brownie led Wendell Joiner in through the witness door. He wore a Western suit with a string tie, the kind that adorn fiddle players in country bands. It was button-popping tight around the middle. No khaki commando toque this time, no blue-coloured mirror glasses. But yes, the Coors belt buckle.

Arthur and I had spent much time debating our approach to the Joiners. Wendell would be surly, a thin shield of bluster over a soft underbelly. Tom would be very scared.

"Do you swear to tell the truth, the whole truth and nothing but the truth, so help you God?" said the clerk.

"Yes, I do."

I was smothering coughs. My cold was still finding new areas of the body to ravage: lungs, and back and shoulder muscles.

"Sit down if you like, Mr. Joiner," said Hammersmith.

Wendell had a startled look. He twisted his head, as if trying to seek the source of those words, finally locating the judge on the dais to his right. "Yes, your worship." Awkwardly, he sat.

Lukey asked a few questions to introduce him to the jury (fisherman, auxiliary RCMP two evenings a week, six years in Tash-Tash). I tried to keep my mind on this, but it made peregrinations into the entangled forest of Ruth and Max, a soap opera nightmare from which one is never going to awake. I had sent five bottles of Cordon Rouge on Saturday, cowardly and extravagant in my guilt. I had not dared phone her.

The cruelty of fate—was my karma so infuriated by a minor, drunken transgression that it would punish so barbarously? Perhaps this was not *my* karma at all, but the collected karma of past, wanton lives.

But I could endure much hell in exchange for a victory in this case. What a sweetness that would be.

Leroy was having the same problems with this witness that I had had in interviewing him at Tash-Tash. Very taciturn fellow.

"Like I followed Corporal Scanks. He saw everything first."

"But what did *you* see?"

"Well, the bodies, like. And Mr. Shiva standing there."

"Tell us in your own words."

"Well, Mr. Shiva was standing there in the middle of the bodies."

"Describe him."

"He was standing there mumbling something. Blood on his face, all around his mouth."

Lukey pulled teeth for about half an hour, then sat down exhausted.

"Something very peculiar about this fellow," Arthur said in my ear as he rose. All through his evidence-in-chief, Wendell had been deadpan. What emotions was he feeling, what had he felt back then? *All those dead fuckin' wind-up dolls. Hey, a guy could sell some of these pics to a magazine for big bucks.*

Arthur instinctively knew where to stick first. "What were your feelings, Mr. Joiner, when you saw this scene?"

"I don't know." Wendell gave Arthur a look from the sides of his eyes, nervous about lawyers' trick questions.

"You did feel something?"

"I was too surprised, I guess."

"Surprise, is that it?"

"I guess I was shocked, too. It looked like a war had happened."

"A war."

"Or something."

"Had you ever been to Om Bay before?"

"Not after these . . . people showed up there."

"Been there since December eighth?"

"Since? You mean after?"

"Yes."

Wendell thought about his answer, as if fearing a trap. "Couple of times."

"Speak up, witness," said Hammersmith.

"Yes, your worship." Louder: "Two or three times."

"Do you mean two or three times after the police investigators had quit the scene?" Arthur said. He was standing beside me at the counsel table, his arms folded.

"I guess."

"I understand you were there the day that all the buildings were burned down."

"I'm not sure what you mean."

"I think you do. You were with a group of men from Tash-Tash Cove who went to Om Bay on December twenty-second and burned everything down, weren't you?"

That's what Benjamin had told me. We knew Wendell would be hard pressed to lie himself out of this one: too many possible witnesses against him.

"I didn't do nothing. That was some of the other guys started the fires."

"A Saturday afternoon, three days before Christmas, and you and a bunch of yahoos from Tash-Tash Cove got drunk, went out to the murder scene and obliterated all sorts of possible evidence. That's what happened, isn't it?"

"I don't know about evidence. The investigators had finished there."

"So you thought it was all right to go in and raze the site, and sink the launch that was at anchor there, is that so?"

"No. I argued against it."

"I can't hear the witness," the judge grumbled, to no one in particular.

"I was against it, your worship."

"You were, were you?" Arthur asked with arched, disbelieving eyebrows. "And how much had you had to drink that day?"

"You mean before we went out there?"

"Oh, the drinking continued all day, did it?"

"I had a few drinks. It was just before Christmas."

"The witness is mumbling so," Hammersmith said.

Arthur filled the judge in. "He said, 'It was just before Christmas.' Three days before honouring the birth of the Prince of Peace, he and a mob of men from town besieged Om Bay, and captured that strategic site after heroic battle, sinking the enemy's entire fleet."

I was laughing and coughing at the same time.

"Were you ever in the armed services, Mr. Joiner?" This was an educated guess.

"Yes. U.S. Marines."

"What year was that?"

"I think 1968." The adventure of Viet Nam. Enlisting in the Canadian forces wouldn't have got him there.

"How long did you serve?"

"Three months," he said softly.

"*Please*, witness," said the judge.

"Three months."

"I see," said Arthur, leaving it at that, letting the jury wonder about the reasons for Wendell's abbreviated military history. One more question might have backfired on us— maybe Wendell had merely suffered a disabling injury in training.

Arthur seemed to be warming up to the task of really doing a job on this fellow when he was—as was much of the courtroom—diverted by what I considered to be an odious display of bad manners. Werner Mundt and Annabelle Beauchamp jointly stood up, shuffled down the bench to the aisle, headed for the door.

People come and go, of course, when a sitting is under way, and counsel are not usually distracted for more than a moment. But for Arthur's former wife to leave in the middle of his cross-examination—with Mundt in tow—suggested contempt for her ex-husband.

Everyone watched them go. I saw a few smiles. Mrs. Beauchamp's proclivities in the area of casual sex had been rich fodder for gossip among the trial set for many years. The walkout must have hugely embarrassed Arthur.

He lost it after that. The cross-examination became turgid, plodding.

He asked a few questions about the murder scene, got answers neither helpful nor hurtful. Wendell hadn't touched the bodies, hadn't talked to Shiva, couldn't remember anything Shiva had said, couldn't remember any trail in the snow. His observation was so vague, it was almost as if Wendell Joiner had never been there at all that day. I wondered: was this man sharing in the payoff that Scanks had received? If so, Arthur did not get it out of him, did not seem to have the touch to do so.

The witness could not remember having seen Bill Wheatley in Tash-Tash Cove on November twenty-fourth, or at any time. He had never met him. Yes, Wendell was a good friend of Eddie Scanks, and they shared a brew or two on occasion, but Scanks had never mentioned receiving any money in connection with this case. And that's as far as Arthur got along that line, Lukey insisting that the hearsay rule be enforced and Hammersmith making the standard speech about how counsel of late have tended to abuse the rules of evidence.

As Wendell stepped down from the stand, I was left with a feeling of emptiness, of incompletion—as if there was much more to be mined from the dank coalfields of this witness's memory. We had abandoned him too early, missing a rich vein.

We broke for lunch and I followed Arthur outside the courtroom. He was striding purposefully. I swore to myself I would have a word with Mundt before things got out of hand. That fellow was a gremlin, prepared to sabotage the defence to quench libidinal thirsts and perhaps vengeful ones as well.

I grabbed the psychiatrist, drew him aside for a private consultation. "You'll be most help to us, Werner, inside the courtroom, listening to the evidence. I don't see Priestman and Wang leaving while evidence is being given."

"Don't lecture me like a school child, Macarthur. It gets quite boring in there listening to Beauchamp take the mickey out of some poor benighted savage like that last fellow. I needed fresh air. Besides, I seem to have become merely window dressing in this case. Quite a waste of valuable time for me to be here at all, if I'm not to be used on the stand."

"I don't like you being out here with Annabelle Beauchamp, Werner, when Arthur is trying to do his job in court. He doesn't do his best under such circumstances. I hope you get the picture."

"You should have taken up the priesthood, Macarthur. Moralizing seems more your line than lawyering. Of which, in this case, you don't seem to be doing much. And speaking of cases, get off mine." He walked away.

I joined Arthur and Annabelle. "You boys will want to talk law, why don't I just let you be? she said. "Werner is going to tell me over a collins all about the patient who thought he was a werewolf." And she tripped off, took Werner's arm.

Arthur almost mashed his pack of Craven A's with his hands as he turned his back to them, put a bent cigarette to his lips. "I think we're wasting time," he said. "These Joiner brothers—they'll leave a bad taste in everyone's mouth, but I don't know how that advanced the cause of our client."

"Tom Joiner may be different," I said. "Unlike his brother, God gave Tom to the world packaged in the normal way, complete with heart." Tom Joiner had helped get my salt-soaked engine going on the docks at Tash-Tash. *I figured you was done a wrong.* I remembered how he had insisted frantically that at Om Bay he hadn't seen nothin', hadn't heard nothin', hadn't done nothin'. If Scanks, an experienced witness, had been afraid of this courtroom, Tom Joiner would be looking forward to the prospect with all the gusto of a virgin tied to the tracks. I had had the feeling that Tom was a weak link in the Crown's case. Cleverly handled, a scalpel not a sword, he could be exploited.

Arthur's thoughts were not, however, on this task. He stubbed his cigarette, only half-smoked. "Joe Whitegoose, that's who I want the jury to hear. When's he due?"

"A couple of days."

"I don't trust Leroy to remember to call him." He lit another cigarette.

Tom Joiner stepped up to the witness stand fiddling with the buttons of his faded, worn suitjacket, unsure which ones should be done up, which undone. He had not cut his blond ponytail, had poked it under his collar. I heard someone suck in a breath as he took the Bible in his two-finger claw hand.

As advertised, Tom Joiner didn't know nothin'. He had brought the fishboat into Om Bay, had watched as Scanks and brother Wendell went ashore in the dinghy, had observed them returning with Shiva, had seen blood on the lips of the accused. (What a horrible image. So easily dispelled if we were to know that Shiva had tried mouth-to-mouth resuscitation.) Tom had heard some "mumblin's," as he put it, from between those lips, but nothing he took note of or could remember. He did say, in vague answer to one of Lukey's vague questions, that Shiva seemed to "come out of it" after a while on the boat. I wondered if Arthur picked this up.

Arthur seemed barely able to pick himself up. He uttered a weary grunt, finally shambled to his feet, looked at Tom Joiner with distaste. Then he went on an attack that rebounded. He accused Tom, as he had accused Wendell, of being a member of the drunken party that had gutted Om Bay and sunk the launch on December twenty-second.

Tom insisted he had not been there, but with such trembling of voice and manner that Arthur did a misread. "You deny being there? And where do you say you were when all the other barroom bullies from Tash-Tash were converging on Om Bay?"

"I, uh . . ." Fiddling with the buttons. "I, uh, think—"

"Yes, yes? What do you think?" Arthur's tone was severe.

"Well, I'm chairman of the parish hall committee down at St. Mary-of-the-Fields, by the Indian reserve at Peale Island. I think I was decorating the hall that day, for a dance."

"I take it . . ." Arthur stalled, ". . . you have witnesses."

"Most of the parish hall committee, I guess."

I had warned Arthur: this man was not cut of the same cloth as his brother. I hated to see Lukey crowing quietly with his junior, hated to see Hammersmith's nasty smile.

Arthur, his pride injured, refused to accept defeat, lashed out at the witness more furiously, attacking him for being purposely vague in his evidence, suggesting in ungentle language that the witness was not merely unobservant but stupid. I think the jury was beginning to feel sorry for the man. "May I suggest that you and Corporal Scanks have agreed that Wheatley's name will not be mentioned in these proceedings? That you have conspired not to do so?"

Lukey kept his seat. Arthur had done no harm to this witness.

"No. I didn't. We didn't." He unbuttoned a button, did it up again.

"You saw Wheatley and two other men in a boat on December eighth. I put that to you."

"Didn't see them. Didn't see nobody that day."

"But you were out fishing then, that Saturday?"

"It was pretty foggy."

"Stop evading, witness. We know you were out trolling that day, and we know there was a salmon closure that day and you went out fishing just the same. No Fisheries vessel is going to find you in the fog, isn't that right?"

"Yeah, I guess."

"Did you have a crew with you that day?"

"No, no one, they didn't go with me. I didn't see no boats I didn't recognize. It was pretty foggy in patches." Again, the faltering voice, as if he were lying, felt guilty about it. Arthur seemed intent on proving that this chairman of the parish hall committee was in reality a doltish brute. I could see it was

not working. That small gold cross around the witness's neck:
the jury could see it, too.

Arthur had picked up on a small contradiction in Joiner's
earlier evidence. "You told Mr. Lukey you didn't go ashore at
all, but I suggest you did, after the police aircraft arrived. You
went ashore then, didn't you?"

"Yes, well, *then,* afterwards, I did."

"And you looked at the scene of the deaths. You wanted to
see all those bodies, didn't you?"

Tom Joiner worked furiously at the buttons. "I didn't," he
said. "I didn't want to see." Something was giving inside him.
"I didn't want to see. Oh, Jesus God." And he put his hands
to his face and began shaking.

This was terrible. Everyone's sympathies were with the
man. Arthur, not the witness, had come off like a bully.
Damn Mundt. Damn Annabelle. They had not come back
from lunch. Mundt, Arthur, and Annabelle were going out for
dinner again tonight. I prayed she would act responsibly.

Arthur seemed to have run out of questions. He sat down
beside me, uttering softly, "Christ, what a hash I made."

"Pause, Mr. Joiner," said the judge just before the witness
stepped from the box. This could be bad. Hammersmith,
unlike many bad judges, usually did not try to embellish
cross-examination with questions from the bench, but when
he did, he could cause irreparable harm. "You used the
expression, 'He came out of it,' when referring to your
observations of the accused aboard your boat. I am not
familiar with the, ah, terminology, to 'come out of' something. What did he come out of?"

"I mean he kind of changed, your honour. Not so much of a
daze, I guess. He said, 'Where am I? Who are you?'"

"He had been in a daze?" Hammersmith asked.

"He was kind of out of it, your honour."

"He was 'out of it' and then he 'came out of it.' How
curious. You may step down, witness."

This was okay. I was relieved. Even though we planned to
abandon the insanity defence, we could use this to suggest to
the jury why Shiva had not given evidence—he had no
recollection, i.e., was out of it. I was hoping Arthur would
follow this up with more questions, but he just sat there
drumming the fingers of his right hand, in sequence, upon
the table.

Arthur could relax through the rest of the day, get himself

together. Just the police scientists left this afternoon, not critical witnesses.

Sergeant Marven, the fingerprint man, came into the courtroom with an armful of charts. Loops, whorls, and arches, recurves and ridge bifurcations for half an hour.

"But most of the prints were impressed into drying blood."

"Maybe there were more underneath, Mr. Beauchamp."

The footprint man: twenty-seven separate impressions from Shiva's boots in the mud near the bodies.

The hair and fibre man: strands of manila fibre found on the sleeves and rope-skinned hands of George Wurz, matching the rope found in the shed. Nothing much we could do about this evidence—we would concede the possibility that Wurz was forced to tie his victims up, but under the gun of the deprogrammers.

Hislop, the ballistics man, was the day's last witness. Half an hour of breech face markings, firing pin impressions, trigger pull, bullet splash, and muzzle blast.

Arthur got a lot of interference from the bench while he was putting the witnesses through their paces. He was on temper's keenest edge all afternoon and finally, frustrated with Hammersmith's rulings, he announced it was the judge's privilege, being a judge, to be "*non rectum esse.*" Which means not to be right in court. Arthur continued to use the Latin for "right," i.e., *rectum*, in his snarling rejoinders to Hammersmith. ("It is the *rectum* of the court to guide us in matters of admissibility." "The court has a traditional *rectum*, of course." "The court, relying on its cherished *rectum*. . . .") During the twenty or so minutes of this pitched battle, the courtroom seemed strangled by an embarrassed silence. Except for me. I kept coughing.

The old judge will be gnashing his teeth all night, I thought, readying some unjust form of retribution for the next day. Hammersmith had seemed not unimpressed with the emerging outlines of our defence, and, less brusquely handled, might be more easily persuaded to give us a fair charge to the jury. However, Arthur was human, not a cold machine of the courtroom, and it was his *rectum*, as it were, to err. But damn Mundt, and damn Annabelle.

*   *   *

After we adjourned, I swiftly changed into my street clothes, Superman in the phone booth, raced my Daimler back to the office, began dictating letters on Augustina's files. John Brovak came ghost-like into the room, his bloodhound-sad eyes studying me as I rattled please-be-adviseds and find-encloseds into the dictating machine.

"Boynton, that smarmy Crown bastard," he hissed.

"Something happen in court today?"

"He ruined my public image. My good name is destroyed." Brovak drew from his pocket a page of transcript. "I asked him would he kindly not, I asked him as sweet as I could, but he did. Right in front of the judge."

"What is it?"

"A little wiretap a year ago, just when Twelve-Fingers Watson was thinking about hiring me." He read from the transcript. "Watson: 'I'm gettin' this new lawyer, Brovak, they say he don't give a fuckin' shit.' Unidentified male: 'Yeah, I heard of him.' Watson: 'Really knows his lines. In fact I did a few up at his place Saturday night.' Brackets laughter end brackets. 'He told me he thinks the system is shit, the cops are shit, the judges are shit.' Unidentified male: 'Sounds like a positive attitude.' Brackets laughter end brackets." John crumpled the page of transcript into an imperfect ball, looped it into the corner where it caromed perfectly into the waste basket.

"Suddenly the judge isn't laughing at my jokes any more. He thinks I am *cosigliaro* to Watson's bagging business."

I gave him an I-told-you-so look. "The Canons of Ethics say thou shalt not toot with your clients."

"You don't sound too empathic, Macarthur. I'm getting fucking short with this firm, man. Everybody drooling with sympathy for poor, innocent, bushy-tailed Augie Sage, and I'm bringing in twenty big ones a month—and that's all going to go by the board if I have to resign from this case."

"You'd better head off the posse. Draft a letter to the Law Society telling them the truth."

"The truth?"

"The truth is you never had Twelve-Fingers Watson up to your place ever, nor did you snort coke with him."

He brightened. "And furthermore, I've never committed such a repulsive, filthy practice in my life. I get your point. I'll tell the truth."

"What's the latest on Augustina?" I asked.

"She's gone fire-fighting. The big burn near Strathcona

Park. Sophie sent her up there to keep her busy. The cops talked to her."

"What did she say to them?"

"The truth, man. She didn't know anything about the escape."

The truth. I felt crummy. So many truths. I thought of Shiva, who would tell no version of it.

I finished dictating and went wearily home.

Dominating all in my mailbox—arrogant among lesser missives such as a bill from my dentist and a bulletin about a lettuce sale—was a thick letter in a blue envelope. Postmarked Mexico City. Ruth's bold ballpoint slants. Dated four weeks ago. The combined efforts of the Mexican and Canadian post offices had ultimately urged this hoary dispatch up and over the continent.

I made a cup of hot cocoa, and settled in to read it.

Darling,

I've had a pina colada or two. Or three, or four. A little tipsy, I think of you. Is that sad or is that funny? Most people drink to forget about others. When I drink, I remember you. I guess that is because pina colada makes me happy, and you also make me happy, and when I drink pina colada I naturally think of you. That make sense?

Wonderful sense, I thought. This *billet* from Ruth was uncharacteristically *doux.*

Marriage. "Grab him off, Mom," Jacqueline says, "before the Macarthur clan finds an innocent virgin of pure blood for him." *She claims I'm not getting any younger. I'm not.*

I started off by listing (see separate sheet) all the yes's and all the no's. The things about you and me that say, yes, it will work. And the things that say it won't. Are you ready to face the break from your family? Can you live with a fussy neurotic psychologist? Can I live with a workaholic lawyer with a martyrdom complex?

The bottom line is this, Max—I'm afraid of commitment. I'm not like your guru—I'm not into surrendering myself.

Suddenly I wasn't liking the tone of this.

The phone rang. A resonant voice rich with poetry.

"'Oh, come with old Khayyam, and leave the wise to talk—'"

"Arthur!"

"'—one thing is certain, that life flies; One thing is certain, and the rest is lies—'"

"Arthur, for God's sake!"

"'The flower that once has blown for ever dies.'"

Arthur recited those lines merrily, and from behind him came a roar, a waterfall of voices and music.

"'Ah, my beloved, fill the cup that clears today of past regrets, of future fears—'"

"Where are you? What are you doing?" Clammy fingers clutched at my heart. Arthur was into it. Well and deeply. "Are you drinking?"

"*Humanum est errare.* It is the lot of humanity to err. I am in a state of abandon. I am also in a state of abandonment. I have been abandoned for a randy goatee. What is a goat that fucks like a duck and is therefore a quack?" He made duck sounds. Their dinner had turned out disastrously. Had the snake-like Mundt envenomed the evening? I had a mental picture of him: a plump serpent with a goatee and a duck's quack, terrorizing our trial. "'Awake, for morning in the bowl of night has flung—'"

"Arthur, where are you? I'm coming to get you."

"'—the stars to flight.' Don't come. I fear I must remain at large. I am wanted for assault with a deadly weapon, to wit, a bowl of French onion soup with which an experimental form of wet cheese-and-onion psychotherapy was performed upon the inestimable alienist for the defence." Arthur could sound incredibly articulate when drunk. "My friend here has some words of wisdom for you."

"Arthur, wait—"

A boozy male voice. "Thish the Blacktop taxshi company?"

"Get the other guy back to the phone!" Little flutters through me, precursors to panic.

"Or is is Bluetop? Black and White. You got Black in y'r name ain'tcha?"

"I'll pick you up. Where are you?"

"Allus use you guys. Besht taxshi company. Hey, can you send a cab to, ah . . . ah . . . ." His voice moved away. "Hey, where the hell are we? I'll call you back."

"No, don't hang up!"

Click.

In utter dismay, I stuffed Ruth's letter into the pocket of my jacket, tossed it over my shoulder, ran in unlaced shoes from my condo, down to the garage. My Daimler squealed into the alley, up Yew Street to Fourth, heading downtown. I felt like murdering Mundt. Quackricide.

Granville Street. Arthur usually started off going up one side of Granville, down the other. I parked in an alley south of Theatre Row and began a fast prowl of the bars. Most would be closing soon—it was after midnight.

Granville Mall, one of Vancouver's more spectacular disasters, had been intended originally as a pedestrian sanctum from downtown traffic, but the idea got corrupted, and now there is a driving lane for buses, taxis, squad cars, and assorted lost tourists from California hunting for freeways. South of Nelson Street, just off the mall, Granville becomes Sleaze Street: strip shows, porno flicks, hash pipes, and French ticklers with hard rubber knobs on them. I checked out the bars here after finding no success in the Mall. Nor had any of the cops or crooks I encountered seen him.

The last lounge I tried was the Blackstone, where I gave cold shoulder to a hype with a jacket to sell. It was a few minutes later that I did a double-take, grabbed him by the collar as he was trying to deal the jacket off to some pool players. It was my two hundred and fifty dollar Italian leather jacket with explorer pouches. I had left it in my car.

"You filch artist," I hissed.

"No way, man, I got it from another guy. Forty dollars. I'll take thirty. Hey, let go of me." And he pried himself loose, ran for a back door. Outside, he was away, lost in the darkness. I went to my car—it had been stupid of me to park it in an alley—and found that neither window nor door had been jimmied. Absent-minded Macarthur had not locked the driver's door.

I sped over to Arthur's place on Cordova. His office was dark, his apartment—a key was kept under the mat outside— revealed an unmade and unoccupied bed.

Arthur could be anywhere within the great emptinesses of this city. But he was a trouper. He would show up for court.

I went home. I remembered: Ruth's letter was in one of the explorer pouches of the Italian jacket. Aw, God. I popped some antihistamines and lay in bed and worried about the morning.

21

○

Bicycle Accident

I can't remember if I slept that night. If so, it was a tense, peripheral sleep. My alarm nagged me out of bed at seven-thirty, and I did a physical checklist as I shat and showered and shaved: low temperature, one ear and both nostrils blocked, a mallet's soft thud in the forebrain.

I drove uptown to the Law Courts Complex, expecting to find Arthur there, hung over but keen for the battle.

But he wasn't in the locker room, wasn't in the library, wasn't at the coffee concession. I was suddenly seized by jitters. I phoned his home and office. No response. I called Amanda, asked her to check the hospitals. An accident—it had to have been something like that. Trials were Arthur's life, and he wouldn't let one drunken debauch ruin his career.

Mr. Justice Let's-Get-On-With-It was in a businesslike mood as he listened to my lies about Arthur's absence. Salmonella poisoning, a misadventure with a tin of smoked oysters, doctor says he'll be laid up for part of the day, my lord. I exuded a lying confidence.

Lukey was ready to go and had his witnesses here: the chief pathologist and two assistants, medical men who had booked this day off at great cost to the state. He and Hammersmith were bristling with an indecent zeal to keep the show on the road.

"I have had the privilege, Mr. Macarthur," said the judge, "of observing your, ah, abilities as expressed in other matters that have come before me. I should think that Mr. Beauchamp shall not be missed for the duration of the day. Learned prosecutor says his witnesses are all straightforward and will be giving the kind of scientific evidence that counsel of your experience will have no difficulty with." He tendered a rare smile. "Particularly since we all heard Mr. Beauchamp advise us yesterday that his junior had briefed himself to cross-examine the medical witnesses."

It was true.

Hell, I was tired and suffering, but somehow I felt ready. And ambitious for this chance. And not wanting to seem cowardly. Once they think you're scared around here, the wolves single you out, a crippled antelope trailing behind the herd.

"I'm ready to proceed, my lord."

Mundt was among us this morning, but was not wearing the suit with the French onion soup stains. He never once met my eyes, and I was intending to wait until I was more settled down before confronting him. No Annabelle. The faces of reporters and courtroom groupies were ravenous and expectant, hungry for sacrifice. Always, the sad-eyed parents of the murdered.

I gravely indicated to the jury that I was proceeding in Arthur's absence due to illness. The jury looked sympathetic.

There was a piece of cross-examination to finish from yesterday. Hislop, the ballistics expert, identified the four .30-.30 cartridge cases that we had entered as an exhibit.

"Yes, I examined these, and concluded all four had been fired from the same gun."

In rebuttal, Lukey asked if the spent cartridges appeared to have been out in the weather.

"Yes."

"Can you say how long?"

"Not at all."

The chief pathologist was an Ichabod Crane whose bones were draped loosely with epidermis and whose voice sounded as if it were coming from inside a funeral parlour. "My name is John Borden Magruder and I am chief pathologist at Vancouver General Hospital." He paused. "Pathology is the study of disease."

I felt sorry for the jury. Brains, livers, lungs, and kidneys. Twenty-two separate sets of these. Mr. Prebbles, our queasy junior, showed many moments of distress, crossing and uncrossing his legs, but he seemed more steeled to gore than in the earlier days of this trial.

In summary, Dr. Magruder's evidence was that all deaths but Emelia Cruz's were caused by propellants ripping through brain or heart. All had died instantly, or nearly so. All had received bullets at close range: there were powder burns on scalps and necks and backs of all those tied and executed, and on the chest of the one victim who had been shot from the front. All but Cruz had died between eleven o'clock in the forenoon and one o'clock in the afternoon, he said.

By noon adjournment, the chief pathologist had finished his evidence for the Crown. I intended to spend the lunch break polishing my questions. My task would be to show the deaths could have occurred at about nine A.M., when Wheatley, Morgan, and Calico were still in the area of Poindexter Island.

But first I grabbed Mundt, on his way to the elevator, spun him around by the elbow, and drew him into a shadowy alcove. "I've heard that half the world's psychiatrists are masochists and the other half sadists. You're an exception. You're both. Only a sadist would so cold-bloodedly go for another man's testicles. And the masochist in you wants to bring this trial crumbling down around our ears. Don't you care any more? We don't let you play, you won't stay, is that it? What did you do to embarrass him? Tell him that you and Annabelle planned to spend the night fucking?"

He brushed away at the elbow of his suit, where I had dared touch him.

"What went on last night?"

He stared dark-eyed and cool at me. "Quite frankly, I'm not sure. She got quite soused, and perhaps a little malicious. I would have been pleased to withdraw if I could gracefully have done so, but I was the host. I really had no other role to play."

"To hell with that—tell me what happened."

"It is debatable how much of my private life is your business, Macarthur."

"Look, you're a smart man, Mundt, so you should be able to digest the following piece of knowledge: Arthur is on a tear. He has disappeared. You've known him, Mundt—a long time. And you know what this can do to him and to our trial."

"Macarthur, one of the traits of personality you possess most bountifully is a certain arrogance. I think you'd love to finish this trial on your own, and win it. Circumstances may have conspired to impose greatness upon you." He took out a small comb and ran it through his hair. I wanted to slap it out of his smarmy hand.

"What happened, Werner? He didn't dump a bowl of soup on you in play."

He began stroking the comb through his goatee. "There was an awkward incident. While he was in the washroom, she leaned over and kissed me. She was quite drunk."

"On the mouth."

"It was quite out in public, I'm afraid. He came back too soon. But everything seemed civil at first. He was in high spirits. He poured himself a glass of wine and downed it. Then, when the waiter brought my soup, he turned it onto my lap. That happened out of nowhere. He walked out. I am not the culprit you make out."

"Bullshit. Did you sleep with her last night?"

"Macarthur, you are exceedingly bold. Incidentally, I have that report about Shiva's breakdown in the 1950s. You'll be interested. I'll courier it over."

I looked disgustedly at him, wheeled, walked toward the law library. "Pick up Scanks yet?" I yelled at Storenko, who was standing about with other police witnesses.

"Be patient," he said.

While in the library I received an urgent message from the office. Amanda had located Arthur in the Lion's Gate emergency room. From Annabelle Beauchamp's neighbour, from the West Vancouver police, from Arthur's physician, she had sewn together the sad story:

Last night, Arthur must have taken a taxi to his former home, on the cliffside over the ocean, near Lighthouse Park. Finding all doors locked, he had found a ladder, climbed up to the tar-and-gravel roof, where he kicked through the plastic bubble which served as a skylight to the master bedroom. In crawling through, he fell, missed the bed, landed on Annabelle's exercise bicycle, injuring his lower back. Annabelle had not been home. At ten this morning, a neighbour responded to Arthur's cries, called the police, who made entry and summoned an ambulance.

It was a drunk's luck there were no broken bones, but a severely sprained back would keep him in hospital for several days, and he would not be able to get on his feet for several more. He was under sedation.

How to break this news to Hammersmith? A possible ten-day to two-week continuance seemed unavoidable. I would seek Arthur's advice at the end of the day.

* * *

"Dr. Magruder, let us eliminate one of your hypotheses. Let us suggest you don't have Corporal Scanks' evidence that the bodies were not in rigor mortis at two P.M."

"Yes."

"That expands the area of time of death, doesn't it? To somewhere before eleven A.M.?"

"Yes."

"A corpse doesn't begin to lose much warmth until about three hours after death, isn't that right? The cooling curve isn't exponential."

"That's right, Mr. Macarthur. The skin surface doesn't begin to cool much until the interior body temperature has significantly fallen."

"It's common, is it not, when seeking estimates of time of death, to insert a thermometer four inches into the rectum and make hourly observations to determine the rate of cooling?"

"Yes."

"And that was done in the cases of each of the twenty-one corpses?"

"I've indicated that, yes. But of course it wasn't until the following morning that the bodies arrived at the morgue."

"However, you did then commence to take hourly readings of the temperatures as the bodies cooled?"

"We can't place too much reliance on rectal temperatures here. Too many variables: size, build of body, outside temperature, wind, amount of clothing worn."

"You are, of course, familiar with the formula of Marshall and Hoare?"

"Yes, they developed a series of theoretical cooling curves."

"Here's one of their examples: a naked body, sixty-nine inches in height, a hundred and sixty pounds—you don't mind if we're somewhat unmetric—lying supine in still air at thirty-two degrees Fahrenheit." He peered at the graphs I laid before him. "This example describes a person of about average size."

"I suppose."

"And in fact if we take the mean of the heights and weights of the twenty-one corpses, the figures comes to sixty-nine point five inches in height and one hundred and sixty-two pounds."

I passed him a pocket calculator. He shook his head. "I'll accept your mathematics."

"Generally speaking, the factor of clothing reduces the body cooling rate by a third, isn't that so?"

"Approximately."

"Taking that into account, taking also into account that the outside temperature was just below freezing on a windless day, and the morgue temperature was about the same, the bodies were cooling at the rate of one point three seconds per hour."

"Let me look at your figures. Yes, one point three, that's the mean."

"At nine-thirty A.M. on the ninth of December, the mean inner body temperature was sixty-two degrees Fahrenheit?"

"Yes, I accept your figures."

"And at three-thirty, six hours later, it was fifty-two degrees?"

"Yes."

"Using the Marshall-Hoare formula, that would bring the time of death on December eighth closer to nine A.M. than to noon, wouldn't it?"

Magruder hesitated. "I can see what you're getting at. Well, all I can say is that's possible."

"You're familiar with the works of Bate-Smith?"

"Yes, he's the author of a major text."

"I quote from a paper he presented to a Hamburg medical conference in 1963. 'Attempts to calculate time of death based on onset of rigor mortis or rate of body cooling, alone or in conjunction, are fraught with potential errors and cannot be presented as definitive or reliable.' Do you agree with that?"

"Well, yes, I'd have to say I do."

"Thank you," I said. "No more questions." I sat down, quite delighted with myself. Nothing like a good cross-examination to drive the gloom from the day.

I dealt quickly with the remaining two assistant pathologists, who did us no damage. Indeed, one of them agreed it would be hard for a layman, even a policeman, to determine whether a corpse had entered rigor mortis unless he were to try, for instance, to bend back some fingers or flex a knee. Scanks had admitted he did no more than look at the faces.

Hammersmith, a man we had described in the Hotel Vancouver washroom as a miserable old vulture, not only laid off me for the day, he even slapped Leroy's ruddy cheeks three or four times for daring to interrupt my crosses. The more punishment Lukey took, the more obsequious and slave-like he became. *Hit me again, O benevolent lord, thou art so good to me.* I, however, was treated like a knight just back from the Crusades. Courtroom 54 was my banquet hall. The day was in honour of Sir Maxelot, Knight of the Swollen Ego.

But my ego whispered to me: don't look into the eyes of Shiva Ram Acharya, the invisible accused.

Later, in the barristers' washroom, where I was taking a hard-earned piss, Lukey engaged me, coming up to the neighbouring urinal.

"It won't be long now, like the man said who stuck his prick in the meat chopper." Lukey gave a contented cowlike sigh as he let go. "Just Indian Joe tomorrow, a few odds and sods to fill out the week. Then I can just sit back, relax, listen to your bullshit. You going to put your Buddha on the stand, Max? Act of God, that the defence?" He laughed, gave a couple of bumps and grinds, and made a one-handed zip of his fly. "Ouch!"

I chuckled. "As you said, Leroy, it won't be long now. Only one thing worse than pecker tracks on your zipper, and that's zipper tracks on your pecker. Maybe you should call off your witnesses for tomorrow. Arthur won't be with us." No harm being truthful: Leroy had known Arthur a long while. "He tore up the town last night, sprained his back. We're looking at a week's layoff at least."

Lukey followed me to the sinks. "Not that I don't trust you guys with your tales of salmonella poisoning and sprained backs, but I'm going to protect my own back. I'll be ready with my witnesses in the morning."

* * *

"*Hic jacet Beauchamp,*" Arthur said groggily. One of his legs was raised in a sling. They had shot him up with Demerol. "No one will tell me what happened."

"You can't remember?" I had brought gifts—A Sony Walkman and cassettes of *Othello* and *Macbeth* with Olivier and Gielgud.

"I awoke in pain on the bedroom floor of my ex-house. Earlier, the last thing I can remember is walking along English Bay beach, reciting from *War and Peace*."

"I'll have to tell the judge you had a bicycle accident. You fell on one. The doc thinks it'll be some time, then you can get a cane. Hammersmith won't like the idea of a long adjournment."

"He can't force you to proceed unless the client consents. Damn, but this is lamentable. What a weakling I've been, what a fool."

"No way, Arthur." I patted him on the arm.

"Max, if you think you can win this, the trial's yours to finish. The Wheatley defence is yours anyway."

"I don't think so, Artie." But I felt the temptation all right.

* * *

At the office that evening, after calling Benjamin Johnson at Tash-Tash, arranging for him to come in mid-week, I joined my partners in the library for an office meeting over a case of beer. Augustina was absent, fighting the big fire on Vancouver Island. Brovak moved we cut her loose, got no seconds.

"You're a dork," said Sophie. "She'll be a good lawyer yet."

Brian Pomeroy, although miffed at a vote censuring him for sneaking off to play golf today (his clients left angrily after four hours), agreed to join me in Court 54 tomorrow in case I needed an extra gun at my side.

"You don't need help," Brovak said. "I popped in today. Hammersmith was sucking your cock."

"He won't like the delay," I said. "Maybe he'll order a mistrial."

"Not his style," Sophie said. "It's his last case. He wants one last, sweet conviction for his memories."

"Are you kidding?" I said. "This is going to be the biggest win since Daniel versus Lions."

"Macarthur," Brovak said, "you always impressed me as having an overstuffed idea of your courtroom talent. Why don't you go for the gusto?"

"I'm going to tell Shiva we won't proceed without Artie." But what a chance I would be giving up, my ego said softly to me.

"Reason for this bout of cowardice, folks," said Brovak, "is if Max blows this case he could look like something the cat regurgitated."

I drew Sophie aside later. "You talk to her?"

"Uh-huh. I didn't lie. I pleaded you guilty, told her I

thought you were scum, but that there were exonerating circumstances. She's reserved sentence. You can try to make repairs this weekend, you've got too much on your plate now."

22

○

Dying Declaration

In court the next morning, Hammersmith and I had a *tête-à-tête* in the absence of the jury.

"Mr. Macarthur, while your senior recovers from his, ah, condition, we cannot have a jury loitering gainlessly in their hotel rooms. We can't keep them locked up for ten days or two weeks like common criminals."

"Mr. Beauchamp has been retained," I said. "The accused has a right to counsel of his choice. Your lordship of course needs no authority for that." I was speaking breathlessly. I had rushed into court late, no chance to talk to Shiva. One of my trusted clients, Louie the Loot, had got busted with a fence's warehouse of stolen goods, and I had been up to the city cells to see him before racing to the courthouse to tell the judge, sans jury, about how Arthur, just recovered from salmonella poisoning, slipped, fell, threw out his back.

Hammersmith began wheedling. "Mr. Macarthur, this court is aware that you are well-tried in battle. Your cross-examinations of yesterday might serve as a primer for some of the more embarrassing excuses for counsel who have been appearing before me. I cannot but think the law schools are negligent. They attempt to imbue their students with much radical zeal for so-called law reform, but nothing of the nuts and bolts of the courtroom. In my day one learned through hard experience. Experience, that is the school." He paused to get back on track.

"But as I say, you are an exception, Mr. Macarthur, and you lack the flabby intellectualism of some of your fellows." Should I have felt complimented? "And I see young Mr.

Pomeroy is assisting you. He has distinguished himself in my court as well."

He was benevolent, grandfatherly. He didn't hold a grudge from the guffawing incident in the Hotel Vancouver washroom.

"If your lordship would consent to adjourn, perhaps until the weekend, we can report then on Mr. Beauchamp's—"

Hammersmith cut me off. "How many years have you been at the bar, Mr. Macarthur?"

"Five."

"Did you know that I did my first murder when I had been called three years? And four more within the next two years. All prosecutions—but it's the same, ah, responsibility, don't you agree?"

I nodded. He was talking to someone hot to be seduced. How enjoyable, I was thinking, to continue being senior counsel for a little longer. Had not my name seen bold print in the morning *Province*? Had not last night's TV announcer so lovingly tongued that same name on the news? And had I not been suffering with ambition for the big trial, secretly masturbating dreams of glory? And was not the trial going our way?

Back to reality.

"I am simply not in a position to alter the fact that counsel far more senior and able than me is on record for the defence, my lord."

"I wonder what your client has to say about this. Mr., ah, James?"

Fast, before I could get to him, Shiva, who had so far not uttered a word in court, who had refused even to take the plea, said from behind me: "I should not only be delighted but honoured to have Mr. Macarthur proceed on my behalf."

When I turned around he was looking right at my middle eye.

All the courtroom seemed quite awed that the man could speak at all: Shiva Ram Acharya, alias Matthew Bartholomew James, part of the quiet decor of Court 54, like the official reporter or the clerk or Patricia Blueman.

I found myself startled at how his quiet words filled this great room. If only the jury were here: a man who speaks so gently and urbanely must be innocent.

"Break a leg," Pomeroy whispered, "you're on."

I found words. "Ready to proceed, my lord." And I suffered a small anxiety attack. I was going in as second-string quarterback with no coaches to send me the plays. Would I throw from the end zone the intercepted pass that would turn the contest against us? (Linebacker Big Bill Wheatley flattens the passer.)

I realized that Shiva in so publicly proclaiming confidence in me had just put me to the test—his test. The courtroom was a laboratory for the study of my ego—how would events swell and twist and warp it? Could they shatter it? And would this Shiva, this avatar of the Indian god of laughter and practical jokes, have a merry time at his lawyer's expense?

The first juror in was always McIlheny, the foreman, and as always he scanned the courtroom, his eyes lighting for a second on every face. He looked at me, in Arthur's chair, then at Pomeroy. And I saw his gaze rove about the courtroom for Arthur, then touch upon the psychiatrists' bench, where sat Mundt the rake.

When my eyes followed McIlheny's to the back of the room, I saw Jacqueline there, neat, unobtrusive. Her mother must have had something to say about the orange hair.

Dear Ruth. I thought: I would get through this trial and heroically remake my life.

"Calling Joe Whitegoose," said Lukey.

Whitegoose shuffled into the witness box, eyes shyly cast down. In his soft Kwakiutl-accented voice, he began to tell the story of December 13. The judge, too gruffly, told him to keep his voice raised, and Joe tried to do so, without looking up, without seeing what was going on around him.

He described finding Emelia Cruz on the rocky beach by his cabin, carrying her unconscious to his bed, radioing the RCMP from his boat, returning to the cabin to make fish soup. It all came out well, and the jury seemed to be giving Joe sympathy, knowing he was very nervous. Lukey, however, acted the subtle bully, standing stoutly by the witness box, gripping the collars of his gown, making his questions sound faintly like accusations.

"Now we should ask the jury to leave, my lord, for the balance of the morning," he said.

"We're not there yet," I said, standing up. "The witness hasn't even mentioned she spoke any words before she died." Get that tidbit out hard and fast to the jury.

Hammersmith excused them until two P.M.

I think the U.S. system is better, where questions of admissibility are usually settled before the trial begins. Here

we were, a few days from the end of the Crown's case,
seeking on a trial within a trial to know whether or not the
jury could be told Emelia's dying words. Mr. Justice Carter
would certainly have been for us. Hammersmith—well, don't
count your chickens, but he had recently been sweet on me.

Whitegoose then described how Emelia recovered briefly,
opening her eyes.

"And what did you say?"

"Making fish soup."

"You said that or you did that?"

"I guess both. I do it and say it."

"'I'm making fish soup.' That what you said?"

"Yes."

"And then?"

"She moves her lips, and I come close, and she says, 'Did
they kill everyone? Am I alive?' And she closes her eyes,
says, very soft, 'Am I alone?'"

Beautiful. I loved him.

"I find no breathing, no heart. I guess she is dead."

"My lord, that is the evidence for the Crown on the *voir
dire*," Lukey said. "Unless my friend has some questions, the
witness may stand down?"

"I have no questions now. I may have some when the jury
returns."

"The Crown takes the position that the words of Emelia
Cruz are inadmissible as hearsay."

"And your friend, doubtless, takes a somewhat, ah, altered
position," said the judge. "I will hear argument."

I went first, happy to have the advantage of laying out the
doctrine of dying declarations in a chronological, develop-
mental way, the kind of argument The Hammer likes, lots of
old cases.

The rule against hearsay evidence is ancient in our law, the
reasons for it still as telling as they were centuries ago. It's
dangerous to subject a person to a trial on the words of those
he can't challenge in court. Nor should one, in fairness, be
entitled to a defence which relies on the words of witnesses
not present. But dying declarations are among the various
species of exceptions to the rule. It has long been held that
words spoken by someone under a settled, hopeless expectation of death are entitled to be weighed: when there exists no
future on this earth, there exists no excuse to be false.

One big hurdle: establish that the deceased knew, when

she spoke those words, she was *in articulos mortis*. The critical thing is not that Emelia Cruz died shortly after she spoke those words—it's whether she knew she was dying.

I gave Hammersmith law from 1633 to 1983, English, Canadian, Commonwealth, and American.

My argument was twofold: Emelia Cruz was so badly injured, suffering so from exposure, that she could not have known otherwise than that she was dying. Her words, "Am I alive? Am I alone?" gave rise irresistibly to a conclusion that she knew she would soon not be alive—and no longer alone.

I wasn't sure what to read into Hammersmith's demeanour. He took notes, marked passages in the Xeroxed cases I handed him. But he listened to Lukey well, too, although he interrupted from time to time, asked questions and gave examples. Leroy made a good argument, I will admit.

I finished my rebuttal with a flourish, pounding home the fairness aspect. Could we risk having a man convicted because a jury was denied evidence to exonerate him, evidence of the most trenchant character? Are our laws to be so rigidly interpreted as to cause such a miscarriage of justice? (Beware of the Court of Appeal, I was warning him. Go into your retirement leaving us one, if only one, memory of fairness.)

"Not bad," Brian said, as I sat down. "But if you think you're in front of Oliver Wendell Holmes, you're dreaming."

"Gentlemen," said the judge, "I shall have to reserve. I dislike to do so, but this matter troubles me. Mr. Sheriff, tell the jury they have the day off. They will not be returning until tomorrow at ten A.M."

Court adjourned. Shiva seemed to be smiling to himself as he left.

I drove Jacqueline to a steak house on Davie Street. "Pretty decadent," Jacqueline said of the swank decor here, a former West End mansion. "Hey, order some wine, then sneak me some. A nice Bordeaux." She gave me a sly look, checked to her right and left for spies. "A certain party is prepared to enter negotiations this weekend. It hasn't been easy, but after Sophie spent an evening with her, I followed up with the old one-two punch. You're worth saving. By the way, you were just gal*van*ic in court."

* * * *

An unexpected afternoon off. An extraordinary September afternoon, the sun resuming a benevolent despotism after a few days of wispy cloudiness that had seemed to write closed, finally, to this endless beaming summer.

By now eighty per cent of the mass of land that is British Columbia had been placed off bounds to all human beings without permits. Those were hard to get unless you were a volunteer. Two hundred and five forest fires had broken out this summer, and forty per cent of those were burning now—an odious record. The people of B.C., an unemployed lot this summer of our continuing recession, had responded with great character to the crisis, and no conscripts were needed by the forest service. The forest is the economy of this province. It is all.

Over a coffee and Vitamin C tablets on Robson Street, I read gloomily the story in *The Province* of how fiery teeth were nibbling at the toes of Strathcona Park, a vast naturalists' paradise. That's where Augustina Sage had gotten permission to go. She was undergoing cremation, she told us on the phone, black with filth and smoke, every muscle screaming. She loved it. She was being repaired in the process.

I was determined to use this free time to repair health, vowed to run and sweat and steam and bring this cold to its knees. I knew I hadn't the strength to best any personal running marks, and dared not try to, and did a jog around Stanley Park in sweatsuit and neck towel, savagely chasing the cyclists from my path. Then I ran six miles back, the other way. The germs poured from my cells with the sweat.

After swimming, steam-bathing and showering at the YMCA Health Club, I was ready for Arthur.

The Walkman was on loud and his private room at Lion's Gate was gently singing with voices from the Old Vic. Arthur was frowning, his leg still raised. He turned the tape off. He smiled when he saw me. "I hear the client forced you on. Did you know he was going to do that?"

"Shiva has a sense of humour. He thinks he's having a joke on me."

"But you got Hammersmith to reserve on the dying declaration. That's very good. I can think of only five times he's ever reserved on evidence in cases I've had. Well, Max, you're now counsel of record. And if you're the lawyer I think you are, you're ambitious for this chance."

"Arthur, I know this is going to come out sounding like something from the script of a B movie, but I'm going to win this trial for you. I don't have your skills by a long shot, but I've watched you in every major trial you've done since I was in first-year law. It'll be your victory because what I'll do will be what I've learned from you."

"Be careful of Lukey. He's a viper."

They hit Arthur up with some pain-killer after a while. I waited until he fell asleep, then drove home. I sat in the sauna for an hour, recovered from that under the warm September sun on my penthouse deck, then more sauna, more sun. I figured I had broken the back of this cold. Everything was going to be good.

On my way to a neighbourhood sushi bar, I saw an interesting headline inside a newspaper vending box. The subhead read, REUNION OF THE M'GARETHYS, and below it, the banner: *MELISSA-JUNE IS GOING HOME*. I dropped a quarter in and pulled out a copy. My preliminary reaction: annoyingly, I had been dumped from the front page. My argument as to the dying declaration had disappeared from page one of the early edition, was now buried in the guts.

Dominating the front page was a group photograph, stylized, like something out of 1920—an oddball family dressed up for the travelling photographer. The three M'Garethys in front, a sorrowful-looking Mrs. and Mr. at either side of Melissa-June, formerly Astral, who looked quite lost. Some business-suited men behind. A young man with strange eyes standing among them, in a robe with a cowled hood.

Melissa-June M'Garethy came back to her parents this morning, saying she had been told to do so by a messenger from Antares.

The three-member M'Garethy family stood united in a bizarre, hastily-convened press conference held at ten A.M. in an anteroom of a Bayshore Inn suite. Ms. M'Garethy, 19, who nearly two years ago deserted her parents' Boston mansion to join a series of religious cults, stood between her mother, Edith, and her father, J.J. M'Garethy, former Governor of Massachusetts and reputed to be one of the richest men in North America.

Behind them, for the four minutes the conference lasted, were Dr. Francis Descartes Mangus, chairman of religious studies at Harvard University, and a group of security men and lawyers. Also present was an unidentified man in a long, hooded white robe.

M'Garethy read a prepared statement about the circum-

stances of the reunion, then his daughter was called upon to speak.

Ms. M'Garethy, who was without makeup, wearing a flower-patterned cotton dress, said simply: "I am happy to be with my parents. I am going to live with them for several months in Switzerland."

One of the lawyers then abruptly called a halt to the press conference, but as the family were being led away, Ms. M'Garethy turned around, and in answer to a reporter's shouted question as to why she was returning to her parents, she said: "I was told to by a messenger from Antares."

Antares is a red giant star in the constellation Scorpius, and is 420 light years from the solar system.

I was out on the street, laughing loudly, enjoying this latest episode of the saga of the M'Garethys. Raba-urt-Jogan, doubtless the fellow in the white robe—was he a mercenary who had decided to tap into the family fortune? "Several months in Switzerland"—a locked-door sanatorium, likely, with expert brain-dewashers.

I wondered if Wheatley et al had anything to do with this brain-napping. But Dr. Mangus, a Jesuit and a leading Catholic philosopher, was unlikely to get involved with such as Wheatley.

The press conference started sharp on the announced hour of ten A.M.—reporters late arriving were barred at the eighth-floor elevator door—with the introduction by one of the lawyers of the three M'Garethys and Dr. Mangus.

In his statement, M'Garethy said he and his wife had spent "several days" meeting with Ms. M'Garethy at a location on the B.C. coast he did not specify. He credited Dr. Mangus with effecting a "philosophical and emotional coming-together" between parents and daughter.

Ms. M'Garethy is known to have associated herself with a series of sects after she ran away from home Dec. 20, 1983. A deprogramming attempt was made last June by Rev. William Wheatley, a Vancouver-based deprogrammer, but was abandoned after kidnapping charges were filed against him.

The article went further into background. No doubt Melissa-June had by now been placed in one of the M'Garethys' executive jets for an Astral-travelling journey to Switzerland.

23

o

The Sword Descends

Before leaving the office in the morning, I received via a delivery service a small envelope from Werner Mundt. Inside was a letter from Mundt (which did not contain an appropriately abject apology that he had decided to render after a sleepless, guilt-racked night), but rather an account for his services rendered. The envelope also contained a two-page photostat of the medical report from Philadelphia we had been waiting for, from a clinic where Matthew Bartholomew James had been committed for five weeks after his breakdown at age eighteen.

A severe depression for the first few days, said the report. Followed by mild manic-depressive states. Lithium carbonate drug therapy had been indicated.

Mundt, with a red pencil, had drawn a rectangle around a paragraph on the second page: *After six days, it was determined to consider the patient for release under a voluntary rehabilitation program, but during one difficult occasion on the seventh day, he went into an extreme rage, throwing and breaking objects in his room, even attacking one of the male attendants, trying to choke him and bring him to the floor. The patient had to be strapped into his bed until calmed by an injection. Rages of lessening force and duration followed for approximately ten days. Much of his conversation during this time seemed to consist of reflections about death. Therefore a twenty-four-hour watch was kept on the young man until it was felt that this dangerous phase had been worked through.*

I was shocked. I had persuaded myself that Shiva was—to an excess—non-violent. No, I didn't like this. I wondered if the Crown psychiatrists had this information. Good thing we had decided to abandon the insanity defence—this little business of attacking an attendant now wouldn't get before the jury.

I tucked the report deep into the Shiva file and went to court. I would worry about it later. Mr. Justice Hammersmith could send this trial's tide to flood for the defence this morning. With a fair ruling, I'd worry less about Shiva's refusal to take the stand.

The judge crept in. A silence. An "ahem" as he adjusted his glasses, peered into the dim wasteland below, then began reciting the facts relating to the dying declaration. Finally, his decision:

"The rule against hearsay evidence is so ancient, so fundamental to the common law, that it has shaped evidentiary jurisprudence." Foggy, heavy words. The law reports had been ignoring the old man of late, his judgments being too political and sour. This was The Hammer's last chance to get into the Dominion Law Reports, Fourth Series.

"The slow erosion of the rule is weakening the very pillars of our laws of evidence." I was getting uneasy. "One rarely argued exception to the rule involves dying declarations. Never in the history of English or Canadian courts has the exception been expanded to include cases in which the declarant did not know he was on the point of agony of death. I will not take the liberty of expanding the exception in this case."

Oh-oh.

"Learned counsel for the defence, who delivered a most able and lucid argument—" the compliment, now the knife— "asks me to find in her words a suggestion that the declarant knew, as she spoke, she was at death's door. 'Am I alone? Am I alive?' My impression is that the words constitute babblings of someone not in her right mind. That being the case, they could not qualify as a 'declaration' at all, let alone a dying one. But if I am wrong, I find these words are an affirmation of her awareness of life. The question, 'Am I alive?' carries the sound of hope, not hopelessness."

I was surprised, outraged. Deep in my heart, in the hungry depths of that ego whose captive I was, I had believed I would win this argument. I had been flattered by my own ambition into thinking Hammersmith had miraculously changed into a reformer in this, his career-ending case.

"I must therefore find the words of Emelia Cruz not to constitute a valid dying declaration so as to be admissible evidence before the jury."

He had set me up. It was vengeance for my vileness in the Hotel Vancouver washroom. I was the kitten, he the sadist, and he had played with me, befriended me, then strung me up with a hangman's noose.

"Learned counsel for the defence makes much point in arguing that the jury should not be denied forceful testimony— albeit from a party not before the court—that might point to the accused's innocence. Hard cases make bad law. Our rules are given to us by centuries of tested practice...."

I stopped listening to this diatribe. Pomeroy, who had been speaking to an adjournment in another court, settled into his seat beside me, and whispered: "Your problem is you're a dreamer, Max."

I don't think the fog of anger lifted even after the jury came back, after Leroy Lukey rendered the witness to me.

I found myself staring at the witness door as Joe Whitegoose came shuffling in. There was silence. I pulled myself to my feet.

"Mr. Whitegoose, on December eighth last year, five days before finding Emelia Cruz, were you out on your boat laying crab traps?"

"Yes." He raised his eyes to look at me. I gave him a weak smile. He looked down at his hands.

"And conditions that day were foggy?"

"Fog here and there. Patchy, you know."

"And you were in waters not far from your home, near the south end of Poindexter Island?"

"Yes."

I showed him a marine chart, one of the exhibits, and he pointed to a spot just off Desolation Sound which I marked with red ink.

"And did you happen to notice any other vessels in the area that day?" Did my voice sound controlled or merely stiff? I was determined to get something back here.

"Yes, one boat. I maybe hear others in the fog, but just see one. I am there three hours from nine o'clock, maybe nine-thirty."

"And did you give a description of that boat to anybody?"

"I give to . . . the RCMP."

"Who?"

"Mr. Scanks."

I glanced at Lukey, who was looking at the witness with a sceptical expression. That, for the jury. Was he surprised by this? Had Scanks kept this to himself, as part of the deal with Wheatley?

"When did you describe the boat to him?"

"He comes from town to speak to me, day after. He ask me to tell him any boats I seen on the Saturday, day before. I said just one."

"What time did you see that boat on the eighth?"

"Just about after eleven."

"How far away?"

"Half a mile, she come out of a patch of fog, moving fast, too fast, so I went to see it through the binoculars. Cabin boat with maybe t'ree men inside, I can see them moving around, and it say *Doodle Dandy*."

"Boat like this one?" I showed him one of the pictures I had taken of that boat. Leroy didn't seem prepared to object, just lolled in his chair, faking disinterest.

"Yes."

"Could you see the three men clearly enough to identify them?"

"No, but three big men, I think." Joe had originally told me three or four men. I was happy with this little gift.

"Now I want to ask you about December thirteenth, about finding the girl." This would be dicey. I was not sure how much guts I had. "It's true she came to consciousness upon your bed?"

"Yes, she opens her eyes."

"And you had conversation with her?"

Lukey growled loudly: "My friend should be very careful."

"You're premature, Mr. Lukey," said the judge, "but frame your questions carefully, Mr. Macarthur."

"You and she spoke words?" I asked Whitegoose.

"Yes."

"What did you say to her?"

"I say I am making some fish soup."

"And she moved her lips, and you came close to her, is that right?"

I struck. This was for Arthur. "And she asked, 'Did *they* kill every—'" My voice was drowned in a gushing, sputtering Niagara of words from the table to our left. I had surprised myself: I had the balls. Now let them cart me off to jail for contempt.

"I ask the jury be removed." Lukey spoke with machine-gun burps. "I ask the witness be removed. An utterly *brazen* defiance... I ask this court to deal with my friend... the jury should be removed, my lord...."

I let the jury see an astonished innocence play upon my features.

Hammersmith looked like a kettle aboil. One could almost make out little spurts of steam from his ears. "The jury will be removed." His voice a terrifying whistle. "We will take the morning adjournment. We will assemble without jury and witness in ten minutes."

As the jury were led out, I caught the eye of Margolis, the economist. Almost a smile there, almost. The rest of them looked scared and confused.

His lordship descended from his dais and I grabbed Brian's sleeve. "Quick, I need a lawyer."

"What are you, some kind of courtroom Evel Knievel?" As Lukey charged, Brian grabbed Phipson on Evidence, twenty-third edition, began scrambling through it.

"Okay, you little cocksucker, I've had enough. I'm playing hardball now."

I exploded back at him. "You bombastic mountebank, you want to play hardball, play hardball, get your big hitters out there, where've you got Wheatley hidden? Put him up there for me to cross, goddamnit—"

"Hammersmith is going to find you guilty of contempt, asshole—"

"Stop playing peekaboo with your goddamn case, get it out front—"

"He's going to thin your wallet, asshole—"

"—and stop trying to hide behind stupid rules of evidence—"

"—and give you a few weekends in the slammer, asshole—"

"Eat it, Leroy."

A crowd of reporters watched all this. I walked out past them. "Get the facts straight, ladies and gentlemen: I told him to eat it."

I stood by the balcony railing, looking over the bustle below. I was glowing within. The jury had heard me clearly. They would understand that some legalistic mumbo-jumbo had prevented them from hearing the most telling bit of evidence of this trial.

When court resumed, Hammersmith, still simmering, inquired of me if I was prepared to show cause why I should not be cited for contempt.

"May it please your lordship," said Brian in his gloomy voice, "I will undertake to show, on Mr. Macarthur's behalf, why there was no contempt. Not a scintilla of it."

Hammersmith squinted, identified the speaker.

"The words Mr. Macarthur put to the witness were not put for the truth of them, but for the fact they were spoken. The jury of course can't consider the dying words as evidence, but merely as words." Brian backed up this gobbledy-gook with passages from Phipson, artfully taken out of context. "On that basis, the jury are entitled to hear the words but must of course be warned not to treat them as evidence of the truth of matters stated." He smiled benignly up at the judge. "Your lordship has ruled the words are inadmissible for the truth, that's all, but the fact that the words were used is just that, a fact, part of the surrounding circumstances."

A long pause. The judge took off his glasses, wiped them, polished them, slid them back on. Had Brian's incoherencies somehow struck a weakened cord in The Hammer's tenacious mind?

"And with respect, my lord, the witness didn't answer the question," Brian continued, seeking to drive in the wedge. "The fact counsel speaks words doesn't make them evidence. Anyway, I think Mr. Lukey interrupted before the jury could get the effect of the question. No harm done."

Somehow Brian stayed the judge's wrathful hand. "I had hoped for better," he said, "considering the name you carry, a name you obtained from a distinguished legal family. It is good for your future at the bar that your question was interrupted in mid-sentence and before the witness could answer. Otherwise, I would consider, ah, sanctions. Bring the jury back."

And they filed in. Now if only Hammersmith could ask them to disregard what I said, my day would be made.

"Members of the jury, if you heard any of counsel's last question to the witness, you will entirely disregard it. What counsel said was not evidence, was spoken improperly, and cannot in any way enter into your deliberations."

Wonderful, I thought. Emphasize it. Leave my words ringing in their ears: *And she asked, "Did they kill every—"* Oh, I had nearly screamed that plural pronoun.

Joe Whitegoose was brought back in, reminded by the clerk he was still under oath.

"Do you have any further questions?" Hammersmith said, his voice sibilant.

"In view of your lordship's ruling, I haven't." I sat down brusquely, letting the jury know the defence had been the victim of a miscarriage of justice.

Lukey sat for a moment, considering. Then he stood. "I have some re-examination, m'lord. In fairness, because of what transpired, I think the Crown might be allowed some latitude."

"I agree," said the judge. That meant that Lukey was being allowed to cross-examine his own witness, to put to him the kind of leading and provocative questions that prosecutors are permitted to ask only of witnesses called by the defence. This was bad.

Lukey went over to the witness. "Joe, how long have you lived up the coast, there?" Patronizing.

"All my life."

"You're a native Indian, no secret about that."

"Kwakiutl."

"Go to school up the coast?"

"Maybe. Indian school."

"What I mean, Joe, is did you ever go to a real school? Learn to read and write?"

"A little, maybe."

"When you talked to Mr. Macarthur in July up there, did you sign a statement for him?"

"Yes."

"And did you read it, first?"

Joe shook his head. But Benjamin had read it to him. I felt sorry for Joe, too afraid to amplify, to explain.

"So you don't know whether it's the truth, do you, Joe?"

"I don't know."

"English wouldn't be your first language, would it? You were raised speaking an Indian dialect?"

"Yes."

"And sometimes you don't hear English too well, yes?"

"I don't know."

"How old are you?"

"About seventy, I guess."

Now Lukey walked to the opposite side of the courtroom, beside the jury. "And how's your hearing?"

"I don't understand, mister."

"You don't *hear*, isn't that it?"

"Maybe."

"And you didn't hear Emelia Cruz very well, either, did you? As she lay dying, her words weren't clear at all, were they?" His voice was up now, hard.

"Maybe," was all Joe could say.

"You told us you had to bend close, and you missed some of the words. I suggest you didn't hear any of the words at all very well."

"I don't know. Maybe." This was depressing.

Lukey lowered his voice a little. "'Did he kill everyone?' Did you hear that? I spoke four words."

"I hear," said Joe.

"What did I say?"

"I think you say, 'Did they kill everyone?'"

I felt air hissing from my pores. Lukey stood chest out like a fusilier guard. "Thank you, witness." He sat down.

I stood up. "Re-cross-examination," I said.

"I deny leave," said the judge. "Your next witness, Mr. Lukey?"

Lukey turned around and looked up at the big clock on the wall, surveyed the galleries, beamed a glance at me that was triumphant in its hostility. "May it please your lordship," he rumbled, "the prosecution closes its case."

I gave a jump, like a startled cat.

Lukey sat down.

"What's this?" said Brian from the side of his mouth.

"I don't know." I stood up. "Learned Crown counsel informed us he had eighteen more witnesses on his list."

"I'm not calling them," Lukey grunted from his chair. "My *friend* can call them if he wishes."

"Are they not to be produced for cross-examination?"

"I won't force the Crown to do so," Hammersmith said sharply, still exacting revenge for my transgression. "Let's move along. What is your election, Mr. Macarthur?"

"Election? The Crown hasn't finished its case."

"Oh, yes, I have," Lukey said.

"What about Scanks? His cross-examination hasn't been finished, my lord. The defence can't be denied its right to complete that."

Hammersmith started. He, and probably Lukey, had forgotten all about Scanks. But my concern was that the judge, having taken a position, would be too stubborn to back down.

"I was under the impression Mr. Beauchamp had completed," he said.

"Not at all, my lord."

"Mr. Lukey, I take it there is no, ah, guarantee this witness will return to us in the next few days?"

"No, he's vanished."

"I see no solution, Mr. Macarthur. Mr. Lukey has suffered, too, he is unable to re-examine his witness. The defence did its damage, and has the better of it."

"Then I move that all of Scanks' evidence be stricken from the record, the jury told to ignore it."

"I will not do that."

"I move for a mistrial."

"Motion is denied."

"We're caught by surprise."

"Are you saying you're nor prepared?"

I would be damned if I'd have it look that way. I'd be damned if I'd get on my knees and beg for understanding.

"We're electing to call evidence, my lord. I ask fifteen minutes to bring my witnesses in."

"We will take the morning break," the judge said.

I didn't want a mistrial anyway. I was prepared. My witnesses were here. That jury would be listening hard to my address. Margolis was mine for sure, I could tell it in his eyes. Two or three other probables, and the rest would be brought along. As far as I knew, Lukey owned no one for sure. But there would be weak people on the jury, gullibles who hold the state can do no wrong, is too even-handed to prosecute an innocent man.

While Brian corralled our two witnesses, I ran down to the lockup to see Shiva. "I haven't thanked you for reposing your trust in me," I said.

He just stared at me.

"I'm going to demonstrate triumph of mind and ego, Shiva. I'm going to win."

"Win your *maya* battle in your *maya* courtroom. Let me recommend this Upanisadic prayer. Pray it tonight. Pray it until you're at peace." He recited in what I guessed to be Sanskrit, then in English: "'From the unreal lead me to the real. From darkness lead me to light. From death lead me to immortality.'"

A cold little worm wiggled up my spine. "'From death lead me to immortality.'" I repeated. "Would you have been happy, Shiva, if they had restored the death penalty for murder? It's martyrdom you want, isn't it? Acharya, the teacher. You think your teachings will spread only if you're crucified in a courtroom. The cult will grow and engulf the consciousness of the masses. I'm not going to play Saint Paul to your Christ."

I flounced up my gown and returned to the courtroom.

Brian came in leading Barney Hinkle as I was halfway through my opening to the jury. We of the defence, I told them, were pointing a deliberate finger at other parties and would continue to build a case of opportunity against the Wheatley group by putting them physically into the rented boat that Joe Whitegoose had seen, proving they were the men who had been racing at eleven A.M. from the direction of east Poindexter Island and Om Bay. I would prove, through another witness, that .30-.30 bullets had probably been fired on that same day, demonstrating beyond peradventure not only that there were at least two killers on the scene, but that the Crown's theory was stuck together like wet tissue.

"Mr. Barney Hinkle, please take the stand."

With his hale, service club voice, Hinkle was an easy, relaxed witness. He described his operation, Tyee Rent-a-Craft, south of Campbell River, and identified my photograph of the *Doodle Dandy* that Wheatley, later I, had rented.

Yes, he could also identify Wheatley, Morgan, and Calico from their photographs, filed as exhibits. No, he didn't see what they carried onto or off their boat. They checked out the *Doodle Dandy* in the dark of the morning, returned it three minutes before noon. He had processed Wheatley's Visa while the others loaded the Winnebago.

He produced copies of the receipt and Visa forms, and they were filed. Wheatley's name was on them clear as neon.

Yes, Hinkle said, they had enough fuel to get as far as Om Bay and back. They had ordered extra fuel tanks.

"You didn't see them packing any firearms?" Lukey asked.

"No."

"See how many persons got off the boat?"

"No, I was busy with Mr. Wheatley."

"When he was paying the bill, did he look like someone who had just murdered a bunch of people?"

"Not exactly."

"That's all."

Benjamin Johnson's evidence went okay. He described the finding of the .30-.30 cartridge cases in the creek and by the willow tree, identified them and the pictures I had taken at the scene, and described the *chaitya* on the hill.

"You don't know when those cartridges were placed there, do you?" said Lukey.

"No, sir."

"Could have been there ten years or two days. Did you see Mr. Macarthur wandering around that area before you found these things?"

"That's a low hit," I snapped.

Benjamin was good. "He was nowhere there before I found them."

Lukey humphed and sat down.

"That is the evidence for the defence," I said. I surprised myself, finishing so quickly: it was only eleven forty-five. I looked at Shiva, who looked at me, and I felt an unease, a tremor of it, in my testicles. The courtroom seemed strangely oppressive.

"You're calling no further witnesses?" The judge peeped down at me, at Shiva, looked at the jury. Observe, he was saying silently, that the accused has not chosen to take the stand.

"The defence is in," I said.

"Rebuttal?" he asked the prosecutor.

Lukey sat there for a while, kind of spread out, then his belly started to roll, and it came to me he was chuckling. My testicles continued to tingle. Lukey stood with a contented sigh, and said, "May it please the court, the Crown's first witness in answer to the theory of the defence is Dr. Francis Descartes Mangus of Boston, Massachusetts."

It was one of those old Perry Mason shows. Voices buzzing. Eyes darting everywhere. Bodies shuffling. The witness door opened. Short, dapper, wry-looking. Intelligent eyes in the shadow of beetle brows. Stepping forth from the back row of that front-page photograph in *The Sun*.

"Do you promise to tell the truth, the whole truth, and nothing but the truth, so help you God?"

"Yes." Mangus placed the Bible down.

"Where do you live, sir?" Lukey said.

He gave an address in Boston.

"And your occupation there?"

"Chairman of religious studies, Harvard University."

My pen was slippery with sweat in my fingers. In my mouth there was dryness.

"Can you tell us what degrees you have?"

"I obtained my priesthood at Le Sacré St. Mathieu in Lyons, France, then took a Ph.D. in comparative religions at Cambridge. Lacking the power to make creative decisions, I became a teacher."

A nice self-deprecating touch. The voice was cultivated, with a Boston sound.

"And you have taught on the faculties of five universities during the last twenty years?"

"My last five at Harvard, where I was offered the religious chair."

"Honorary degrees?"

"Notre Dame, Arizona State, Chicago, Tel Aviv, the University of Berne. Another one . . . I can't put my handle. . . ."

He was a hit with the jury, the absent-minded professor.

"Yale. It's no wonder I forgot."

Chuckles.

"You are the president of the Society of Jesus, New England Province?"

"It's almost an honorary position. I'm afraid I don't work very hard at it."

"And you're the author of several books, doctor?" Lukey was beside the jury, a winsome smile on his lips. I was having trouble not squirming. What was up?

"Yes, several. Well, eight, but three are merely texts. The rest of them, rather stuffy religious tomes."

"Did one of them win some sort of prize?"

"*Estasy and Guilt: Religions of Western Man*. The Sonnenschein Prize."

"And you've written a book about cults in America?"

"*The Excursive Religious Experience in America*. It never made mass-market paperback." The wry smile.

"And you've written learned papers?"

"I've written, yes, mostly for academic journals."

"How many times published?"

"Oh, I never stopped . . . perhaps a hundred and twenty or thirty."

"And your subjects have included cults, deprogramming, that sort of thing? I know I'm leading, my lord—"

"Carry on," said the judge.

"Yes, well, I've made studies of so-called cults. I prefer to define them as excursive religions; the word cults has a somewhat pejorative ring to it. So, I suppose, has the word deprogramming. I use it, but in the sense of awakening a person's mind to the reality of personal religious or philosophical choice."

"And have you performed any deprogrammings?"

"I've participated in a number. Out of professional interest, I might add, not for a fee."

"In fact, you've recently been in the news with respect to such a matter—the M'Garethy case."

"Yes, it's the matter that brought me back to Canada, to your province. I recently spent a few days with the M'Garethy girl. We had some interesting talks."

"Culminating in a reunion with her parents."

"It seems a truce, as it were, has been joined."

The jury would know this, too. Only stories of this trial were clipped from their newspapers.

"You know a certain Reverend William Wheatley?"

"I do. I met with him on the weekend."

"And when did you first come to know him?"

"Last year, in the month of December."

"I will ask you to relate the circumstances of that."

Mangus wrinkled his nose as if it had encountered an unpleasant odour. "Mr. Wheatley. Yes, well, I met him at the M'Garethys' fishing lodge. Maybe I should start earlier. I was requested by Mr. and Mrs. M'Garethy to assist in this matter perhaps a year or more ago, a few months after their daughter, Melissa-June, vanished into the religious wilderness. I consented to counsel the girl—if they found her—on condition that she would agree to talk to me."

The jury were all cranked forward. I was nothing more than a petrified pair of ears attached to a scribbling hand.

"Early last December I was summoned by telephone to the M'Garethy—"

"Don't tell us what he said, professor, what did you do as a result?"

"I cancelled, to the relief of many, three days of classes. I flew here to Vancouver, then was met by one of Mr. M'Garethy's associates and flown by amphibian craft to his lodge."

"His fishing lodge," said Lukey. "And where is that?"

"Two hours by air up the coast, and I can hardly be more specific than that."

"How far from Poindexter Island?"

"I think it's nearby, I can't be sure."

"He doesn't know," said Hammersmith, "leave it at that."

The M'Garethy fishing lodge. I remembered the newspaper story: "a location up the B.C. coast he did not specify." M'Garethy had hideaways all over the world, why not his own lodge in the world's finest salmon waters? I had never heard of it; M'Garethy was wealthy, could keep his places secret. *How far from Poindexter Island?*

"Continue, professor," said Lukey.

"I arrived there on Friday, December the seventh. The plane that brought me there left. Mr. and Mrs. M'Garethy were alone there—I was surprised, there's usually a retinue. I was given to understand that Melissa-June would be brought—"

I was too frozen to object, but Lukey cut the hearsay off. "You expected to see her?"

"Yes, the next day."

"All right, what happened the next day?"

"Hang onto your britches," Brian whispered. I could hear the click of the guillotine as it released above my neck.

"At about seven-thirty in the morning, Mr. Wheatley and his two ... friends arrived at the lodge. A rented boat."

The blade descends slowly, a nightmare.

"Mr. Calico and Mr. Morgan?"

"Yes." He smiled.

"And what did you understand your role to be at that place on that day?"

"I would, as I said, have been happy to counsel Melissa-June. I think Mr. Wheatley had his own plans."

The blade descending.

"Please don't tell us what anyone else said. What did those three gentlemen do that day?"

"Well, really ... nothing. To be quite frank, I arrived there in some innocence and was never apprised as to how Melissa-June and her parents were to be brought together. It struck me that the M'Garethys seemed surprised that their daughter was not in the company of Mr. Wheatley and his two friends when they arrived."

"Okay, what happened?"

"I had a mild row, I must say, with Mr. Wheatley, and with the M'Garethys, as well. I knew Mr. Wheatley by reputation, and frankly—and I told him to his face—I wasn't pleased to see him there, particularly if he were proposing an act of force with respect to the girl. It was a difficult matter. I insisted to Mr. and Mrs. M'Garethy that I should leave. Apparently Mr. Wheatley abandoned any plans to take Melissa-June forcibly—I hope at my insistence—and became quite gentlemanly after that."

"Yes?"

"We all had tea. Mr. Wheatley used the two-way radio to try to arrange a flight out for me, but apparently nothing was flying in the weather, very fogged in. I agreed to return to Vancouver Island in Mr. Wheatley's rented boat and catch a ferry from there."

The guillotine blade touches skin, begins a gentle incision into flesh, into the bone that protects the spinal cord.

"And you left by boat with Wheatley, Morgan, and Calico?"

"Yes. To Campbell River. To a fishing boat rental. It took us two hours. We were running dangerously fast, I thought, in a patchy fog."

"What time did you leave the lodge?"

"It was a few minutes to ten. We got there, oh, about noon."

The head bounces into the waiting basket. Leroy threw out his bosom like a cock at dawn: "Did you by any chance *stop* anywhere en route to Campbell River?"

"No, sir."

"And for what period of time that Saturday, December eighth, were you in the company of Wheatley, Morgan, and Calico?"

"Seven-thirty in the morning until—it was one-thirty in the afternoon when their Winnebago dropped me at the ferry near Nanaimo."

"And while they were in your presence, Dr. Mangus, did they happen to *murder* anyone?" The penultimate word was elephant-trumpeted.

"I'm afraid not," Mangus said.

I remember thinking: how oddly he phrased that. *I'm afraid not*. I reluctantly have to admit. It seems a pity, but. They *do* seem the type, but they didn't do it, and I regret the inconvenience to the defence.

Lost in morbid contemplation, for a moment I didn't know where I was, what I was doing here. Obviously I was part of some medieval ceremony, monks about me in black robes, the high priest—a large, sunny-faced man—swirling in gross ballet. I can understand amnesia now, for I was in that state of nowhere in that courtroom. Just my moving hand, a pen writing but forming no words on the lined paper of my binder, furious-looking, Schaeffer-nibbed, five-pointed stars, row after row.

The high priest flapping onto his chair with a contented cackle like a hen to roost. His words: "Your witness." I recognized that voice. *I'm playing hardball now.* The dam broke and the whole disaster came flooding over me. I knew what I was doing here; I was simmering in a kettle of coconut oil while the cannibals drooled all around me.

"Any cross-examination?" said the judge.

"Get it on, get it on," Brian was urging beside me. I looked at his mournful, grey silhouette, past it to the big clock on the wall, twenty after twelve, ten minutes to lunch break. Arthur Beauchamp might have had the stamina to come out counter-punching, but Max Macarthur could seek only to be saved by the bell.

I felt my knee joints click together, and I was in a standing position. "Since it's moving toward the noon break, my lord, perhaps we could adjourn now to avoid interrupting my cross-examination."

Dr. Mangus gave me a sympathetic smile. He was a nice man.

"We'll resume ten minutes early then," said Hammersmith. "Ten minutes to two, everyone."

"Order in court!"

As everyone stood for the judge, I turned around. I met the eyes of Shiva Ram Acharya. They were laughing at me.

24

o

Dies Irae

"Drink this slowly," Brian said.

Sprawled on a soft chair in the barristers' lounge, I groaned, accepted from him the carton of chocolate milk.

"You look like the revenge of God," he said. "I heard one of the radio reporters at a pay phone. 'The defence counsel was visibly shaken.'" He waved some breeze into my face with his clipboard.

The milk slid like sand down my throat, met the bile in my stomach. I breathed slowly in, slowly out. Brian extended to me a tuna sandwich.

"No, just the milk." I groaned again. "Hardball's one thing, but he didn't tell me he was going to throw a strike at my head. What am I going to do?"

"You get in there like Rocky Balboa. You finish the fight." He gave me a funereal look, sat down beside me.

"Let's brain this, Brian. Shoot something by me. An answer."

After a moment: "All right, Max, there's a conspiracy here, and that smiling, self-deprecating religioso is in on it. We're talking about M'Garethy megabucks here, enough to buy Mangus and Harvard University, too. He's too goody-good-good. Too damn holy and wryly Jesuit. He's a phony. Go after him."

He said this in a turgid voice without conviction.

"This guy is a Catholic mensch, Brian."

"Expose him. Do the cross of your life."

"He has no axe to grind, despises Wheatley. He's straight. S-T-R-A-I-G-H-T. As in shooter. As in arrow."

"Then make him unstraight. Bend him a little. *Put* things to him."

271

"Maybe he still beats his wife. Maybe he used to masturbate."

"Maybe he's been promised a hundred square miles of downtown Boston."

"Maybe he doesn't brush his teeth every morning."

"Maybe he was a witness to these murders, Max. Didn't do anything about them, didn't say anything, fears he'll be an accessory."

"Uh-uh."

"They've threatened to kill him if he tells."

"Not even a good try."

"Wrong day. It was the Saturday before. Absent-minded professor—turn that to your advantage." With each suggestion, Brian seemed more lugubrious.

"I know what he'll say. 'I'll never forget that day, Mr. Macarthur.' They've got the M'Garethys and Wheatley and his two dodos to confirm all this." I sat up hard. "My God, Brian, I have wronged those men. Why did they keep silence?"

"Lukey made some kind of deal with Wheatley to suck us in," Brian said.

"A *ruse de guerre*," I said. "We were farm boys at the skin show, and Wheatley was the shill. Lukey even got us to abandon our insanity defence. But why that prepared alibi of Calico's and Morgan's? Why the bribery of Scanks? Something's out of kilter. Think, Brian."

"Mangus is a fraud, an actor hired to impersonate the famous religious philosopher. Lukey wants this conviction so bad he had the real Mangus chloroformed, put in a locked closet."

"Come on."

"Wheatley hypnotized him so he can't remember the stopover at Om Bay. Mangus fell asleep, missed the whole thing. Maybe Hammersmith will let you reopen—you could call Mundt."

"Mundt." I laughed hoarsely. It would be like retaining a Red Army terrorist to guard the Saudi jewels. "No, no Mundt."

"So what's your answer?"

"Maybe I'm defending a guilty man."

"Max, you've hitched your wagon to Wheatley, and you are just going to have to ride it."

"Even if it goes over the cliff."

* * *

Back in court, I mustered a shallow air of confidence, so transparent the jurors looked upon me with pity. I think most of them had begun to like me, and were embarrassed.

I guess it was the worst cross-examination I have ever done. Pecking around for flaws, uncertainties, inconsistencies, I only had the witness repeat his story, add body to his evidence.

I tried to alter the time frame, chisel out a little unaccounted-for half hour when they could have been at Om Bay. I tried to get Wheatley, Morgan and Calico arriving at the lodge at eight-thirty, not seven-thirty. I put it to Mangus he was a forgetful man, and he agreed, was deferential, but had no doubt of Wheatley's arrival time at the lodge.

My questions began to take on the tone not of an accuser, but a believer, and the jury could tell I knew in my heart of hearts that this was a man of credit.

I explored at the fringes, inquiring why he had agreed to help counsel Melissa-June after having left the M'Garethy lodge in anger ten months ago. After Wheatley's bungled try last June, the M'Garethys had apologized to him, he said, and agreed to let him try to counsel the girl without interference.

I hinted weakly about offers of rewards, and Mangus scolded me like an errant child. Only expenses had ever been paid. No bequests, no advantages given to himself or any institution. As for Eddie Scanks, the professor had never met with nor heard of him.

My fuel tank emptied fast and as I sat down I sensed an air of finality in the courtroom. The drama had been mis-staged, the climax had been brought on too early, the verdict would be a mere clerical act, a conviction stamp on a Form Five Warrant of Committal.

"Calling Mr. J.J. M'Garethy," Lukey said.

The billionaire ex-politician came briskly through the witness door, as if rushed for time. Strain was buried in furrows upon his face, hard lines where his jaw muscles worked.

Leroy Lukey went confidingly close to his witness, prattled about how, in this difficult time, when he would wish to be close to his daughter, we would try not to detain you long, sir.

M'Garethy spoke with a brittle, crystal voice; his words were splinters. There was not a wink of humour about him. "I had announced a fifty-thousand-dollar reward for information leading to my daughter. On November thirtieth last, Mr. Wheatley contacted me by telephone."

"I'm afraid you can't tell us what he said. We have silly things like rules of evidence."

"Get *on* with it, Mr. Lukey."

"What did you do as a result of the conversation with Mr. Wheatley?"

"He flew to Boston at my request. We made an arrangement."

"What was that?"

"Shortly put, he would rescue Melissa-June and bring her to us. My wife and I would help him convince her to return home. I paid him a hundred and fifty thousand dollars. We later arranged we would do this at my fishing lodge on Bute Inlet. I insisted on Father Mangus attending. We met—my wife, myself, Father Mangus—at the lodge Friday evening, December seventh. Mr. Wheatley had told me—"

"There, that's the kind of stuff, I'm afraid—"

"Sorry. I was under the impression that Melissa-June would be brought there the next day by Wheatley, but he and Calico and Morgan arrived by boat early in the morning without her. There were several sharp words between Wheatley and Father Mangus, and under the circumstances I told Wheatley to abandon whatever plans he may have made as to my daughter. I didn't ask him, frankly, what those plans were, and I don't know to this day."

Nor time nor words wasted. A man whose empire turns over a hundred thousand dollars in the time it takes him to complete a syllable.

According to his evidence, the *Doodle Dandy* bearing Big Bill, Wimpy, and Jack arrived just after seven-thirty, as a printer was rattling off the week's closing trends on the N.Y.S.E. The three, accompanied by Mangus, left precisely at ten A.M., just before M'Garethy received a scheduled one P.M. e.d.t. call from his attorneys in New York.

Om Bay and the east side of Poindexter Island, he testified, would be a half-hour run by boat from his lodge. At no time had Wheatley, Morgan, or Calico left that lodge until they departed with Mangus.

"I understand Mrs. M'Garethy will not be gracing us this afternoon," Lukey said. "Perhaps you might be so kind as to tell the jury why."

"We felt it was important for her to be with Melissa-June

on the flight to Europe. I suppose we have to thank you for not forcing a subpoena on her."

At the mid-morning break, I walked quickly and alone from the courtroom, avoiding all eyes. I went to a toilet cubicle in the barristers' washroom, pulled down my pants, sat. What had I been saying only three months ago, leaving the courthouse after taking the Hammering on A-OK Books and Novelties? About the human shells the courtroom casts out, about fearing I'd be crippled by the harsh practices of the criminal law? That fear was on me hard again.

My anal muscles kept their grip. Maybe that was a good sign.

I had nothing to lose now by asking open-ended questions. I needed information—something to hang a defence on.

"Mr. M'Garethy, you're aware that twenty-one persons were murdered that day you speak of, December eighth, at Om Bay, not far from your lodge."

"I know what I've read and heard about it."

"Did you know where your daughter was that day?"

"No."

"Hadn't Wheatley told you he believed she was at Om Bay—"

"Objection!"

"Sustained."

"You feared she was one of the murdered, didn't you?"

"I took some trouble to ascertain she was not."

"We can assume you greatly cherish your only child, your daughter Melissa-June."

"You can and should."

"I read in the papers that you had a yacht designed and built for six million dollars. A hundred and fifty thousand seems a comparative bargain for your daughter." I was urged on to recklessness by my despair.

M'Garethy gave me an icy stare and spoke icy words: "The hundred and fifty thousand was paid in advance as Wheatley's expenses. I told him if he were to succeed in getting her back to us, I would pay him two and a half million dollars."

That brought a stir in court. I was shocked at the sum.

"And you've paid the two and a half million?"

A hesitation. "I don't know if my dealings with Wheatley need be matters of public fact."

"They may be matters of interest to this court, however."
Perhaps I was onto something.

Lukey to the rescue. "M'lord, the defence shouldn't be
allowed to go on a fishing expedition."

"Not unless the object is to catch fish," I said. "I assure the
court my questions go to relevant matters." Not much
Hammersmith could do about this.

"On that assurance, proceed," he said.

I looked down at Brian, who gave me a why-not-go-for-it
look. "You've paid the two and a half million dollars."

Another hesitation, like a little nibble on the line. "In total,
I've paid slightly in excess of that sum."

"And in what instalments did you make these payments?"

"In mid-June of this year I was instructed that Wheatley
had located Melissa-June in a Universal Church lodging near
Vancouver. I paid him seventy thousand dollars."

"In expenses. Cash?" I recalled those thousand-dollar notes
in Wheatley's wallet.

"Yes."

"In addition to the hundred and fifty thousand paid for the
previous December's aborted kidnapping?"

"The word kidnapping was never mentioned, Mr. Macarthur. I
didn't discuss Mr. Wheatley's methods with him." I felt
another tug on the line. Resistance.

"It's called turning a blind eye, Mr. M'Garethy."

"Please get on with it," said the judge.

"And the next instalment?"

"Five hundred thousand dollars."

"In cash, expenses, no receipts given?"

"If you like."

"When?"

"A month ago."

"And the next payment?"

"Two million."

"Surely not in cash?"

"It was arranged by my lawyers through a bank in the
Bahamas, I know nothing more."

"Why have you recently paid him this huge sum, Mr.
M'Garethy? Did Wheatley have something to do with the
recent rescue, as you would put it, of your daughter?"

"I can't see that that is relevant."

"Mr. M'Garethy, you determine what's relevant in your
boardroom, but his lordship makes those decisions for the

courtroom." Lukey started to get up, thought better of it, sat down. "Please answer the question," I said.

"He did have something to do with it."

"What?"

"He, well . . . put it together."

"That's not very plain. The half a million given to him a month ago—that's a lot of expense money. What costs was it intended to cover?"

"I hope you know what you're doing, young man. Certain matters aren't within the knowledge of my daughter."

"Not within mine, either. We're dealing with twenty-two counts of murder in this courtroom, sir."

M'Garethy looked to the bench for help, but the judge said nothing.

Raba-urt-Jogan, from the star Antares, those guru eyes in the photograph. The world coming to an end at dawn on last Saturday. Love Apocalypse. Go with Raba. Yes, half a million dollars could buy such an extravaganza. I spoke slowly. "It sounds as if this latter operation was a costly production. Where did you find your daughter last weekend? Where was her commune?"

M'Garethy gave me a look of biting hostility. "At a place I own."

"Your fishing lodge?"

"Yes."

"You hired a group of professional actors."

"I didn't make any of the arrangements. Mr. Wheatley did."

"But you knew those arrangements had to do with hiring actors, about a dozen for this little religious order of Raba-urt-Jogan from the star Antares. Tell us about it, Mr. M'Garethy."

He drew a tongue over his lips. "Very well. I believe you were the attorney for the Moonies when we were in court last June, Mr. Macarthur. Wheatley failed to deprogram my daughter on that occasion. He argued for another chance. I acceded on the basis that no violence would attend her rescue and that we would use Father Mangus to counsel her. We knew through our detectives Melissa-June had escaped from the Moonies and was living in some sort of hippie den in Victoria. Wheatley retained an actor through an agency in Los Angeles."

"And he made contact with her."

"Yes."

"And played the guru very well."

"My daughter is in sanctuary now, but if she hears about this, I will hold you responsible, Mr. Macarthur. I don't know what you think about her, young man, but her psychiatrist advised us that although she's quite intelligent, she's capable of falling quite rapidly under the power of suggestion. In other words, she hypnotizes easily. That's what these people do, you know." And he actually gestured at Shiva. I could see how M'Garethy got his reputation for being ruthless.

"So you're saying the man Wheatley hired was a hypnotist as well as actor?"

"I believe he had done night-club performances in that field."

"So I take it your daughter was under hypnosis during that press conference yesterday in the Bayshore Inn."

"She was not."

"And maybe throughout the deprogramming done by Dr. Mangus."

"She was of free mind, able to make open choices."

"And that half-million to Wheatley—that was to fund the costs of this dramatic production?"

"Most of it." M'Garethy seemed to regret this answer. "I don't know."

I dove in like a cormorant. "Who else did he pay?"

M'Garethy tongued his lips again. "Do I have to answer these questions?"

Hammersmith waved Lukey back to his seat. "You're in a court of law, Mr. M'Garethy," he said.

"I believe," the witness said slowly, "he may have paid someone off."

I ploughed recklessly ahead. "Who did he pay off and how much?"

"He promised there'd be no interference from the police."

"Police protection?"

"I don't know the details."

"This drama was staged at your fishing lodge. What RCMP detachment has jurisdiction there?"

"The Tash-Tash RCMP, I'm told."

I walked blindly into it. "Corporal Scanks."

"As I say, I don't know him, I don't know the details."

"Wheatley told him what was going on at the Raba-urt-Jogan commune, with its actors, and Scanks promised not to investigate. And he was paid on August twenty-ninth at that

meeting on Quadra Island. That money in his safety deposit."
It was as if I were talking to myself, but very loud, in front of
the jury, answering their last remaining questions about
Wheatley's alleged role in these murders. Scanks had been
paid off to keep his mouth shut—but not about murder. He
had been paid not to interfere with the fraud being perpetrat-
ed upon poor, simple Astral.

That entire, brilliant, throat-cutting cross-examination by
Arthur of Scanks: it was all dust at our feet.

Could the defence reach a yet lower ebb? No doubt: when
Lukey produced Wheatley, Morgan, and Calico, men whom I
had blithely painted as murderers. The jury would be inflamed at me.

I lost my fight again. I had wasted myself on damaging
irrelevancies. For the next fifteen minutes I tried to pry a
little early-morning time from M'Garethy, a little splinter of
time after Wheatley left Campbell River and arrived at the
M'Garethy lodge. The absurd implications of my questions
were choking me. A two-minute rampage as twenty-one
persons were bound and executed.

I sat down.

"We're dead," I whispered to Brian.

"Feels that way."

The court was my tomb.

Lukey stood up and hitched his thumbs under the shoulders of his gown. "May it please your lordship, the Crown
rests its case in rebuttal."

No Wheaties, Morgan, or Calico.

I realized: Holy God, all the evidence is in.

Hammersmith studied the clock. "I see we have some time
left. But rather than starting with the jury addresses now and
having to interrupt them, we'll begin at ten o'clock. Call the
court to order, Mr. Clerk."

Everyone was staring at me. I felt like a hobo who had
wandered into an elegant tea party. Some of the parents
looked at me with what I felt was disgust.

I let Brian lead me out, following behind like a whipped
animal. At the door I wheeled around and saw Shiva watching
me. A smile as distant as the stars.

I got a pass and went to the cells.

"Okay, you win. I have religion. I am aware. The radiance
of your divine eye has reduced my ego to ashes. I see all now.

Your magic was awesome. Now save me." I realized I was shouting.

Shiva, with the expression of an innocent child, was twirling fingers through the curls of his hair. He seemed unconcerned about me, abstracted.

"I accept—not a cloud of doubt mars the clarity—that while we were ignoring you in court, you have single-handedly and single-eyedly shaped this trial as a teaching tool for your estwhile contumacious pupil: me, the former Maximillian Macarthur, whose spiritual name will henceforth be Samarpan. That stands for surrender, right? I am yours, Shiva Ram Acharya. Work your will. But I've an idea. Now you demonstrate to the world that you truly are a god. You turn the tables on the prosecution, winning a spectacular acquittal. I am drugged on you, Shiva. Demonstrate your powers."

"This is very boring of you, Maximillian."

"Are you hearing me?"

He shook his head. "Not when you mock."

"I want to know what the hell happened in there, Shiva. I want enlightenment."

He went on curling his hair. "But you are blind. I tried to explode you out of the darkness, but you clung to it like a terrified cat. The truth of even this trial eludes you, because you've been unable to look within. Seek ye the truth, for the truth shall make ye free. Your truth, though, not the court's, not the jury's." He seemed split: part of him in this time zone, part somewhere else.

"Shiva Ram, I have a report from a clinic in Philadelphia that says you flew into psychotic rages, tried to attack an attendant."

He looked blandly at me. "I don't remember."

"Amnesia, I suppose."

"Perhaps."

"At eighteen, you were obsessed with death."

"I was?"

"And you may still be. It's been a favourite topic in recent dialogues."

"Only when you look at death does your flame of life burn joyously." An odd grimace, almost a smile. Not quite.

"That kind of thing."

"Isn't it a joy to be alive?" And with that, out of nowhere, Shiva lifted his head and loudly laughed. "And to see it all as humorous? God has a sense of humour. Our trial is a divine joke." His chubby face was shaking. "Oh, laugh, my friend, laugh now because it will never be as funny again. Laugh and be free of it."

"Did you kill them?"

He stopped laughing.

"Look at me for the truth," he demanded. My eyes went into his, slammed into them. "Fall into me." His pupils seemed like two black motes sucking the world inside them.

"They were my children. I loved them." His words pierced me and his tears came.

"I loved them": words echoing through my aural channels.

"Follow me," he said. All my senses came alive with strange sensation: a dog barking, the smell of burning meat, a roofline above some trees.

"Follow me," Shiva cried.

And into those trees a fire explodes. Burning meat, a dog barking, fire, two bodies in gross coupling.

"Follow me because I love you."

Because I loved you, I had to kill you. The flames race toward us.

"Follow me."

No, came a whisper from deep within me. Do not follow him into that fire. *Because I loved you, I had to kill you. Because I love you, Maximillian....*

He is a madman, said the whisper within me.

I am under his control, and his madness is within me. Retreat from his flames, return from the abyss.

I broke contact with his eyes and swept back to the cells of the Law Courts Complex.

Shiva began to laugh again, softly at first, chuckles bubbling from him, his holy, roly face beginning to bounce, and the tears disappearing into his beard.

Manic-depressive.

I pulled my hands away from his.

The little interview room was dancing with his merriment.

One of the deputy sheriffs looked in, shrugged, went.

Shiva was wiping his eyes with his sleeve. "Didn't you see? Waving his wand? Garth Vader, is that the name?"

"Darth Vader." The Empire, psychotic, strikes back.

"Why didn't you follow me? Oh, it is quite funny. Darth Vader. And Mao Tse-tung with holes in his head." He burbled with pleasure.

I told him I had to go to prepare my address.

"Life is such a comic mystery," he said as they led him away. "Goodbye, Maximillian. I have waited many lives, and am at the flowering."

Holes in his head.

I sneaked quietly into the locker room to change but encountered Dumptruck Hooper. "Just finished my address, I gave a winner, I think. Not guilty, maybe, but at worst only manslaughter, three years. How's your trial going, Macarthur, not so hot, I hear. Told you, stick to doing pornos."

As he talked, I changed at my locker. Got to take these dirty shirts to the laundry one day—this place smells like a slum.

"You got more guts than brains taking on a case like that without senior counsel. You could've asked around, maybe someone would've given you a hand."

I straightened my tie. That empty mickey of Smirnoff still in here. Five books of stubs from the Civil Liberties Association raffle. I had failed to market any of them, bought them all.

"Those witnesses Lukey hid on you—Christ, everyone's talking about the job he did. Lukey will be getting his judgeship over this one."

From the floor of the locker I removed a can of shoe polish, pried it open, and rotated it on his nose.

He screamed epithets at me as I walked out.

I didn't go to my car, but walked to Burrard Street and turned south. The late-afternoon sun was golden on this eighty-second day of our everlasting summer. I went over False Creek on the Burrard Bridge, looked down at the gay bustle on Granville Island, the bright tin-roofed bars opening now for the late-day crowd, the buzzing pleasure boats, farther up the gut of the inlet the Expo 86 construction site, bustling with activity.

Was it really hard at all to understand how Shiva had been capable of rendering into putty the minds of his twenty-two followers? My critical, doubting-Thomas mind had succumbed to his afflicted one, to the mystic twists of his magnet. How much easier to hypnotize devotees who had surrendered themselves to him like people drugged.

So easily the madman had manipulated me. So accepting of his innocence I had been, so simple-minded. Amnesia? Had I really believed that?

I walked on, to Kitsilano, turned off the bridge to the Planetarium and Maritime Museum.

Perhaps the worst mistake had been abandoning the insanity. We should have stayed friendly with Mundt. This would go down in history as the worst-botched defence ever conducted. Lawyers will talk about it for decades: the case that broke Max Macarthur—you know that old wino who keeps bumming clients from Legal Aid? He fucked it up.

Darth Vader. Silver angels. A land of amber moons. And we abandon insanity.

I stood by the seawall and saw the West End spires reflected in the bay. Vancouver. Hard town to make it in as a lawyer. Should have started off in Dawson Creek or Prince Rupert.

I crossed Kits beach, letting the sand dust me. Volleyballers and Frisbeeites. A fat family eating French fries oiled and stained with vinegar and Ketchup. I should have been a historian. Straight A's in all classes.

Had they all been lies, Shiva, all part of your joke?

Back to Cornwall Street, then right again to Jericho Beach, west toward Point Grey. Dry-eyed and brave.

"Ladies and gentlemen of the jury," I recited aloud, "we have come to the end of the evidence, and it is my duty and my pleasure to address a few comments to you."

Locarno Beach, where I used to hang out as a kid. A case of Labatt's Blue in a rucksack. Bundling on the sand.

"The trust of centuries is imposed on you because throughout our history the common law has stood as a fortress of protection for the innocent." A hand-holding couple stared at me as I walked past. Spanish Banks East, Spanish Banks West, the wet, umber sand stretching for half a mile from shore, the beach sucked empty by a new-moon tide.

Why did you do it, Shiva?

"This, ladies and gentlemen, is a classic case of circumstantial evidence. . . ."

* * *

Not wanting to endure sympathy from others in the El Beau Room, I returned to Kitsilano after my walk around Point Grey and found a gloomy corner in a neighbourhood pub. I ordered a beer and sandwich. The first sip of cold Tuborg was like a knife going down. I nibbled my grilled cheese in the

manner of a trapped and watchful rat and, out of a twisted
sense of masochism, studied the front page of *The Sun*.

To Rescue Daughter

BILLIONAIRE BUYS PHONY CULT

What is this? I am painted as the hero who uncovers the
Antares conspiracy, while my burial by Lukey, Mangus, and
M'Garethy is buried itself, on page eight. But on the front
page, an inch below that towering headline, in big boldface,
is the name of Max Macarthur. Under cross-examination by
that skilled barbecue artist, the ex-governor concedes he paid
for a police bribe.

I looked like the other MacArthur, capital A, accepting the
Japanese generals' surrender.

Absorbed in the newspaper, I jumped when a lanky figure
slid into the chair beside me. He put a fresh Tuborg in front
of me, beside what looked like a scotch double. Foster Cobb.
I didn't want to be with a lawyer. Especially not Wheatley's.

"Hi, Fos. You live around here?"

"My bar."

"How's Jennifer?" His girlfriend, a lawyer.

"She's why I'm drunk."

"Oh, you're drunk."

"She said she'd be home two hours ago. My Johnny Walker
ran out fifteen minutes ago. Don't ever take up with younger
women, Max. She's fourteen years younger than me. I'm
fifties, she's sixties. I'm scotch, she's pot. I'm Bach, she's
rock. I hear the bomb dropped on you today."

"Let's talk about the weather."

"I tried to warn you."

"Yeah, I know. A very, very, very friendly warning. I
thought you were bluffing."

"I couldn't tell you more—I was under instructions. I was
hoping to ward you off so you wouldn't get my boys in
trouble. I didn't want them to get popped for bribing a cop."

"So you knew what they were up to, this Raba-urt-Jogan
thing."

"It must have been quite a scene, Mr. and Mrs. M'Garethy
walking down the hill to their daughter with the rising sun at
their backs on the morning the world was to self-destruct."

"Poor girl."

"But you've made it a big year for me, Max. Now that
Wheatley's rich, his lawyer can afford doubles of Johnny
Black." He waved to the waiter for another.

"They arrested him yet?"

"I don't think the police want to be too precipitous. There are discussions going on."

"Like what?"

"State secret."

"You've really been suffering from a case of solicitor-client privilege, haven't you, Fos? I know Lukey and Wheatley set us up. What was your role?"

Cobb shook his head. Then he sighed. "Okay, I can tell you about the deal that was made last month, you've probably guessed that by now. Don't blame me. Lukey sought me out after you spaded up some muck about my client. I assured him my guys had an alibi as tight as a popcorn fart and gave my permission to talk to them. He did, and I guess he saw his chance to really stick it, metaphorically speaking, up the undefended asses of the defence."

"With his metaphorical member."

"Wheatley agreed to co-operate with the Crown, keep mum about his alibi until you fellows slipped a noose around your necks. It was Leroy's idea, not mine. But I had no alternative but to go along: I was gagged. As you say, a bad case of solicitor-client privilege. Leroy was even behind that concocted story the defence was to hear if you made inquiries. Out doing the laundromats—Calico told me how they fed that one to you at a McDonald's restaurant."

Yes, they had seemed like real dumb bozos. Lukey had strung a trail of candies for us children to follow. Brilliant.

"The .30-.30 Remington—the one we figure you tried to filch from the Winnebago—that's in storage. It's not the one that produced the cartridge cases you found at Om Bay. Test it if you want. Max, Wheatley's a flim-flam man and a hypocrite. But he's not a murderer. I'm almost sorry about that."

"I'm going to feel naked in front of that jury tomorrow."

"Addresses tomorrow?"

"Then Hammersmith will need the weekend to prepare his charge, and we'll go to the jury on Monday." I vented a half-groan, half-wheeze. "I wish I could pick up all the pieces. There's still a lot of stuff scattered on the ground."

"You never prosecuted, did you, Max?" Cobb had been one of the best, but had quit the Crown counsel office two years ago after being passed over for Senior Vancouver Crown.

"This was my first."

"You didn't have the resources in there, Max. You needed backup, someone with field expertise. You're a lawyer, not a detective. If you want someone to pick up the pieces, why don't you give Honcho Harrison a call? He's taken out a private investigator's license. You know him, eh?"

"Yes." Most of the criminal bar had been at his banquet last year. James Orval (Honcho) Harrison, retiring at sixty after forty-two years a Vancouver policeman, the last twenty of those as senior homicide detective.

"Kind of late to bring in a private eye," I said.

"Honch is a friend of mine, Max. He's also very fond of Arthur Beauchamp. He's been following the case in the papers, and I think he has some theories."

"What theories?"

"Why don't you talk to him? I'll call him for you. Let him fine-tooth the files. Maybe all he'll do is pick out a better case against Shiva, but if he does, it lightens the burden of conviction for you." Cobb looked at his watch. "Almost midnight. At eight o'clock she went out to something called a bio-energetics class. That was supposed to last an hour. Where do they go after they're bio-energized? Another drink?"

"No, thanks." I bought him one, then went home. I thought of Arthur Beauchamp. I hadn't had the guts to see him.

25

○

Dies Infaustus

Friday, September Thirteenth. I am a scoffing Scot, an unbe-
liever of superstition. I have survived many Friday thir-
teenths, and among them were good days and bad.

As I sat down at the counsel table, I touched its wood.
Then I took a deep breath and turned to watch the deputies
bring Shiva from the prisoners' door. No manic laughter. No
shouted recognitions of Darth Vader and Mao. But he had a
vacant look, and when he sat he began, as yesterday, to twirl
his fingers in his hair.

My jury address was minutes away: I was a high-strung
horse in the paddock—a long shot. Lukey Stables had slipped
some dope into my oatmeal, but I intended to set a pace that
would force that fat pedophile to gallop at the end. An
acquittal was unlikely, but I knew I had a chance at getting a
deadlocked jury. If I could hang them, convince a stalwart
one or two to vote against conviction, a new trial would be
directed.

But Lukey had the advantage of last speech. Once the
defence calls evidence, it gives up the right to address the
jury last: another of those subtle procedural iniquities built
into our court system.

Brian joined me as the court rose for the judge. He had
done my dirty work, had gone to Lion's Gate Hospital this
morning. "He says do your best, then come by for a hit of
Demerol."

"How does he feel?"

"He feels, as we all do, for you. He says *nil desperandum*,
never despair. Give them the old Lord Russell, make them
weep."

287

"Mr. Macarthur?" said Hammersmith.

I stood up without notes, walked to the jury, stood before Mrs. Marrypole, second from the left, front row. Mrs. Marrypole, why can't you look me in the eye? Mr. Prebbles, such a sensitive, tidy man, think of the pain this young lawyer has suffered, feel for me. Margolis there, you're my soul-mate on this jury, you can't convict. Jock McIlheny, we are both sons of Scotland.

"Ladies and gentlemen of the jury, I want to say hello to you first of all." To my surprise, my words were calm, my hands steady. "We haven't been formally introduced. As you all know by now, my name is Max Macarthur. I have a condo in Kitsilano, I run, and I'm five foot five and two-fifths inches tall. I'm about the only lawyer in the courtroom you haven't had to look up to. I don't know anything about you, but you seem like people in my neighbourhood, pretty friendly, caring, intelligent."

They relaxed quickly.

"You don't seem the kind of people who are capable of being overwhelmed by appeals to passion or prejudice, nor do you look like the kind of people who'll condemn a man because he's, well, different. And you look like people who're going to ask yourselves questions."

I saw that my father had walked in. He gave me an encouraging smile.

"And one question you're going to ask, and ask again and again, is this: how could one man, the accused, by himself, do all of this? One man! It's the theory of the Crown that my client forced George Wurz at gunpoint to hogtie seventeen persons, and shot him, three others along the way, before executing the seventeen. You are going to conclude that is an impossible theory. The killers had to be more than one. What single man could have the power to kill twenty-one others without resistance, and how could there not have been resistance when the hogtying began?"

I avoided the judge's eye. "At the end, you'll ask not the question did he kill everyone, but did *they* kill everyone."

That was my central theme: too big to have been done by one, too complex, too incredible.

I played the cards I had. The .30-.30 cartridge cases: that suggested at least two men and rifles. The .303 hadn't been traced to anyone in the commune, no ammunition for it was found in storage. Surely killers who knew it couldn't be traced had left it there.

But why? I heard a juror ask.

Shiva's bloody fingerprints upon the rifle—that meant he picked the gun up after the shootings.

But why pick it up at all? someone inquires.

The blood on his face and garment meant only he had come down to the scene after he saw the killers leave, and had checked for life, come close to the bodies. Where had he been? Why the *chaitya* on the escarpment. You heard Benjamin Johnson describe it, a place with candle nubs and cushions of cedar boughs. You'll remember the footprint trail in the snow, leading from there.

But why, eyes were inquiring, hasn't he told us this himself? Explain that, says Margolis, and maybe I can fight for you.

I dealt frontally with his failure to take the stand. There was no obligation on the part of an accused to prove innocence. The entire onus rests with the Crown to prove the reverse. But at any rate, they would recall the evidence of Tom Joiner: Shiva was "out of it" when arrested, and a man who has not a memory makes not a witness.

"Let me talk about the Wheatley business. Whatever we have or haven't proved about him and his partners, we've shown how easily someone else could have committed these murders. We haven't been trying to prove anyone else guilty: what we've been doing is demonstrating a possibility that other killers exist."

I had a good feeling about Margolis then, a barely perceptible message, a fraction of a head nod. You're my main man, Margolis. Some of these other folks look a little dubious, so you have to show leadership.

The lesser prize—a stalemate, a hung jury—I'd settle for that, and I made the pitch. "You'll be discussing the evidence in detail after his lordship charges you. As you have seen, a criminal trial is made up of lots of arguments, and because lawyers are lawyers, and because lawyers are human, too, they argue. And you're human, and you'll argue in the jury room. I urge you to stick to your guns if you believe you are right."

I hammered that right into Margolis's third eye. I could hear the judge coughing in reproof behind me: one is forbidden to solicit hung juries.

I talked for a while about the circumstantial evidence rule. *Hodge's Case:* there may be no conviction unless the evidence is consistent only with guilt and no other rational conclusion.

And toward the end I banged away at reasonable doubt. "That most fundamental evidentiary pillar, the concept that distinguishes our common law from lesser systems, a concept that towers. Reasonable doubt." I quoted by heart from Lord Sankey in the *Woolmington* case, great words: " 'Throughout the web of the English criminal law, one golden thread is always to be seen: if at the end of and on the whole of the case there is a reasonable doubt, the prisoner is entitled to an acquittal.' I tell you that and his lordship will tell you that on Monday. And I tell you that in the twilight of your deliberations, when you've sifted through the sand of evidence one last time, when you're asking yourselves: how could one man have done this, then are you not asking yourselves if you're satisfied beyond a reasonable doubt? To ask that question is to answer it. I know you will join, all join, in that answer. The answer is no, *no.* Not guilty."

Maybe a little florid at the end. It wasn't Clarence Darrow and it wasn't Lord Russell, but it was okay. Margolis for sure, maybe a couple more. But what had those other expressions been saying? *Maybe he's innocent, but we can't take a chance on letting a monster loose among our children. It's obvious he hypnotized and shot them, Macarthur. I see it in his face, he's guilty. What difference does it make, he's just a freak anyway. They wouldn't have charged him if they didn't believe he was guilty.*

I had been an hour and a half. I walked out with Brian for the morning break.

"I hate to say it, but that was good."

"Hurricane Leroy will blow all the reasonable doubt away."

"He'll blow it, all right. Too excessive. The judge wasn't making any notes, maybe he'll hand you an appeal, forget to put the theory of the defence to the jury. Whatever that is."

My father came up. Brian shook hands but politely departed. It was a time for a man to be alone with his father.

"That was a fine speech. I'm very proud of you, son. Myrtle seems to think I haven't been able to say that to you."

"I gather you had a talk." I smiled. "You related."

"She and you talked, too. You told her to bear with me."

"I told her you're a Charter of Rights man, we need you up there."

"Not that you'll be permitted to appear in front of me."

"I think she just wants you to spend more time with her. She loves you."

"Yes, well, so do I. Her." He cleared his throat.

"This trial has almost killed me, Dad. I've been knifed up pretty bad."

"All good counsel wear scars, son. Bestmunderson, a rape murder, that gave me mine. Another man later confessed, but by then the appeals had been completed."

"It's a famous case, Dad. Hammersmith thirty years ago. He hasn't improved with age."

"I didn't do any more criminal work after that. Bestmunderson was stabbed to death in a riot; the case was never reopened."

We shared, for a brief quietness, our two failures. Father fought for a smile. "I had a crank call yesterday. The secretaries usually catch them, but this fellow got through. Said I should be taken out, drawn, quartered, and left to the crows. For defending a mass killer. That's what I get for being so conceited as to name you after myself."

I laughed. We were called to court. Dad patted me on the shoulder and went.

Lukey was by his table with some of the court staff, who were laughing at his jokes. Lukey with victory in his talons.

When court resumed, Patricia Blueman stood up for the Crown. It was Leroy's flamboyant gesture: the case was so confidently locked up that he would give Ms. Blueman a chance to get some harmless practice in.

She blinked at the jury, smoothed down her robes with her hands, and opened her mouth.

And she began to slice the defence into thin bacon.

"The defence was a house of cards that collapsed yesterday, and this morning Mr. Macarthur in his speech to you wasn't able to pick any of them up. The entirety of the defence at this trial has been directed to a single, misbegotten theory, and it died a quick and merciful death with the evidence of the Crown's last two witnesses. I hope it will be buried now. Innocent men have been vilified in this courtroom, accused of murder. It was a desperate tactic."

"Who is that masked woman?" Brian whispered.

Patricia Blueman, the zero, the tinfoil decoration at the Crown table, who hadn't seemed to be following the evidence all that well. Patricia Blueman, wielding a keen, cruel edge, peeling off the case for the defence like transparent bologna.

"Fact: there was blood on his robe and hands and face and mouth. Mr. Macarthur says, oh, well, he went over and touched some bodies. The shoulders of his robe were *soaked* with blood, ladies and gentlemen. Blood that must have spurted from the victims' wounds upon each execution.

"Fact: his footprints were found near each body. Fact: he said, 'Because I loved you, I had to kill you.'"

Brief. Lucid. Subject before the verb before the object. No fat to be trimmed here. And the jury so open to her, giving her this chance.

"Counsel for the defence asks: how could one man have done this? Well, I ask you what powers can be exerted by mind upon mind. These were followers of the accused. Cannot we conclude they emptied their minds for him, let him control them? And maybe there was some resistance. Three were shot in the back, another in the anterior chest. A struggle for power, maybe? George Wurz, one of the resisters, was he forced at gunpoint to tie the others? We don't know the whole of the picture and perhaps never will. But we know enough, we know enough."

She went over all the evidence, tied it in with the Crown's theory, then gave an exhortation to their sense of evenhandedness, made no plea for blood, for vengeance. She asked for a fair verdict, without malice. The Crown was dispassionate, seeking only justice. She sat down.

I felt like applauding.

"Well, that's all she wrote," said Brian.

As I looked at Pat Blueman, she gave me a wink. Funny how you get fooled.

"We've made good progress." Hammersmith was pondering his watch. "In view of the fact the jury is, ah, sequestered and will probably want to get home this weekend, I will commence my charge at two P.M. I intend to give the matter to the jury by the end of the day."

Let's get on with the conviction. Addresses, charge, verdict, sentence, grind it out.

Lukey wore the expression of a cat going to the lavatory.

Shiva, laughing silently.

"The Hammer's expecting a fast verdict," Brian said.

"The Kangaroo Express on its final run. I'm getting out of this profession, man."

A large man in a rumpled hat, laughing with a rich, gravel voice at some joke he had passed with a few policemen, detached himself from them, approached, stretched out his hand to me: James Orval Harrison.

"I remember you, kid, you juniored in the Garvey prelim, the car bomb attempt. This guy Pomeroy, he acted for Laszlo Plizit, who is now where deceased buttonmen go. How's Artie?"

"He'll be in a truss for a while," Brian said.

Harrison's great hand swallowed mine up, disgorged it, took Brian's.

"A truss. That ain't a pleasant feeling. Foster Cobb said drop in and see Max Macarthur."

"He says you've been following the trial. You have some theories."

"You want some help with this, kid?"

"We can't afford much. Anyway, the jury's going out tonight."

"This jury will be a day or two. I seen lots of juries. I'll do it as a loss leader, a business opener. I want to get back on the street, kid. I miss the smell of it. I been smelling things for a living for forty years, and I got one of those good noses. From the newspaper stories about this case, I've been getting the full bouquet. Bill Wheatley and Wimpy Morgan—I know those guys, I know their smell."

"I think we've lost their scent permanently, Mr. Harrison."

"Maybe you should sit down with me. Maybe I can pick it up."

"What've you got to lose?" Brian said.

"Nothing. I've got nothing to lose."

"You going to need your files for the rest of the day?" Harrison said.

"I'll get the transcripts boxed up for you. Why're you volunteering, Mr. Harrison?"

"I told you, I don't like Wheatley. Also, I don't like the shit on Artie's face. Doesn't look good on you, either, kid. Okay, buy me lunch. I like spaghetti, steak and whiskey today, how about Iachocho's, downstairs. We can talk. I want to know everything."

* * *

My work wasn't over—there still could be exceptions to be taken to Hammersmith's charge—but I let myself get a little loaded on Bardolino, returned to the courtroom engulfed in a warm mist of grape fumes, the better to withstand Hammersmith's standard charge for conviction.

In a high and almost emotionless voice, he recited the standard charge on the law—judges must always give it to their juries: onus of proof, presumption of innocence, reasonable doubt, circumstantial evidence. Hammersmith could do this after thirty-three years without his glasses; the words were finely chiselled into his brain.

He defined murder for them, then dealt with the facts. "If I seem to express any opinions about those facts, you are free to, ah, disregard them." Judges constantly say that to juries: it gives them licence to promote their bias.

All through his summary of the evidence were to be found plums and candies to decorate the Crown's case. He had forgiven Lukey for his prattling and prancing, and now gave the prosecutor a reward in penance—a sodomizing of Macarthur which Leroy could enjoy vicariously.

An example: "I am unable to conceive what weight can be given to the finding of .30-.30 cartridges a hundred metres from the bodies or the existence of some hollow tree or marks in the snow which are claimed to be, ah, footprints. Mind you, this is my opinion and you don't have to accept it."

When it came time to dicuss the Crown and defence theories, he gave them straight Patricia Blueman—her words as he'd written them down—and short shrift to the defence.

"I have reviewed with you the evidence concerning Wheatley, Morgan, and Calico upon the assumption the defence hasn't abandoned its case against them, although from Mr. Macarthur's remarks this morning, I was left in doubt. Counsel for the defence say there was opportunity for others to have done these murders, and a reasonable doubt therefore exists."

He smiled at the jury and shook his head. What foolishness, he was telling them—in a way that would never get on the record. "As I've instructed you, a reasonable, ah, doubt is a doubt based on reason. It is not a fanciful doubt, it must be real, based on your consideration of the evidence. You don't leave your common sense at home when you go into the jury room."

He instructed them they had to be unanimous, then slapped me around a little bit more, castigating me for having urged jurors to "stick to your guns, as counsel rather inappropriately put it." Verdicts were brought about with good fellowship and compromise, mature discussion among adults.

"You have twenty-two counts. The verdict upon each of them must be guilty or not guilty. There is no other verdict. Insanity has not been raised as an issue at this trial. Ladies and gentlemen, the deputy sheriffs will take you to the jury room, and you may begin deliberating in a few minutes."

They were led out. "Mr. Macarthur?" said the judge. I was being invited to make exceptions to his charge, suggest matters upon which the jury might be redirected.

I was feeling choleric. The wine had been sitting in me for an hour and a half, giving me a raw feeling. "It is my respectful submission," I said, "that that was the most one-sided and biased charge that has been made in these courts in the last two decades. To be consistent at the end, your lordship should have instructed the jury to convict. I apply to have the jury recalled and redirected with a completely fresh charge omitting your lordship's opinions."

Arthur would have done it.

"Thank you," said Hammersmith. Not a bat of an eye. "Mr. Lukey?"

"Your lordship's charge was fair and thorough, and I apologize on behalf of the bar for my young friend's intemperance, not to mention bad manners."

"Aw, stop being such a suckhole, Lukey. You make me sick." I found myself saying that out loud, but I didn't give sweet dick. I bent down and started packing my files into my briefcase.

Lukey was spurting and spitting, but the judge cut through this. "Mr. Sheriff, tell the jury they may deliberate for two and a half hours until six o'clock when they will be taken out for dinner. They will start again at eight o'clock—unless of course they have a verdict. We will adjourn."

Adjourn it up your ass.

"I will see counsel in my chambers."

Oh, God, here it comes.

Brian said, "Oh-oh," and started picking up the files. "I think I'll just sit down with Honcho Harrison as we planned. See you later." He escaped.

Lukey, smiling, followed me and a deputy sheriff to Hammersmith's chambers. "He's going to ream you, and I don't mean with a rectal thermometer. You won't be able to sit on it, shit with it, or fart."

The deputy was waved away by the judge, standing at his window. His robes hung on a closet door and his hands gripped a pair of blue suspenders. "Sit down," he said amiably.

Leroy and I chose chairs at opposite sides of this commodious room, decorated with English hunting prints and a big framed photograph of the judge when he was forty years younger.

"Well, that's another one out of the way," Hammersmith said. "One thousand and twenty-seven trials now. Yes, gentlemen, I topped the thousand mark early this year. I don't count, ah, guilty pleas and I don't count contested chambers matters. Trials. One thousand and twenty-seven."

"That's a lot," said Lukey.

"Doesn't count what I prosecuted," said Hammersmith. He leaned against his desk, contentedly popped first one suspender then the other, grabbed them again in his frail, age-freckled hands. "Did the Crosby murders, you know that? Fifteen, not as many dead as here, and all on different days. But fifteen murder convictions. That was back in thirty-nine, stands as the record. Not the same as here, you've got all the bodies in one place. Now what would you gentlemen like to drink, my poison is scotch but there's vodka and, ah, rye. Mr. Macarthur?"

"Scotch, thank you."

"Same for me, m'lord," said Lukey. "Can I help?"

"Sit down." Hammersmith made the drinks at a little recessed bar behind his desk. "Thirty-three years, and I've never seen a wrong verdict. Not in my court. The Bestmunderson conviction, where that door-to-door peddler later confessed. But he retracted it. That was the only one that gave me pause. Thelma Taylor, after all those exercises in journalistic impudence, and all those books written about it, she was as guilty as Satan. Killed her own child. I think they made a movie of that one, didn't they?"

He came over with our drinks.

"Thank you very much, m'lord," said Lukey. "Cheers."

"Eighty-seven murders in all, don't think anyone has sat on more than that. That many and half again of rapes. What do they call that now?—aggravated sexual assault. Ridiculous. A rape is a rape in my book."

And that's all that happened. Not a mention of our trial, his

charge, my comments afterwards. That's another one out of
the way. Another day, another trial.

At the end of our drinks and a few more reminiscences,
Lukey and I stood up to go and were graciously ushered out.

"If you were my size, I'd take you outside and kick the
smile off your face," Lukey said in the corridor.

"You just do that, bimbo. I'll give you the weight advantage."

We cursed at each other until we parted.

* * *

There is no tension of the human soul greater than the
disquietude that seizes a defence attorney as he waits for a
jury. One cannot read, one cannot converse, one cannot
organize thoughts. One paces a lot.

I am doing most of my pacing in solitude, up on the
seventh tier, back and forth near the door to a small interview
room, stopping once in a while to look over the railing. Look
at the carrion eaters down below, outside 54, waiting for
Macarthur to give up, stop squirming, die. Cops, reporters,
courtroom thrill-seekers. And the parents, woeful and watchful, always the parents. Lukey wandering amiably in and out
of the courtroom door.

A smaller group outside Court 53, where Hank Hooper's
back-alley brawl murder has also reached its final stage,
waiting for the verdict.

I go into the witness room, crack a beer. Brian Pomeroy
is here, reading the *Bulletin of Atomic Scientists*, pulling
from an Old Style. He has smuggled up a case.

"Says here it takes ten minutes for a missile from a Soviet
sub to reach a coastal city. Like Vancouver, say. But it takes
fifteen minutes for the people of a city to be alerted. That's a
minus five minutes advance warning we get. In other words,
the bomb goes off and five minutes later they warn us."

"Stop it, Brian."

"Since there's no defence from submarine launchings, a
growing chorus of responsible military men in the free world
are suggesting we nuke them first."

"Brian."

"Have another beer, Max. The imminent annihilation of all
life forms puts this trial into perspective."

I have another beer.

At six o'clock we break our vigil to have dinner. We return

at eight. The Law Courts Complex gives off a sick, forbidding air in the evening twilight.

The court reporter: "Not a whisper from the jury room."

I don't have to suffer Lukey, who is probably up in the Crown office. I begin to pace again, sending off vibrations of ill will, keeping everyone at bay.

Eight-thirty, nine, nine-thirty.

The courthouse seems haunted by small, dark spirits. An incessant murmur. Air conditioning? Soft voices, grumbling, mumbling trying to tell me something. Perhaps that I was cracking up. A communicable psychosis.

The deputy sheriff flags me down. "Jury's coming back."

Panic. "What for? This early?"

"I don't know. I'm off to get the judge."

A quick verdict: it would almost certainly be for conviction.

I try to collect my scattered pieces and get them inside Court 54.

The prisoner is brought in. Lukey strolls bumptiously in with Blueman. Now the judge, dreaming of his thousand and twenty-seven trials, working his way slowly up to his throne, and perching there, blinking behind those spectacles.

The jury. If they avoided my eyes, that would be a sure sign, a sign I didn't want to receive, so I avoided them, doodled furiously, great overlapping circles, arrows.

"I understand there is a question," Hammersmith said.

The foreman stood. "We wanted to know, sir, if persons are persuaded by somebody using hypnosis to consent to be killed, is that murder?"

Hammersmith was quiet for a moment.

A terrible question. It demonstrated the jury's bent: they were not asking themselves who did it, but by what means the accused had done so. And maybe they were guessing very close to the truth.

"There is no evidence on hypnosis," Hammersmith said. "The question does not arise." A pause. "Does it seem unlikely you will reach a verdict tonight?"

"I think it's very unlikely," McIlheny said.

I was studying them. No eye contact, not even from Margolis. They seemed embarrassed, being told like that they had gone off on a wrong track.

"You had better get some sleep," the judge said brusquely. "You'll attack it in the morning with a fresh zeal."

The foreman and his flock followed the deputy sheriff out.

"Any comments?" said Hammersmith.

Lukey and I had nothing to say. I don't know about Lukey, but I wouldn't have been able to get a squeak out anyway.

The jury would be convicting in the morning. I had no other expectation.

26

○

The Manic Depressive

I drove to Gastown yinning and yanging, feeling hot and cold flushes. The heat came with the manic, the cold with the depressive.

Craziness. Was it a nervous breakdown, or had I picked it up from Shiva like psychotic measles. I would be seeing Darth Vader walking out of the Shillelagh and Shamrock in the company of leprechauns. My dementia had begun in the traditional way, little failures of memory, becoming more serious, delusions at Oakalla and at Om Bay.

I parked behind the tracks, walked to our building. Outside the nightclub were not leprechauns but odder beings, some in spangles, some in leather, some even in furs this warm September night. Many looked like large black cats. Everyone was violently coloured. Silver gods. Martians.

The big banner draped across the front of the building, just below our office windows, advertised: "Grand Opening, Friday, September 13th, The Black Cat Ball, Drinks Half Price." Beneath that where had been the Shillelagh and Shamrock sign, the new management, opting for the drag crowd, proclaimed this recent addition to Vancouver cosmopolitania to be the "Kinks and Queens." I laughed a crazy laugh.

In my boring suit jacket I walked through the crowd, attracting a few whistles, and went up the stairs to our offices. I had not been here for two days, and I didn't particularly want to be here now, but a dog's obedience to the duties of running an office had been ingrained into me.

I leafed desultorily through the collection of messages: clients and others screaming for my attention through the medium of pink memo slips. Mrs. Claxson, five times—finally wanting her retainer back. Mr. Howard, thrice—he being the vicious tax collector to whom Revenue Canada had assigned my file. Greg Ranjeet from Civil Liberties, although I had told him I was off call. Nothing from Ruth.

My in-tray: many threatening letters from opposing lawyers. Criminal documents from prosecutors. A letter from Civil Liberties. I stared at it numbly. I had won the raffle.

I phoned Ruth and Jacqueline answered.

"She's left, I'm afraid. She got dressed up and even put some makeup on, then left with a bottle of champagne. I don't know what gives, Max. We had a big fight two days ago. We haven't been talking. She is *la belle dame sans merci*."

"Give her my love if and when she returns." I hung up, balled the letter from Civil Liberties, zinged it against the vine pot in the corner.

This was the day's final clanger, my ego had been Hammersmithed and Lukeyed and Worobecked into a pathless pulp. It was time to surrender, to shout the Sufi mantra Hoo and dance the dance of Shiva.

I was about to ball up another paper, but I noticed it was the first page of the information charging Louie the Loot with operating his fencing factory.

Entering deeper into my depressive phase, I studied it, seeking sanity in the wondrous technicality of the law, searching for defects of form and substance. A five-page information prepared by a greedy prosecutor, sixty-seven specific counts and a basket charge for items not traced to their owners.

Perhaps I could find here an Italian leather jacket with explorer pouches.

From between the floorboards seeps rough vocal sounds, a tenor screech: "Take us back to the days of marital aides," was the repeated refrain.

My eyes did a double-take, skipped back a few lines. Who is this familiar-sounding guy, Swindon C. Durkee?

Count number twenty-seven of the information: "Louis Keegan on the tenth day of September, A.D. 1984, was in possession of property knowing it to have been obtained by theft, to wit, three silver goblets, the property of Swindon C. Durkee."

Major Durkee. Who had testified about his house being broken into, about a Lee-Enfield .303, among other items, going missing.

Louie, what were you doing with the major's silver goblets?

I trotted the two blocks to the jail and endured the crankiness of the night staff, and with Herculean effort persuaded them to wake him up, bring him to an interview room.

Louie sat down, studied me.

'You been asleep?"

"Who can sleep when you get a drunk with heebie-jeebies down the hall?" His hair straggled in unkempt strands across a balding scalp. He was morose.

"I want to talk to you about the three silver goblets."

"It's nearly midnight. You want to talk about the three silver goblets. You feelin' okay, Mr. Macarthur?"

"You're a professional, Louie. You don't deal with strangers. Who sold them to you?"

"I shouldn't of took them. They had little initials scrolled in their sides."

"s.c.d., I'll bet. Swindon C. Durkee. He had his house broken into a year ago last August. The West Marpole area, Seventy-first off Arbutus. A silver setting, portable colour TV, a coin collection, pair of ivory tusks, a .303 Lee-Enfield, the three goblets, some other minor stuff. Who brought you the goblets?"

"Goblets, silver setting, coin collection, they came in at the same time. I wouldn't handle the tusks, that's crazy, and I don't do guns, as you know. I was able to move the coins real fast, made a coupla dollars, also the silver setting, good stuff. I don't like to name names, Mr. Macarthur."

"Louie, I'm going to ask you to. You know I wouldn't unless it was important." But I was asking him to break the tightest code of our society.

"He's out of the Killarney Street gang, Mr. Macarthur. They been known to commit assaults and batteries."

"Listen, Louie, if this works out, I may be able to get some kind of deal for you on these charges. It's about the rifle. I'm on the trail of a mass murderer. Nobody's going to fault you for that."

He thought about it. "Okay, tell him I said you can be trusted. It's about your cult murders, isn't it? When I read about the Lee-Enfield, I wondered if it might of been the same gun. I told Angelo I wasn't interested in it. Angelo Lucchi. They call him Angel. It was November, third week, around there. I don't know where he took the ivory and the rifle. He didn't say what he planned, I didn't ask."

"Killarney Street gang—they hang out someplace?"

"Archie's Steak House on Kingsway. Late nights, Angel has been going to a place called The Blitz Creek, a kind of body contact dance bar on the docks."

"I know where it is."

I hurried across to the Public Safety Building to confer with the late-shift detective in Stolen Property, Nick Corshiu.

"Poor Louie," he said, "he just can't stop. He doesn't mean harm, I think he just got stuck in a klepto phase during his childhood, never grew out of it. We used an undercover, a young dick from Edmonton, he scored a half a dozen ghetto blasters from Louie, all from the Radio Shack on Commercial. I like Louie, but he's got to smarten up."

"There are some silver goblets mentioned in the information. You know anything about them, Nick?"

"It's Detective Halversen's file. He comes in at eight tomorrow. Since you're here, Max, there's something maybe you can help us with."

"What's that?"

Corshiu disappeared into the back and came out with an Italian leather jacket with explorer pouches. "You been missing something?" he said.

"How did you know?"

"Nice jacket. Real leather. You can't afford to lose things like this. A harness man caught some pathetic little junkie trying to hawk it in a bar couple of nights ago. He said he got it from a friend, but he wasn't believed. Funny, though, when we checked our sheets, we didn't find any record of a jacket of this description."

"Yeah. I guess I forgot to report it."

"A good citizen reports such things."

"As you know, detective, the police never solve these crimes anyway. How'd you trace it to me?"

He pulled a fat air-mail envelope from the pocket. "Addressed to Max Macarthur, West Second Avenue, your address. Except she forgot to put the name of the city or province or zip. It's a wonder this ever got to you."

I hadn't noticed that. She had been into the pina coladas, all right.

Corshiu smiled. "I guess we have to hold on to this as evidence for a while."

"Keep the jacket, give me the letter."

Grinning more broadly, he handed it to me, along with a stolen report form. I was blushing as I left.

Back to the car, off to Archie's, Ruth's letter warming my behind in a buttoned seat pocket. Archie's was still open. It was a rounder restaurant, kept late hours. The bartender said he had never heard of Angelo Lucchi, but I suspected he was lying. But I knew one of the customers, Bad Czech Jerzy Janek. Yeah, he'd seen Angel around, and would put the word out, get Lucchi to call me.

Any time of day or night, I said, and slipped him fifty dollars. "Tell him he'll be rewarded even more richly."

The Blitz Creek was an illegal after-hours bar on the fifth floor of an old warehouse by the East End docks. Midnight to six A.M. to take up the small-hour slack. On the dance floor, people throwing other people against still other people, a form of dance. No Angelo Lucchi. I passed some paper to the bartender. He would get the word out.

Then I sat in my car and read Ruth's letter beneath the map lamp. From the top.

Darling,

I've had a pina colada or two. Or three or four. . . ."

By the time she had got well into this eight-page letter, she had had more, I suspected. Her handwriting began to show poor discipline.

She chatted about herself, her feelings for me, for Jacqueline. She had gone into counselling because she felt obsessed with relationships: how they work, how they don't, the things that glue them, the things that poison them. And she talked about Jacqueline's father.

I guess I was stung bad that first time. I was eighteen, but I'd been brought up to watch out for myself. I believed everything, believed he wasn't married. It was the sixties, for God's sake, and people were all suddenly sweet and honest.

Anyway, where am I? Well, where I am is at a little table in the courtyard of the San Pedro Hotel in Mexico, and the waiter is just setting down another pina colada on my table. Where I am is about relationships. About you and me. About why I'm afraid.

Where I am is about love, I guess. I love you.

Commitment. Ouch. Loss of emotional sovereignty. When I say I love you I feel invaded by you. Be delicate. These are fragile goods.

She reminisced for a few pages, a little embarrassingly. Some decidedly erotic allusions. Then:

Your poor, apologetic proposal, Max—it made me want to cry. In fact I did, later that night. Don't feel you have to ask me again to save my pride. (But I'm not stopping you.)

Did that mean yes?

She ended abruptly. *I'm kind of pina colada'd to my eyeballs here. I'm going to pop this into an envelope and mail it before I say something terrible.* Three big X's. *Love, Ruth.*

I remembered her words in my apartment as Augustina's form lay prostrate in my bedroom: *You didn't get the letter? Gee, that was going to make things a lot easier.* I felt like a skunk.

Depressive phase. Sitting here, sunk into the soft leather car seat, studying the blurred whorls of the polished oak dashboard, unable to find the switch to turn on the windshield wipers, everything in front of me distorted with a wetness. I was weeping, uncontrollably.

It was not my habit.

I sat there for a while until my weather cleared up. The tears purged my anxious soul: I began to feel relieved, then happy. As I drove down Main Street to Prior I began to smile. Relief that Ruth was able to commit herself to me that way. I began to laugh. Manic phase.

Star Wars triple bill at the Broadway. Big cinema poster of Darth Vader swinging that big laser stick. A throb in my head, wang, wang, wang, as though someone was trying to lug it somewhere.

Honcho Harrison. I should have phoned him, told him about Angelo Lucchi. Too late now, after midnight.

Today the jury convicts.

West on Broadway to Yew, turn north, back to the water, to home. The various pieces of Max Macarthur must sleep tonight, mend. I turned the ignition off and the engine protested and choked and died. I needed to take this machine out on the highway, clean the carbon out. Maybe drive into the Interior on Sunday, pack my hiking gear and go up into the mountains. Get away, alone, knit my broken spirit in a tent by the lip of a glacier.

At the condo, I unlocked my door, hung my jacket in the hall closet, undressed as I slouched toward the bathroom, draping pants, shirt, socks on divers chairs en route. I turned on the faucets in the Jacuzzi tub. Room enough to drown here if a man wanted.

I went to the living room to get a book from the bookcase that Ruth—was it only a week ago?—had deposited on my head.

"Hi," she said.

Mao Tse-tung. With holes in his head. Here on the fourth shelf is the history of the Chinese Red revolution.

"I said hi."

I slowly turned around to face the low maple table, champagne in ice upon it, the woman I knew as Ruth on the divan behind it.

She looked at my naked form critically.

"As you grow older you will become knobby-kneed and pot-bellied. But you look cute now. Kind of sexy."

I stared at her dumbly.

She lifted a glass of champagne to her lips, sipped with a smile under dark, Mongol eyes. She wore a short, low-cut, pearl-white dress that fanned out on either side of crossed knees, and one silver, slim, high-heeled shoe dangled from the big toe of her left foot.

"I didn't expect you," I stammered.

"You never do."

"You look beautiful."

"You look pretty good, too."

"I better cover up."

"So shy? Have your bath. But a glass of bubbly first." She reached down, tilted the bottle over a glass, extended it to me.

"This is what's been happening to me," I said. "The Wheatley business backfired. The jury is asking questions about hypnotism. Shiva sent me a message about a dog barking and a fire and said he saw Darth Vader and Mao tse-Tung." I blurted out these things in a disconnected way.

"I see," she said, closing one eye, squinting at me with the other.

"It's been a long day. There's a new club below our office. The Kinks and Queens. Black cats and drag."

"Is that where you got so stoned?"

"And Louie the Loot knows who stole the Lee-Enfield, a guy called Angel. Angel is going to tell me that someone from Shiva's ashram bought the rifle from him. I know that."

"Or are you having a nervous breakdown?"

"I was at Archie's Steak House and at the Blitz Creek. I addressed a jury, and my father admitted he loved Mom and I had lunch with Honcho Harrison. I insulted the prosecutor and the judge poured me a scotch later in his chambers."

"You're falling apart, Macarthur."

"It's been a *hell* of a long day."

"It isn't over yet." She stood up, clinked her glass against mine, delivered a light, dancing kiss on the mouth. "And your trial isn't over yet."

"It will, by about noon tomorrow, that's all I give it. Sometimes I'm sure Shiva killed them and sometimes I don't know. He has terrible powers, Ruth."

"Honey, I think you're in bad, bad shape. Those whom the gods seek to destroy they first drive mad, and you've been out for a drive, I can see that." She picked up my abandoned socks, shorts, shirt from chairs, led me to the bathroom. "You haven't been smoking grass, Max, you know it doesn't agree with you."

"No, I'm stoned on beer and confusion."

After testing the water, she helped ease the wreckage into the tub.

I groaned, sank slowly to the bottom, let the waves bubble over my chin. "Oh, sweet Mary, mother of the Lord Jesus, but does that feel good."

"I'll get your champagne."

My scattered pieces began to lock together. "Why are we celebrating?"

"Let's *find* a reason." She went out, returned with the champagne glasses and my pants draped over her arm. "I'm wilting in here, it's hot," she said. She shook the trousers, began to fold them.

"Don't go, I've been suicidal. Keep talking to me."

Her letter dropped out of the right hip pocket and she stooped and picked it up.

"Oh," she said, startled, recognizing it.

"As you see, I carry it everywhere. You'll notice you didn't address it properly. It could have gone to Second Avenue in New York or Tallahassee or Kokomo."

She began reading it. "Oh, *God*," she said, putting her hand to her mouth. "I must have been *drunk*. Ouch."

I could feel the hot water caress my body, healing sore muscles, sore mind. It was good, at last, to have Ruth close by.

"The other thing that happened to me today—I cried. I read your letter and cried."

"How very un-Macarthur of you."

"You wondered if you could live with a workaholic lawyer. Don't give it a second thought. I'm going to become a history teacher. I'll do the dishes every night. I'll take you out to dinner at least once a week. I will play your favourite card games and watch your favourite TV programs. We will canoe your favourite lakes. I will join the Polish-Canadian Association. I will let you psychoanalyze me constantly. I will not relate to other women except on a professional basis. I'll enter into a marriage contract, name your terms. I am a second-stage male."

"And you'll sign this all in blood?" She put her glass down and began unbuttoning her blouse.

"My father loves you, my mother loves you, and if that isn't enough, I also love you. Jacqueline wants me to be her stepfather. I won't do dynamic meditation, I'll pick up my clothes and I'll learn to make a perfect bloody Mary. I'll encourage you to finish your Ph.D."

I discreetly ogled as she undressed.

"Is this another of your proposals then?"

"I believe it is."

She nudged a toe in the water, then delicately vaulted in behind my back. She put her arms around my chest, pulled me back against her, nuzzled the nape of my neck. "Still want to marry me, huh?"

"Still."

"Augustina called me at the office yesterday from some-where up north. She's fighting forest fires, for goodness' sake. Maybe it's therapy—she says she's happy. We had a good talk. She claims she used you as a sexual substitute."

"It's true."

"Tied you to the bed, did she?"

"I was drunk."

"A coward's refuge. I intend to be possessive, Max. And you're going to have to work. There are going to be no easy jumps with me, no leaps into transcendental bliss. Life is work. Partnerships are work. *Being* is work. But it's good work, it's honest, satisfying, you can put your slippers on at the end of the day, and stroke your cat and know you've earned some happiness."

"We don't have a cat."

"We'll have a cat. We'll have a little place in the country where we can take it weekends. We'll call him Mao. And we'll have a dog. Lech."

"Lech? Is this your response to my proposal?"

"Was it a real proposal, no guilt at having seduced me and used me so cruelly for the last five years?"

"No, I'm asking you because it would be trendy and chichi to marry a Polish worker's daughter."

Her long fingers made circles on my stomach.

"I'm getting horny," I said.

"Pardon *me*."

"Catholic church wedding if you want."

"Let's keep it civil, embarrass fewer people that way."

"Does this mean you're accepting?"

"I practically proposed in my letter."

"Say it: I accept."

"Propose right."

"I offer this wounded knight to your lifelong service, dear lady. Wouldst marry me?"

"That's sweet. I do. I mean, I will."

I whooped a war cry.

I turned my head, and we kissed, and her lips slid from mine and touched along my cheekbone to my earlobe. She nibbled. I was suffused with happiness. "As soon as this trial is over, we're taking a break together. I've won two tickets on an Alaska cruise next month."

"I have to work."

"Tell them to shove the job. Finish your Ph.D."

"You'll support me in that?"

"Sure."

She sighed. "Okay. I'll pay you back."

"Don't be silly. We're going to be *married*." I slapped the water with glee, then began rubbing my hands.

She began to laugh. "Aren't you something, Max. Just like a kid. Now you just forget about your goddamn trial until the morning." She slid around to face me, encircled my hips with her thighs, and her fingers slithered to beneath where our abdomens met.

A kind of transcendence.

27

○

Silver Angel

A night of dreams, all vividly remembered, their colours many shades of russet, colours of earth and flame. Macarthur racing from the fires that howled through the forests, trees bursting with the sound of shots. The voice of God thundering above me: *Seek ye the truth, Maximillian.*

The secrets of Poindexter Island pull me like a magnet in my dreams, and the fires raze cedar shacks while drunken, boisterous men dance a wild dance and the many hands of Shiva beat hypnotic rhythms upon his drums. *Our trial is a divine joke. Oh, laugh and be free of it.*

There is gunfire, but I cannot flee from Poindexter Island.

Naked now, atop the building, lawyers loudly hawking advice in the bazaar below, and I am pleading to the jury, and the fire is creeping, creeping toward us, and the jury takes face and form: Wheatley, Scanks, Mundt, and the parents of the dead, sad and featureless, their multitudes fading into the fiery distances, and Shiva stands up to announce the verdict, and he is wearing a toga, and he extends his arm, and the thumb descends. . . .

"*Mea culpa!*" I scream, for the guilt has seized me.

"*Mea culpa?* Holy mackerel, Max, wake up."

The deputy sheriffs grab me by the shoulder, roughly lead me to that concrete windowless jail.

"But I'm going to get married," I muttered.

"We'll have time to do that later. Right now you've got company." Ruth shook me again. I opened my eyes to see her hovering above me, brown hair falling over her eyes, over her pale, sculpted face. She stood up, tightened her bathrobe cord. "Sorry to interrupt your nightmare—God, I'm going to

310

send you in for some shock treatments—but there's a person at the door. I think it's a person. He's all in silver."

"It's all right," I moaned. "Shiva must have sent him. One of his angels."

"That's odd. That's how he introduced himself. Angel."

"Angel!" I sat up. "Make him coffee."

"He needs it."

I quickly showered away the sweat of the night, climbed into weekend jeans and Expo 86 T-shirt, then went to the living room to find him standing in front of the fireplace, staring at my antique candelabra, a family heirloom.

He had a square and handsome chin, blond, curly hair on head and chest, over which dangled a brilliant, round, silver medallion. The shirt was also silver, great flounce sleeves, open-buttoned to the gut, pants metallic satin, skin-tight. Every few seconds he would snap his fingers. He was high, perhaps on many things.

"You're Angelo Lucchi," I said.

He turned around, looked me over. "Right. I just come from the Blitz Creek. I got your note."

"You're a dancing man," I said.

"Dancer, right. I dance all night. Except when I work." His eyes wandered to my stereo and my portable TV. Dance me the dance of Shiva, Angel.

"You know who I am?"

"Yeah, you're the lawyer for that guy in the big murder. I seen you on TV."

"I'm also Louie Keegan's lawyer."

"Louie, yeah. I hear he got bulled over."

Ruth came from the kitchen with mugs of coffee, milk, sugar.

"My fiancée," I said, proclaiming proudly.

"Yeah." He took a mug from her. "Thanks."

"Maybe you can help Louie."

"I'm willin' long as I don't get in no trouble."

"I guarantee it. Sit down, Angel."

"Naw, I'd rather stand, you don't mind." Little clicks from his fingers.

"They found three silver goblets in Louie's warehouse." Silver goblets, silver gods, silver angels. "A certain party brought these goblets to him, plus some other stuff."

"Uh-huh. Maybe I know about that certain party."

"He was also in possession of some ivory."

"Two tusks, yeah."

"And a .303 Lee-Enfield British army rifle."

Angel looked at Ruth, who discreetly disappeared into the washroom, shutting the door. I heard the shower start.

"That could be right."

"But Louie doesn't handle guns."

"I un'erstand that" what he told the certain party."

"So where did this person get rid of it?"

"I don't want to get mixed up in your trial, Mr. Macarthur."

"It may mean I can do a deal for Louie. Help a friend. I just want to know where the rifle went, Angel."

"Louie never dealt me no bad cards, but I ain't a squealer."

"I'm a lawyer. It's not squealing. Anyway, there's a reward for information." I started to go for my jacket in the closet, where my wallet was, but Angel was shaking his head.

"Naw, I don't want that."

"What do you want?"

"I need a lawyer."

"You got him. For whatever you're charged with."

"I sapped this clown who was tryna wolf my old lady."

"Yes, I do assaults."

"And there's this quiff who's also haulin' me into court. They call it a filiation."

"A certain party got the quiff pregnant. Yeah, we can handle that."

"Oh, yeah, and I'm charged with a breach of probation on that assault."

"No problem."

"Plus, I'm out on bail on six B. and E.'s."

"Jeez, you got a bit of a shopping list here."

"There's also a carrying a concealed weapon, but I done the prelim on it."

"That's it?"

"It's enough."

I sighed. "Okay, Angel, I'll do them all. No fee."

"It's the same rifle, I guess, the one that turned up in that Om Bay. I met three guys in the Yale Hotel last fall, around October. I don't know no names."

"Three guys." My heart skipped. "Three big guys?"

"Naw, just one. From outa town. Fishermen, they was, from up north, one guy who owned a boat and two skinny little Indians I guessed who worked for him. Drunk Indians.

The guy, the boss, like, he gave me forty bucks and I took the rifle up to his hotel room."

"Describe him."

"Easy, he had three fingers missing from his right hand. Looked kinda like a claw."

PART THREE

○

Day of Judgment

Because thou lovest the burning-ground,
I have made a burning-ground of my heart—
That Thou, Dark One, haunter of the burning-ground,
Mayest dance thy eternal dance.
The ashes of the dead, strewn all about,
I have preserved against thy coming.
                    —Bengali hymn to Shiva

28

○

Revelations

I watch the white cloud, and am enveloped by it, swallowed in its pathless way, and I burst free, the propeller churning the mist into wisps, and the sun conquers again. Below us, the perfect green of the sea, silky, rolling, no wave or whisper of froth upon it.

I dip a wing and see below the scattered, toy-like farms on Texada Island: fat dots of cattle and sheep on yellow fields, shake-grey barns and sheds, high scrub and forest, yellowing cedars and maples. Then the rich and silent sea.

"Don't bump into a mountain, is all I ask," James Orval Harrison yelled over the roar of engine. I had met him at Fort Langley, by the Fraser docks where my father keeps his Cherokee float plane.

The mountains were to the right of us—the Coast Range with its white spires and milling, massive glaciers. Probing deep between them was the crooked witch's finger of Jervis fjord. To the left, haziness over Vancouver Island from the smoke of the glutton fire which still browsed the marges of Strathcona Park, where laboured Augustina Sage.

Behind us, an hour to the southeast: Vancouver, where a jury deliberated, and Brian Pomeroy kept the morning and afternoon watches. His task was to delay a verdict until we got our job done here. He would call by telephone at regular intervals.

Bliss had descended, and I had achieved a form of enlightenment. Shiva was not guilty. I was being permitted to serve, after all, the cause of the innocent. Yet part of me continued to wonder: was this an elaborate joke he had fashioned by

means of a magic, psychic power? Shiva, the god of the
elaborate jest.

It was a new paradigm. It had all come together magically,
a Rubic's cube abruptly solved after those weeks and months
of twisting and turning. Tom Joiner has testified he'd been
out fishing on that morning of death. Quite a grisly catch. He
had denied having any crew with him. How nervous on the
stand he'd been, fidgeting with those buttons, nearly collapsing. A tortured man, a monster lurking behind the curtains of
his innocent show.

Arthur had followed a right instinct in going for his jugular
on the stand. I had been sucked in by the little crucifix and
the good deeds.

Last night, during his study of transcripts and exhibits,
Harrison had discarded the Wheatley theory. When I told
him this morning about the Tom Joiner connection, he de-
duced that it wasn't Wheatley that Eddie Scanks had been
protecting.

And Harrison had noticed, in the photographs, that several
of the victims had been tied with double clove hitches, the
kind of knots mariners but few others might be expected to
know.

"How did I miss that?" I had said.

"I been casing stiffs since before you were born, kid," he
had said.

It felt good to have beside me some tough old fellow
capable of loosening up witnesses (teeth, too, if the legends
be believed) as I answered the petition of Poindexter Island
on this last Saturday of the summer of 1985.

I nestled the plane close to the sea as we came into
Desolation Sound. Below, a tug strained, wakeless, slow, long
rafts of fresh-cut timber inching along behind. Sails down,
windless and dispirited, a ketch motored toward Refuge Cove
on West Redonda Island. As the channel widened, I saw
Chaco Point, a rocky spit, the southern dagger of Poindexter.
I felt the island pulling me, drawing me into its ghost-ridden
forests, urging me to reach within and wrench its secrets
away.

In a few minutes we could see Tash-Tash, a sprinkling of
grey roofs up the hillside, and now we could see the boats,
the docks, the old hotel, the square, graceless buildings at
the centre. I did a pass, checking for flotsam and boat traffic
while Harrison had a good look at the town. I came into the

breeze in front of a clear channel, levelled, throttled down, and we skipped on a roll of sea, and fluttered into the bay.

Here were my friends Benjamin and Susy Johnson, who had got my message this morning and were standing by the seaplane dock.

I jumped out and tied up, and Honcho, blowing out his cheeks with relief at the prospect of terra firma, lumbered out after me. I made introductions.

"Who's the law here now?" I asked Benjamin.

"Law?" He shook his head. "No law here on Saturday. We get law on Tuesdays and Fridays. Constable comes in from Powell River. Ever since Mr. Scanks deserted us." A wry smile. "But Saturday, no law except Wendell there."

I caught a glint of sunlight from the mirror sunglasses of Wendell Joiner, who was standing on the wooden decking outside the Tash-Tash Lodge.

"I'll be the law," Harrison growled jovially. He was pleased to be back in harness. He squinted in the direction of the lodge—a boisterous dozen of the seabillies that Wendell hung out with were drinking beer outside. "Tom Joiner there, too?" Harrison asked.

"Tom went out on his dinghy a half hour ago," Benjamin said. "Maybe he got some crab traps somewhere."

Harrison was still peering at the crowd outside the lodge. "Guy who wears sunglasses and a khaki toque, he's got to have puny balls." He looked down at the blushing Susy. "Pardon me, ma'am."

"He's been drinking ever since Scanks took off," Benjamin said.

"Tom Joiner had a couple of crew members last winter," I said. "Who are they?"

"Wild boys," said Benjamin as we began walking up the dock to town. "I think from Ladner, down near Vancouver. City boys. They worked for Tom, October into December, when we had the big openings, but they went away somewhere before Christmas, never seen them since. Joe Gibson and Gordie something."

"Tom was fishing December eighth, in the morning," I said. "Those guys go out with him?"

"Don't know. I didn't even see Tom's boat go out. Only boat I saw go out was the police, in the afternoon, Scanks and Wendell."

"Tom wasn't with them?" I said.

"No. I seen Mr. Scanks and Wendell, like they was running to the police boat, and then I saw it go off into the fog."

"They were running?" Harrison said. "What for, I wonder." Slope-shouldered and bear-like, in his old suit and a hat that seemed as often sat upon as sitting atop his head, Harrison looked what he was: a cop with a veteran's confidence. His eyes were always moving, taking notes. Shy Susy seemed lost in his shadow.

"Wendell's a piss-tank these days, eh?" he said to me. "I'd like to scare him a little, get him talking. I'm a confession expert, kid."

"Wendell isn't a talkative man," I said.

"Ve haff vays." He told Benjamin and Susy to hang around their boat, and he'd talk to them later, and he and I went to the Firetrap Arms. "Wish I had old Swede with me. Lars Nordquist. We did a good Mutt and Jeff routine."

"I'll be Jeff," I said.

"You'll be nobody, kid. Stay out of the way if I get some action going."

Wendell was inside the bar now, working up some armpit sweat at the foosball table. Harrison and I took stools by the bar and watched him.

"Set you up?" The bald bartender—if he recognized me from my last visit, he didn't show it—swiped the bartop with a cloth. He had a mirthless, perspiring face, eyes buried like secrets in his skull.

"Two beer," said Harrison.

"One for me," I said. "What's new?"

"Don't know," said the bartender. "Don't keep track."

Harrison downed his first glass in two slow pulls, then relaxed over the second.

Wendell's concentration was impaired by drink and possibly by the knowledge we were staring at him. He slammed the foosball table with the fat of his fist as his opponent scored.

Harrison wandered over. "I'm betting on you, Wendell," he said. He looked him over, the toque, the mirror glasses, the big Coors buckle.

"Fuck off, Jack," Wendell said.

I moved to a stool nearer them. Wendell popped another ball into play.

"I'm betting you're a man who likes to make a deal. A man

who don't like the idea of doing a long bounce in the federal pen."

Wendell flubbed a good chance. The other guy scored on a shot from the defence.

"I'm betting if you do the bounce, you're gonna get your guts cut out in there. They kill creeps in the pen, that's what they like to do. All someone's got to do is get the word out, then Wendell Joiner, doing a lifer for the Om Bay killings, gets his guts cut out in the laundry room."

Wendell's arms seemed frozen. "Take a walk," Harrison told the other man. "Out of earshot." The man backed away from the table.

"Who're you?" Wendell said.

"Harrison, Detective James O. Harrison." He proffered his old Vancouver detective shield—an item which the copper must have forgotten to turn in when they retired him.

"Honcho Harrison. I heard of you."

Harrison smiled. "I'm on special assignment. We know everything now, Wendell." He spoke softly, menacingly. "They asked me to come up here and talk a little deal with you. We know Tom bought the .303 last October from a thief in Vancouver, at the Yale Hotel. If you had nothing to do with it, better start talking to me now. Otherwise we charge you both with murder."

"Not sure what you're talking about." Wendell was white.

Harrison reached up and slipped Wendell's mirrors off before he could react. "I like to see a man's eyes when I'm being friendly with him."

"Gimme those back."

"On the other hand," Honcho said, folding them into his shirt pocket, "if Tom wants to be the first to co-operate, we'll do the deal with him. I'm offering to you first, pal. Cause I like you a lot." He sipped his beer.

"You're tryin' some trick."

"Let's take a walk in the sunshine, Sunshine."

"I ain't goin' nowhere."

I surveyed the bar: three Indian fishermen at the far end, Wendell's foosball competitor at the bar with the waiter and bartender, a dozen guys still outside staring at us.

Wendell tried to sidle away, but Harrison blocked him with a straight forearm, and Joiner bounced off, staggered back a step. Then he tried to duck under the arm, and Harrison grabbed him by his shirt collar, jerked him back. "Listen, you fuck, I'm talking to you."

When Wendell tried to slap his hand away, Harrison, with an incredible, almost invisible speed, batted him so hard in the kidneys that Wendell's face opened up, fragmented. Trying to catch his breath, he could utter nothing more complex than an extended, polysyllabic grunt.

"You heard of me, eh, Wendell?" He turned to me. "He don't need a civil rights lawyer hanging around. Why don't you pay a visit to the Scanks house, see what you can find? Wendell and me are going to take a walk down behind the fish plant warehouse."

Joiner had both hands plugged into the area between groin and belly, was still gasping for breath as Honcho, tightly gripping him by the biceps muscle, pulled him toward the exit doors.

Here was the great civil liberties lawyer standing by ignobly, witness to a classic case of police brutality. Wait—this was ex-police brutality, an emergency for which corners had to be cut.

How was that jury doing?

Cool, like Alan Ladd in *Shane*, drinking sarsaparilla while the cowhands sized the little gunfighter up, I sipped my beer while I waited for Brian's three-P.M. call. I tried again to pump the bartender. "What's happening, man?" I said.

"Dunno, don't get involved."

I went into the lobby. Brian's call came on the dot.

"The word from the sheriffs is they're for conviction, nine to two, one even."

"We've only got two?" My voice cracked. Margolis and one other. Could they hang on one more day? "Brian, don't let them give a verdict, no matter what happens."

"What am I going to do, hold a shotgun on them? Max, I can't buy time unless you let me release the Angelo Lucchi statement."

"No, we're on the verge of breaking this. I don't want anyone alerted. Honcho is just now talking to Wendell Joiner. And if Tom Joiner finds out there's evidence connecting him to the massacre, he'll run before Honcho can get to him and extort one of his famous voluntary confessions. Fake a heart attack, phone in a bomb threat, use your famous imagination. Call me at six sharp, after the jury takes their dinner—"

Brian cut me off. "Hold on, Max, here's Lukey."

I could hear Brian's voice away from the receiver. And Lukey's. Brian came back on. "Scanks has just turned himself into the police at a motel near Lethbridge. Leroys says he hasn't got the details."

"Are they bringing him back to Vancouver?"

"By plane tonight. Leroy asks what we want to do."

"Surely to God Hammersmith will give us until the morning now. Apply to reopen so the defence can finish Scanks' cross-examination. He can't deny that now."

"Don't count your chickens. I'll call at eighteen-hundred hours."

A sticky marine stench followed me up a gravel road past some faded houses to the brow of the hill. Below me, the fish plant buildings, the fish dock thrusting into the salt-chuck. The town was hidden behind a high promontory.

The Scanks house had both a good view and a good smell of the plant. A path went down to it directly. *You live above a pile of fish guts, you learn to hate the fucking fish.* A memory from that first, hostile talk with him.

It was a prefab house, lapped wood siding, ranch style, painted, of all colours, turquoise. It must have been a helicopter job because there were no delivery trucks here, just a few beaters and this RCMP four-by-four collecting dust in the carport.

As I crossed the weed-tufted yellow lawn, my nose picked up whiffs of burning meat. The sound of a dog, woofing.

A remembrance swallowed me. Shiva Ram Acharya swept into my mind. *Follow me. Follow me.* His laughter.

Behind the house I saw another roof-line, partly obscured by trees.

Again, his laughter, his roundness of face in front of me. *Oh, it is quite funny.*

I shivered. Had his demented, divine eye picked out, from the infinity of sensation that I might in a lifetime endure, this time and place?

The woofs kept a one-second beat. Numbly, I followed them and the smell around the side of the house.

A voice high-pitched: "Oh, yes, oh, yes."

I tom-peeped from between evergreen branches. The burning smell came from a brick barbecue several feet away from a picnic table upon which a couple were in loud congress. I assumed it was Mrs. Scanks and her enamorato, the fish plant manager, Cosgrove. Their feet were toward me, his pants hanging from his boots, his arms gripping either side of the table, and he was woofing with every stroke. Her heavy thighs were apart, a summery dress was above her waist, and peach-coloured bikini panties were dangling from a knee into an open mustard jar. My trespassing eye also observed on the table relish, pickles, butter, onions, and hamburger buns.

Wimpy Morgan should have been here to rescue the meat. Four patties were sizzling to a blackness on the grill, and their smoke was swirling away in the breeze.

"Sweet Jesus," cried the man, in his throes. The relish jar fell over, slopped contents on a six-pack of beer on the ground.

Cosgrove decelerated quickly, and as he slumped loosely atop a complaining Mrs. Scanks, I snaked my way among the trees, out of their view, then found myself standing before a structure of cinder-block walls, bare and ugly, unadorned even by windows, a flat tar-and-gravel roof through which a stove-pipe poked, a heavy metal door open a few inches, a power line entering at the doortop.

"My God, the hamburgers!" Mrs. Scanks' voice.

Pitch black in here, but I found a light switch and turned it on after closing the door. Fluorescent lights crackled from the ceiling and popped into life. It was cool and musty. Junk items were stacked against all walls: old chairs, at least two old beds broken into their pieces, springs, mattresses, bed-steads against the far wall. An oil heater in one corner, some packing cases, plywood sheets, a worktable with tools, rags, oil cans. The ceiling and walls were lined with a soundproofing material.

Harrison would be unhappy if I touched anything. I turned the light out, squeaked the big door open and heard from behind the trees his easygoing drawl. "I saw smoke, thought there was a fire."

"You from the forest service or something?" came Cosgrove's voice.

"Harrison, Vancouver Police."

I plunged into the trees, picked my way out onto the road in front of the house, retraced my steps to the back yard.

"Here he is now," Harrison said. "Thought you were going to come direct here, kid. Mindie Scanks, Mike Cosgrove, this is the lawyer Max Macarthur, who's co-operating with the authorities in this case. Right, Max?" He tucked his shield away.

"Right," I said, shaking hands. Mindie Scanks was about thirty-five, her full bodice was heaving with recent exertion and she was nervously combing her hair.

I remember Cosgrove from my visit to Tash-Tash last July: a loud clown quaffing beer straight from a jug.

"We're reopening the investigation," Harrison said. "I've been appointed special investigator."

Cosgrove bent down, pulled up the six-pack and began wiping relish from the bottles. "You guys like a beer?"

"You're the manager of the plant, right?"

"Yeah, that's my job, I gotta confess to that." An attempt at laughter.

Harrison and I declined the beers. I was still feeling strange. Shiva's laughter was echoing somewhere. Was he around? *Why didn't you follow me?*

"What were you doing on the morning of Saturday, December eighth, last year?" Harrison went right to work.

"Aren't you going to read my rights? Honest, I didn't do it." Cosgrove chuckled.

"There's nobody who ain't suspect any more, Cosgrove."

"What's going on?" he said.

"Mrs. Scanks, I wonder if you'd mind going into your house. I want to talk to you alone later."

She gave a nervous flutter and entered the house.

"Let's take a load off, Cosgrove." Harrison sat on a lawn chair, Cosgrove on the picnic-table bench. I stayed standing, buzzing.

"My wife, Laura, is in a wheelchair most of the time with M.S. We were just going to wrap some burgers up, Mindie and me, and go down to my place."

"Mike, from the front of the house you can see your fish plant, also the dock."

"This house?"

"Yep."

"I guess you can."

"From the front bedroom in fact."

"The bedroom? Yeah, I guess. I hope nothing's being insinuated."

"I don't insinuate, ain't my style."

Cosgrove's hand slipped down to his crotch as if he had forgotten to zip his fly.

"Let's get back to December eighth. Where were you?"

"I guess I got up around nine, made some breakfast for

Laura and the kids. It was Saturday, hell, I don't know, did chores. Listen, you guys want to take home some big chinooks, so red they look like raw steak, be my guests. You fly in on that plane this morning?"

"See any boats come into or leave your dock that morning? From the vantage point of the bedroom window here?"

"What are you trying to say?"

"You're so coy you make me sick, Cosgrove." Harrison got up, knelt, and with the lead end of a pencil raised a pair of peach-coloured bikini panties from the grass beside the table. A gob of mustard rolled off and fell. "You wanna put these in a bun with some relish, grind a little pepper on top."

Like one of his chinook salmon, Cosgrove noiselessly opened and closed his mouth.

"Eddie Scanks took off that morning and you came up here to visit, okay?"

"I don't think anybody's got any right trying to ruin people's lives. I got a wife. I told you she has M.S. Have a heart."

Harrison let the panties drop from his pencil. He'd been holding his notepad with the other hand, but slipped it into his pocket. "Well, Mike, maybe we don't have to tell the whole world about certain things."

"I'm always willing to work with the law."

"Course y'are. Just help us out a little here, okay? You help us enough, we don't have to involve you."

"We're off the record?"

"Man to man."

"I been seeing her. It's not easy at home, you can imagine. Eddie doesn't know."

"December eighth, Mike, tell us all about it."

"My house is about four lots further down the road. I remember waking up maybe seven o'clock, heard a boat engine down by the fishdock, and I heard Eddie's voice down there. It was Tom Joiner's boat—he'd left it at the fish dock the day before. We finished breakfast, I took a little stroll, and I dropped in to see Mindie, see if something was up."

"And was something up, Mike?"

Cosgrove turned surly. "This is a small town, Mr. Harrison. Nobody knows Mindie and I—"

Harrison lost his friendly tone. "Yeah, and nobody wants to get involved around here, I picked that up already. What did you see from the window?"

"Well, I guess Tom's boat came in. Tom Joiner."

"What time?"

"Noon."

"And?"

"It dropped off Eddie and Wendell, then took off, went to the Harbours Board dock, that general direction, couldn't see where it went exactly. Eddie and Wendell started coming up the hill, so I scrammed and went home, but I know from Mindie Eddie changed into his uniform, stuffed his old clothes into the washer."

I sat down. Shiva laughing. *Why didn't you follow me?*

"Wasn't Scanks supposed to have been breaking up a wild party earlier that morning?"

"I heard about it," Cosgrove said. "Guys with drugs up at Neeley Wilde's cabin. I think Eddie shut it down about seven."

"He said it went on until later."

"I don't know about that, I wasn't there. Wendell was, I heard, and maybe Tom."

"Let me confer with my colleague," Harrison said, and drew me aside while Cosgrove stoked up the barbecue.

"Just to fill you in," Harrison said, "Wendell ran away. Half-drunk he staggers faster than my flat feet can run. I'm not worried—he can't exactly get a taxi out of town."

"Scanks has turned himself in."

"Poor fucker, my heart bleeds."

"Honcho, I have something to show you."

Harrison called to Cosgrove: "We're gonna talk about how we can protect you nice folks from unnecessary scandal. Why don't you relax there for a few moments." He followed me behind the grove of firs to the squat building behind them. I took him inside, switched on the lights.

Harrison took it all in, bedpost by oilcan. "I'll be fucked."

"Why?"

"It's an indoor firing range." He pointed to the soundproofing and to chalk marks on the concrete floor: thick yellow lines. "Stand here, and pow," he said, firing an imaginary handgun at the far wall, on which a couple of boxsprings and mattresses were leaning. He went to the work bench. "Gun oil. See those mounts on the wall? Set up for six rifles. Hearing protectors in this drawer." He was shuffling through things. "Here's something interesting—looks like a scorecard. 'W'—that's Wendell, he's got the best score. Ain't this grand. These boys had a hobby to keep them out of trouble."

He went to his hands and knees, sifted through the rubble on the floor. "What were they using for targets?"

"I think I know."

"Hope you didn't get your prints over everything."

I went to the back, started hauling down the mattresses. Darth Vader all right, advancing toward us, swinging his laser sword, just like the posters outside the movie theatres. Except here he was ragged with bullet rips from head to pelt. The poster to the right was an enormous head-and-shoulders of Mao Tse-tung, smiling, with holes in his head. Behind were thick timbers in which many slugs were imbedded.

"They must have been in the habit of picking up most of their spent shells," Harrison said, slowly standing up with a creak and a groan. He came over, held out a handkerchief with three spent handgun cartridges and one rifle cartridge. "Two of these are .32, probably the standard police issue. This here's a .45. Someone packs a heavy heater around here. Wasn't Wendell in the U.S. Marines once? They use a Colt .45 service pistol. The long one, that's a .303. There's got to be more. Let's talk to them shy lovers again, then we'll search this place an inch at a time."

29

○

Dance of Destruction

The sunlight stretched through the west-facing windows of the lobby of the Firetrap Arms, causing the desk clerk and me to look yellow and burnished. The cloud-scattered sky, hazy with carbon from the fires of Vancouver Island, hinted of a prodigious Pacific sunset.

It was a quarter past six, Brian had not called, and we hadn't found Tom Joiner nor rediscovered Wendell. We were entangled in the unravelling coils of December eighth, but the whole had not come, nor enlightenment.

Mindie Scanks had told us, yes, Eddie used to have different friends over for target practice, not just Wendell and Tom, but other guys from town. Yes, they all had rifles and guns—but practically everyone around here has a firearm of some kind, to hunt with or kill seals with. Yes, Eddie had come home about noon on the eighth, had rushed away without a word. No, Eddie hadn't contacted her since he disappeared last weekend, and she couldn't help us any better than she could help the RCMP investigator who had come by several days ago.

Eighteen hours, o-seven minutes, eighteen seconds on the clock. The scythe of time sweeps quickly on. What was happening in Vancouver? Had the jury come back, was that why Brian had not been able to call?

I had desultory conversations with the desk clerk, a young man with a flat expression on a flat face who, like the bartender, didn't get involved. *Tom Joiner? Can't say. Maybe he went off to Peale Island, bingo tonight in the St. Mary's hall.* Tash-Tashians are taciturn folk.

As for Wendell, we had checked his boat late this afternoon, found it deserted and locked. Then we discovered he had been living for the last three months with a Portuguese woman, a fish scaler. She hadn't seen him all day. Esmeralda, a short, weary woman who squinted distrustfully at us from her doorway, seemed uninterested in Wendell's whereabouts. "Mebbe ees boozing at house of some guy." She wore a purple ring under her left eye.

"He have any guns in here?" Harrison asked.

She closed the door on us.

We had stopped by the co-op store, where the liquor agent told us Wendell had been around two hours earlier, a couple of local decadents in tow, and picked up two bottles of Wiser's De Luxe. We hadn't wanted the trail to grow cold, but were forced to return to the hotel for my six P.M. call and to calm the growling beasts in our stomachs. While I waited in the lobby, Harrison was ordering from the chalkboard menu in the lounge.

Outside, the sun continued to paint, and inside, the round wall clock—another bland, expressionless Tash-Tash face—thumped the seconds noisily away. We would soon be abandoning all hope of returning to Vancouver tonight. Although fool I had been about many things, I was not fool enough to bring a float plane into the Fraser River at night.

A fool about many things. Well, I was only thirty, too young to be very smart. I uttered a mirthless chuckle, and the desk clerk blinked his eyes at me.

Suddenly a vicious pain shot through me, in the back of the neck and the head, and I was immobilized by it, felt it cutting into my brain, and then it utterly disappeared, and I was again with the expressionless desk clerk and the clock that said six-forty, and the sun turning everything into worthless gold.

I rubbed the back of my neck, and blew out slowly.

"You feelin' okay?"

"Pinched nerve," I said. It had happened to me before. Such things come from tension.

The phone rang and the desk clerk handed it to me. Brian. "Hammersmith's just put the whip to them. Called them in fifteen minutes ago. 'You ladies and, ah, gentlemen seem to be having a problem.' Then he adds, 'Or one of you has.' And he's practically staring at Margolis as he says this, Max. The word from the jury room is it's eleven-to-one. The judge gave the spiel about there's got to be give and take, the cost to the state of a new trial, et cetera. He told them to relax over a pleasant meal and come back at eight. I think Margolis will buckle before the night's over."

"His lordship refused the adjournment, eh?"

"Roger, you read me. Scanks or not, he says *technically*, as he puts it, once the case has gone to the jury, we can't reopen unless there's new evidence, and Scanks is old evidence. Do I tell him about Angelo Lucchi?"

"Brian, we're still waiting to talk to a certain gentleman Lucchi had dealings with." Nearby, the clerk pretended not to be listening. "Give us until after dinner. Call me in two hours."

"Another thing: Shiva. Apparently he's down in the cells laughing his head off."

"Enjoying his joke."

"What?"

"Nothing."

We rang off. Kneading my neck muscles with my fingers, I went into the beverage room, where were Honcho Harrison and about twenty other customers, all ochre with the light that flowed through the big plate windows, from the sun falling into the smoky distances.

"I ordered some Ukes for us," Harrison said. "We're gonna be here the night, kid. Wendell will be so snackered by now he won't be able to talk until the morning. I wonder if his brother may've found out we're here and lammed." He peered through the windows to the bay. "What a show." The sun flattening red as it touched some distant, purple peaks.

Harrison looked like a hobo in his lumpy suit, grease-stained at the knees from crawling about the floor of Scanks' shooting gallery. Forming one of the lumps in his suit were eight spent cartridges, six shorts and two longs. Five from a .32. One from a .45. One from a .303. And one from a .30-.30. Using a magnifying eyepiece, Honcho had compared the .303 case with enlarged photographs of the cases found near the bodies. They matched. He was sure the .30-.30 would also match the cartridges Benjamin and I had found.

The waiter brought a couple of paper plates: two double orders of Ukrainian sausages within greasy crusts of garlic bread. "Looked like the top item on the menu," Harrison said. "You hungry?"

"You bet." I could have endured oolichan grease. The waiter placed condiments on the table, two more glasses of

beer, accepted our money with a grunt. The other customers
were just quietly drinking, watching, waiting. All the town
knew of the humiliation of Wendell earlier at the hands of
this grizzled old cop from Vancouver. At two joined tables,
some fishermen and plant workers cast sullen glances at us
from time to time. I remembered some had been with
Wendell during my visit here in July: the evening I had
called him a contemptible boor.

"You armed?" I asked Harrison. I pried the slices of bread
apart to view the ugly creature inside.

"No, why?"

"There is unfriendliness here."

"Relax, kid. Mustard?" He passed me a yellow squeeze
container with a nozzle top. "I'm kind of turned off mustard
right now. You think Cosgrove eats it outa her snatch? I heard
of honey and I heard of gumdrops, but never heard of
mustard." He bit into his Uke and chewed contentedly. "I
remember one guy he liked to eat raw weiners right outa the
joy trail, picked up dames turning out at The Corner, Hastings
and Carrall, the ones with the syph sores all over them, he'd
give them twenty bucks to eat a raw weenie outa them—
never used mustard though."

I was holding the mustard container over my sausage,
repelled by the thought of the stuff oozing onto those old,
wizened tubes of meat upon my plate. There were valid
reasons for being a vegetarian like Shiva.

"Had a homicide once, Tommy Lucero, he ate strychnine
outa his old lady's snatch, but we only nailed her for a
manslaughter, three years." He swigged from his glass and
patted a burp from his belly.

"Mr. Macarthur," the bartender called. He pulled an extension phone from under the counter. "You can take it here."
I preferred the lobby with its fewer ears, but went to the bar.

"What's up, Brian?" Had the jury, like me, lost appetite?
Or merely decided to convict before dinner.

"We have the adjournment." But the voice was burdened
with more than its usual freight of doom. "Get a grip on
something, old buddy."

"What?"

He seemed unable to say it. Finally: "There was a knifing.
In the cells. I think maybe he's been killed. Shiva."

On the six-inch timber post was a rudely-lettered cardboard sign: "No shoes, no shirt, no shervice." Beneath that someone had scrawled, "No shit."

"You there, Max?"

"Yeah." I cleared the phlegm from my throat. "Yeah."

"As much as I've got is this: Hank Hooper had a jury out all day, too. A punk about eighteen who smashed some guy's head with a tire iron in a back-alley brawl. The jury didn't give Dumptruck the expected manslaughter, so the punk got life. An hour ago he went into a rage in the cells, maybe had some drugs in there, I don't know."

The sky outside the windows, horizon to skyward: red, red, red, as if the mountains to the west had exploded. Golden boats in the bay danced on the sun's reflected flames.

"Max?"

"Yeah, I'm listening."

"I'm here with Leroy. He says because it's Saturday, they were on weekend security downstairs, a couple of rookies who didn't know the prisoners were to be kept separated. The punk had some kind of homemade shiv, stabbed Shiva from behind, just below the scalp."

Lukey came on the line: "Max, they've just taken him away by ambulance to VGH emergency."

"He's alive."

"Maybe just. The jury's going to be recessed until Monday, that's the word from Hammersmith's chambers."

Sudden tumult around me. The door from the lobby swings sharply open, and Esmeralda, Wendell's girlfriend, comes stark-eyed into the bar. "He ees go crazy, go crazy!" She turns to me. "He wan' keel you!"

I am in shock, can't react. Now a gunshot from somewhere, and a smashing of glass, and the hotel clerk bangs backwards through the lobby door, ashen-faced. Following him, Wendell Joiner. Dressed in jungle fatigues. Holding a .45 automatic in his left hand. Something else in his right. A grenade.

He is unhinged with drink. His eyeballs bug and look feverish. I have a surplus and unnecessary thought: where are his blue-mirror glasses? Still in Harrison's pocket.

"Nobody fucks with me!" The muzzle of the gun moves in an arc. "I am the law!"

The muzzle goes up, and an explosion screams through the room, and plaster falls from the ceiling, and Wendell's shrieking voice: "Nobody fucks with me! Nobo'y!"

The black shadows of men and women trying to sidle

toward doors, and another shot, and Wendell screaming, "Ever'one sits! Nobody goes!" Stiff bodies ease into chairs. I am benumbed, holding the receiver of the telephone, setting it gently down on the bartop. Lukey's distant, scratchy voice: "Max? Max?"

Wendell hears that noise, looks to the side, at me. I am still standing, all joints soldered.

"I seen you somep'ace." He blinks, trying to fix me in some part of his anarchic memory.

"I need your help, Wendell." It's Harrison's voice, from across the room. Wendell wheels around, squints at the bulky shadow seated near the big plate window.

"I'm the law! Nobo'y fucks with me!" He takes a shaky bead on a pitcher of beer on a nearby table, and the gun bellows again, and the pitcher shatters and two men scramble underneath that table. "Nobody move! You fucks! Don' you know, there's fuckin' *war* on! Fuckin' Commies!" He turns again to me. "I know what you are, you're a fuckin' spy!"

Three more hand grenades tied to his webbed khaki belt. This is not a movie. He is real and I am real, and I may die. Poindexter Island, death brings me here, and its spectre haunts me here.

"I need your help on this one, Wendell." Harrison's voice is calm but remote. Wendell turns to him again.

"You ol' fuck, I c'n take your head off with one shot, whatcha say t'that?" He whirls his gun back at me. "You tryna get behin' me? Sit down! I know you, y'r the lawyer. Siddown, y'r un'er arres'!"

I find muscles that will answer, and back slowly away from the bar, Brian's voice crackling from the receiver: "Holy Jesus, what's happening?"

Near Harrison, I find a chair at a solitary table. "Let's work together on this one, Wendell," he says. "I hear you're a good auxiliary cop, and I need a deputy. Sit down, I'll buy you one."

"I flush't y'out, didn' I, you fuck. You're un'er arres'." His voice sails: "Nobo'y fucks wi' me! I c'n shoot y'r fuckin' face off!"

From the corner of my eye I see Harrison, with measured slowness, raise his glass of draught to his mouth, sip, let it settle on the table. Wendell staggers a few steps toward us. He is protected from all but the most foolish attempt from anyone behind him: his fingers hold the ring of the grenade, and if that ring is pulled, attacker will become martyr, as perhaps will Macarthur, from whom Wendell now stands six feet away.

Sun-dyed russet faces. Esmeralda cowering on the floor against a wall. The hotel clerk on a barstool, rigid. The bald bartender who doesn't get involved behind him, crouching below the bar. He has a door from which he can exit. He doesn't go, but a few people slide out through the lobby door.

"I seen you somewhere," Wendell says to me, squinting. He is swallowed in a fiery bath. "You tried t'fuck wi' me, didn' you?" He comes closer, studies me, then Harrison. "You *both* tried t'fuck wi' me. Y'know what I do t' people try t'fuck with me?" And he fires three times past us, through the big pane of glass, six feet high, between Harrison's table and mine, and the glass splinters outward, sending shards wheeling onto the deck and the wooden railing, onto the rocks below.

"He ain't gonna kill anybody, kid," Harrison reassured me, his voice eerily relaxed. "He's just having some fun with us."

Some fun. Max Macarthur was about to get married, was about to have a summer cottage and a dog named Lech and a cat named Mao but not before Ruth and he went on an Alaska cruise. He is only thirty, has his whole future.

Wendell extends his right hand, with the grenade. "Yeah, it's live. What d'you say I stuff it down y'r fuckin' Commie throats?" His back is to the bartender, who is creeping up slowly, a steel pry bar in his hands.

"I've got your sunglasses here, Wendell," Harrison said carefully, plucking them from his shirt pocket, extending them. "I been saving them for you. I want to be your friend."

"You ain't gonna get me, y' ol' fuck. 'Cause y'ain' gonna *live* t'get me. Y'r gonna *die* for what you done!"

Out of some deep-rooted instinct, Wendell reacts to the bartender's soft footfall, turns his head slightly, then whirls.

He fires twice. The bald man steps back with an astonished look on his face, a spatter of blood at the centre of his chest.

The .45 whips back toward us, but in the elapsed two seconds Harrison has hurled the table at Wendell, whose shots go wild as he dodges it, and I drop to the floor, beneath the window ledge, and Harrison has stumbled with his effort, goes to his hands and knees, and as he scrambles up, Wendell is screaming, "Die with me, you fucks! Die with me!" And there is madness in his febrile eyes and he is fixing the ring of the grenade into his teeth.

He pulls it. He lifts his thumb from the grenade trigger.
Four and a half seconds.

"Nobo'y fucks wi' me!"

It is a frenzied kaleidoscope. A shadow moving hard to my
right, now flying, a man with a ponytail and a hook for a
hand. A powerful collision of bodies. Wendell driving forward
with amazing momentum. The grenade trickling from his
hand. Wendell's boots stumbling past me as he tries to catch
himself and brace and fire. My hands grasping his ankle,
sending him tripping backwards over the splintered glass of
the window ledge. His *whump* as he falls upon the cedar
planks outside.

And Tom Joiner dropping to his knees in front of me,
getting to that grenade first, lobbing it with a quarter-second
to spare, underhanded, out the window.

Where Wendell is.

Was.

I lose all my air, feel a great crunch of pain and dizziness as
Harrison's huge body lands on mine and in that same instant
in the fury of blood and sunset, the grenade explodes on the
deck, a wood- and bone-splintering crash that sends shudders
into the huge piles upon which sits the old hotel, then three
more blasts from the other grenades tied to Wendell Joiner's
belt, and showers of glass and wood splinters and blood, and
waves of percussion and heat, and some of the pilings below
collapse and the floor begins to tilt crazily down.

I sense Harrison dragging me up by my arms, and we are
scrambling behind Tom Joiner up the tilted floor, shouts and
screams, people pushing and struggling through the door into
the lobby, dragging the body of the bartender, as the Tash-
Tash Lodge flickers red not with the fallen sun but with the
flames that are licking up from the dry cedar planks outside,
from the tinder shingle walls.

Before Harrison pulls me gasping through the lobby door, I
turn around and see the hole torn from the deck, and the
bloody stump of a leather-booted leg beside a burning railpost.

I could hear the wild dance, the dance of destruction.

I sat on the grass outside the front doors of the burning
hotel, collecting my breath, my senses. People were climbing
down the rocks to the beach, avoiding the wooden walkway,
now wonky and bent. They carried away the body of the man
who doesn't get involved.

"You all right, kid?"

I had some cuts, one slow to clot above a knee, but not deep. The window ledge had been sufficiently thick and timbered to save us from the impacts.

"I'm okay, you're not." I ripped my shirt into lengths to cover a flesh wound. A bullet had nicked him in the shoulder. I was able to stanch the blood flow.

The flames raced onto the shake roof of the hotel. In a town without water, only God could save this building. God didn't care. God was still unhurriedly colouring the western sky, and this work mocked His puny fire on Poindexter Island.

Only one other person was out there now: Tom Joiner, squatting, his head in his hands. Tom, who had killed his brother. He was crying.

Harrison crouched beside him. "Time to talk now?"

"Yeah, it's time. I didn't have nothin' to do with it. It was Wendell and Eddie."

The flames flared with a loud fizzling sound in the parched fronds of the cedars that draped their branches over the roof.

From the north, a wiggle of lightning, fingers spreading from it. A growl, a distant clap.

30

o

Flagrante Delicto

Red sky at night. The Village of Tash-Tash Cove was burning.
A fresh breeze from the ocean had flung Wendell Joiner's
death fire deep into the trees and salal; it was chewing its way
up the hill to the houses at the top. From my vantage point at
the bow of the *Black Cormorant*, Tom Joiner's gillnetter, I
could see the top of a fire billow out like an incendiary bomb,
sending flaming branches to the tar-shingle roof of the Scanks'
house. Mindie and her lover would be by the fish plant,
which was upwind and whose generator-driven seawater pump
was wetting the area around. It would be saved. Most of the
homes would go up.

The wind caused anchor drift, a final pull toward this evil
place, undergoing its final evil triumph, screaming its dying
declaration.

I sat high on the snub of the bow, holding a guy wire, my
legs dangling over the side above waves that slapped past to
the east, and the boat and I rocked in the dance of the wind
and water. I saw God dance, too, in the flames, Shiva in his
aspect of Nataraja, the dance king. Shiva who danced the
universe away and danced it back again. Shiva who demands
human sacrifices. Shiva Ram Acharya, teacher of fire.

Distantly, the fire spat and sang; closer, the wind whined
through the stays, and when it lapsed I heard the voices
through the transom behind me. Honcho Harrison, flattering,
cajoling, threatening. Getting it.

I had reached a cold and lucid state. I was savage in the
triumph I felt at seeing this cruel town die. How many here
had kept the secret? As with the affair of Mindie and Mike—
everybody knows, nobody talks.

338

Some townspeople were gathered by the fish plant; others were on the docks near the boats, and many, like us, were out on them. I could see their silhouettes around me, unmoving, bronze outlines facing landward.

I heard the report of a fire-split cedar trunk. A memory from July.

I remembered how lovely this island had seemed to me when first I had come here.

A lurch, and I turned and saw Harrison with a signal lamp. "Two short and a long when you hear the helicopter. Keep repeating the signal until you know they see it." His left arm was in a sling.

I nodded, took the lamp, nodded toward the cabin where Tom was. "How is he?" I said.

"He's good, he's good."

The helicopter came a few minutes later, and found us quickly. When the pilot signalled toward one of the two small islands in the cove, we hauled anchor and Tom took us close in to the lee of it, and the helicopter settled onto the grass, waiting until we came in the dinghy.

Three uniformed RCMP officers and a man with a medical bag hopped onto the dinghy and departed. I followed Tom Joiner and Harrison into the aircraft.

"Hello, Frank," I said.

Storenko, beside the pilot, was half turned to us. "The judge wants you before he'll hear our application, Max," he said. He looked at Tom Joiner, who slouched into a seat, head cast down. Storenko's eyes met Harrison's.

We belted ourselves in and the big blades started churning, and the nose dipped a little and we moved into the sky.

Outside, the dinghy moved through the choppy water toward what was left of the town. Law and order were returning to Tash-Tash Cove.

* * *

On the flight to Vancouver, I read the statement of Tom Joiner, question-and-answer form in Harrison's confident, large penscript:

Q: When were you first approached to go to Om Bay?

A: About three days before the eighth. Corporal Scanks, all he told us was he was going to make an arrest there, under the Immigration Act. He asked me to take him and Wendell.

Q: How did you and Wendell and Ed Scanks get together that morning, the eighth?

A: Wendell and me were at a party up at some loggers, and Ed came by there about seven in the morning to shut it down, and me and Wendell went with him to my boat and took off from there. I had the boat down by the fish dock.

Q: What kind of condition were you and Wendell in?

A: We were a little loaded. Wendell had snorted a lot of cocaine all during the night that those loggers brought from Nanaimo. I wasn't too bad.

Q: What time did you get to Om Bay?

A: Eight-thirty, it was just getting light.

Q: Were you armed?

A: Wendell brought his .30-.30 from his boat, and I had the .303 on board the *Black Cormorant*. I never touched the gun all day. I had nothing to do with this.

Q: Tell me what happened.

A: We tied up to the commune's boat. Ed took the .303 and Wendell had his rifle, and they went in on the longboat. I stayed on the *Black Cormorant*. They went into shore where the creek let out and a bunch of people from the commune came to meet them. There were some shouts back and forth, and I guess these people were objecting. And then things started happening.

Q: What things?

A: I saw someone grab the barrel of Wendell's rifle, and must have jerked it. It's a real hair-trigger, that's the way Wendell likes to keep it. Liked to keep it. Anyway, it fired, and the guy took a bullet in the chest. I don't know what got into Wendell, if it was the coke or what, but he went kind of crazy, kept shooting, and he hit someone in the back and another guy in the leg when they were running.

Q: Yes?

A: Then there was some shouts from Ed and Wendell, I didn't hear their words exactly, but most of the people stopped running and began raising their hands. One girl got away, behind some trees, and ran for the forest.

Q: That was Emelia?

A: I guess. I just stayed where I was, I didn't want no part of this. They all disappeared toward where the campsite was, and Wendell was holding his gun on them. There was about half an hour, and I could make out yelling, and there was one shot, Wendell told me later a guy had started to run as everybody was being tied up, and then I heard about twenty more shots. Wurz, the guy they made help Wendell tie the people up, he was shot in the back, and the others were shot in the head.

Q: Who told you this—Wendell or Eddie, or both?

A: Wendell, later. Eddie didn't say nothing, he was white. Anyway, to get back, after a while, after the last shots, Wendell and Eddie came back to where the creek was, and they dragged the two bodies from there to the campsite, and after, they threw a lot of snow over the blood where the two bodies had been. It was starting to snow again pretty hard, anyway.

Q: And they came back to your boat?

A: Yeah, in the dinghy, and there was a lot of blood on Wendell, not so much on Eddie, or I didn't notice. Wendell was really hyper, his eyes bugging out, kind of, and he told me he and Ed decided to do away with all the witnesses.

Q: What did Ed say about all this?

A: All he said was Wendell used the .303 because it couldn't be traced, and I could get into trouble because I had bought it, and he knew from a serial number check it was a stolen rifle and I better keep my mouth shut. He still had the Lee-Enfield with him.

Q: Did he shoot anyone?

A: I don't know, but I guess he had his rifle trained on them when they were being tied up.

Q: Did you go back to Tash-Tash?

A: Yeah. Things were pretty mixed up. They decided to go back to town, and we were going to ditch the rifles, but they got scared and decided we should change clothes in town and then go back to Om Bay.

Q: Why?

A: There was the girl, Emelia, and the guru guy, Shiva, nobody seen him. We came in at the fish dock, and I let them out there, and I went to the big dock and tied up near the police launch. Ed told me to warm it up and wait for them.

Q: Why did you agree to go back with them?

A: I was scared not to. I didn't want to get in any deeper, but I was just out and out scared. I wasn't going to have nothing to do with anything, just run the boat, and I was scared they'd use the .303 to tie me in. Anyway, after a while, Wendell and Ed, he was in his uniform, came running to the police boat making lots of noise so I guess people would notice us leaving for somewhere. Ed told me in case anyone asked to say we'd been home until then, about twelve-thirty, and that we were going to Om Bay to answer a complaint from someone at the commune.

Q: And you went back to Om Bay?

A: Yeah, but I stayed on the boat just like before. When Ed and Wendell went to shore, back to the campsite, I guess that's when they saw Shiva babbling away with blood all over him, he was out of it, so they arrested him.

Q: For murder.

A: That was the idea. He was completely out of it, even when they brought him to the boat, I thought, but he got a little better, said he couldn't remember nothing.

Q: And the rifles?

A: Well, they decided to leave the Lee-Enfield there with the bodies because it couldn't be traced, and that really scared me. That's why I couldn't say nothing. Even though Wendell was my brother, I might of said something except for the rifle. The .30-.30, Wendell's, he threw it into the saltchuck, in the bay, while we waited for the RCMP planes.

Q: Have you made this statement voluntarily, without fear of threat or promise of favour?

A: Yes, it's all true.

Signed, Thomas Joiner.

31

○

Change of Venue

Mr. Justice Hammersmith's big house, tricked out in the Victorian style, was stuck square on a treeless lot in South Shaughnessy, lights on in every window. Storenko parked in front of Brian's motorcycle, and we got out.

Brian put an arm around my shoulder. "You okay?"

"I feel fine." My thin cloth jacket was next to my naked skin; I had abandoned my tattered shirt.

"Harrison?"

"He was supposed to go direct to emergency, but he's probably gone to the RCMP lab. He told Storenko to get a ballistics man down there tonight."

"'I know what you are, a fucking spy.' That was the late Wendell Joiner? Off-the-wall phone call, man."

Storenko walked past us, toward the house. "See you up there." In the lit verandah were Lukey and Blueman, none of the court staff, but a third person, tall, rangy.

A wind spun down this quiet street, whipping leaves into small uproars. The air had changed taste, become colder, juicier.

"Storenko was evasive," I said. "Still alive is all I got. How is he?"

"It's very bad. They've had one emergency operation to the lacerated blood vessels. They're going to finish obtaining their baseline data, then go in again about midnight."

I checked my watch: nine-thirty now.

"The knife apparently went up into the fourth ventricle, possibly brainstem damage, maybe into the medulla. That controls the breathing functions. The operation: a suboccipital craniectomy. I got this from Vaughan Pascal-Forbes himself."

343

Dr. Pascal-Forbes was a notoriously high-living and flamboyant neurosurgeon—but brilliant.

"He volunteered for this one."

"What are the chances?"

"Without the operation, one in five he'll live, one in twenty he'll ever recover normal brain functions. With the operation, better odds on both."

"Get Pascal-Forbes to call me if you can. Hammersmith's manservant will find you a phone."

"Just a small sidebar to the story. It wasn't Margolis who was holding out. One of the sheriffs told me it was McIlheny, the ex-RCMP instructor. I wonder if he remembered Scanks from ethics class. The corporal, incidentally, had two hundred grand U.S. in his motel room."

We began walking toward the house, along flagstones through a prettily kept garden. "Who's the cowboy in there?" A long-boned man in a Western suit, string tie.

"It's Harry Rogers from Calgary. Minus his twenty-gallon hat and his guitar."

I recognized him. Rogers was a flashy Alberta trial lawyer whose hobby was the construction of his own legend. Rancher, daredevil flier, TV panel-show personality, he got big cases all across the country.

"What's he doing here?"

"Represents Scanks. He's had him a couple of days, I think, but turned him in only this afternoon. You ready for this?"

"I'll never be readier." The ghastly events of these last few hours had acted like a strop to my mind, cleaning out the rust, the numbness, giving me a sharp, bright edge.

I gave Leroy Lukey a cold hello, but he clapped me on the arm. "Hey, bantamweight, looks like you're the hero of the day. Weirdest phone call I ever had. So maybe we should talk, Max, before we see the judge."

I introduced myself to Harry Rogers, six feet, eight inches of smile. "You've had a few sessions with your client, I hear. What kind of deal did you make with Leroy?"

"Partner, you're asking for privileged information. I have a client who's standing up to his eyeballs in a shit-filled sewer line, a poor, easily led boy who has never known a break in life. The pathetic guy, he called me from a motel, and when I got there he was throwing up. I've always taken great pride in fighting the cause of the underprivileged."

"Especially when this easily led boy has two-hundred thousand U.S. bucks."

"'Fraid that may have gone missing." A broad smile from the top of this Calgary skyscraper.

"If we can do this by consent, Max," Lukey said, "it'll be—"

"No," I said. "Let's see the judge."

The manservant pointed Brian to a hall phone, then led Lukey, Blueman, Storenko, Rogers, and me into a large parlour. It was expensively furnished, some Regency pieces or very good replicas, some early Canadian painters I recognized, an Axminster English carpet on the floor, old porcelain vases, a bookcase along one wall with English adventures, also an array of hardcover detectives: Sayers, Chesterton, numerous Christies. The manservant silently slipped out and closed the door.

"Take seats, gentlemen." But Hammersmith himself intended to stand. He was leaning against an eighteenth-century walnut secretaire, his thumbs hooked into suspenders, the sleeves of his white shirt rolled up over bony elbows. I was even more informal: faded, ripped jeans and a grimy jacket with red stains on it.

Across the room, Lukey dropped onto a spindly comb-back Windsor chair that audibly groaned under his weight. I found a gilded-wood armchair, set my soiled rump on it.

"You will forgive the, ah, informality. After the first of the abhorrent incidents of this evening, I couldn't bring myself to return to the courthouse. I don't imagine there is any desire to do so on the part of any of you gentlemen, either."

Patricia Blueman, I thought, was simmering at being unacknowledged.

There was a memory of another woman in here: a large, framed photograph on the wall, a young woman of refinement with a distant, dreaming look. It was the kind of camera portrait they did in the old days, fuzzy around the edges, the colours unnaturally blurred. Hammersmith's wife, I realized. She had died of tuberculosis forty-two years ago, aged thirty-one. He had never remarried.

"Have you had a chance to read the Crown's material, Mr. Macarthur?" Hammersmith said.

"I looked at their affidavits. Corporal Scanks has turned himself in and the RCMP want permission to talk to him."

"On the Friday before he took his, ah, sudden leave, I

instructed him in very careful language not to discuss his evidence with anyone."

"The police would not conceive of acting in contempt of your lordship's order," said Lukey. "What we're seeking is to have your lordship untie our hands." He tried to make that a joke, chuckled. Hammersmith looked at Lukey's hands, then Storenko's, finger-locked around a crossed knee.

"Your lordship will realize the police never like to stale-question a suspect. Apparently Scanks is willing to co-operate in the investigation—Mr. Rogers is here representing him as you know, m'lord—and the inspector would like to have a go at him as soon as possible."

Hammersmith's squirrel eyes scampered across the room, lit on me. "The inspector would like to, ah, have a go. What do you say, Mr. Macarthur?"

"No. I think he should be recalled to court."

Lukey looked around the room to see if anyone else found this as preposterous as he. "The accused is dying. He won't survive the night. It means the end of the case. *Mors omnia solvit.*"

Hammersmith snapped one suspender, then the other. "Mr. Macarthur, tragically your client is unable to take his place on the witness stand. He is soon to undergo a danger-ous operation. Whether he will survive is a very, ah, moot question. And if he is fortunate enough to do so, he will be in no condition to return in good time to court. Do you not think I must call a mistrial?"

"I would consider that most unjust. After all that has happened, my client should be entitled, at the end, to one fair thing. A verdict."

The judge's eyes broke contact with mine. "Mr. Lukey is correct," he said. "The death of a party dissolves the action."

"He's not yet dead."

"In any event," said Hammersmith, "by law the verdict may not be taken nor may the trial conclude without the accused being present in the body of the court. Obviously he cannot be brought to court. I see no way in which you can obtain your formal acquittal."

"With your permission, my lord, I'd like to ask a few questions of Inspector Storenko."

"We're not in court," Lukey said.

"I have a right to apply to cross-examine him on his affidavits. Give me a damn break, my lord."

"We're abusing his lordship's hospit—"

"Proceed, Mr. Macarthur."

I turned toward honest Frank Storenko, locked with his cool, quicksilver eyes.

"You're not under oath, inspector, so could we just be friendly about this?"

"Of course."

"Well, we got down fast from Tash-Tash tonight, didn't we? Because you picked us up in an RCMP helicopter."

"If that's a compliment for quick work, thank you."

"You couldn't have been far away. Harrison radioed you from Tom Joiner's boat, right? Where were you at that point?"

"We were stationed at Campbell River. No, it wasn't far away."

"And so you'd prearranged contact with Harrison?"

"That's so."

"He kept saying to people he was on a special assignment. I thought he was kidding. When did you fellows hire him? It was before Friday. On Friday I thought *I* was hiring him."

"It was on Thursday, Max."

"Why? You were trying to get someone into the enemy's camp?"

"It was just that—we knew you'd found out certain things. Mr. Beauchamp's cross-examination of Scanks revealed that. Maybe you'll recall we asked you last Monday what you had, and you wouldn't turn the information over to us. Frankly, we were very anxious to find out. No harm meant."

"Tricky. It was Foster Cobb who helped set this up, wasn't it? I talked to him Thursday night. He volunteered to send Harrison to me." I caught a little glance from Storenko to Lukey. "So it must have been Cobb."

"I'm going to protest, m'lord," Lukey said.

"Please don't," said the judge.

"Yes, Foster Cobb, Bill Wheatley's lawyer, approached the prosecution early this week, that's right, isn't it?"

"I believe that happened, yes," Storenko said in slow, measured words.

"And a deal was made." It snapped together for me then. A deal had been made with Foster Cobb: his three muscle-bound Jesus freaks wouldn't be charged with a criminal offence. "Wheatley was not going to face indictment for offering bribes to an RCMP officer. I'm right so far?"

"That's right, I'm afraid. It was necessary, you know how these things work." Storenko seemed not so unflappable now.

"I wonder if I might be allowed a few minutes to talk privately with the inspector," Lukey said. "He wasn't anticipating this."

"Request denied."

"And in return they, Wheatley et al, offered to provide certain information."

"Correct."

"And you also agreed not to charge them with respect to any offence their information might divulge, yes?"

"Correct."

"What information *did* they divulge?"

"This is hearsay," Lukey rasped.

"I don't care," said the judge.

"Am I bound to answer, my lord?"

"I wish you would."

A long pause while Lukey fidgeted and the witness studied the carpet. "Yes, well, it had to do with the murders at Om Bay."

"Wheatley had evidence he hadn't previously disclosed?"

"That is right."

"And that was information pointing to the murderer as being other than Shiva Ram Acharya." I said it as a statement.

"It tended that way."

"Let's hear it."

"Well, Scanks contacted Bill Wheatley last fall saying he thought Melissa-June M'Garethy was at Om Bay, and Scanks was aware of the big reward being offered for her. It was Emelia Cruz, we now know. Wheatley told us he went to Tash-Tash on November twenty-fourth and they began to discuss a joint scheme to rescue the girl from the cult. Scanks wanted a cut of the reward, hinted about that, anyway. After meeting with Mr. M'Garethy, Wheatley got together secretly with Scanks about five days before the murders, and they worked out a plan."

"And what was it?"

"Under the ostensible authority of Scanks' powers under the Immigration Act, he would visit the commune and arrest the girl for having been in Canada more than six months without a visa. He would bring her to Tash-Tash, where she would be released into the custody of an agent of her parents. Wheatley himself, in other words. He already had a written authority from the M'Garethys. The girl was to be arrested on the morning of the eighth, and after bringing her to Tash-Tash, Scanks was to radio the M'Garethy lodge, a coded message to Wheatley to tell him to pick the girl up."

"That message was never sent," I said. "Something went wrong with the plan."

"Obviously. Very wrong."

"And Wheatley held his silence, and he had Scanks in his clutches, and Scanks had to co-operate with the Raba-urt-Jogan business that later went on in his jurisdiction."

"Plus he was paid well for it."

"And so Wheatley and his two assistants aren't being charged with bribery, they aren't being charged with being accessories, they aren't being charged with a conspiracy to kidnap. They're walking, two million dollars richer. What a low-camp comedy. But it gets worse, doesn't it?" I could feel anger rise like steam through me, from where I was boiling.

"I'm not sure what you mean."

I looked from face to face: of those here, only Mr. Justice Hammersmith, for all his faults, was innocent.

"When did Wheatley, Morgan, and Calico make their statements to you?"

"We contacted Foster Cobb early last week after we were unable to locate their whereabouts. Cobb came in and made his offer on, I guess it was Wednesday. We took statements from his clients the following day."

I looked at the man in the shadows, at the back of the room, Harry Rogers, the cowboy. Wheels in wheels, deals on deals, what was his role in this?

"You're saying that on Thursday, as the final evidence was being called, you knew Shiva was not guilty." I turned to Lukey. "The trial was a charade, and everything we did there at the end was a joke, calling the defence witnesses, Dr. Mangus, J.J. M'Garethy, our addresses, your lordship's charge. It was a joke."

Patricia Blueman had a startled expression. A harsh glint behind Hammersmith's spectacles.

"Would you have gone so far as to let them *convict*, Leroy?"

"Don't be preposterous," Lukey said.

"We will hear from you, Mr. Lukey." The words strained through Hammersmith's narrowed, rigid lips.

Lukey wiggled on his comb-back chair. It creaked, but no

sound came from him for a while. Finally, he said: "M'lord, we also learned on Thursday that Mr. Rogers was in contact with Corporal Scanks. It just seemed we should continue going through the motions of the trial until we had our facts collected."

Hammersmith gave him a look that said this wasn't good enough.

"Mr. Rogers flew to Vancouver that Thursday night, and we had some talks." A pause. "Well, frankly, we were worried that if we dropped the charges against Shiva too quickly, Scanks, who was in possession of a great deal of money, might disappear on us forever. There were certain matters that had to be discussed before Scanks would give himself up. We weren't able to come to terms with Mr. Rogers until this afternoon."

Hammersmith said nothing, waiting for more.

"And in the meantime, we were sending Detective Harrison to Tash-Tash Cove to try to get statements from Wendell and Tom Joiner. He would be able to use means the regular police couldn't. If the Joiners heard about the charges being stayed, I don't think *they* would have stayed." His chuckle faded quickly in the gloom.

"What if the jury had come back with a verdict, Mr. Lukey?" the judge said softly.

"It was our intention to forestall that. We would ask for an adjournment. At the worst direct a stay."

"You weren't going to indulge in the ultimate thrill of convicting an innocent man?" I exploded. "My client was tortiously and unlawfully imprisoned and now he's dying! I'm goddamn mad about that! I'm mad about the way these guys think they own the court system. I'm outraged that they've been allowed to kill an innocent man!"

"I say!" Lukey cried.

"You're a party, damn it, a party to his death! And I'm going to sue your dirty fat ass off! My client is stabbed in the neck and the brain in the courthouse basement while you're hoisting a beer in the Lawyer's Club with Harry Rogers over there, celebrating your deal, and a story is going over an international wire service quoting informed sources saying the jury is eleven-to-one for conviction. And you sit here talking about a stay. 'At the worst a stay,' he says. We've *got* the worst. You helped kill a man, Lukey, a man who couldn't physically damage a fly, you wasted him, you bastard!"

I was standing now, hands bunched into fists, spitting my denunciations at him.

"My lord, I don't want a stay, I don't want a withdrawal, I don't want a mistrial, I want a verdict. A verdict! My client is entitled to his final hour in court."

In counterpoint to my outburst, the judge's velvety whisper: "Mr. Lukey, did you have the sanction of the Attorney-General for this?"

"M'lord, it was one of those cases you have to fly by the seat of your pants." In so saying, Lukey shifted the seat of his pants, and the comb-back Windsor chair uttered a splintered cry of pain. Something had given in it, but Lukey maintained a wooden smile, sat still, pretended nothing had happened.

Hammersmith closed his eyes, perhaps was meditating in his way. Then he opened them and turned to me.

"Do you have an application, Mr. Macarthur?"

"Yes."

"And what is it?"

"That we recommence the trial at midnight. In the operating theatre of the Vancouver General Hospital. If the accused can't come to the trial, the trial can come to him. He *can* be present in the body of the court. Your lordship has the power to designate any place as a courtroom."

Lukey was making the kind of mouth-pops a pipe smoker makes when he blows rings. "That's impossible. I'm entering a stay of proceedings."

"If you attempt to do that," Hammersmith said, "I will address some very pointed remarks in open court with respect to the, ah, ethical history of this matter."

"I'd like to appear to protect my client's interests," Harry Rogers said from the back of the room. "If you have no objection, sir."

"You have no status."

Brian interrupted, opening the door without knocking. "I have Dr. Pascal-Forbes."

"May I, my lord?" I pointed to a phone extension on his desk.

"Yes."

I didn't have to do much explaining to the showy Pascal-Forbes. He told me there was ample seating in the sealed-off gallery for the jury and court staff, and standing room for the press—which, the doctor knew, included such international luminaries as Charles Rubinstein of the *New York Times*. I put the phone down. "He'd be delighted."

The judge blinked behind his big spectacles. "You have heard the application, Mr. Lukey. Any comments?"

"It's ridiculous."

"I'm sorry, Miss Blueman, did you have something to say?"

She had been making agitated noises, throat clearings. "I just want to explain that Mr. Lukey doesn't speak for me." She was embarrassed over her effrontery, but held her head up boldly. Leroy was silently apoplectic.

"I see." Hammersmith looked around as if he were in strange surroundings. He studied his wife's photograph for a while. "Yes, well, the application is granted."

32

o

Non Omnis Moriar

We are in the Vancouver General Hospital, a labyrinthine monster, a city within a city. It spreads wings north and south between Ninth and Twelfth Avenues, across streets named not for forgotten aldermen but lovely growing things: Laurel, Willow, Heather, Oak. About it is the professional sprawl that surrounds all medical megalopolises, high-rises with proctologists, posologists, and nosologists; drug stores, laboratories, optical shops, all sucking like parasites from this beating heart of Vancouver, this place where life begins and where life ends.

From north- and west-facing windows of this hospital, the front can be seen coming, with its play of light over Howe Sound, the sky splintering into whiteness upon every tenth heartbeat. We can feel it. The throat softens. There is a sweet foretaste in the mouth. The rains of autumn. And the taste is bittersweet: the end of summer.

The rains march from the northwest behind a buttressing cold front born above the Bering Sea. By now, five minutes to midnight, Augustina Sage and her comrades will be singing and dancing, because God had decided to save Strathcona Park. By now, the downpour has overwhelmed the fiery holocaust that has been ripping across Poindexter Island. Om Bay itself has been forgiven.

As the rains approach the city, Matthew Bartholomew James alias Shiva Ram Acharya lies strapped to an operating table tilted at a forty-five-degree angle. Bent forward over the high end of that table, his shaved head is suspended on cushioned props. We watch the pattern of his heartbeat on the computer screen.

This hospital associates with the U.B.C. medical school, and students watching from the gallery of the operating theatre have seen many famous operations, many brilliances—for there are Arthur Beauchamps in this other great profession, and they cut as sharply and exactly. Arthur is in the gallery tonight, in fact, sombrely smiling encouragement at me, his cane across his knees. So is Harry Rogers here, and many media people, although their cameras are forbidden. The only working camera in this place is on the floor, focussed on the wide hole in a cloth atop Shiva's shaved head. The camera's unblinking eye peeps from among plastic tubes that rise from the area, unseen, of his facial orifices. A panoply of stainless steel machinery surrounds the operating table, and above them a computer screen blinks out coloured graphs. On the green tile wall, a printed sign: "Have you hugged your surgeon today?"

Five men and three women stand about the table below us. The one in charge gives orders in a clipped, hard voice. He is Vaughan Pascal-Forbes.

Pascal-Forbes and I are both operating tonight, he in his greens and I in my blacks. But his adversary is death, and mine is only Leroy Lukey, who is no longer interested in this trial, has abdicated. He is standing, looking down through the oval formed by windows at the scene below.

Behind a table at the far end of this long gallery is Mr. Justice Hammersmith, impassively gnome-like in his red gown. The jury are seated in two rows to one side of the glass roof of the operating room, and we have court clerk and reporter, deputy sheriffs and counsel on the other side. And at the end facing the judge, the witness, Edward Scanks.

"Corporal Scanks," says the clerk, "you are still under oath."

"Administer it again," I say.

Scanks solemnly swears he will tell the truth so help him God, and he kisses the Bible afterwards. Coached to do so by Harry Rogers.

At the judge's invitation, Scanks slowly goes down on a metal chair.

"*This will be an absolute bugger. Vince says there's a soft spot in the occipital artery wall. Is that going to leak?*" The voice comes from a speaker, Pascal-Forbes, through his gauze mask. "*Let me see those CT scans again, Chuck. And Jane, put the electrocardiograph tracings on the screen.*"

There are sounds of suction: waste fluids going up tubes.

"Can the sound be turned off?" Hammersmith says.

One of the doctors below slicks out some commands on a computer keyboard, and EEC tracings appear on the big yellow screen. To my right, a deputy sheriff is looking for the speaker control.

"*Life stats, please.*" Eight squiggling lines of different colours bip and bop horizontally along the screen. "*Christ, this isn't deep sleep, it's almost total inaction.*" He is pointing at the blue line, the EEG, I guess, dipping and rising like the surface of a gentle sea.

"I'm looking for the switch, my lord," says the deputy.

"*Okay, give me the Hudson drill, we'll go in just above the external occipital protuberance. Let's be sharp, ladies and gentlemen. . . .*"

His voice fades.

Shiva, I dare not look at you. They've said there's a possibility your brain will die and your body live. And your soul will remain trapped within, in purgatory, unable to escape into the universalized, liberated soul. Better that you die. But all that will happen to you is known by you, isn't it? It doesn't matter. There is no choice.

"This will be quick, witness," I say. "I am going to read a statement signed by Tom Joiner in which he implicates you and his brother in the murder of the twenty-two victims of Om Bay."

The jury, looking startled, gazes upon Scanks with mixed horror and guilt as I put Tom's words into the record. At the end, I say, "Do you admit this statement is true?"

Scanks responds in a low, cracked voice. "Your lordship, I object to answering any questions on the ground they may incriminate me, and I seek the protection of the Canada Evidence Act." That act protects a witness from his answers being used against him later, except for perjury.

"I have taken note of your objection," says Hammersmith. "You are protected but you must answer the questions."

"Is what I read to you true?"

"No, it isn't, not the part about the killings."

"Then I will take a few minutes." Of your precious time, Shiva Ram Acharya. I am sorry. Be patient with us, my guru. "Witness, you're under suspension by your police force, yes?"

"That's right."

"And you face criminal charges of accepting bribes from Wheatley and criminal negligence in the execution of your duties."

"Yes." He is looking at the wall.

"But you're not charged with murder."

"No."

"At least yet."

He said nothing. Wheels and wheels, deals and deals, we are all caught in the corrupt machinery.

"Last fall you entered into a plan with Bill Wheatley to pick up the girl you thought was Melissa-June, a plan to stage the abduction under the Immigration Act."

"I'm sure that's all in Mr. Wheatley's statement. I don't deny it."

Obviously Scanks has been counselled not to contradict Wheatley. "And you knew you were entering into a criminal conspiracy, didn't you?"

"Not necessarily. I believed the girl was in Canada illegally, without a visa. I did accept an unlawful payment from Mr. Wheatley."

Lukey is still uninterested in this, keeps his eyes fixed on the operation below. I am trying to erase from my mind all thoughts of what is happening there. With difficulty. (What will the doctors find in your alien brain, Shiva, in your transcendental tissues?)

"At seven o'clock on the morning of that day you set out for Om Bay in the company of the Joiners, on Tom's boat, the *Black Cormorant*."

"I have to tell you I'd been quite ill that morning. I woke up at five-thirty with an extremely bad stomach ache, and had to go out on a call to break up an all-night party. Both Wendell and Tom were at the party, at a cabin, Neeley Wilde's, and I guess I didn't realize until later that they had taken some drugs, I believe cocaine. I found some at the party and destroyed it. I was almost doubled over with pain by the time Tom's boat got to Om Bay."

I begin to wonder: does it matter? My task isn't to convict Scanks here, but acquit Shiva, and quickly.

"When you arrived there, Tom stayed on board the *Black Cormorant*, you took the .303, Wendell the .30-.30, and the two of you went ashore in the longboat."

"That is absolutely untrue." He says this with vigour. "I

stayed aboard the big boat and the other two went to shore. I was in terrific pain."

This is his defence. He will admit the side crimes but not the big one, the mass murder. No matter how hard the courts will come down on the corruption and criminal negligence, on being an accessory after the fact to murder, he can look to parole. But they will never free this man if convicted for the executions.

"In his statement, Tom Joiner said he observed you and Wendell land the longboat on shore where the creek let out. He says you were met at the shore by a group of young people who protested your arrival."

"That is wrong."

"What do you say happened?"

"It was like in Tom Joiner's statement, but he's deliberately put me in his place. He and Wendell did it. I saw the first couple of people killed up by the creek, and I heard all the shots later. There was nothing I could do. I was throwing up by now. I was trapped on an anchored boat, and Tom had taken the key ashore. I was greatly horrified."

I glance down to the operating room where the doctors fight their trial. *Death is merely the loss of information, an episode. It only changes the skin. Life after life we remain the same.*

"I suggest it was you and Wendell who killed them."

"That isn't so."

"Tom Joiner says it's so."

"Then he's lying, sir."

"You're lying. You lied under oath last week, and you're lying under oath today. You've lied a thousand times and you'd lie a thousand more if you could. You lied about Shiva's words, 'Because I loved you, I had to kill you'—all invented. Yes?"

I don't wait for the answer. "You lied about that visit to you from George Wurz: Shiva controlling people's minds. It was an afterthought to justify an official visit to Om Bay."

I look over to Arthur. Can you believe they would have gone so far, Arthur? They are heartless. Everybody talks, everybody walks. And, as Mr. Bumble says, "The law is a ass, a idiot."

"You returned to Om Bay to seek and kill Emelia and Shiva."

"I don't know why I went back. I was scared and panicky. I

hadn't decided on a course of action yet, whether to make arrests or whether I was in so deep I couldn't get out."

"When you saw Shiva babbling and dancing, blood all over him, that's when it came to you he could be fixed with blame for these killings."

"It wasn't my idea, sir."

"Oh, of course it was. Wendell was too dumb and Tom too scared, and Tom had stayed on the boat anyway. When Shiva took the rifle you handed him, that was proof he was out of his mind. And this untraceable weapon was left among the bodies, and that's where you'd tell the detectives you'd found it."

"You give me too much credit."

"I give you none."

I take a deep breath and turn to the side, and take a view through the glass. The head of Shiva is hidden among bending, green-robed figures. The multi-coloured worms on the computer screen make phosphorescent paths, proving life.

Shiva, you are the god of the game, the god of humour. And is this a part of your joke, Shiva? And did the joke begin as you saw the police launch coming into the bay while you stood in grief among your children? Did you fog minds and feign madness? And did you carry on that joke at the expense of the former prisoner of logic who defends you? Amnesia...?

I turn back to Scanks. "He's still living. The man against whom you bore false witness. Pray that he lives, Scanks."

"All I've been doing for the last week is praying."

"A special pleading for your own condemned soul. Let's finish this. You arrested Shiva, thinking to frame a madman. It was a big collar for the Tash-Tash RCMP. It all held together, and even Emelia Cruz didn't live to tell but a few words of her story. But there was the problem of Wheatley, wasn't there? That man and his pals had information that could put you at Om Bay that Saturday morning. And you came under his thumb after that, didn't you?"

"If you mean the actors he hired for the M'Garethy lodge and all of that, yes, I felt it wise to co-operate."

"Especially with an offer of two hundred thousand dollars."

"It was enough for me to start my life over."

"Where's the money now?"

"I lost it. I had a rented car and someone jimmied the trunk. The police have the car, they've seen it."

"You buried the money. You're hoping you'll make parole some day."

"It was honestly stolen from me."

Honestly stolen from me. I don't know whether to laugh or cry.

"And then it all started to collapse, right? When we started to prosecute Wheatley, he started to feel edgy about carrying the secret of your plan to raid Om Bay. Maybe they talked to you, and maybe because they were panicking, you panicked, too, under cross-examination—when it started getting hot for you in the courtroom. Then the stampede was on, you got your money and ran to Alberta; Wheatley ran to his lawyer who ran to the police."

Why cross-examine? Set the whole thing out on a platter for them, like a basted fowl.

"And you came to the prosecution with this stuff about being a frightened bystander, and when you found out from your lawyer that the Lee-Enfield rifle had been traced to Tom Joiner, you saw your chance, and you made a deal to testify against the Joiners."

"Yes."

"So it's only your word against Tom's now, right?"

"I don't know."

"That's the best one of all." I turn to the jury. "Can you believe it? The final deal gets him off the murder charge. He pleads guilty to everything but the kitchen sink and murder, and he'll get concurrent time and walk out with a tidy profit from his investment. And there's the accused." I point with a furious index finger. "The *accused*. They're trying to save the life of the poor bloody *accused!*"

Still my fury, Shiva.

"You know what's going to happen, folks? Ex-Corporal Eddie Scanks is going to give evidence against Tom Joiner on twenty-two counts of murder. And when the jury realizes there is not a thread of honesty knit into this man's soul, they'll give the verdict to Tom Joiner."

I scan these twelve racked faces.

"You know what that means? It means no one will ever be convicted for this bloodbath. Not one of those unoffending, God-searching kids will ever be avenged. Not to mention the man who's lying there, whose brain is under a knife before us. My God, it's no wonder the legal system is despised by every layman from Hong Kong to Houston. Justice: what a

farce! And what a costly price is paid for it in the case of the
Queen versus Shiva Ram Acharya. What a cruel price! Give
us what we've paid for in pain. Give us your declaration to
the world that Shiva is innocent!"

I turn to Scanks. "You will pay the price. I'm going to get
Lukey removed from this case. His deal isn't going to hold."

"I didn't kill them."

"I have no more evidence, my lord, let's have the jury's
verdict."

After the heat of my words, the judge's sound whispery
and hollow. "Have you anything to add, Mr. Lukey?"

"No, my lord. . . ." He is distracted. "My god, there's
something happening!"

I turn to look below.

A spurting burst of blood, green gowns splattered. Hands
move in feverish dance above Shiva's neck and head. The
electric air of profound emergency sweeps up to us from the
operating room. Lukey rushes to the sound control, and
Pascal-Forbes' voice pours through. *"Clamp, clamp, clamp!
It's a hematoma!"*

"He's gone into shock!"

The life system lines are erratic on the monitor. *"My God,
maybe it's something else!"* Jagged peaks and deep valleys,
lines of pulse and blood pressure and kidney function and
brain pattern dancing a capricious dance upon that screen
like a last explosion of life, a last sucking away of its brilliant
mystery. Nataraja, the dance king, dancing his universe to
destruction so ordinary mortals may not proclaim his innocence.

And the lines on the screen begin to falter.

Why, Shiva?

Whys cannot find answers.

"Blood pressure down, pulse going!"

"Give us the verdict, Mister Foreman!" I say.

"I think he stopped breathing."

I feel release, as if some part of me has taken wing with his
soul.

"Ladies and gentlemen," says the judge, "do you have a
verdict? Stand and signify."

"Pound it."

"There's nothing left!"

McIlheny stands. "I find the accused not guilty of all
charges."

There is just the hard rasping of breath from the speakers.

The next juror stands. "Not guilty." The next person. "Not guilty."

Straight and furry lines on the monitor. From the operating room: *"Yup, he's gone. Finito."*

Finito. Infinito. The finite and the infinite merge, do they not, Shiva? As death merges with life.

"Not guilty."

"Not guilty."

"Not guilty."

Disloyal Margolis: "Not guilty."

"He's gone all right."

"Not guilty."

Are you not going to rise from the dead, Shiva? Isn't that the punch line? Rise now. I will be the first apostle. Send a little blue blip onto the screen, a message for me.

"Not guilty."

The soft hospital hum. But it seems—only seems—there is another sound, a threnody, voices in soft chorus and his whisperings. Or is it a memory of them? *I can die at this moment because I am fulfilled. I will remain a part of the uncreate, a universalized soul.*

"Not guilty."

"Not guilty."

Non omnis moriar. I shall not wholly die. Acquit my soul, free it from the burden of Karma and rebirth.

"Not guilty."

"But he's dead," says Lukey.

"The verdict will be recorded," says the judge. "Mr. Sheriff, proclaim the close of the assize."

"Oyer, oyer, oyer! The court having disposed of all business before it, I declare this sitting of the court duly closed. God save the Queen!"

Having disposed of all business.... There, below me, the disposed business of you, Shiva Ram Acharya, your discarded chrysalis. I am in tears. I do not know whether they are sadness or tears of joy. Has death kissed you with life, teacher?

The Legend of the Tandava

A god can exist in supreme indifference to the honour which men would like to confer by their belief. Still, since a god has all the time there is with which to play, he can afford to take a moment to render clear to obstinate and clouded minds his real presence and his power. So Shiva, though tranquil, let his overflowing love and grace impel him to the gesture of visiting the sceptical sages in their forest hermitage to show them the truth.

On his arrival at the forest glen, Shiva was received with the violent reactions of men who face a fact that doesn't fit their orthodoxies. Shiva smiled.

Somewhere within the soul of that great god a faint strumming of uncertain sound began to stir. So faintly it began that he turned his whole mind inward and distinguished a slow and stately rhythm rising from his overflowing grace. A hand which held a drum began to tap it in the slow and even cadence of a pulsing heart. The movement of his legs picked up the rhythm. The fire in his left hand traced the gestures of the accelerating tempo. Graceful arms and hands declared the motion of his ecstasy. Surging legs lifted in leaps of joy. His body glistened and glowed with dazzling splendour as he danced.

The heretic sages prostrated themselves to be his dancing floor. The gods came down from their heavens to watch the joyful dance. As Shiva moved with stately grace and gay abandon, as only a Shiva could do, mist began to form in the outer reaches of the universe. The torch he waved aloft flared forth in pulsing rhythms of the dance, and stars expired before its dazzling brilliance. All that was not Shiva dancing began to fall apart, disintegrate, evaporate into the thin vapours of apparent nothingness. The dance of joy became Tandava, the Dance of Eternity, a dance of universal death and joy.

At the climax of the nothingness Shiva paused, and then began again—as slowly as before. He had danced the worlds out, now he danced them in again, flinging stars into their heavens, evoking life upon the earth, a kinesthesis of overflowing grace and love. So Shiva danced a new world and a new age into being, and had himself a day of lovely sport and playful joy.

When he brought the world very near to where we stand, the dance closed quietly and he slipped back to the cosmic fellowship. After all, it matters not to god to dance a world out or in, or whether wise men will believe in him or not. He danced. It was enough.

—from <u>Stories of the Hindus</u>

ABOUT THE AUTHOR

Following a career as a journalist, WILLIAM DEVERELL started a law practice in British Columbia in 1964, and is currently practising in Victoria. A former president of the British Columbia Civil Liberties Association, he describes himself as a political, cause-oriented lawyer.

Deverell's previous three best-selling novels, *Needles*—winner of the $50,000 Seal Award and voted Book of the Year by the Periodical Distributors of Canada—*High Crimes*, and *Mecca*, have been published in Canada, the U.S., and U.K., in hardcover and paperback. They have also been translated and published in numerous foreign-language editions.

Robert Littell
Author of
The Defection of A. J. Lewinter
has now written his most ambitious book yet—

THE SISTERS

"A sinister twisting roller-coaster ride,
the fastest since *Day of The Jackal*."—Joseph Wambaugh

Francis and Carroll are minor legends in the Company. Brilliant, eccentric and extremely dangerous, these two men are considered the Company's odd couple, for they complement each other exquisitely: one will see forest where the other sees trees; one leaps in the general direction of unlikely ends, while the other, a pedestrian at heart, trails him, lingering over means. Somewhere along the line one of the CIA's army of PhDs dubbed them "The sisters Death and Night." The name stuck.

But only a handful have an inkling of what the Sisters actually do for a living.

What they do is plot.

And what they are plotting one perfect August day is a perfect crime.

"What Elmore Leonard is to mysteries, what Isaac Asimov is to science fiction, and what Stephen King is to horror—well, that's what Robert Littell is to the novel of intrigue. He's a first-rate writer." —Susan Isaacs

THE SISTERS

Available wherever Bantam Books are sold, or use this handy coupon for ordering:

Special Offer
Buy a Bantam Book
for only 50¢.

Now you can have an up-to-date listing of Bantam's hundreds of titles plus take advantage of our unique and exciting bonus book offer. A special offer which gives you the opportunity to purchase a Bantam book for only 50¢. Here's how!

By ordering any five books at the regular price per order, you can also choose any other single book listed (up to a $4.95 value) for just 50¢. Some restrictions do apply, but for further details why not send for Bantam's listing of titles today!

Just send us your name and address and we will send you a catalog!